The 1

Cat McCallum wants her
Raymond Kidd is nowhere to be found. In fact, ...
flaw in the fabric of space and time to an earlier life as Oliver Cole, sailing
ship captain in mid-nineteenth century Halifax.

Cat does have help. Angle and Octave Daggon, two ghosts from the
basement of Raymond's seaside house, have come to life again. Former
school teacher Octave has a crush on Cat and former pirate Angle once
preyed on Captain Cole and wants to make amends. The three make a
dedicated crew, but they need yet more help to retrieve someone who no
longer exists.

More help is available. The flaw in the fabric is still open. Unfortunately,
there's no telling what else might come through it.

Evil loves doors.

Praise for Jim Lindsey's *The Flaw in the Fabric*

"The writing is enticing, the story multi-layered. I enjoyed falling under its
spell. Well done. Simple. Draws you into the story from the first page."
—Judges for the 2012 Annual Book Awards,
Bay Area Independent Publishers Assn. (BAIPA)

"Wildly imaginative black comedy. The gripping opening drags the reader into
the nightmare of Raymond's brush with the supernatural, with the threat of
the invasive sea in the basement suffocatingly real. The details are surreal and
horribly convincing. Lindsey has an enviable turn of phrase."
—Jean Gill, France

"How to write like a pirate! Superb writing style and a captivating story filled
with shining and disappearing characters, ghostly insights and laugh out loud
humor. Great read. I'm hooked. Bring on the sequel, prequel or any work by
this author. It's just that good."
—C. L. Sumruld, Nashville Tennessee

"The style is unique, the colorful language and characters endearing. The
gentle choice of words in intimate moments is both sweet and believable. The
author connects with the thoughts and passions of both young and old. He has
quite carefully and sensitively taken me in and stirred my heart."
—Judy Jones, Texarkana Texas

Book 1 of *A Travellers Guide for Lost Souls*

THE FLAW
IN THE FABRIC

JIM T. LINDSEY

SeaStorm Press
SeaStormPress.com
Mendocino, California

To my mother, Moja Yvonne,
and my teacher, Khenpo Tsultrim Gyamtso,
the carefree wanderer

Acknowledgements

The author would like to express his appreciation to Suzanne Townsend for her editing efforts, to Deborah Luscomb and Barbara Taylor for the hours they spent listening and commenting and helping with research, to his sister Lynn for her generous support, his nephew Jordan for his technical and artistic expertise and to his sister Leigh Anne for shepherding him through the publication process. Without them this book never would have been more than the series title that came in a dream.

Contents

The Flaw
in the Fabric

Chapter 1

A New Prescription

The muttering in the basement began again, and again in the master bedroom of the very old yet very new house, Raymond Kidd lay awake listening.

Two hundred and ten years earlier, 7 Lands End had come into being as a shoebox with six cramped rooms, a simple shoreside cottage on a coast where the topsoil lay as thinly on the granite bedrock as the hair on a balding man's head. There was no basement then. The idea of digging an underground room in such rocky ground never entered the original builder's mind. Nor was there a master bedroom upstairs. The upstairs was an attic for storing fishing gear. Two hundred years later, however, when young Nora Lee of the Mi'kmaq tribe became the lead attorney for Canada's Assembly of First Nations, she flexed the muscles of her newfound prosperity by buying the cottage for fifty thousand dollars and carrying out two hundred thousand dollars worth of renovations that included a boathouse and woodshed, a new wing, a basement, the conversion of the attic, and a ripping out of walls to make the six rooms one big open one. After the makeover, the only doors were on the bathrooms and closets and the new basement. The contractor protested against adding a basement because of the natural underground flow of the marsh behind the house down to the sea in front. But Nora had insisted, because the basement was to be not only the laundry room but also her exercise room, where while the washer was washing and the dryer drying she could mirror the movements of the obviously successful and splendidly built young men and women on the TV she ordered built into the basement wall.

As it turned out, the new basement flooded with every moderate rain and spring tide and stayed damp even after being pumped out. The sump pump couldn't handle the influx nor a dehumidifier the mildew. The door had to be kept open to improve the ventilation. But these were minor problems for Nora. The major ones were that her husband-to-be, a talented young Haligonian movie director, abandoned her for Hollywood;

1

and her older sister, while skating on a remote lake in northern Manitoba, plunged through thin ice to a watery grave.

The TV was never built in. Nora moved to Winnipeg to take care of her sister's seven children, which accorded both with tribal custom and the call of her own broken heart. She sold 7 Lands End to the newly arrived American immigrant Raymond Kidd, accepting his ridiculously low offer because he professed to be a poet and because she wanted her dream that had almost come true to be appreciated by someone with imagination.

Whether Raymond was a real poet or not was anyone's guess. He had certainly written reams of the stuff and published a couple of thin volumes. But that he was possessed of a vivid imagination was unquestionable. As he lay upstairs listening, he was certain he heard ghosts conversing, that their conversations originated in the basement where the door was always open, and that it was important to his destiny that he understand what they were saying. Strain his ears as he might, though, night after night, year after year, he had never made much sense of it. It was like a radio broadcast so faint and staticky that only a word or two was ever intelligible.

Usually this was enough, because the listening distracted him from the problems on his mind. This particular November night, however, he determined to know more, to get out of bed and go down to the basement and get to the heart of the matter.

He did not have to throw back the covers. They were already off. Having once again awakened from a dream of irreparable misfortune to find himself stewing in his own juices, he was letting bed and body dry out in a cross draft of gentle sea breezes from the open windows at either end of the long room and the open skylight overhead. The skylight was another of Nora Lee's additions, one that Raymond found pleasing (unlike the perennially flooding basement), especially now with the moon casting a silvery sheen down through it onto the exposed left breast of Mimi, the young Québecois woman beside him. The romantic effect was not spoiled at all but even enhanced by her snoring, that was soft and regular as the beat of the distant surf it accompanied.

By daylight, Raymond would have experienced this intimate exposure more warmly, would have been tempted to touch and fondle, but the moonlight (a light once removed as it were, essentially ethereal) had moved him beyond passion. Had he still possessed a camera, he would have pho-tographed Mimi, but the camera had gone with his wife Cat when they had separated the year before. So he simply lay there, admiring the silvery curve of that breast as if it were a wind-sculpted dune in the desert, until more muttering from the basement reminded him of his resolve.

Still not fully awake, with his first tentative steps he stumbled in the dark into the closed door of the bathroom. He could have gone in and splashed some water on his face—the idea was appealing—but he feared he might wake up too much and lose the voices, so he simply reached in to slip his house robe from its hook before continuing on, groping his way groggily along the hall to the stairwell.

At the landing he paused. What if he did find something down there? What if it was something he didn't really want to find? He went one step down, and then another. Along with the muttering he now perceived laughter, a sort of veiled amusement that swelled with his approach. His mouth, from drinking too much wine with Mimi, was intolerably dry, and licking his lips with a tongue like a cotton swab was no help.

By the next to the last step, he was no longer sleepy at all, and no longer afraid that the voices would escape him but that he might not escape the voices.

On the last step, with the open door and deeper darkness of the base-ment before him and his heart doing a doomsday drumroll, he was seized from behind, at the back of the neck, by a hand cold as ice.

"Now, you see," said Mimi, who had stolen down behind him, "how unpleasant it gets a person when you leave her lying in the bed half-un-covered and all alone."

As he turned to go back up, his hand in hers, Raymond thought he heard a last noise from below, a sort of contemptuous chuckle, but Mimi seemed oblivious, and so he let himself be led away, his mission unaccom-plished.

In the morning, Mimi was gone. Raymond sensed this without open-ing his eyes even before he felt the empty space beside him with his hand. There was only her scent, a subtle fragrance he could not quite name. Per-haps *sky flower*, or something else that was only imaginary, as it sometimes seemed to him that Mimi herself was, since she appeared and disappeared always by night. Once she had been an occasional factor in his everyday life, the receptionist for his financial advisor, someone whose ready smile and French-accented patter and consistent and outstanding décolletage he had found far more engaging than the investment magazines he might otherwise have read while he waited. But she had left that position, and when she came to him in the dark, when he was already in bed with the lights out, she never wanted to talk very much, and never at all about where she had gone or what else she was doing.

He was sad to have missed her departure again, though impressed that she was able to make it so consistently before dawn, still in the darkness and with no alarm, for without an alarm it took light to rouse Raymond. He was so sensitive to sunlight that he had never been able to stay asleep in its presence, a condition he sometimes regretted and that he particularly regretted this morning. First light always woke him, no matter how tired or hung over he was, and this morning he was both. Extremely both. He would rather have slept in.

Obscured by heavy clouds, it wasn't much of a first light, but it was enough to bring Raymond to that part of waking where his hearing kicked in, and what he heard was not the gentle sea breeze of the evening before but a howling blow that scoured the room between the two open windows, flailing the drawn shades and whistling through the cranked-open skylight over the bed. He opened his eyes with a start to find himself in the middle of what looked like a blizzard of bizarrely large snowflakes. Then the flakes resolved themselves into sheets of paper, which he then realized were the manuscript of the book he was writing, a commentary on a traditional list of obstacles and antidotes in the Buddhist practice of meditation, a manuscript he had never bothered to number because why should he when it was always lying there on his bedside table with its pages stacked in the proper order.

The chapter on which he had been stuck for the past seven years concerned the obstacle of laziness.

He extracted the page that had managed to furl itself into his wineglass and laid it dripping on the top of the low Japanese chest that served as the night table for the low Japanese futon he slept on. The wine that was left in the glass he finished in a gulp. One of Mimi's homemade reds, it had seemed palatable enough under the influence of sexual arousal. He concluded with a grimace that it did not improve thereafter.

He further concluded, as the pages of his manuscript danced around him to the wailing of the powerful wind, that something must be up.

One of the four antidotes to laziness was, of course, exertion.

He dragged himself up, got his robe from the bathroom, closed the windows, stacked the manuscript in an order now totally random, and proceeded to the shrine room by the second floor landing. The Japanese *noren* that covered the shrine room's open doorway streamed out toward him, its two fabric panels fluttering wildly. Here too the windows had been left open, and here too there was a whirl of papers, in this case from a liturgy left unbound in the Tibetan style and unclosed by Raymond after his last practice session. On the walls Raymond's thangkas of Buddhist deities flapped and clanked, while all the white silk scarves that normally draped the framed photographs of his Tibetan and Japanese teachers had blown off. The most elegant of the scarves, that had the eight auspicious symbols and normally ornamented his root teacher's photo, had landed over the offering bowls on the shrine and was stained a bright yellow by the saffron water in two of the bowls.

With a heavy heart that now matched his heavy head, he closed the windows and put the chaos back in order here too. Lighting candles and incense on the shrine, he took his seat on his meditation cushion. In front of him was the long low puja table on which the liturgy had lain. The half of the table that was his was covered with a rich brocade cloth and the traditional implements of his practice—bell and dorje, kapala, hand drum, a bowl of offering rice, a dish of mustard seed for dispelling harmful spirits. The half of the table that had been his wife's was bare and dusty. He traced a heart in the dust with his finger.

"If you in the basement are still in the basement," he said at last, when subsiding emotion allowed, "please let go." He repeated these words over and over in the monotonous chanting style of his tradition and thumbed the bone beads of his mala as if counting the recitations of a mantra. He threw rice toward the shrine and mustard seed in the direction of the basement. When the smell of the incense became that of ashes, he dedicated the merit, bowed and got up. For a while, till the blood and feeling flowed back into his left foot that had grown numb from sitting cross-legged, he stood there listening to his heart trying to outrace the threatening wind.

The disturbance that moved Raymond so had in fact only touched him with the tip of its out-stretched fingers. Thousands of miles to the south, its full embrace had snuffed out the lives of one hundred and forty-three citizens of the Caribbean countries of Haiti and the Dominican Republic, some by drowning, others in mud slides, one infant in her mother's arms by driving a beer bottle cap so hard into her forehead that the cap remained there with its logo facing out. First remarked as a depression, the disturbance had gone on to be recognized as a tropical storm and finally a hurricane, the sixth of the season. The weather services dubbed it Noel. For itself it had no notion of any of these names. It simply held out its arms and moved northward in search of other lovers. The journey was taxing, however. By the time it reached Nova Scotia, Noel's wind speed had diminished and therefore its status. The forecasters reduced it to, "Noel, a post-tropical storm," and those said to be in its path for the most part began breathing easier and going about business as usual.

In the province's low-lying coastal communities, the prospect of a tidal surge with fifteen-foot waves made the difference between a post-tropical storm and a hurricane less readily apparent. In the village of Prospect, both fishermen and pleasure boaters were slipping their moorings and moving their craft out of the already white-capping harbour into the shelter of local hurricane holes.

Had Raymond still owned a boat, he would have done the same, but the loss of his bookstore to creditors had forced the sale of his yawl *Happy Cat*. Since then, and even more since the departure of his wife, for whom the yawl had been named, he had paid little attention to the weather. If it blew it blew, and if he was taken by surprise, so much the better. He had not heard of Noel at all. There was no mention of the storm on the websites he checked, he had given up television twenty years before, and his old pickup truck had no radio. As he drove into the city to work he was moved by the passionate flailing of the trees but thought no more of it.

Along the Halifax waterfront, proprietors of the many taverns had lain in extra stocks of refreshments in expectation of an even more crowded evening than usual, for while a true hurricane might be bad for business, a near hurricane was an added attraction. As it whipped the long harbour outside their big picture windows into a rousing turbulence, so it would whip their clientele into an appreciative drinking frenzy.

The Stag's Head was not one of these bars, properly speaking, being on the other side of Lower Water Street and having neither harborside frontage or windows. In the mid-eighteenth-century, it had been Alexander Keith's private haven in the basement of his Lower Water Street brewery, a place to bring guests and entertain investors. Now however it was part of the regular tour of the brewery, a tour being conducted in spite of Noel, for the Stag's Head was the part of the tour where the beers were sampled, and management knew the pub crawlers would make it come hell or high water.

The four couples on the final tour at eight o'clock were wet and rowdy university students. They plagued the guide of the first part of the tour, whose part it was to show them the old copper vats and explain the original brewing process, with ridiculous questions. They wanted more to drink, not a history lesson. When the actor playing apprentice brewmaster Mac finally brought them down the stone stairs to their destination and rapped at the door of the Stag's Head, supposedly to summon their host Mr. Keith, they hooted and laughed.

"Right, like he's really in there."

"Who cares? Just deliver me to the beer."

"I care. I need a new sugar daddy."

"So do I. Come on out, sugar, and give us a lick!"

The script called for Duke the bartender to appear rather than Mr. Keith, and since it was Raymond Kidd's day and shift to be playing Duke, it was Raymond who opened the door. Before he could begin his scripted greeting, however, the students interceded.

"That's Mr. Keith? Doesn't look like him."

"Oh, another man in an apron. I just love men in aprons."

"Only pussies wear aprons."

"Yeah. Listen, apron guys, can we cut the spiel and get on to the beer? If you have to keep *entertaining* us, do it after we're served. Then you can do whatever you want. Shakespeare. Whatever. You can make like you're *real* actors."

The other students found this last comment hysterical, so smirking in triumph and spurred on by the laughter, the boy who made the comment tried to elbow Raymond aside. Raymond reached for the boy's arm, partly to detain him and partly to regain his own balance, but instead, because he had new glasses and was not yet used to the progressive lenses and their disruption of his depth perception, he mistakenly grabbed the boy by the neck. It was a thick muscled neck, of a piece with the thick muscled build of its owner, whose hooded sweatshirt read ME VARSITY.

Raymond was floored by a punch that he never saw coming, that the boy threw without hesitation like a snake striking.

Back in the dressing room, Raymond sat holding a paper towel on his split lip.

Tyler Robb, who played Mac, pulled his round-collared white period shirt off over his head. His long slicked-back black hair contrasted sharply with the corpse-like pallor of his thin bony torso. "What do you think, Pops," he said, "We need to call somebody?"

"I'll be all right," Raymond said.

"Nine dollars an hour still worth it, you think?"

Raymond tried to smile. It hurt his lip.

"I mean, I'm only nineteen. I'm just getting started. But you, a man of your years with your history—cowboy, sailor, businessman, poet—isn't it hard sometimes to have come down to this?"

"I don't look at it that way. I always wanted to be an actor. And anyway, I'm not an antique, Tyler. I'm just middle-aged."

"My father's middle-aged and he's an antique. He sits in his easy chair in front of the television and never moves. I take my friends in to see him. Sometimes I polish him up, like I polish the copper vats here." Having slipped into the tight black jeans and hooded black sweatshirt that were his invariable street costume, Tyler hung his brewmaster costume on a hook in the crowded locker he shared with another guide. "Okay, let's get out of here. You want me to help you up? I don't mean to be offensive. It's just that I've got a date and I'm running late."

"No, I can manage. So, you finally asked Regan out?"

"Don't say the name, Pops. If you start saying the name, you'll forget you're not supposed to say it and you'll blurt it out in front of everyone."

"I'm not senile, either. And stop calling me Pops."

"Sure, Pops. Of course you're not senile. Maybe a little on the outer space side sometimes."

"I remember many things, sometimes."

"Of course you do. So, I hear it's going to be a lot rougher out where you are, with Noel getting here at high tide and all. You taking any special precautions?"

"Noel?"

"You're kidding, right? You heard about it. The big storm? No? What planet did you say you were from? Look, Pops, I gotta go or I'll miss my bus. Will you lock up? The code's one two two eight two. I'll write it down."

Raymond thought this was what it must mean to be *knocked into next week*. His head would not stop spinning. He lost track of how long he sat waiting to be able to get up off the dressing bench without falling down. When he did finally get up, he retrieved from between two stacks of shrink-wrapped beer-case-loaded pallets the bicycle that would take him to his truck. At ten dollars an hour, he could not afford the parking charges that would have let him park nearby. The brewery had its own parking lot, but the lowly tour guides were not allowed to use the spaces.

Carrying the bike out a side entrance into the light of the street lamps, he was greeted rudely by a huge roaring wind far beyond the morning's, and a driving rain that soaked him to the skin in an instant.

From the brewery to Raymond's truck a mile away, the streets were uphill and at first very steep. Usually Raymond walked the bike up the first demanding stretch instead of grinding out the distance pedaling, but the wind was so strong behind him now that the pedaling was almost effortless. He gained momentum, his body a living sail, till he was fairly flying along, his tires flinging wide the water streaming past him down the streets. He concentrated fiercely on not being blown over altogether.

He was flying past the entrance to Camp Hill cemetery when he noticed that the gate was open.

Instantly, even as he thought how unusual it was that the gate should be open so late in the evening, he swerved between the stone arches to get out of the traffic and take the short cut through the cemetery up to Robie. That this was one of his usual lamebrained mistakes was his next thought as within moments the light from the street lamps faded and the darkness of the cemetery rang down around him like an iron curtain. He was going so fast he could just make out the headstones racing past on either side like the teeth of a pair of jaws into which he was racing. The speed was nightmarish and, as if in a nightmare, it made no difference at all when he stopped pedaling completely. He squeezed the hand brakes but they didn't slow him down in the least. Still he thought he might make it. He seemed to have the hang of the breakneck navigation, and a marker that was a low pyramid of stone cannon balls indicated he might be more than halfway through. Then a treacherous cross-gust caught him and sent him careening willy-nilly into a monolith of rose-pink marble.

When he came to, he was sprawled on his back on the ground with the rain driving down in his face and a man in a leather vest and a three-cornered hat bending over him. By the dim flickering light of a handheld lantern, the man was contemplating him with concern. In the man's other hand were Raymond's glasses, the metal frames of which were twisted and one of the lenses shattered.

"Well," said the man in a kind way, with a kind smile, quite distinctly through the wind and rain yet not at all loudly, "So you're not one of us yet. You've only had a little spill, so you have, and mangled your spectacles somewhat."

Raymond was too groggy to catch all the man said. There was no doubt about the message his nose was giving him, however. "What's that awful smell?" he said.

"'Tis the fish oil," said the man, indicating his lantern. "It doesn't burn well, and it stinks like the devil, but it's easy to come by in a port city."

"Very authentic. And I love your hat. I'm amazed it stays on in this wind. I wish I got to wear a hat like that on my tour. I'm a guide down at Keith's. What tour are you with?"

"My name is Burton Latimer, sir. I am on the tour of lost souls, a tour of duty, you might say, and I fear it is not worth the hat. Could I remove it, I would give it thee, but I cannot. This hat and I are fastened together for all eternity. It *is* within my power to restore your spectacles, however. Would you like that?"

The man's image blurred, doubling and even tripling before returning to normal. Raymond became aware of a pounding in his head and realized on putting his hand to his temple that not only his glasses but his bicycle helmet was gone too. He looked all around, at the base of the monolith, at the twisted wreck of the bicycle, as far into the rows of graves as the dim fish oil lantern allowed.

"My helmet," he said. "I'm missing my helmet."

"Perhaps it was not well secured."

"I think I've … hurt my head."

"Tis likely you have. I said a *little* spill, but judging by the damage to your conveyance, it must have been rather nasty. It certainly made the monolith ring again. Nevertheless, I must ask you to attend, sir, to this matter of your spectacles. Shall I set them to rights? A simple yes or no will do."

"Fix my glasses? How can you … how would I get them back? I need to get home now."

"My dear boy, it's the work of a moment. I can do it right here. Yes or no?"

"Well, sure, if you can. But how can you? The glass is smashed. You'd have to be a magician."

"I have my tricks," said Burton Latimer. Looking up from Raymond into the sky, he held up the glasses as if offering them to the storm-torn darkness, and cried out, "Hear me now! He has given consent! The words have been said, and the words have been heard!"

Setting the lantern down on the base of the monument, the man made a loose fist, passed Raymond's glasses through the fist and knelt and placed them back on Raymond's face. Raymond blinked in wonder. The smashed lens was whole as before and the frames were like new and fit perfectly. And the rain—the rain did not obscure or even seem to alight on the lenses.

The face of the man, now sharply in focus, Raymond saw was deeply lined with a bold beak of a nose and sad blue eyes, so sad Raymond could feel the sadness in himself, deep inside, as if the man's gaze were transferring some unbearable loss into his heart. He let himself be helped to his feet. His helmet, produced as if from nowhere, was quickly and deftly strapped back on his head.

"Now," said Latimer. "Until we meet again, farewell."

Then the bike, undamaged and in perfect working order, was back in his hands and he was alone in the furious weather in the dark in Camp Hill Cemetery. The only light was a faint glow from the rose pink monolith, just enough for him to make out the epitaph inscribed on the side:

God Rest Ye Merry Gentleman
Burton Latimer
1768 – 1820

The bicycle was borrowed.

Rose and Will Renneker, who no longer kept a car, let Raymond use their parking space in the graveled parking lot behind their row house on Henry Street in exchange for the occasional use of his truck. In addition to the parking space they had a tiny fenced-in yard with a diminutive garden and a shed no bigger than it had to be. That spring Rose, who had just retired, dedicated herself to the garden. As she no longer needed her bicycle to ride to work, she wanted it out of the shed to make more room for her gardening gear. Suspecting that she might one day want to ride the bicycle again, she was against selling it, yet she had nowhere else to keep it. This dilemma was on her mind the day Raymond first arrived to make use of his parking spot. On Raymond's mind was the problem of the spot being so far from the Brewery, a good twenty-minute stroll downhill and a determined thirty-minute hike back up. The upshot was that Rose had lent Raymond the bike. He was several sizes too large for it, and it was a girl's bicycle, and the back wheel was out of true and did wobble a bit, but since the loss of his bookstore he had become quite a believer in the old adage *beggars can't be choosers*. Anyway it wasn't that hard to ride, and he didn't mind what people thought of him. What he did mind was two weeks of sharp comments about his lack of a helmet from Wade who served him coffee at the Trident, so he had bought a used helmet for ten dollars, because as Wade said *it was the law and he couldn't afford to be in trouble with the law.*

He couldn't really afford to be in trouble with anyone, because although he was still a big healthy-looking bruiser of a man, he had become quite delicate. In his fifty-fourth year the anguish of his separation from Cat had scrambled his heartbeat and sent him to the emergency room where he had almost died of a blood clot. He didn't want trouble with Rose Renneker tonight, but he knew she would be waiting for him—her husband was away—and he didn't want to be with her. Usually sex with Rose was a welcome relish in his life, like a jalapeño-stuffed olive, but tonight he had no appetite. His head hurt from the sucker punch at work and from his accident in the cemetery and he was frightened by the excessive power of the storm. Also a ghost had just fixed his glasses. Home was all Raymond wanted at the moment.

He threw the bike in the back of the truck and was backing out when the porch light came on and Rose in her nightgown and slippers rushed out waving and calling his name.

"Raymond, are you all right? You're so late! I was so worried about you! Oh, you *have* had an accident. I knew it! Just look at you, all muddy and bloody and soaked to the skin. And still wearing your bicycle helmet! You're in shock, aren't you, sweetheart? Come inside. I'll take care of you."

He would have liked for someone to take care of him. He would have liked to wake up in his bed with his mother sitting beside him, stroking his hair and telling him soothingly it was only a nightmare—not just the incident in the cemetery but in fact the whole mad business of growing up and growing old. He might have let Rose take care of him if she had not leaned in through the open window to kiss him, because when she did her lips shriveled away and her teeth were left pressed to him. Then the rest of her features evaporated and he found himself joined at the mouth with a grinning bared skull.

He jerked back in horror. When he did, the skull jerked back too, and Rose reappeared outside, looking like her usual self except that the rain had flattened her bobbed blonde hair and made a ghoulish mess of her mascara.

"Ray," she cried, "what's wrong?"

"Rose," he said, gripping the wheel with both hands and looking straight ahead away from her and over the dash, "You're very good, but I am *very* tired. I am tired in the way of being tired of all things, and I beg you will excuse me. I must go home, and I must go home *now*."

The windshield wipers beat time to the awkward silence that ensued, while the wind blew the rain through the open window so it splattered across the steering wheel and speedometer.

"Ray, why are you talking like that?" Rose said finally.

"Like what?"

"Like a character from your beer tour! Do you think this is funny?"

Raymond did not think it was funny. He knew what she meant, was quite aware that he had spoken strangely, archaically strangely. But he had not meant to, and now he was doubly bewildered. First his eyes had betrayed him, and now the words from his mouth. He sat stunned while the rain poured in and Rose's nightgown billowed up around her in the wild wind.

"Ray, please come in," Rose pleaded. "I think you've got a concussion. You don't need to be driving right now, especially not in this weather."

"Forgive me," he said, reaching out and taking her hand. "I am not who I was, nor quite yet who I will be, and I forget who I am."

He had no idea what he was saying. The words came out seemingly of their own volition. He gave her hand a last squeeze and put the truck back in reverse. He made an attempt to reclaim his own voice.

"I think you're right," he said. "I must have a concussion."

"Then why are you going?"

"Emergency. I'm going to the emergency room."

"Let me go with you. I'll just throw something on. It's only a few blocks to the hospital. I won't be a minute."

He thought of her there beside him in the truck, turned skeleton from tip to toe. He shook his head and was about to say, No, I've to go alone, when the strange voice pushed past and he found himself saying instead, "Madam, God be with you, for tonight I cannot be."

As he drove away from the forlorn figure in the sodden gown, he waved to her out the window. She in turn held a hand halfway up, wanting to reply in kind but not having the heart. In a small dispirited voice she called after him, "Oh, I like your new glasses, by the way. They're very becoming."

Raymond did go to the hospital, but when he walked in through the emergency room entrance, his vision continued to betray him. The variously damaged people waiting in the rows of bolted-down orange plastic seats, and the medical personnel coming and going and seated in the admissions station, all were transformed in an instant into animated skeletons.

A big skeleton stroked the skull of the little skeleton crying in its lap and said, "It's all right, sweetheart. Everything's going to be all right. I promise."

Raymond got as far as the admissions station, but when the skeleton in the nurse's uniform behind the counter told him to take a number and have a seat till his number was called, he fled.

His half-hour drive home from downtown Halifax to the village of Prospect was another kind of nightmare. The trees no longer danced but whipped themselves in a mad frenzy and sent their broken limbs flying across the streets and roads. A wheeled refuse bin trundling along by itself spewed fish heads and rotten papaya skins across the truck's windshield. At the last turnoff, a parted power line snaked and snapped and sparked across both lanes, narrowly missing the truck as Raymond swerved and sped up to avoid it.

Arriving at last at his house by a thundering sea, Raymond hurried inside, stripped off his wet clothes (though he kept the bicycle helmet on), and put on all three of his house robes (summer, fall and winter weight), along with his fleece-lined winter boots. On the stereo he put Bach's cello suites and turned the volume up to mask the shrieking of the storm. Then he lowered every blind in the house, upstairs and down, warmed a mug of whiskey in the microwave and in the living room area of the big main open room settled himself deep in the overstuffed turquoise leather chair by the turquoise leather couch and cradled the warmed mug against his belly. He sat there, helmeted and robed and booted, a very unlikely warrior, and sipped, and felt the house vibrate like a tuning fork, and listened to flapping and knocking noises as parts of the roof began to work themselves loose.

He thought about Burton Latimer and the magical repair of his glasses. About Rose Renneker's lipless teeth pressed to his lips. He revisited the skeletons in the hospital. Then, in search of a safer subject, a saner one, his mind veered to Cat. He told himself he was glad that she wasn't there with him, in a sea-level house with the sea at the door and a hurricane riding in on the waves. Then he wished she *were* there, in his lap in the overstuffed chair, holding onto him and he to her, each comforting and reassuring the other. Then he noticed the dent in the living room wall where she had thrown her coffee cup at him the night she left, and he was glad she was *not* there, with her rages black and wild as any hurricane. Then, because he missed her so, he wished aloud he had it in him not to father such rages, and the tears ran down.

He knew with an awful certainty he would never escape into sleep on such a terrible night. And in a matter of five minutes he nodded off.

The tears dried. His grip loosened and the last of the whiskey spilled into his lap. He dreamed he was back in junior high school, wandering the corridors, wondering why he couldn't find his next class on an exam day of all days. He had just found the room, and was at his desk staring confounded at an exam whose questions made no sense at all, when a sound like a car crashing into the house shocked him awake.

He half-expected to see a wall collapsed or some other evident damage, some blatant intrusion, but there was none. He struggled out of the overstuffed chair and went to the front door, halfway between the living room area and the kitchen and dining room area, in the middle of the long southern wall facing the sea.

The front door and its storm door were glass. For privacy, Raymond kept a shoji screen in front of them. He swung the screen aside now and flicked on the porch light.

He should have seen his front lawn and the graveled lane called Lands End and beyond it his boathouse and dock and ramp down to the cove. In the lawn, on the band of exposed granite along the lane, there should have been a whale's rib, ancient and starred with orange lichen and with the flowering hens and chicks in the cavity at the top that Cat had planted there. And leading to the house from the lane should have been the short curling walkway of pale granite paving stones that had once graced the streets of old Halifax.

Instead in the light there was only the sea, the dark rolling sea, all the way to the doorstep, where it foamed and licked and pounded at the lower half of the glass storm door like a slobbering beast wanting in.

And then the light went out as the bulb was smashed by a piece of flying debris.

He couldn't call. The regular phone wouldn't work and he couldn't remember where he'd put his cell phone. He couldn't leave because he was too scared to go out to his truck. Yet he couldn't stand just standing there and being so damn scared—scared out of his mind.

He tried going back to sleep. He tried first in the overstuffed chair, but the sounds the sea made as it lapped at the wall near the chair were too close, like someone whispering in his ear, *please let me just swallow you whole and alive.* He tried next in the guest room further inside the house, but the room was so small that when he lay in bed there he could touch the walls from either side, as if he had been buried alive and they were the walls of his coffin. He tried in his usual bed upstairs, but the skylight just above the bed was like headphones to the fury outside, and the foam earplugs that had always kept out Cat's snoring had hardened in the nine months since she had left and would not stay in his ears. Also each time the plugs slipped out he had to remove his helmet to put them in again, and it seemed very important that the helmet remain on his head.

Another thing he couldn't do was get his glasses off. Each time he tried to sleep he tried to take them off, and each time they stuck to his head. He told himself it didn't matter, that there were worse things to worry about. But it did matter. It was like the last straw in going crazy. After giving up on the earplugs, he lay pulling on the glasses till he was afraid his face would come off with them.

As a last resort, to find something he *could* do, he went to the shrine room to meditate.

At the heart of the practice of sitting meditation, or so Raymond had gathered after twenty-two years, was a refuge from ignorance. He knew he could not escape fear any more than he could run from his shadow. Fear had to be faced. Fears were just thoughts, and thoughts had no substance. He could let go of fear because in fact fear was not really there to hold onto. He just had to sit down with it, let it be there, look into it. He had practiced this way all those years. He was surprised he had not done so already tonight. Even there on the lee side of the house, the walls vibrated around him and the wind forced its way through the seals of the double-paned windows with an eerie low whistling, an incessant summons as if for an unwilling dog. Tonight there was no lack of substanceless fear to be faced. So with determination, he sat. Yet for Raymond the unwilling dog, tonight the heart in his mouth seemed so very substantial he imagined he could taste the blood.

He got up from the cushion where he was sitting cross-legged and lit another stick of incense. From a bookshelf he took a notebook of songs. Nerving himself to take his seat again, he opened the notebook on the low table before him and began to sing.

Father, protector of wanderers ...

It was a traditional song from the Buddhist saint Milarepa, meant to bring a practitioner's teacher strongly to mind and to invoke that teacher's fearless compassion. Raymond sang the song loudly, both to encourage himself and to drown out the wind at the windows. After singing it several times, courage did indeed start to return, slowly but surely. As far as his hearing was concerned, however, the loud singing had the unusual effect of making him hear more rather than less. Not only was the wind not drowned out, he began to discern a whole range of melodies in it. In a growing accompaniment, he heard the surge of the sea along the sides of the house, the humming of the air recirculation system, the refrigerator cycling on and off down in the kitchen. He could even make out, after a while, more murmuring from the basement, a murmuring which was now in two-part harmony.

What he could not hear was the sump pump. This caught his attention and cut short his singing, for the sump pump was what kept the basement from flooding. Normally it cycled on regularly to keep the water table from rising into the basement with the rising tides. With a heavy rainfall it would cycle on even more often. With the sea now at the door, it should have been working overtime, with its distinctive hum much in evidence. Yet there was nothing—nothing but the steady beeping of the alarm that indicated that the pump was so far underwater that it was either overwhelmed or not working at all.

His cell phone rang while the dismaying implications of this were sinking in and so he was slow to answer. The first few bars of When The Saints Go Marching In had played and stopped four times before he roused himself and found the phone in the sleeve of the innermost of his three robes.

"Hello?"

"Hello. What are you wearing?"

"Cat, is that you?"

"Yes."

"Why are you calling me?"

"I said, *what are you wearing*?"

"You're calling me for phone sex in the middle of a hurricane?"

"You used to be pretty good at it anytime."

"Cat, this is not anytime. This is definitely not a good time."

"Not a good time for who? I'm lying here in a cold bed with a spilled margarita, I can't sleep for this godawful wind, and I'm missing my husband. What is it? Are you with someone?"

He searched for the right thing to say—something endearing, for he missed her too, and yet something that would let her know what a hard time he was having without making him sound crazy. As he considered, the photos of his teachers on the wall before him vanished and were replaced in their frames by grinning skulls whose jaws moved and whose creaking laughter dovetailed with the sump pump alarm in a macabre counterpoint.

What he wanted to say, what he thought he was going to say, was simply *No, no one's here with me I wish you were here with me I need you*. But as with Rose Renneker, the aberration of his vision was followed by one of his speech, and again the words of another person from another time with another intent came out.

"My dear Catriona," he said, "I've the sea in my lap, the unforgiving sea, and must go down. Pray for me."

He left his robes on the ground floor landing and took the steps to the basement in only his boxer shorts, his glasses and his bicycle helmet. At the very last step, he stepped into scummy water to his shins and waded through the open door. The water was a foot high and rising up the sides of the deep freeze, washer and dryer that lined one wall. Taking a flashlight from the shop table against the adjoining wall and putting it between his teeth, he got down on his hands and knees and went through the low square entrance leading out of the basement and into the dark flowing crawlspace. The water was icy against his chest and belly and genitals. The joists of the floor above brushed the top of his head. He came to the place where the new house ended and the old house began. The concrete floor ended. On the other side of the plywood lip, polyethylene-sheathed rock sloped slightly downwards into a natural declivity. Raymond slid down the slippery plastic till only his head and the flashlight in his mouth were above water. The light showed water spurting in through all three outside walls.

Half-swimming, half-slithering, he made his way up the slope toward the corner where the sump pump was housed. The squealing of the alarm was now piercingly loud. Scanning the corner with his light, he saw the problem immediately. In the outlet high on one wall where the alarm and the pump plugged in, the pump plug and cord were nowhere to be seen.

Someone had unplugged the pump. Who the hell would have unplugged the pump?

There was no time to think. He took the flashlight from his mouth and propped it on a crosspiece just below the outlet. The illumination was indirect and poor but it relieved his aching jaws, and he didn't need much light anyway to grope in the murk around the pump. When he found the plug, he wiped it dry with an old rag the plumber had left on a nail by the outlet the last time he serviced the pump, then with shaking hands he guided the prongs into the outlet.

The pump sprang powerfully to life and began to suck. How it had become disconnected Raymond could not even begin to imagine, but at the moment, with it working again, he did not much care.

Then the pump went quiet again. The whole house went quiet. The only sound left was the storm, and down here that was muffled and distant.

It dawned on Raymond that the problem now was that the power had gone out.

"Well," he said, "Why not just drag me right on down to hell?"

At that he was seized by his ankles and dragged backward. His eyes stayed open as his head went underwater. The last thing he saw was the dim radiance of the flashlight on the wall, dim and growing rapidly dimmer. And then there was nothing.

Chapter 2
Angle & Octave

Captain Oliver Cole emerged from another interlude of absent-mindedness and immediately took stock of where and when and who he was. Yes, he was in downtown Halifax on Lower Water Street. There to his left was the harbour, and to his right, a block further, the granite walls of the brewery of Alexander Keith. And the time? He was certainly back in the present. Along the piers of the harbour, the ships were sailing ships, their crowded masts and spars in the slow-falling snow like a winter wood stripped of leaves. And the street was paved with granite paving stones, and the conveyances that made up the traffic were all horse-drawn.

And yes he was Captain Oliver Cole, though he walked now with the aid of a cane and though he made his way slowly like a doddering old man, for there waiting for him, across the street under the archway of his friend's brewery, was his wife Josephine in her best blue dress and bonnet already holding her gloved hands out to greet him, and his daughter Amélie in a bonny red cloak, half as tall as her mother already.

He wondered how long it had been. The snow, a gentle sifting that made its unhurried way downward in large separate flakes through the calm lamplit evening, was not a first falling. The curbs on both sides of the street were heaped high.

Overwhelmed with emotion, he paused in crossing the street to remove his top hat and bow to his loved ones, and consequently was so nearly side-swiped by a coach and four that he lost his balance on the slippery uneven paving stones and fell.

"Here now, guv," said a rough voice as a hand took his arm. "Up you go."

The Captain felt his pocket being picked as he was heaved to his feet, and grabbed at his purse. "No, you don't, you blaggard."

"Just taking my thanks in advance, like," growled the man, wresting the purse easily from the Captain's feeble grasp.

"Help! Help, thief!" the Captain called. "Josephine, Amélie, call for help, my dears! I'm being robbed!" He flung both arms around the pickpocket and held on for dear life as the man dragged him off his feet trying to escape. "No you don't! You can't!"

The man stopped and locked the Captain's neck in an iron embrace in the crook of his arm and leered close into his face with bloodshot eyes. "Sure I can. And I can break your face too. Is that what you're after, old dad? 'Cause that's what you'll get."

The thief's braided hair had escaped his Monmouth cap and hung over his shoulder and down by his whiskery chin. "Why, you're a sailor," the Captain said, staring at the braid and at the golden earrings in the man's ears.

"What's it to you?"

"If you're down on your luck, I can get you a ship. I'm a captain. Only give back my purse. There's no money in it, anyway. Only something important to me."

"If it's important to you, Cap'n, it'll be worth something to someone."

"No one knows how to use them but me. Wait! My wife will have money!"

"Let go, damn and blast! Well, I warned you."

The man wrenched the purse free and struck the Captain across the face with it. The clasps broke open in the event and two golden objects spilled out and went skittering across the stones. One was a bell with a handle, the other a double-headed sceptre no longer than a handspan. The thief dove for the objects, but was interrupted in his pursuit by the passage of a carriage, and secured only the bell before the advent of several men running to the fallen captain's aid persuaded him to leave the little sceptre and take to his heels.

The Captain lay in a heap. Looking up, he saw his wife and daughter beside him.

"Oliver," said Josephine, stooping, "Oh, Oliver."

"Pápi?" said Amélie.

"Hello, you two," said Captain Oliver Cole. "Hello again. More bad luck, I'm afraid."

His eyes would not stay open. Letting them close, he felt the snowflakes kiss his eyelids, then his cheeks.

Josephine, Amélie—had he lost them again? Or were they not his to lose, and only dream people in a desperate dream? But if he was dreaming, when had the dream started? The night with Mimi? Or had he been injured in the crash in Camp Hill cemetery, and was he now in a hospital bed? Everything since the crash had been much like a dream. Burton Latimer. The magical repair of his glasses and Latimer's proclamation. All the visions of skeletons. Being dragged by some demonic creature into the depths of an abyss in his very own basement.

Who was he? When was he?

He felt around him without opening his eyes. It wasn't a hospital bed. It was Raymond Kidd's bed, in Raymond Kidd's house, at 7 Lands End. And these were his old flannel sheets and his quilted down comforter. And this was his Japanese chest at his bedside, a little dusty on top, and his lamp and his phone. And his manuscript.

And this was Raymond's bicycle helmet, still on his head. And these were the glasses that wouldn't come off.

He took a deep breath to steady himself. And found that he smelled like the sea, as if he had been scented with seaweed and salt water.

"If I'm going to be stuck in a dream," he announced to the room he had yet to look out on, "at least let me be young. And stop taking my lovers away."

Then the pickpocket spoke to him again.

"Better stuck in a dream than stuck in between. But you ain't dreamin', Cap'n. You're awake, all right. Now you just lie there quiet-like till you get your bearings, eh?"

"The part of the dream with you in it is over," said Raymond. "You got the purse. You got the bell. You ran away. Now leave me alone. I'm going to wake up now."

"Beggin' yer pardon, sir, but it's like I was sayin'. Yer already awake. You just need to open your eyes. When you do, you'll see me. Leastwise, I'm pretty sure you will. I'm outta yer basement, and I show up in your mirror there, and you're already hearin' me. But don't you worry. I ain't strange lookin'. No rope burns, no ax wounds, no bullet holes. Nothing bloody or horrible. Nothing out of the ordinary."

Raymond opened his eyes. There beside him, in a plain wooden chair from the kitchen, was the pickpocket. The eyes were no longer bloodshot, and the whiskery chin now sported a fully grown beard, but the braid and the earrings and the weatherworn deeply tanned face were the same. The only thing really different about the man were his clothes. They were Raymond's. The ragged white sweatshirt and sweatpants were his latest painting outfit, splotched with the same turquoise that covered the house. The black rubber sea boots had CAT painted on them in dribbly red letters.

Raymond stared, and blinked, and touched his glasses. His visitor, with his arms folded over his chest, smiled back amiably, neither disappearing nor becoming a skeleton.

"Just ol' Angle Daggon like he was in his prime, sir, reportin' for duty."

The name stirred Raymond's memory. "Angle Daggon?" he said. "When I moved here years ago, my neighbours made a point to tell me a story about an Angle Daggon who was a pirate who used to live here. I thought they were putting me on. They said he threw a wild party one night and went out for a breath of fresh air and lay down in the snow and passed out. Was found frozen to death the next morning. Are you *that* Angle Daggon?"

"I am. That I am. Or, as you might say, that I *was*. Though that story is out in a few particklars, for it was not lyin' down but sittin' up I died, and I never passed out but simply went to sleep a'contemplatin' matters. Furthermore, it wasn't only me as froze to death. My brother Octave died right along wi' me. But he weren't no pirate, and so he gets left out o' the story."

Raymond ignored the particulars. Still staring, he said, "Then you're a ghost."

"Well now, sir ..."

"You're one of the ghosts in my basement."

"Beggin' your pardon, Cap'n, we did sling our hooks in your basement, but we ain't no ghosts. Never have been. Never will be. *Lost souls* is what you want to say. Octave and I talked it over, over and over—people lived and died while we was talkin' about it—and we come to the conclusion that we ain't ghosts 'cause we don't haunt no one. Nor never wanted to. We sort of lost our way is all. And while I'm at it I might as well tell you that we know you mean well, but it don't do no good you sittin' up there with your candles and your incense advisin' us to *let go* every time you hear us talkin'. We know what you mean, all right, but you don't give no practical instructions, and we ain't got no idea how to go about it. If we did, we wouldn'a been here all this time, stuck in the doldrums for what seems like all eternity, first out o' doors, and then in a basement that floods for a nothin', where there's never a breath but is that thick with mold you could chew it and swallow it."

"I'm sorry," said Raymond. "I didn't mean to insult you. And I didn't think about instructions. I did put in a dehumidifier. I know it broke. I've been meaning to get a new one, but they're expensive, and ..."

"Never you mind, Cap'n, sir. I ain't here to complain."

"Why *are* you here? And why do you keep calling me Captain?"

"Well, sir, I'll answer your last question first, since it's easy. Your name is Kidd, see, and it's many the time you sailed off in that ol' yawl o' yourn, out to sea all by yourself, and Octave and I watchin' (which we can see through walls at least), well, we called you that just for a laugh—Cap'n Kidd! After that there famous Scottish privateer what got hisself hanged for a pirate, right? Ha ha. So I guess I got into the habit. But it ain't no sign o' disrespect, sir. For I was in that line myself, the privateerin' line, that is, and still retain a few fond memories, even reformed as I am. Speakin' of Octave, sir, I wonder if we might not continue our conversation down where he is, in the basement still with all that nasty water, so as not to leave him all alone. He ain't used to my not bein' there, see. Not since we died. We been together—right close together, no one else to come between— ever since, and that is quite a while."

"And why are you wearing my clothes?" said Raymond, who had not stopped staring. "Why aren't you dressed in your own, from your own time? The ghost in the graveyard last night, he had his own clothes still. And why is your brother still down there? Why didn't he come up here with you?"

"Well, he can't. Not so far. And in fact he's some disturbed and more'n a little put out that I can. Cap'n, there's mysteries everywhere, and I'll tell all I know, but can we please first set poor Octave's mind at rest? And perhaps you might do us the honour of bringin' a bottle o' whiskey along. Against the cold, like."

"You get cold?"

"In course we do. Which we was used to what is felt there in the in-between, where it ain't never quite warm, but now we're flesh and blood again, it's summat worse."

"You're flesh and blood?"

"For a fact, Cap'n, for a fact. And if you prick us, we bleed. But please, sir, now to Octave, and then you can ask all the questions you like, broadside after broadside."

"Angle … can I call you Angle?"

"Well, there's no sense pretendin' we're newly acquainted, havin' shared the same digs all these years."

"Angle, truthfully, I'm a little scared to go down there. The last time I did, something awful happened. Something I have trouble even thinking about."

"It worn't us, Cap'n. I'll swear on a stack of bibles it worn't us. We may ha' been a little behind-hand in stoppin' it, but we did fish you out soon as ever we could, and you're livin' proof that we did it in time."

"How do I know it won't happen again?"

"We ain't goin' under that part of the house. We'll just stay in your shop. It always was safe in your shop."

"You'll swear to that?"

"Bring out your good book, sir."

Raymond's good book, since he had not been a Christian for twenty-odd years, was not a bible but a Buddhist text entitled Pure Appearance. He chose it because for some reason it had been pulled part way out from the other books in the shrine room bookshelf, a coincidence that seemed auspicious. For his part, Angle would not enter the shrine room to swear on the text, said he could not, and when outside the room he did press the palm of his hand to the yellowed white paperback cover, he could be seen to lose his composure and break out in a very unghostly sweat. Nevertheless he did swear and swear heartily and Raymond was persuaded. As they descended the last short flight of stairs to the basement, Raymond armed with the bottle of whiskey he had retrieved from the kitchen, the ghostly howl that issued from the open basement door gave him pause, but he was reassured by the swearing and complaining that followed, for it was very human if somewhat unusual.

"Ow! Sacred purple! Name of a chicken! Dam up my eyes! The blamed thing bit me. Oh, oh, oh! Dead once and almost killed again! Fool! Meddler! Head of a moose!"

"That's our Octave," Angle said, speaking up to Raymond from below him on the stairs, "Don't you mind him. Harmless as they come. A little exotic of expression when he gets riled, mayhap." Two steps further down was the open door of the basement with the water there brimming to the top of the first step. "Now, Brother, compose yourself," he called ahead. "I've got the Cap'n wi' me."

Raymond waded in after Angle to find Angle's brother perched dripping on the broad white lid of Raymond's top-loading partially submerged deep freeze. Pieces of Raymond's small black auxiliary pump lay scattered around him on the lid. Across the lid lay the ends of two hoses that had been attached to the pump. One hose led into the water, the other up and out of an opened window behind. The air reeked of burnt plastic.

"Mr. Kidd," said the perching man, visibly trembling, his face red with pain and embarrassment, "my apologies. I have witnessed you operate this pumping device, and was convinced it was within my capabilities to do the same. Yet it would not function when I *turned it on*, as you say, and when I disassembled it to inspect its inner workings, it came alive in my hand and delivered a most dreadful sensation. Had it been followed by a clap of thunder, I would swear I had been struck by lightning. I was propelled willy nilly into the water."

There was nothing out of the ordinary about this second apparition, either. He had a round pinkish face that was clean shaven but for a thin blonde mustache neatly trimmed to the ends of his thin upper lip, sparse blonde hair that had receded halfway up his scalp, and a short pointy nose. There was some family resemblance in the broad openness of his face, and in the widely set blue eyes, but not much. Like his brother, however, his clothes were Raymond's clothes, in this case the jeans and black mock turtleneck pullover Raymond had dumped down the laundry chute three days ago. Both man and clothes were soaked and dripping. The puddle of water underneath him was an inch from the disassembled pump, and the distance was lessening as the dripping continued.

"The power must be back on," Raymond said. "Have you unplugged it yet?"

"I have not. I am afraid now to touch any part of it."

"Don't move!" Raymond sloshed to the wall, reached behind the freezer and unplugged the pump. "There. Now you're safe. You were almost a dead man."

"Thank you," said the crouching man, shivering and hugging himself to keep warm. "I have been a dead man for the better part of two centuries. It is only a matter of hours since I ceased being one. I am not anxious to return so soon. But *safe*? *Safe*, you say? I wonder. For the nonce, yes, but is anyone safe for long with this flaw in the fabric exploited? With the borders between here and the hereafter laid open? With a demon underneath who is our …"

"Brother," interrupted Angle, "where's your manners? The Cap'n here's our guest. Not only that, he's our *host*. You're to welcome him properly 'fore you commence to pontificatin'. Sir," he said, turning to Raymond, "he ain't always like this. It was him as spent all eternity teachin' *me* how to behave."

"It's understandable," said Raymond. "He's not only been shocked, he's in shock. So am I … but in his case I think I think it's nothing that dry clothes and whiskey won't fix. Here." He extended the bottle.

"My name is Octave, Mr. Kidd. Octavius, properly speaking, and I will be very frank. I will be very h-h-honest. I am indeed in a state of unaccustomed and even overwhelming agitation, but it is not due altogether to your devilish device. Devilish forces are indeed at work, but on a far far grander scale. Oh, make no doubt. I had rather not welcome you at all down here. Upstairs would be much better. In the kitchen, perhaps, by the woodstove. Very close to the woodstove, I think. And if you would do me the favour of lighting a fire in the stove, and brewing a hot cup of tea …"

"I thought you couldn't go upstairs."

"Which he couldn't," said Angle. "He bounced back like a ball. Here, Cap'n, I'll take that bottle, if you don't mind. No use lettin' it go to waste."

"A rejection as c-c-certain as the one from your device," said Octave, "if less painful. Certainly less of a surprise. One thing you learn early on in the in-between, s-s-sir, is the reliability of boundaries. When you wander out of doors, you are bound by the limits of your community—in our case, our village. That is not a hard and fast boundary—when you pass it, you s-s-simply get weaker and weaker till you cannot go on. But when you come in, your sh-sh-shelter becomes your jail, and you cannot go out again. Not through an open window, not through an open door."

Angle guzzled a full quarter of the bottle of whiskey before handing it back to Raymond. Wiping his lips with the back of his hand, he said, "Aaaaahhhhh. If there was anythin' worth waitin' for as long as we waited, now that would be it."

Raymond capped the bottle. Not only was it far too early in the day—the situation called for sobriety. He had begun to feel that this was not a dream, that he had indeed awakened and that he was being called on somehow, in a way that required that his attention be clear and complete. "But you're not a ghost anymore. You're flesh and blood again, apparently. So why would you be bound by the rules of ghosts when Angle isn't?"

"What you say is true, sir, according to the logic of the l-l-living, except for the reference to ghosts. I was never a ghost and have never haunted nor hurt anyone nor abandoned my mother's code of right conduct in the l-l-least. So I find the term offensive and ask that henceforth you not employ it. Now, why am I still bound by the rules of *lost souls* when my brother is not? I do not know. There is your answer plain and simple. Were I to elaborate—and I do not favor elaboration, mind you—I would add that it might have something to do with the fact that this house was once divided, and that my half was moved elsewhere and no longer exists. This was Angle's half. One might guess that affords him greater liberties. But as I say, I do not favor elaboration. It is the play of an idle mind."

"You didn't just live here, then. You owned the house together."

"The old part. *Before* its division," and here he gave Angle a look of admonishment, as if to remind him of something in which he had erred.

"You built it?"

"No, our father took it from a man. Now, s-s-sir, before we continue, can we not go upstairs? I would be happy to tell you our story right from the beginning, but I find that my sh-sh-shivering is impeding my s-s-speech. And before you object, let me s-s-say that I believe I *might* be able to go up if you invite me. You are the owner now of the house as a whole, both the old and the new. An invitation from you could very well bridge the difference."

"All right, then. Come on up."

"More formally, if you please. S-s-say my name."

"Oh, all right. Octave, would you …"

"More formally yet. S-s-say *Octavius*."

"Octavius, then …"

"And the last name. Angle told you."

"Yes, he did, but how …"

"Just s-s-say it, sir, please."

He thought perhaps he shouldn't. He had agreed to say something the ghost in the graveyard had wanted him to say, and now his glasses were stuck to his head and he was seeing skeletons and reconstituted spirits. What awful bargain might he be entering into now? Still and all, the poor man looked so cold and pale, he couldn't help himself. "Octavius Daggon, come in, please. Come into my house." He gestured toward the stairs.

"You go before."

He went through the door and started up the stairs, only to hear a splash and a curse behind him. He turned around to find Octave on his back on the floor in the water, rubbing his nose.

"What happened?" he said.

"It was just as it ever was," said Octave, disconsolately, struggling to his feet. "That's what happened. Like colliding with a wall. Perhaps your invitation was less than sincere. Perhaps your heart was not in it."

"It was, though," said Raymond.

"After all, why would you want us in your life? We'd only make things difficult for you. We're just *ghosts*, as far as you're concerned."

"Look, I really tried. I really want to help."

"What you want," interrupted Angle, as he reached out, relieved Raymond of the bottle again, unscrewed the cap and took another swig, "is to *order* him up, not invite him. You're the Cap'n, after all."

"I always hated it when you drank in the morning," said Octave. "Not to mention any other time. But when you do it in the morning, then I have to put up with it all day. I thought you had changed. I guess once a drunkard always a drunkard, no matter how long between drinks."

"An order is the *ticket*, boys. That's how you get things done. Now Yer Honour, if you please, really put yourself into it. Imagine yourself at the wheel of your boat and your mate Octave down below in the cabin. The weather has changed and you need him on deck. Call him up. Call him up like you mean it. You're the Cap'n, for chrissakes. Really put yourself into it!"

Octave's implication that he did not care stung Raymond, because he feared it was true. The most hurtful thing Cat had ever said to him was that he was incapable of caring. Her accusation echoed in his ears even now. So he seized on Angle's suggestion with a vengeance, without considering the ramifications any further.

Closing his eyes, he imagined himself back on the deck of his yawl, with the big stainless steel wheel in his grip. He had no trouble *really putting himself into it*, for not only did he miss the boat more than he ever acknowledged, but he also had trained in visualization for years as part of his meditation practice, and it was no strange Eastern deity here of another color and any number of limbs and bizarre ornaments, but something perfectly familiar. The sweet sheer of the Cat, the spray flinging back from the bow as it plunged, his steering in a fine balance with the set of the sails and the angle of heel, the mizzen mast firm at his back, the living ocean beneath. A lightning-shot darkness ahead and the breeze muscling up. That freedom from the land that was glory itself.

Something deep stirred inside him. The words arose effortlessly.

"Mr. *Daggon*," he boomed out, "On deck to shorten sail. Look alive there!"

Quite pleased with himself and quite certain his command would be obeyed, Raymond opened his eyes.

There was no one else there. In the dim flooded basement was only himself. An empty whiskey bottle floated on the flood.

Every mortal day of her life, Nettie McEachern walked. Since the time she had put three steps together and been applauded by her parents for it, neither illness nor bad weather had held her back. She had struggled out of bed delirious with fever and, imagining her room as the highway to heaven, had strolled the perimeter until an angel took her hand and tucked her in again and said the Lord would see her soon enough. She had walked not only through rain, sleet, snow, and hail but also three hurricanes. The tale was still told in the village of how Hurricane Able was *able* enough to fling a ten-year-old Nettie, who was no slip of a girl, through Mort Christian's front window; and how Mort, who was spooning with his missus on the couch to pass the troubled time, had made no more remark than, "Didn't no one ever teach you to knock, Nettie Keddy?"

In her day she had walked all around. Like the back of her hand she knew the High Head, where the seagulls dropped crabs on the rocks to break them open for eating, and where the waves as they broke on the rocks would give her a little love-tap of spray if she walked close enough to the edge. Down in the salt marsh of the barachois she had become as familiar with the inhabitants as if they were kin—otters, golden eagles, owls, eels, even the elusive yellow rail—all creatures that were mostly gone now with the developers bulldozing everything to sell oceanfront lots to wealthy come-from-aways with no idea what they were killing off.

Nowadays she mostly walked the road. She had walked it as dirt, she had walked it as gravel, and now it was paved. She had walked all five miles of it from the village to the head of Prospect Bay, where it ended in the mainland road to Halifax. She had walked off her grief on it after her husband and two other fishermen motored out into a winter gale and were claimed by the sea. She walked the road now because it was a level surface and easier on her aching legs, and because with her children grown and gone she could find occasional company there. There were a few other regular walkers, and she could wave at familiar faces driving by, faces however which were fewer every year.

On the return leg of her constitutional the morning after Noel, Nettie paused beside the village graveyard, at that point where the road fell away sharply and the village below and the ocean with its necklace of islands around and beyond appeared so suddenly it took her breath away no matter how many thousands of times she had seen it. Noel's power was still evident in the waves that thundered against the High Head and broke high over Bald Rock in the offing and marched white-maned and glittering all out to the horizon under a sky as blue and clear as it must have been on the first day of creation. She closed her eyes and inhaled deeply. The inshore breeze was mild and pure, scented only with that pure scent of salt sea that raised her spirits till it made her almost dizzy with delight— an emotion she would not have expressed to any one at any time. She was a lean, wiry old woman, reticent about matters of the heart, a natural match for a coast called The Granite. Between her inner delight and her outward expression was a gulf that would no more be crossed. She did have a ready smile, however, a very civil one if modest, and a curiosity for any news there might be, so on her descent into the village, when she met young Sheila Littlefair toiling uphill with her infant son in the carriage, they naturally engaged in a neighbourly visit.

"Good morning, Nettie."

"Good morning, Sheila. I hope I see you and little Benjamin well."

"Well enough, thank you. Neither of us slept much last night, what with all that clattering and banging and shrieking and the whole house shaking like it was about to shatter. I mean, *I* could have slept, I think—I was that tired—but not little Ben. He screamed and cried for hours."

"Well, it was quite a commotion. Al*most* a hurricane, the weatherman said. More than almost, if you ask me, from the looks of things down by the water."

"Yes, I'm glad Ty took our boat out to the Roost before it hit, much as it scared me not having him here. If he had left her in the harbour, she would have been on the rocks for sure, like she was after Hurricane Juan, all stove in and the insurance denied."

"As it was altogether, to everyone, with every fixture in the harbour swept away but for Paddy Coolan's stage with its stinking open bait tub, that deserved it most of all. Ah, the ways of the Lord are for the Lord alone to understand. And so are the ways of the insurance companies, the back of my hand to them." Nettie peered into the carriage at its well-wrapped occupant. "Well, well, look at that. He's quiet enough now, isn't he? Sleeping away, little angel."

"He wore himself out fussing, poor thing. Wouldn't be comforted."

"When he wakes up he'll be fine though, as if it all never happened." She sighed, straightened and shook her head. "And then we grow up and it never stops happening—all the bad news. Did you see poor Booda Ray? The surge took his boathouse and set it in the playground next door again, just like with Juan. When I saw him this morning, he was sitting in his front yard on that old whalebone, head in his hands. Said it cost him three thousand dollars to have the boathouse moved back the last time and where was he going to find three thousand more. I said he should thank the Lord he had a boathouse that was still in one piece when everyone else's got beat to splinters the first time around. He just looked back at me real funny and didn't say anything. I guess it's because he's a Boodist and doesn't believe in the Lord."

"I did see him. I didn't talk to him though. He was still in his house robe. I thought he might be drunk."

"Oh, he's harmless enough. That's just his way. When he first got here thirteen years ago he used to come out dressed like that and muck around in the cove at low tide, collecting old trash like it was treasure—broken dishes, old silverware all salt-corroded, clay pipe stems, pieces of porcelain dolls. Now he hardly ever comes out at all. Bought a boat and had to sell it. Bought a bookstore in the city and had to sell that too. Got married and couldn't keep his wife either. He had me over to clean for him once. I found sprouts growing out of his shower drain. He wouldn't let me touch them. Said they were new growth, however acc-i-dental, that was bound to make it to the light no matter what, and so they were a sign his luck was changing. God love him."

"Well, these are trying times. Crazy weather, crazy economy, crazy terrorists. Enough to drive anyone crazy. Lucky for Ben and me that Ty's in disaster management and doing better than ever. Haven't I tried to get another job? Nettie, you take care, I have to get along now if I want to get my walk in."

"You know what Maddy Ryan says we ought to call that boathouse?" Nettie called after her as Sheila pushed the carriage away up the hill.

"No, what?"

"Booda's Ark. 'Cause it sails away with every flood but it never has anyone in it."

"Oh, that's terrible!"

"Isn't it?"

Naked, itching from bug bites, and sensible that they were no longer invisible, the two brothers hunched in a thicket of blueberry bushes a hundred feet back from the shore, peering through the foliage at the parade of vessels—fishing boats, motor cruisers, sailboats and a single rowboat—that was leaving the shelter of the high-sided cove through its one narrow exit to the west.

"Rogue's Roost," said Octave. "I might have known."

"How might you have known, Brother?" said Angle, scratching his side. "Since the day we woke up dead, I find there is precious little I might have known."

Octave slapped a black fly on his ear. "Because one, as I told you before, we shouldn't have fooled around with the living. And two, because you never learn."

"Well, for my part, *one*, we didn't have no choice about foolin' around with the livin'. We ain't dead no more. And *two*, how could I know that what I was thinkin' would still move us around? And right out of the house! As for it bein' the Roost, I couldn't help it. When I was tellin' the Cap'n to give you the order, it just natcherly put me in mind of our dad, *as he was*, and when I think of our dad *as he was*, I think of Rogue's Roost. This is where me and him was most often together, on the old *Queen Mab*, alyin' in wait and lookin' out for the main chance."

"We should have kept to ourselves in the first place, that's all."

"You mean, and let the Cap'n get pulled down by the one we don't name? I'm surprised at you, Brother. It was you as made a decent man of me, all those years in between."

"Angus Daggon, there is a flaw in the fabric ..."

"Would you just bugger off with your *flaw in the fabric*? That ain't our concern. Our concern is *we ain't dead* now. Don't you get it? We got to think about stayin' alive. I say we hale that yellow dory there. We're stuck here if we don't, since thinkin' ourselves back into the basement ain't workin'."

"You suit yourself. I'm not convinced I want to stay alive."

Shaking his head at his brother in sheer disbelief, Angle stood up in the thicket and waved his arms back and forth over his head and cried "Hey! Ho!"

The yellow dory was the last in the line of boats leaving shelter that bright morning after Noel, and had reached the mouth of the cove when the rower, a white-haired old man in a red and black plaid jacket and a black leather cap with a bill, saw a naked man run from the bushes onshore, waving and calling out, to be followed by another naked man who proceeded more slowly, with his hands cupped over his privates.

The old man lay on his oars for a moment, observing and contemplating and working a chew of tobacco, and then rowed back to within a few yards of the shore.

"You gentlemen forget something?" he said.

The bearded gentleman, who had a gold earring, a tattoo of a dagger through a rose on his chest, a rooster on one ankle and a pig on the other, replied, "Reckon we did."

The other gentleman, who had none of these things and was cleanshaven but for a thin precise mustache, nodded sheepishly in confirmation while keeping his hands in their place on his lap.

"Names?"

"Angle and …"

"…Octave Daggon."

"Daggons, eh? From the village?"

"That's right," answered Angle.

"I know all the Prospect Daggons. Don't recollect ever meetin' you two."

"Not likely you would."

"Been away, then?"

"In a manner of speakin'."

"Quite a while?"

"A while longer'n we care to remember."

"Just so. A pair of prodigal sons. Well, I ain't comin' in any further. Wade on out and I'll ferry you home. Mind your step on the bottom. The rock there is covered with seaweed. You don't want to slip and fall and bruise that pretty skin."

When they had clambered in and settled themselves, Angle in the bow and a shivering Octave in the stern, the old man took to his oars again and rowed them out of Rogue's Roost and as far as a rock-toothed gut between Hearns Island and Burnt Island before he paused. Beyond the gut lay open sea that was whitecapped already with the stiffening breeze. In the distance the tiny white steeple of the village church marked Prospect Harbour.

Backing water with his oars and spitting high and wide over the side, the old man said, "You look cold, Octave Daggon. You'd do well in the future to remember your clothes. Folks require 'em—them as venture out-doors and are subject to changes in temperature. Now it's sloppy out there after last night's commotion. When the spray wets you, you'll be colder still. I wish I had somethin' to cover you up. As a rule I would have. I always carried dry gear. But the last time I came out, I didn't care if I got wet. They told me I had cancer and I'd have to quit fishin' and take to my bed. But I was eighty-five, boys. I knew if I took to my bed it would be my grave. So I went out one last time. Told Marjorie I was just goin' to bring home my nets. Not plannin' to come back, I brought nothing with me but this." He patted the corked earthenware jug between his black rubber boots. "However, such as it is, you're welcome to it. You'll be warm on the inside, at least."

The two brothers regarded the old man with raised eyebrows.

"You're d-d-dead, then?" said Octave.

"Still dead," said the old man. "Not like you. Never seen anything quite like you two. Live again, yet movin' around like you was still spirits. And still able to see me. You're an unlikely pair, so you are. But that's as may be. Have a drink. It'll either taste like rum, or mornin' mist. Either way, you got nothin' to lose."

Leaving the sheltered water of the gut, the dory met the waves with a lurch. Much of Octave's first sip missed his mouth and went up his nose. "Gimme that, you tarnal landlubber," said Angle, taking the jug from his choking and spluttering brother. In the manner of one born to the billows, he cradled the jug with his elbow and tilted and swallowed without spill-ing a drop.

"Now when you've taken the edge off," their labouring saviour said, raising his voice over the splashing and crashing of their slow windward progress, "maybe you'll do me the favour of employin' those two hand-lines. Here directly we'll be over the Cabbage Patch, and if we don't load the odd cod or two there, my name's not Victor Cooley!"

The incense stick in the bronze burner burned into the ash and was replaced by another, and then another.

After contemplating with dismay the removal of his boathouse to the playground next door—its second visit in four years—Raymond had spent much of the day in his yard dealing with what else the surging ocean had deposited. He had forked the seaweed into several piles he could use to mulch his flower gardens against the winter. He had filled several trash bags with the manmade debris he picked out of the piles. He had stacked the driftwood to be hauled away by the government. Now he sat in his shrine room, sometimes meditating, sometimes falling asleep from fatigue. Whenever the smell of incense turned to the smell of ash, he would look up at his teacher's scarf-draped photo on the wall above the shrine and say three times, with his palms pressed together:

Whatever arises is fresh, the essence of realization.

It was disconcerting that the photo kept flashing a skull on and off in place of his teacher's head, but the enchanted glasses would still not come off, so there was nothing he could do about that. He could only sigh, and when it came time, replace the incense. And then he would sit, and again let his thoughts go their way.

One thought was that he had never had so many thoughts or such wild ones. It was like watching a lawnful of grasshoppers on speed. He thought …

… he was mad as a hatter, as a hatter's hatter …

… that his luck had surely bottomed out when even his ghosts left him …

… that there was no one he could tell about any of this …

… that maybe he could remove his hallucinatory glasses with a pair of wire cutters …

… that maybe this was all a flashback from his acid years …

… that he was so lonely that his heart felt like a drain not a pump …

… that even his finest incense did not smell as fine as his honey-butter wife …

… that he had never had an enemy as awful as his honey-butter wife …

… that he missed his teacher who was ill and maybe dying in Seattle …

… that he missed his mother who was incapacitated with Alzheimer's at the family ranch in California and certainly dying there …

… that he missed his sister in Steamboat Springs and his brother in Houston but was jealous yes jealous that they could afford to go visit his mother…

… that he missed all the children he had never had in any country …

… that he would roar louder than any wounded lion if he could only afford a good PA system …

… that he would like to be back on the deck of his old yawl, with the sails full and his heart full and his course set for the horizon …

… that he wished that his heart would stop beating so loudly …

… that it would stop beating at all …

… that someone was clearing their throat and it was *not* him …

"Er, yer Honour."

"Angle?"

"Aye, sir. It's me."

Raymond blinked. He had been half asleep. He wanted to rub his eyes, to make sure he was awake now, but of course there were the damn glasses, immovably in the way. He turned his head to the shrine room entrance. There under the noren were a pair of legs in his own paint-spotted sweat pants. It was Angle, all right.

He realized with a start that he was definitely not happy to see him. Also, that he was going to give in to this definite feeling of unhappiness.

"What are you standing there for?" he said. "It's just a curtain. Nothing to stop a ghost."

"Beggin' yer pardon, sir. You're angry, and I don't blame ye. But it weren't exactly our fault we disappeared."

"How not exactly?"

"Well, sir, I just thought of somewhere else, and suddenly we was there. I've known it happen in the in-between. I didn't think it could happen on this side. We didn't mean to jump ship, sir. Honest. It just happened."

"Angle, don't just stand there. Come in. I don't like having a conversation where I can only see the other person's legs."

"Which I can't come in there, sir."

"What's the matter? You allergic to incense?"

"Allergic? I don't know what that means. What it is, if I was to come in, I'm pretty sure I'd disappear for good. That's it, pure and simple, frank and plain. There's spirits in there as would banish me for bein' unnatural. You've asked 'em in yourself, over and over, time after time. Them Boodist spirits o' your'n."

"Angle, I'm the Captain, right? What if I ordered you in, like down in the basement—wouldn't that do the trick? Couldn't you come on in then?"

"Please don't, sir. Octave and me, we're kind of countin' on gettin' to know you. And speakin' of Octave, and beggin' yer pardon, I was wonderin' if you might see your way clear to accompanyin' me down to the basement again, for he's been took a mite poorly and needs yer attention."

"*My* attention. Why does he need *my* attention?"

"He asked for you, sir. When he was able to speak."

"Now, sir, do not mind the fish," Angle said as they stood once again at the door of the basement. "We come back as we left, all of a sudden like, and the fish they just come with us. I think they was meant for a gift."

The fish, all cod and enormous, as much as three feet long, lay in a great heap on the basement's cement floor, some still flopping and quivering, their gills flexing as they gasped. On top of the heap lay Octave, still mostly naked—a cod covered his loins—and mostly inert but for his hands and his feet, which stirred as weakly as the fins of the cod.

"He still gets seasick," said Angle.

Raymond laid a hand on Octave's foot. "Why, he's cold as ..." he started to say 'death' but with an on-the-fly sensitivity changed it to "... one of these fish. He's not just seasick, Angle. He's hypothermic. Here, you take his shoulders and I'll take his feet and we'll carry him upstairs. The shower in the first-floor bathroom has a steam unit. That's the quickest way to get him warm."

"Oh, I'll just throw him over my shoulder, Cap'n."

"No, we've got to be gentle with him. Come on."

"As you say, sir."

"Now," said Raymond, when they had Octave propped up between them on the wooden bench in the large shower stall with the steam clouding around them and the wet heat prickling their nostrils. "Now I'd like to hear what's going on. I'd like you to start with your own story, so I'll know more about who I'm dealing with here, and then I'd like to know what's brought you back to life, if it's alive you really are, and then anything you can about what's been happening to me, about these damn glasses, and that trickster in the graveyard, and that thing that dragged me down, and your disappearance, and, and ... that impossible pile of fish in my basement!"

"Well, sir," said Angle, pursing his lips and stroking his beard, "I'll do my best, and maybe Octave when he's summat thawed will chime in with the rest. Our story? Near as I can tell …"

The telling took them through the steam bath into the kitchen for hot fish soup, which Raymond made from one of the monsters in the basement; thence into the guest room where they put Octave to bed; then, when Octave had fallen asleep in the middle of his own memories and conjectures, back down to the basement to clean and put the rest of the cod away in the deep freeze—cod of a size that hadn't been seen in the waters off Prospect for a hundred years or more.

When that was done it was late and Angle too took to the bed in the guest room.

Raymond was too tired to shower or bathe or even wash at the sink. Determined, however, to record while it was still fresh in his memory the story of Angle and Octave (and all that had led up to its telling), he took his laptop computer to bed with him and typed till he fell asleep, leaving several fish scales on the keyboard in the process—one wedged inextricably between the Enter and Shift keys.

Raymond's mother Angelina Kidd no longer checked her email because in her oblivion she no longer knew what email was. Her computer was kept on a table at the foot of her bed with a slide show of family pictures continuously running on the screen. Normally unmoving and seemingly unaware, she would object with a sudden show of life and wordless cries to any attempt her husband Eldridge made to remove the monitor to create space for her medications or for flowers.

Raymond knew these things not from his father, who was a reticent man, but from his sister Sarah Marie, who had written him after a visit. So when he woke the next morning with his laptop computer still in his lap, the first thing he did was to email his mother about the strange things that had happened. He did this because his mother had always been his confidante and always kept his secrets safe. He knew she could no longer read, yet writing to her made him feel less crazy.

What Raymond could not know was that when the email arrived, at that faraway house on a hilltop among the redwoods and madrones, his father would be sitting at his mother's bedside holding her unresponsive hand, as he frequently did, in a silent one-way communion with the woman he had wed as a teenager. Eldridge Kidd, hearing the little fanfare of trumpets that meant his Angelina had received a message, went to the computer and opened the message and read every last word of his prodigal son's unlikely tale of Angus and Octavius Daggon, *Two Lost Souls Found*.

"They were two brothers who lived here in Prospect a couple of hundred years ago in this very house.

"Angus took after his father Captain Willard Daggon and Octavius after his mother Letitia. The father being a privateer with a letter of marque and the mother the village schoolmarm, the brothers turned out quite differently.

"Angus like his father became obsessed with coastal shipping schedules. A hard violent calculating young man (by his own admission), he haunted the Halifax waterfront taverns—fraternizing with sailors, buying them drinks till they were muddle-headed, playing hail-fellow-well-met while at the same time extracting the information he needed. What ships did they sail with? Which had they heard might be sailing? What cargoes, how armed, when leaving, where headed?

"A real privateer would not have met with much success in this manner, since only American ships were lawful prey and would not have been found in their enemy's port, but Angus and Captain Will and the rest of the crew of the *Queen Mab* were privateers only when it suited and outright pirates the rest of the time, for it was easier to lie in wait in friendly waters than to sail south and risk confrontations with American warships.

"The favorite waiting place of the *Mab* and her company was Rogue's Roost, a sheltered basin near Prospect. A lookout atop Roost Island kept a constant watch seaward. When a likely merchantman appeared, no matter what its flag, they sailed out from their hiding place and took it by surprise. On attacking, they hauled up the American flag with its fifteen stars and bars, but they did not depend on these false colours to keep their treachery a secret. They also left no survivors to carry any tales.

"Eventually word got out, however, and on a foggy May morning in 1813, the *Mab*, a 6-gun topsail schooner, on emerging from the Roost to sail to Halifax and top up her stores, was met and sunk by *HMS Fantome*, an 18-gun brig-sloop of the Royal Navy, which had crept in with the fog and itself lain in wait, gun ports open and slow match smoking.

"Captain Will, taken unconscious from his sinking vessel, was revived and hung from a yardarm of the Fantome. His son Angus, who had been blown into the water during the schooner's destruction and had swum ashore, watched the hanging from behind a blueberry bush by a large standing rock. He was stuffing his mouth with the tangy sweet fruit when the drum rolled and his father dropped.

"His mother, greeted with the news, showed no distress. She neither fainted, screamed, cried, clutched her bosom or even sighed. She just nodded, kept rocking and put her nose back into her book—Gibbon's *History of the Decline and Fall of the Roman Empire,* the sixth and last volume. Not till she reached the end of the chapter did she look up and say, 'Well, there it is, then. And now I am supposed to wear black, when I detest black. The house, of course, belongs to you and Octavius. It was Mr. Daggon's wish, in the event of his demise, that I rely on your charity. When I detest charity, too. I neither expect nor would accept it of *you*, and I will not ask it of Octavius. I shall move into Halifax and find occupation there, for above all I detest this awful outpost in the wilderness. Once I thought its beauty worth its ignorance, but that thought has worn thin. And the thought that *love* was worth anything has worn out altogether.'

"Letitia never spoke to her son Angus again, and when she spoke of him, which was rarely, she would not use his given name but referred to him pointedly as *Angle*, for his part in baiting the poor sailors to give up the knowledge that cost so many lives.

"Once she had set off by wagon with the few possessions she had agreed to take (years of Captain Will's gifts from many prizes having been coldly declined), Octavius took his mother's place in her rocker, with her abandoned copy of the sixth and last volume of Gibbon's Rome in his lap. So much did his general attitude and posture resemble that of his mother that Angus swore all his brother needed was a wig clapped on his head and his dainty little mustache shaved off to look just like her.

"Octavius also took Letitia's place as the village schoolteacher. This added little to the Daggon household income but suited the younger brother's studious and retiring temperament. It failed to suit Angus, however. Angus wanted a partner. With a partner, he insisted, they could return to the prosperity they had known under their father. Angus would find a vessel to replace the *Queen Mab* and command her himself, if only Octavius would take his place as their 'agent' in Halifax.

"The heated arguments that frequently spoiled their neighbours' sleep had as much to do with the quantities of rum Angus consumed as with the persistent refusal of Octavius to have anything to do with piracy, privateering or in fact the sea in any way. They did not come to blows—Angus said it would have been like hitting his mother, and only his father was allowed to do that—but there was violence in their dissension, and it came to a head on a night when Octavius, patient and softspoken and peaceful though he normally was and ever strove to be, made the cutting suggestion that if Angus didn't like it, he could take his half of the house and go elsewhere or buy the other half and have the whole place alone.

"They had been sitting by the stone hearth, Octavius sipping tea as he read, Angus taking long swigs from a jug of rum and staring moodily at the fire. The suggestion came out of a pure silence, resuming a conversation that for a fortnight had consisted solely of grunts, growls and muttering from Angus and from Octavius only a steady turning of pages.

"Angus looked slowly away from the hearth. When his gaze encountered his younger brother, it was as if the fire that had been reflected in his eyes now resided there, for they blazed anew.

"In a menacing low voice that was like a bear growling he said, 'You cook like her, which is in your favour. Otherwise I'd make an end of you, brother, for you also sit in that infernal chair and read and rock and forever turn pages like her in that selfsame high and mighty way, as if butter wouldn't melt in your mouth, and when you do condescend to address a poor bugger, it's only to make him feel stupid. Yes, you are more like our dear Ma than not, so I wonder you still covet these ill-gotten gains, for you know not an inch of this house was ever bought but won and won with blood, and the money that would purchase your half likewise won. Mayhap it's you who should leave, and like her wash your hands of it all.'

"'I will not,' said Octavius, keeping his nose in his book. 'I will keep what our father bestowed, or be reimbursed for its surrender.'

"'Good. Good,' replied Angus. 'Then make a fine breakfast come morning, for I have business in the hours till then that will forge a fine hunger.'

"As his mother so often had, Octavius fell asleep in the rocker by the fire, book in hand, comforter over his lap. The comforter was another thing Letitia had abandoned. Though stitched together by herself, the fine Italian brocade on the outside had been more of her husband's plunder. Its gold and silver embroidery glowed faintly in the fading firelight, but the reading lamp having guttered and gone out, the room was mainly in darkness when Octavius awoke. Normally it would have been a need to use the chamberpot that woke him. That night, however, it was his drunken brother Angus on the peak of the roof with a long saw, sawing away, at work on dividing the house.

"Indian summer prevailed that year long enough for the job to be finished without the brothers suffering overmuch from the inside of their house being exposed. Before the first snowstorm, Octavius and a congregation of sympathetic neighbours, mostly fishermen, moved his half of the house, on rollers made from cut saplings and with horses to pull and men to push, to another part of the village. There they cobbled together a sort of lean-to construction to close the halved house to the weather till spring when a proper rebuilding could be accomplished.

"Octavius never disputed the division. When a friend recommended he employ a barrister from Halifax to intercede, he replied, 'No. As I see it, my brother has done me a favour. I only hope that, cooped up by himself, he will not do himself harm, as a snake in a net, finding nothing else into which to sink its fangs, will in its fury bite itself.'

"In his half of the house, Angus greeted the first snowstorm by hosting a revelry for as many of his cronies as he could gather. Over a barrel of west Indian rum that had been bound for Boston, they reminisced and joked and plotted and sang. "The Cap'n is dead! Long live the Cap'n!" they cried, toasting Angus, for they meant for him too, like his father, to lead them, at the helm of the first likely vessel they could lay their hands on. As the level in the barrel lowered, so the level of their aspirations rose, from a calculating practicality to a visionary frenzy. Someone shouted, "A place of our own, a place in the sun, where there's plenty of women and plenty of rum!" and the rest took up the chant. They would sail south to the west Indies, by God, and make a whole damned island their own, with sandy beaches and shady palm trees and sunny days the year round, and leave a frozen fucking granite coast to the Devil who spat it out in the first place.

"At some point in the night and some level in the barrel, Angus imagined that his house was still part of the original whole and that Octavius was still in it, keeping to his room and away from the festivities out of mere stubbornness. He decided that as captain it was his duty to overcome such stubbornness. Octavius should see how much his older brother was admired. Revered even. Octavius too should raise a glass and call him Captain, as he had when they were boys and their swordfights with the other boys of the village had been conducted with palings pulled out on the sly from Baskin Hardiman's fence down the lane.

"So Angus went to fetch Octavius. But when he passed through the door that should have led to his younger brother's room, he found himself outside instead, in a roaring darkness with the snow blasting at him sideways like canister shot.

"In reality, in his half of the house on the other side of the village, Octave, in his mother's old rocker, was fast asleep and dreaming of his mother. In his dream, he was part of a heavenly choir. He was the foremost singer in the choir, and they were praising the Heavenly Mother, who was his own mother, except smiling as he had never seen her smile, with a bliss that lit the heavens and beamed down on the Earth.

"Angus smiled as he headed into the wind against the blinding stinging snow, so wonderfully refreshing after the dense stifling fug of the party. He was Captain now and no longer had to put up with that belowdecks miasma of crowded unwashed bodies and foul breath and stale tobacco smoke. He was Captain and pleased to be out in the open, pleased with the pure if painfully cold air being driven into his lungs, grateful that his brother was not as near as he had thought, not in the least brought down by the recollection that their house had been divided. Hadn't he done it himself? Ha ha. Bugger all. They would both laugh their fill about that once he found the other half of the house. Which had to be around there somewhere.

"The village rector had nicknamed him Octave for the range of his voice, which spanned a full three octaves without resort to falsetto. It was a blessing, the rector had said, and he was high in the upper reaches of that blessing, pouring out to his mother the praise she should always have had.

"It was fine to be among the other angels praising her, and finer still to be the one who praised her best of all.

Angus found himself in water. Not deep water, not above the tops of his boots for his feet were still dry, but flowing fast enough that he could feel the pressure. He could not see the water in the darkness nor feel it when he reached down. All he felt, at the height of his knees, was the snow. He moved his feet. There was ice around his ankles. He had broken through ice that was under the snow.

He took stock of his whereabouts. What it was, he figured, he was in the upper reaches of the inlet at the end of the lane where Octavius lived. He had passed his brother's half of the house and was now on his way to the High Head. Oh well, he thought, he wasn't in a mood for turning back, and anyway it was late and Octavius was probably asleep in his rocker. Little Octavius. And he needed his rest, didn't he, for he was none too strong. *Let you rest then, dear brother.*

"Strangely enough, Angus was in Heaven too and also in the choir. Angus who was not only a great sinner but also a tone deaf one. What was he doing up here? Octavius turned and stormed back through the rows of angels, furious at the thought that Angus had managed to cheat his way even past the Pearly Gates. This time he would show his older brother, for he was a powerful angel. He would pull the wings off Angus as easily as he would off a housefly. He would himself cast the Pretender out, and watch him fall.

"The sea cliffs of Prospect were not tall and unbroken but instead a great jumble of granite slabs and boulders that were low enough that at high tide with a strong onshore wind the breaking surf against them would throw spray over the top. The tide and wind were right now, but the snow dampened the surf and the spray fell short of Angus where he sat in a sheltering cleft at the cliff's edge, singing softly in his off-key manner to himself.

> *Oh don't you see that broad broad road*
> *That lies across the lily leven*
> *That is the path of wickedness*
> *Some call the road to Heaven*

"Past the last row of angels was an edge, and beyond that empty sky. Octave tried to stop, but his wrath and the momentum of his charge carried him over. And now he was falling. Not his brother but him. He had cast himself out. And his great wings were gone.

And don't you see that bonnie road
That winds about the hillside so
That is the road to Elfland fair
Where you and I this night maun go

"Octavius woke in the rocker, in a muck sweat under the comforter, certain that something was wrong, wrong with Angus. And now he felt only concern, not a hint of the hatred he had dreamed. Yet there was somewhat left of the dream, for his brother still sang. He could still hear him singing.

Oh they rode on and farther on
And waded through rivers aboon the knee
And they saw neither sun nor moon
But heard the roaring of the sea

"With his greatcoat and boots thrown hastily on, his winter hat shoved down hard and a lantern clutched to his chest, Octavius shut the door of his house and turned instinctively toward the High Head.

Twas dark dark night with no starlight
And they waded through red blood to the knee
For all the blood that's shed on earth
Runs through the springs of that country

"All the way to the Head, Octavius followed the singing. He knew where he would find his brother. Boy and man Angus had sat in that same cleft near the edge, contemplating his troubles while singing the old country songs, songs their mother had taught them, that he would not be caught dead singing anywhere else. It was their mother, knowing exactly where Angus took refuge, who often and often had sent Octavius there to fetch him home.

"Some yards before the cleft was a gap in the rock that had to be leapt or skirted. It was a wide and deep gap and ordinarily quite evident. Tonight, however, the snowfall had filled and disguised it. Unable to see it, and not remembering it, Octave stepped into the gap and disappeared.

"As the snow and wind lessened, so a break in the clouds let the moon appear on the horizon. Angus finished his song and sat silently watching. A smile broke slowly over his cold-stiffened face. *If only Octavius were here*, he thought. Octavius would know what to say seeing the moon shining like that, over the waves all the way straight to the cleft where he sat, starting as a pinpoint and ending as a broad golden path. Octavius would have the right words. Something short and pithy, like, *Brother, that is the genuine article. That is Heaven's open door.*

"Never was such a brother, Angus thought. And where was he now? Never mind. They were close. He could feel it. No matter what happened, they would always be close. Close as moonlight and the sky it shone through.

"There were those in the village who said it was murder, who were attached to the schoolteacher and knew how he had suffered at the hands of his rogue of a brother. This faction wanted Angus burnt like a diseased animal and only Octavius given a Christian burial. But the Octavians were in the minority. The majority, who feared the vengeance of the pirates, were for burying the two frozen brothers together, side by side, in the village cemetery at the back of the church along the back bay shore. After all, they said, anything could have happened. For all anyone knew, Octavius could have found Angus paralytic drunk there on the Head and been on his way back to the village for help when he fell in the snow hole. He was frail in body and could never have brought Angus back on his own. It could have been like that. Or they could both have frozen to death on their own. All that was certain was that they were dead, and should be laid to rest. The whole incident should be laid to rest, along with the history of that inglorious branch of the Daggon family. There were other Daggons in the village, anyway (this fearful majority whispered under its breath) who valued their good name and did not need a scandal broadcast through the land.

"These virtuous Daggons also valued the two brothers' expensive if ill-gotten belongings, so much so that they quietly and methodically sacked the two half-houses the afternoon after the burial."

Eldridge Kidd finished Raymond's email and to his surprise found it good. He thought his problem child just might amount to something after all. He had friends who had friends in the publishing world. He would speak to them.

He would have to speak to Raymond first, however, because what came after the story of Octave and Angle was not so good. When it became Octave and Angle and *Raymond Kidd*, it was not so good. Eldridge valued his family name as much as any Daggon. He did not need a son dragging it into the dirt with crazy claims that he had met and was harboring ghosts.

He lay a hand on his wife's covered foot at the end of the bed, and said, "Angel, I find I must leave you a while. There are things that a man must attend to in person."

And he replied for her, since she no longer spoke, "Yes, my darling. I quite understand."

In the guest room of 7 Lands End, in the pale morning light, Octave Daggon lay awake, his brother's tattooed arm across his chest, his brother's snoring loud in his ear. They were alive again, two centuries farther along.

He was terrified.

Chapter 3

Dagger and Rose

An invitation had gone out and been accepted, but the guest had not arrived in time. From Africa to the Lesser Antilles, forces had arisen and come together to form the storm the humans called Noel. Noel had been all that was asked for, but too soon. In Hispaniola, Haiti and the Dominican Republic, Noel's power had been well-nigh perfect, but the invitation had not issued from there, and so only flooding and mudslides and a hundred or so deaths had resulted. The essence—the fabric of things as they are— had not been affected at all. And in the long journey north, the fine edge of the storm had worn off. By the time it reached Nova Scotia, where the fabric was stressed and worn thin as required, a dulled Noel had been able to sever only the odd thread and no more, creating a mere flaw where a major unravelling was what had been sought.

It takes time, lots of time—ages, epochs, eras, eons—for an invitation of such magnitude to be prepared. Once prepared, however, its renewal can be issued without hesitation. Two mornings later, while Noel was disappearing over Greenland and the human citizens of Nova Scotia were having breakfast and in their gritty but short-sighted fashion going out to continue dealing with the damage they could see, another invitation was already on its way.

Raymond's three robes were not meant to be worn all at once. The lightest, a thin cotton yukata with a printed pattern of golden carp amid waves, was meant for the warm days of summer, which in Nova Scotia are never many. Of the three therefore, the yukata was the least worn and in the best condition, with the fewest holes, tears and frayed edges. His black and white plaid, a robe Cat had made, of a slightly heavier brushed damask cotton with a red cotton lining, was more ragged yet more effective against the chill foggy mornings of spring and the darkening grey days of fall. His heaviest robe, another of Cat's creations, of Polynesian ikat in muted earth colours with a tan cotton lining and unravelling cuffs, was proof against winter except on those days when he could not be bothered to make a fire. On those days it was his custom to wear all three robes at once, with the addition of a wool cap and a pair of sheepskin boots with gaping holes in the seams. Otherwise he wore all the robes only when he was feeling too alone and too vulnerable, as he had during Noel. Usually two of the robes hung on hooks in the bathrooms either upstairs or down. All had holes in the neck from this practice.

He would have liked to have hidden in all three this morning. Instead Angle wore the yukata, Octave the ikat, and only the black and white plaid was left for him. The three robed men, now housemates perforce, sat sage-like at the table of shellacked knotty pine in Raymond's kitchen area.

They were having breakfast, and the meal was cod again.

"A crew of gib cats couldn't look more glum," said Angle. He sat at the side of the table by the glass sliding doors to the porch, the blinds of which were drawn. "What's the matter? My cookin' don't suit ye?"

"It isn't your cooking," said Octave. "It's the cod." He had eaten only half the great slab on his plate and was twirling his fork idly in the remainder.

"What do you mean? That's prime cod. You'll never eat better."

"I don't care if I never eat any more at all. What I mean is, brother, I am tired of cod. Now matter how you serve it, and I'll grant you have been ingenious …"

"Cod and peanut butter sandwiches, good grief," said Raymond, whose fork and knife lay by his plate and whose own portion of cod lay untouched.

"…there comes a time when it is just too much, meal after meal, day after day."

"There comes a time when it is mostly all we have," said Angle. "And it's thankful we should be for the generosity of one Victor Cooley."

"Well, not to cry the fellow down," said Octave, "but what else would he have done with a boatload of cod? He doesn't need it where he is."

"He didn't need to've given it to us, neither."

"Boys," Raymond said, "The problem is not with the cod—not that I could stomach another bite if it was manna from Heaven and God's own chef served it up—it's our situation. Look at us. What is wrong with this picture?"

"*Wrong*, sir?" said Angle. "I'm warm through and through, I can eat and I got plenty to eat, I'm with friends, and I'm out of that godforsaken basement. I got *possibilities* again. All I can see is what's *right*."

Octave tapped the table with his fork. "Point of order, Mr. Kidd. We are not *boys*. We are in fact your elders. By a long chalk, as Angle would say. It would be more correct to address us as *men*."

"Octave, this is the twenty-first century. If you want to fit in, you have to stop being so formal. Men call each other boys now. Women call each other girls. And you should call me Raymond. And Angle should stop calling me *sir*."

"I take it back, sir," said Angle. "There is one thing as seems wrong, and that's having the blinds on all the windows drawn. Why, there's nothing like sunlight to cheer a fellow up."

"On the other hand," mused Octave, "if you take the point of view that it is you who are the elder—because we died in our thirties, while you are in your fifties—for us to call you sir or mister would be proper, would it not? Even in this socially degenerate age, a greybeard like yourself rates at least that much respect, does he not?"

"On the other hand," Angle said, chuckling as he got up, "there's nothing like fine ale for breakfast to cheer a man up, and we've plenty of that." He removed a tall can of Keith's Amber Red, his second of the morning, from the cupboard in the corner. "Lord, what a job you have, Cap'n. Free beer and wages too. How could you beat that? The sojers in my time, they got plenty, a whole gallon a day, but they had to march and kowtow. And then again someone might shoot 'em."

"It's not free," Raymond said. "A tour guide makes ten bucks an hour. The beer is meant to pacify us. It doesn't pay the mortgage. It doesn't buy groceries. It doesn't pay property taxes or insurance. It won't move my boathouse back. It won't allow me to accommodate two guests who need what humans need but can't work for it. Besides that, tourist season is almost over. Soon I'll be getting just two shifts a week. You want sunlight? Let's figure out how to get you back into it. How to let the neighbours see you without me having to explain who you are or what you're doing here. It's a village, remember? Everybody minds your business. Or maybe *you* could explain yourselves to them. Maybe someone will believe you and take pity on you. Maybe they'll treat you to a birth certificate so you can get a job!"

Red in the face, Raymond left the table and went upstairs. He came down dressed for work and went straight out the door without saying goodbye. His pickup started slowly because of the salt that that the sea breeze had blown into the engine and onto the spark plugs. The gravel of the driveway crunched under the tires as he shifted into gear. As he drove quickly away, there was the simultaneously increasing and decreasing drone of the engine.

The brothers looked at each other over the table.

"You should use your napkin," Octave said. "There's cod in your beard."

"Pardon me, brother," said Angle, combing the morsel out with his fingers and popping it into his mouth, "but is ten dollars an hour not a whopping great sum? I seem to remember it taking folks weeks to make that much."

"Times have changed. We have a lot to learn. Maybe too much."

"Well," Angle said, swigging beer, "We got nothin' to lose."

"I wonder ..."

"What's to wonder? Bein' alive beats bein' dead, and that's flat."

"I mean I wonder if what set him off was my referring to him as a grey-beard."

"Hmm. Mayhap. He's a sensitive sort, is our Cap'n."

"Our *captain*, as you persist in calling him, long after the humor has worn off, is a very curious fellow altogether. Very touchy for someone who spends so much time praying—or meditating, as he calls it—to achieve peace of mind."

"Brother, I don't know what he's tryin' to achieve and I don't care. I don't call him Cap'n for a joke no more. You can go on with your philo-sophical explanations if you like. As for me, I don't believe we'd be here if it weren't for him. He guided us back. I can't prove it but I know it. And he welcomed us on board because why? He don't know us from Adam. It's *because he's the cap'n*, that's why. And I think we'd do well to do our best for him. Mayhap he ain't used to the job."

"Angle, is that a tear in your eye? Have two beers in the morning made you maudlin when it used to take rum by the keg? Show me your chest."

"What for? There's naught wrong wi' me, and any gate you ain't no doctor."

"I want to see your tattoo. Do you remember your resolve?"

Angle parted the yukata and looked down at his chest. Just above his left breast was a dagger through a rose. "In course I do. This bein' always wi' me, and you always remindin' me of it, how could I forget? *A man can turn himself around.*"

"A good motto. I believe it has had its effect. It's a dagger through a rose no longer, but a rose that has swallowed a dagger. You are a pirate no more. Now excuse me."

Between the kitchen and the dining area was an island that on the kitchen side housed a dishwasher and a double sink and on the dining side a glass-doored cabinet. The wooden countertop that extended toward the woodstove was common to both sides and on the dining side had two barstools parked beneath its overhanging lip. Over the dishwasher and sink was open shelving that reached to the ceiling. Raymond had added the shelving at Cat's request so the dishes they used the most often could be easily accessed from either side of the two areas. Since he was an indifferent carpenter with no eye for wood, the one by twelve pine he had used was cupped, bowed, twisted, crooked, checked, knotted and waned, and the golden shellacking had runs. On the outside of this crazed construction, reachable from the closest barstool, hung a cordless phone. The phone was playing a snippet from a Congolese rhumba. Octave went and picked up the receiver.

"Brother, you shouldn't," said Angle.

"Hush. I've seen it done, haven't I? And we've got to start somewhere."

"Hello, Is this Raymond Kidd? Raymond Kidd, you have just won ..."

Octave listened intently to the prerecorded message. "She says I just have to call a certain number and we can win a hundred thousand dollars."

"Brother ..."

"Hush," said Octave, furiously punching the receiver's buttons. "I've got to call right now to qualify."

Angle knew a ruse when he heard one, but he also knew there was no deterring Octave once his stubborn younger brother set his course. Any damage would just have to be made good later. Meanwhile, Angle had an inspiration of his own. Surreptitiously, while Octave's back was turned, he filched an entire eight-pack of the Amber Red from the corner cupboard and slipped out the sliding glass doors and onto the back porch—out into the wide world and under the shining sun again at last.

With a mixture of love and irritation, Dawn O'Keefe dried her hands on her apron and looked up the ladder through the open square in the round ceiling at the little round face so like her own that looked down.

"Shannon O'Keefe," she said, "What are you doing in the turret? If you're not feeling well, it's to bed you must go. And if you are feeling well, it's to school you must go. The turret was never a choice."

"Mother," said Shannon, "it's my responsibility. Miss Bootleer said we all had to look out for each other, because there's terrists everywhere. So, it only makes sense to look where I can see the most, and that's from up here. With Daddy's binoclars, I can see the whole village."

"Shannon, put your father's binoculars away, back in their case, back on the hook, and come down here right now. Ms. Boutilier is a good teacher and we do need to look out for each other, but that doesn't mean spying from windows. That's for old gossips with nothing better to do."

"*Mother*," Shannon said, "I *saw*—and *that's* why I *called* you—a terrist just *now*. He's got a long robe and a beard, just like on TV, and he just sneaked out of Booda Ray's house and stole Booda Ray's rowboat. So *there*."

Before reincarnating had cost him his ability to see through walls, and to see faraway things as if they were near, Angle had watched Raymond Kidd put to sea many times. Octave had sometimes watched with him, but Angle had watched always. It was partly his old yearning for the sea and partly the odd obscure kinship he felt for Raymond. He had been with him, as it were, from Raymond's arrival in the village and his first foray out in his little gaff-rigged sailing dinghy, through his glory days in his yawl *Happy Cat* when he roamed up and down the coast a hundred miles either way, to his current demotion to the smallest craft of them all, the little plastic rowing dinghy which had been the yawl's tender, which leaked and was a risk to take out of the harbour on any but the mildest of days.

Angle knew from his long vigil that Raymond's oars were in his boathouse just inside the door, and his two handlines in an old canvas mailsack on a peg beside the oars. Despite the boathouse having been tossed into the playground next door, these items were still in their places. Angle put them in the rowing dinghy (which had washed up in the playground sandbox), dragged the dinghy by its painter across the grass and over the lane and down the seaweed-strewn ramp to the cove.

He shoved off with some trepidation, for fog was a thing he had never been able to see through, living or dead, and a large bank of the stuff from offshore, having already swallowed the outer islands, was now stealing into the harbour. He also shoved off with some difficulty, for it was low tide and there were five yards of gluelike black mud between him and the water.

He was just at the edge of the mud when a voice called out behind him, "Sir! Excuse me, sir!"

He pitched himself awkwardly into the dinghy, smearing the white molded interior with his mud-caked feet, and hurriedly shipped the oars.

"Sir, I have to ask you what you're doing in that boat!"

She stood at the foot of the ramp, a short slender woman with a flowered apron over her faded blue skirt, her blonde hair bound up in a red kerchief, her hands in their yellow rubber gloves planted in fists on her hips. A slight forward curve to her spine made it seem as if she were about to launch herself after him. A little blonde girl in a pink houserobe peered out from behind her and in a high young voice called out too, "Yes, we have to ask you what you're doing in that boat!"

Even as he pulled madly away into the fog, the humor of his flight was not lost on Angle. He called back, "It's nothin', my dears. Just an old sea dog goin' out fishin'. A very harmless old sea dog. Don't you worry. I'll bring her back, oars and all. And if I catch anything, we'll all share."

"What goes on?" said Dawn O'Keefe. "He was wearing a houserobe."

"That was Booda Ray's robe," said Shannon. "He wears it sometimes when he comes out and mucks around at low tide."

"What kind of thief would run off … row off … wearing nothing but a houserobe?"

"Miss Bootleer says you can't understand about terrists. You just have to shoot them."

"You go back inside, sweetheart—you in your houserobe too, what's the world coming to—and you stay there. We'll talk about what Ms. Boutilier says later. I've got to go find a man to do something about this. I've got dishes to finish, for heaven's sake."

Gordon Daggon was thankful for many things.

Thankful he was no longer a detective in Halifax but a fisherman again in Prospect, operating out of his own village with his own stout Cape Islander. Done with the mysteries of others. Returned to the mystery of his childhood, the sea.

Thankful Noel had not destroyed his dock and stage like Juan. Getting disaster relief from the government had been a long road and an uncertain one, especially since drawing a pension he technically was not dependent on his fishing.

Thankful he did not have to list all the things he was thankful for.

It was nicer on this mild post-Noel morning to just sit on his dock there between two stacks of lobster traps, out of the chill breeze, deep in his comfortable old brown chair with its stuffing working out of the worn places, sipping his hot toddy and feeling his arthritic fingers relax as the rum circulated, resting his eyes on the fog.

He thought with a smile of his friend Joel Peters, a Newfoundland fisherman, who said you could not trust the Nova Scotia fog. The Nova Scotia fog was like a woman, he said, capricious and unpredictable. If you leaned too much on it, the moment you got really comfortable it would slip out from under you, and there you would be in the drink, overboard.

Newfoundland fog was more dependable. It was so thick they could bury you in it like a good wool suit.

Gordon could see no further through the fog than his boat at the end of the dock with its cloud of raucous seagulls still hovering overhead. Now and then one of the birds would dive and emerge with a severed head or some guts from Gordon's early morning catch.

However, if he was to make a list, Gordon mused as he sipped, it would include:

... his current wife, a fine wife, twenty years his junior, who still loved to make love yet was happy to give him his times and his toddies alone on the dock ...

... the new government-paid-for power line that led to his stage and powered the hotplate that heated his toddies ...

... these silly clowning gulls, the only company he really craved, these sad and restless gulls ...

"Gordon?"

To the voice that broke into his revery, he answered reluctantly, "Yes, Dawn." He knew she was standing at the open door to the stage. He didn't look around at her. He didn't want her to be there.

"Gordon, I think someone has stolen Raymond Kidd's dinghy."

"No, Raymond's in it, Dawn. I saw him row by in the fog just a minute ago."

"That wasn't Raymond. It was another fellow in Raymond's houserobe. Shannon watched him sneak out of Raymond's house, and then we both went out and saw him pushing off in Raymond's boat. When I asked him what he was doing, he said he was just going fishing and would bring the boat back. But while he said it he was rowing away just as fast as he could."

"Well, I guess I could have been mistaken. It's pretty thick out here. Probably one of his friends, though, don't you think?"

"He hasn't had any visitors lately, Gordon. Not any proper visitors. Shannon would have noticed. Maybe you could just go out and talk to him and see what's going on."

"All right, Dawn, all right."

"And then maybe you could check Raymond's house too. His truck's gone, but he could still be there. They could have stolen the truck too."

"I'll check on it, Dawn. I'll check on everything. I'm getting up right now. See?"

"Thank you, Gordon. You're a dear."

"I'm a retired detective, and you know it, and I wish you didn't."

While Gordon, the aging descendant of Angle, eased himself cautiously down the ladder to his blue-hulled Cape Islander, Angle, the ancestor of Gordon, rowed through the dense fog with the fine reckless vigour of a man in his prime. The little tender fairly leapt with his stroke. Yet he was not in any tearing hurry. He'd committed no crimes to be hung for in this day and age. A little stooped slip of a woman and her daughter held no fear for Angle Daggon—not for long. His initial anxiety at being discovered had yielded almost immediately to the simple overwhelming joy of being alive again and in a boat, however small. He rowed like the devil just because he could.

He remembered as if it were yesterday how it felt when the scend of the sea—that upward surge, that living lift—first occurred, how it lifted his spirits then as now. He also remembered where that placed him, in the dogleg from the inner cove to the outer harbour where the depth dropped off from five to fifteen feet. And though he could see little in the fog except through vague windows that began closing as soon as they opened, his inner compass still told him the angle to take to the mouth of the harbour, while an even finer sensibility steered him clear of the four moored sailboats in his path.

And then, and at last, he was out in the open sea once again.

He tempered his stroke to accord with the waves, easy low rollers that nonetheless if he were not careful would send the dinghy with her flat bottom and considerable leeway onto the rocks of Redmond Island just yards away to port. He could hear the waves kissing the shore. At the sound of breakers, he knew Redmond's was behind him and he was passing the shallow ledge off its point that the low tide would have exposed. A bell clanging at intervals to starboard guided him further. He knew of the new-fangled ringing buoy from his long-distance vigils of Raymond. It marked for one headed seaward the relatively deeper water inside Prospect's sheltering string of outer islands.

He shipped the oars, wrenched an ale free of the eight-pack and opened and drank half of it in a single gulping swallow. In the headiness of his freedom, he shouted out the names of the islands in their looping order east to west, "Bald Rock, Hopson's, Duck, Betty's, Mosher, Ryan, Shannon,

Roost, Burnt, Hearn!" He remembered his turns as a lookout on the rocky top of Roost. He held up his hands as if the spyglass were still in them.

He went on past the buoy till he was upwind of the Cabbage Patch, that bed of seaweed nine fathoms down on the bottom where the cod liked to gather. There he dropped anchor and began to pay out line. When his estimate put him over the Patch, he tied off. The boat swung to the breeze as the anchor line went taut.

He unreeled Raymond's handline on its square wooden frame till its big silver jig hit the bottom and the line went slack. "Now," Victor Cooley had said, "bring it up a few turns and make it dance there, right over the weed. They'll come up for it." He took a few wraps of the line around the frame and began to jig, intermittently tugging the line so the lure would rise and fall and glimmer and deceive down below. Every few tugs, he took a sip from the can he had opened.

He had finished one can and was opening another when Cooley himself called to him out of the fog. "You'll never catch 'un like that. They ain't there where you are anymore."

"Well, where the hell are they then?" Angle called back, somewhat testily.

The yellow dory glided just into view. "They're over here," said the old man.

"That ain't enough distance to make any difference," Angle growled.

"It ain't the space, it's the time," said Cooley.

"The what?"

"The *time*. The time *you're* in, there's scarcely any cod at all. The time *I'm* in, there's plenty. More'n there was when I was alive. Bigger too. Well, you saw. Cod like there was a lot longer ago, like in the time you came from. Cod to span a man's table. Can't quite figure it. Wasn't like that till you and your brother showed up. No sir. Something's come adrift somewhere. But that's how it is."

"Maybe Octave's right," said Angle. "He says it's come a time, mayhap, when time and times are done. Any gate, Mr. Cooley, how it is with me, I'd like to load a few big ones, all right. Fellow who has our house now, he don't make enough for hisself, let alone the three of us. I'm aimin' to sell me some fish to help out."

"Imagine that. A right cutthroat like you, sellin' fish to help out. What *has* the world come to."

"Amen, brother. So how do I get myself into your time?"

"Well, you have to come over here," the old man said patiently.

"I'm at anchor, Mr. Cooley. Why don't you come over here?"

"You have to come to me. That's how it works. Also, the boats can't touch. You'll have to swim over."

"*Swim* over?"

"You want into my time, you have to swim over. Might as well shuck that silly get-up you got on, too. You know clothes don't pass."

"Well … hell," Angle said. He started reeling in his line.

"Don't bother with that, son," Cooley said. "Someone's coming. Leave it there and come on."

Angle heard it too, the sound of an engine chugging toward them. He slid out of Raymond's robe and went over the side. The dinghy tipped with his weight, almost overturning and shipping a good deal of water in the process.

Gordon Daggon steered less by instinct than experience. With *Severence* his 27-foot Cape Islander at low throttle, his exit from the harbour was not a mad dash like that of his returned ancestor Angle Daggon. Still he steered clear of all the unseen obstacles just as easily and surely.

He had known these waters all his life, had fished them with his father before a young man's ambition and a declining stock of cod had precipitated him into the police force in Halifax. He could have pushed the boat faster, but he was not really in pursuit of anyone. He was simply doing what it took to placate a troubled neighbour. Dawn O'Keefe thought someone had stolen Raymond Kidd's dinghy—had been quite animated, full of conviction and responsibility—and so Gordon Daggon detective retired had interrupted his toddy-enriched contemplation to put her mind at ease. And while he never drank once aboard, he would take a pipe, and he had. And wasn't it almost as pleasant, he thought, to be at the wheel, smoking and steaming along at his leisure, at a pace that let his friends the gulls come too?

He determined to take a turn around AM 62, the nearest bell buoy, and come back. That was Raymond's exercise route, and Gordon was pretty sure it was Raymond he would find. Who else would take, in broad daylight, an almost worthless little plastic dinghy and row off with it into the fog out to sea in his houserobe? A thief would have taken the boat in the night and just tossed it in the back of his pickup. If he could have done that. Not much went on in the village that escaped notice. It had been three years since the rash of car break-ins in the village, and then it was only that half-witted teenager Oley Mullins, their modern-day equivalent of a village idiot, trying to support his marijuana habit after Gordon had taken his plants away and burned them. No, Dawn was likely mistaken, for whatever reason. He would overtake Raymond and have a friendly word, all in the space of one pipe, and that would be that.

Several pipeloads had expired by the time Gordon steered *Severence* back into the harbour. He had found the unoccupied dinghy at anchor with the handline still dangling down. And he had come alongside and looked down into it. And he had seen Raymond's robe, with its blue waves and golden carp, sinking slowly out of sight beside the boat.

The two men in the yellow dory in the realm of lost souls watched and conversed in low murmurs as the Cape Islander idled nearby and its occupant smoked and contemplated on the back deck. When Gordon Daggon lifted Raymond's robe with a gaff to examine it and punctured the fabric with the big hook in the process, Angle Daggon winced and bit his fist to stifle a protest. He knew he was hidden by more than the fog, yet he remained wide-eyed and motionless, like a rabbit surprised in a field, while Gordon pondered and peered all around, looking longest in their precise direction. The former pirate remained frozen as the retired detective retreated to his deckhouse and refilled his pipe and smoked the whole load standing with his radio mike in his hand, pressing the transmission button and releasing it again, over and over, without ever saying a word.

Victor Cooley regarded his anxious visitor with amusement. When the Severance was quite gone—the wake of its departure dissipated, the sound of its engine diminished to nothing, the smell of its diesel swept away by the breeze—he remarked, "Well, he ain't reported you, but ten to one there'll be a welcoming committee when you row back in."

"Can't I get back like I did before," said Angle, "Straight into the basement?"

"That's as may be," Victor said. "I don't know how it works, exactly. Worth a try. What about your ride, though?" He indicated the dinghy with a jerk of his grizzled chin. "You just gonna leave her out here?"

"Reckon so," Angle said. "For the time bein', anyway. Hell and death, I need a drink. Pity I couldn't bring the beer. Funny how you can't bring nothin' with you."

"Worse than dyin'," Victor said, chuckling. "You die, at least you get here with your duds on. Sure, they're imaginary, but I ain't complainin'. Everything's imaginary here. Anyway, never you mind about your beer. I've got rum, and I reckon it's a better choice for a nekkid fellow. Keep you warmer, leastwise on the inside."

"Makes me drunker too. And I can't afford to be comin' home drunk ever day. I got to be a pervider. Octave as a brother is all a feller could want, but all he can do to pervide for hisself is teach, and there's problems with that. One, what he taught in our day, it might be out o' date these days. And two, he's got no papers. Till he puzzles that one out, he can't work anywhere at anything. Neither of us can. Well, I can fish with you, but he'd rather be dead again than come out here again."

"So … you agree to the bargain we were just discussing, then?"

"A boatload a day? A prime boatload?"

"Not a one wouldn't grace the Queen's table. And in return, once you're flush and your brother's took care of, I go back in your place. If I can. And if I can't, I don't hold it agin ye."

"That's a right hard bargain, Victor Cooley."

"You're free to do as you please," Victor said.

Angle spat in his palm and held it out. The old man spat in his and they shook.

"Am I free?" Angle asked. He rubbed himself vigorously all over, took a long swig from Victor's jug, and tried imagining himself dressed and warm. It didn't work. He shook his head. "A better man I may be," he said, as the fog thickened between them, "but I feel like a fool."

Chapter 4
A Threshold Too Far

Mac the assistant brewmaster from the year 1860 met his employer Mr. Alexander Keith's newest guests from the year 2007, and watched without blinking as the whole roomful turned to skeletons before his very eyes.

It was the fourth group of guests in the day to have done so, and no longer a novelty.

He was a little irritated at the size of the group. They not only filled all eighteen seats around the mahogany dining table—*shipped from Italy to Halifax where Mr. Keith's cooper carved the Keith family crest, the stag's head, in the center*—but they also lined the walls, pressing against the blue-green-and-black tartan curtains of the windows on the courtyard wall—*that Mrs. Keith herself made up special for Mr. Keith's birthday last October, of the Keith clan tartan*—and threatening with their bony heads the lanterns on the opposite wall, whose bulbs imitated flickering candles.

It was a fleeting irritation, though, and after making a mental note to complain to the supervisor that tickets for the tour had been oversold yet again, the character called Mac made his way cheerfully through the eerie crowd toward the door at the opposite end of the room through which he would lead them into the next section of the tour.

He apologised that Mr. Keith himself was not there to greet them—*He's meeting with the Antigonish Highland Society about the upcoming summer games, our first ever*—and promised the great man would join them later.

As he made his way around a carriage with a squalling baby skeleton in it, he had the poise to kneel down and extend a finger for the bizarre little creature to grasp, which it did, and which pacified it wonderfully.

On the next tour, Mimi appeared. He recognized her not by her bones but by her accent. Coming close to him in a way that once would have brought her bosom against him, she said, "Alo, Mr. Mac. So 'appy to see you. Doan worry, I not going to kiss you. I just have to tell you, dese people, dey all from Quebec, and dey doan understand hardly nossing. So, you have to speak slowly, and clearly, and plain. And den I will translate."

In the ingredients room, where he showed samples of barley, yeast and hops, the script called for him to make a joke, one with off-color connotations he had never liked. He had to ask for a volunteer, preferably a comely young woman, to grind some barley with a mortar and pestle, and then he had to remark, *Why, you're an expert grinder. Where did you learn to grind like that?* It rarely got the laugh it was half-intended to get, it always embarrassed him to fish for such a laugh in public, and today, given the appearance of the audience, it seemed downright absurd. After Mimi's translation, however, the Quebecois crowd of skeletons clapped and tittered.

"I tell dem," Mimi said with a simper and a clack of her fleshless jaws, "now it going to get really pornographic!"

On the tour after that, as if he had not had enough, there was Cat. Her mere presence as a skeleton would have bothered him. What really unsettled him was that she was *not* a skeleton. Alone among everyone he had seen since the supernatural alteration of his glasses (except for Angle and Octave), Cat remained herself, her voluptuous figure intact, her skin glowing with health and glittering with a novelty makeup she sometimes wore for fun, her green-gold eyes twinkling, her lips dark red and pencilled fine. As was her style, she was dressed in thrift store clothing in the style she called *elegant gypsy.* Her scarlet red bra plainly showed through the ivory lace shirt that was cinched with a wide leather belt over a pale yellow and finely pleated full skirt with a ruffled petticoat underneath. Her elaborately embroidered and appliqued denim jacket clashed with her other garments to just that degree shy of being completely outré that was her trademark. The knee-high leather riding boots had been with her since high school. Only her wide-brimmed sea-green fiber hat was new.

Cat did not stay close like Mimi, and she did not make remarks. She let the flow of the crowd determine the distance between herself and Raymond, and did nothing but watch him and smile. Her smile, however, had lost its usual cool distant yes-we-knew-each-other-once-long-ago quality and reverted to the subtly sensual I-can-see-right-through-your-clothes quality it had the day he first rolled into Halifax fresh from the States and parked at his sight-unseen rental in Spryfield and she strolled into the driveway from her flat across the street and greeted him as if she had been lying in wait like a cat for a mouse.

The juices that flowed in response to that all-seeing smile were an unwanted addition to the already complex chemistry that possessed Raymond. His left eye and cheek began to twitch. His heart boomed and faltered. He felt clammy and faint. His step became unsteady and his presentation forced. Still he got the facts out and the jokes accomplished and the tour delivered to the Stag's Head in the brewery basement. There with the skeletons of his colleagues he served the several flavours of Keith's beer and sang his required drinking song. That concluding his part of the script, he was on his way out for his usual break before the next tour, when Cat accosted him at the door.

She moved in close then, not touching but so close that her scent cast its spell—her mysterious scent that owed nothing to any perfume but was like the innermost essence of perfume, like the oil of the heaven tree rooted in blackest earth.

In that moment, the boundaries of separation, time, tumult and tears vanished for Raymond as if they had never existed.

In the next moment she took his hand and pressed something into it. "Here," she said acidly, "are the keys to your place. That you had to have back. Asshole."

He pocketed the keys without a word and turned to leave.

"And here," she whispered sweetly, turning him back around and pressing his palm once again, "are the keys to my place. I won't be in till late tonight, but when I do get there, I'd like you to be waiting for me."

During an off tour (one for which no tickets had sold), the actors usually congregated in the dressing room by the lockers. Wanting to do what was usual, feeling it might steady him and let his heart slow down and sort itself out, Raymond sat on a metal folding chair among the seated skeletons of his colleagues, having identified them either by their voices, their sizes, or the sheet on the bulletin board that had the names of those scheduled for shifts pencilled in.

The one who played Maggie, the female version of Duke the innkeeper, was apparently asleep, her feet up on a second chair, chin resting on her breastbone. It was hard to tell if she was really asleep because of her lack of both eyeballs and eyelids. This was Tanya, normally a short plump sweet-tempered pretty rugby-playing lesbian ballerina from Sambro who worked two jobs along with attending university and regularly staying out late drinking. Normally her apron would have been thrown over her mob cap and the fringe of her long period skirt would have lain on the floor getting even dirtier. Now, with neither flesh nor clothing, she was like a dinosaur fossil arranged on a frame.

The girl who played Annie, who led the first leg of the tour and rejoined it in the Stag's Head to help bartend and sing soulful Scottish ballads, on this shift was Ellen, another Dalhousie student. Alternately she pecked away with her phalanges at the keys of her cell phone, sending text messages, or talked to Tanya as if she were awake.

"It doesn't bother me that you're gay," Ellen was saying to Tanya now. "I mean, you are a little skanky maybe, but I still like you. Anyway, I think you should concentrate on your dancing, because acting sucks. I'm quitting acting to become a scientist—did I tell you? Oh, excuse me, gotta check this. It's my boyfriend. I never had a boyfriend before and I'm not sure how I feel about it, so we're chatting a lot."

The character Archie was a 'ne'er-do-well' that Mr. Keith purportedly employed out of the goodness of his heart. His particular duty was to take the tour into an old-time games room in the Stag's Head and there play an old timey card game called Three Card Brag with as many as could fit at the table while the others looked on and hopefully laughed at his roguish jokes. Today Archie was the slouching, hulking, hyperactive Sean—all day, for both shifts, just because Sean loved to work. At present, he was swigging a soft drink, scoffing day-old sweet rolls from the courtyard bakery, listening to music on his cell phone, swinging the tibia and fibula of his crossed leg in rhythm to the music and even frequently singing along, though he had shipped headphones out of deference to the others.

Raymond endured for as long as he could. It was not helping, however. It might have been the usual thing to do, hanging out with the gang, but with them all being nothing but bones, and Sean's food disappearing into nowhere, it was just too bizarre. He excused himself—there was a nodding of skulls in acknowledgment—and left.

The Stag's Head was only in use when there were tours going through it. When there weren't, it was empty. Raymond fled to that emptiness. As soon as he stepped into the quiet cool solitude of the basement barroom's lantern-lit, stone-walled, plank-floored illusion of antiquity, he felt more at ease. At the bar he drew a mug of lager (from a fake oak barrel that was really connected to a pressurized aluminum keg under the counter), and then adjourned to the nook they called Mr. Keith's own den, "the heart and soul of the Stag's Head Inn", where they took the occasional one and two-person tours for a feeling of intimacy.

In his time, Mr. Keith had actually kept such a room, one to which he and his closest friends could retire for more private confabulations. That room had been dismantled long ago, after Mr. Keith's death, when the entire basement including the barroom had been converted to a storeroom for kegs of ale. The current sitting room's reconstruction was in the same general area of the basement as the original and was furnished as nearly like it as could be made out from old documents. It had a desk and chair, two easy chairs, a fireplace with flanking bookshelves, a standing hat rack and umbrella stand, and a couple of paintings and a mirror on the walls.

One of the easy chairs, Raymond had discovered, was actually a modern recliner. He stretched out in it now and contemplated his surroundings. The bookshelves held two dozen volumes of what their jackets described as *The Brewmaster's Guide,* but which really concerned any number of subjects, had been purchased from estate sales or used book stores, and had nothing to do with the brewing of beer. In the nonfunctional fireplace the charred logs at least were real, and above the fireplace, in an ornate gilt frame, the portrait of Mr. Keith as a smiling and successful and young gentleman, in tweeds and mutton chop sideburns, was also genuine.

In a corner of the mirror on the wall behind the desk, Raymond could see himself lying back with his mug. In the middle of the mirror was a painting on the wall behind him of a snowy lamplit evening along the Lower Water Street side of the Brewery. The snow had been cleared from the sidewalk and was banked against the building's ironstone wall. From a shadowy archway in the wall, a woman in a long blue dress and bonnet and a little girl in a red hooded cloak waved in greeting to a white-bearded gentleman with a cane and top hat who was toiling his way towards them along the walk on the opposite side of the cobblestoned street, almost out of the picture.

It was the scene from his dream on the night of the hurricane. Though what had happened in the dream was beyond his recall, the setting for some reason was still as fresh in his mind as if he had just been there, and the characters as oddly familiar as if they had just parted ways.

He sensed a mystery, but he was not dwelling on mysteries. He had simply been looking for something on which to rest his eyes—to avoid closing them, for he was afraid to close them—and this painting was it. A family reunion in the making—it pacified his mind, and his was a mind that desperately needed pacifying, for its thoughts were like a flock of pigeons endlessly startled and flying off in all directions.

He dozed off nevertheless and was too slow in waking to the can-can music from his cell phone to answer the call before the caller hung up.

After a minute the voice mail icon on his cell phone screen signalled that he had a message. He dialled in for it.

"Hello, Raymond," the voice said. "Gordon Daggon. Hope this finds you. Funny thing happened. Dawn O'Keefe said she saw someone stealing your dinghy. I thought I saw you in it, rowing by in the fog, but she insisted it was someone else. So I went out to check. Found the boat anchored over near Hearn's with nobody in it and one of your bathrobes in the water alongside. Now, I don't know what's going on, and I don't mean to be prying into your business, but I thought I ought to call. So call me back, please."

Raymond weighed the pros and cons of calling Gordon back. The cons were, first, that Gordon hadn't left his number. Raymond knew there were ways to get the number, but he couldn't remember what they were and he didn't feel like trying to find out. His heart was beating even faster than before and irregularly now and he was finding it hard to concentrate. Second, even if he could call Gordon, what would he say? *No, it's only a guest of mine? Ghost of mine?* On the other hand, if he didn't call back, he ran the risk of arousing the retired detective's suspicions. Gordon might call the police, and what would Raymond tell them? What could Raymond tell anyone?

Feeling panicky and as if he might faint, Raymond called Cat. And got her voice mail. And said yes he would come over, and did she know he had ghosts in his house, and did she have any idea what to do with them, and would she please not think him crazy he needed her now more than ever, and would she please please please consider coming home?

He flipped the phone shut, pocketed it, and extracted Cat's key. Lying there in the leather recliner in the dim cool den, he rubbed between thumb and forefinger this bit of cut brass that represented her unexpected invitation. He wondered what else he should do. He thought he should probably call Gordon. He thought he should go refill his mug. As he grew paler and clammier, he thought that he might also consider calling an ambulance. In the end he decided to just close his eyes and relax and let it sort itself out—his erratic heart. And perhaps everything would sort itself out. Eh?

Once again, in answer to the invitation, a guest had arisen and come.

From the Sun, a plasma of charged particles, electrons and protons, had streamed out as a wind, a solar wind. A gentle gust had wafted toward Earth a clutch of magnetic fields that, when they arrived, spread themselves over the Earth's magnetosphere and squeezed and cracked it like a nut. Through the crack, a mighty torrent of plasma entered and blasted the planet below. It did not uproot trees or tear the roofs off of houses or cause coastline-inundating tidal surges. It was not a coarse blow but a fine one, invisible to human perception except as light or the lack of it.

Both by night and by day, in arcs, curtains, and coronas of ghostly greens, reds and blues, auroras appeared in the sky far beyond their usual northern climes, as far south as Texas, Hawaii and Italy. Electrical light was extinguished throughout the Canadian province of Quebec as the power grid failed with a great sparking flash and a raw ripping sound at the base terminal as of a galactic phonebook being torn by a truly strong man.

A pod of fifteen bowhead whales migrating south from the Chukchi Sea through the Bering Strait altered course one hundred and thirty-five degrees and drove blindly northwest onto the rocky shore of Nunyamo Bay on the Siberian Peninsula at a shamanic gathering place known to archaeologists as Whalebone Alley, there to be greeted by the jawbones and ribs of their ancestors that were already arranged in mysterious arches along the beach in a display renowned as one of the masterpieces of Arctic culture.

In Turkey, during a thousand kilometer race from Manisa to Erzurum, a formation of competing homing pigeons exploded in all directions. The bird known as Greased Lightning, that its South African owner had recently acquired for a hefty 600,000 Rand, flew as nearly straight up as it could, more and more slowly as it went, until at a height of half a mile a Maltese falcon apprehended it, scarcely dislodging a feather, while loafing along on the level at a leisurely twenty miles an hour.

Meanwhile in northern Manitoba, in the Land of Little Sticks, Sky Colomb, a Nehilawe man of the Black Sturgeon Nation, remarked to Jackie Richcoon, as they sat side by side in lawnchairs drinking beer by the remote majestic lake called Keewatin, that the dance of the spirits was disturbing that day. There was something about it that he did not trust, something wild, like a woman with seduction in her eyes and nothing but destruction on her mind.

In Nova Scotia, where the invitation had its origin, the guest made a relatively restrained appearance, striking only the stretch of waterfront in Halifax Harbour that included Alexander Keith's Brewery. In that quadrant all six transformers were fried, sending a more than raw electricity surging through the system, causing the bulbs of all the buildings there to flare with an unnatural brightness for an instant before shattering.

In the Brewery, in the living room where the guests first arrived, the ten-minute video about Mr. Keith started by itself and ran backward on the gilt-framed screen over the fireplace. The taped sounds of a working brewery tripled in volume, so the great copper tuns and kettles and fermenters in the brewhouse all gave a fever-pitch performance, bubbling and threshing and clanging and shrieking, before the tape players shorted and all went silent as the grave.

In the staff room, to the dismay of Ellen, Tanya and Sean, their cell phones began speaking in tongues.

Down in the Stag's Head all the taps flew open and the five types of beer spewed and mixed indiscriminately till the aluminum kegs under the fake wooden kegs were all empty and the narrow stretch of floor behind the bar overflowed with multi-flavored suds.

In Mr. Keith's restored den, Raymond's empty mug cracked in half on the side table by the recliner where he had lain, that now was occupied only by his assistant brewmaster's costume.

A smell of singed hair hovered in the beery dark.

Chapter 5

Back in the Way Back When

"Pápi," said the little girl in the freshly ironed pink pinafore at the invalid's bedside, "Pápi, *réveille toi*. Oh, do wake up, Pápi. It's been so long, and every day I have to sit here, and I've run out of things to say, I really have, and today it's nice and sunny and I could be out playing Graces with Gina and Lisbet."

Her lower lip quivered and her eyes filled with tears. Putting a hand on the covers over the invalid's heart, she added, "And besides I miss you, Pápi, and Mama misses you too. Please wake up."

She had come to this room every day now for forty-nine days, each time for an hour, and each time, as her mother had requested, she spoke to her father as if he could hear her. He had never answered.

Now Captain Oliver Cole opened his eyes, blinked several times to clear them, and looking not at his daughter but up at the damascened claret-coloured linen canopy overhead, said in a hoarse halting voice, "I was dreaming of a squirrel."

He freed an unsteady hand from the neatly tucked-in covers and placed it over the little hand on his chest. "And not just any squirrel, my dear Amélie, but a giant one. A giant red squirrel with a great bushy tail … being led on a rope by a bear. A bear of the usual size and yet—and you could see this plainly since they both went along on their hind legs—a bear only half as big as the squirrel he was leading.

"The bear had a patch over one eye. A black patch.

"The two were passing through a clearing in a wood, and I … I was watching from behind a very slender young pine that scarcely hid me. I knew the bear was looking for me, and that he meant to turn the giant squirrel loose on me. And I knew the squirrel was perfectly savage and loved nothing more than the taste of human blood.

"I had offended the bear somehow. Perhaps I was responsible for the loss of its eye. I'm not sure. I only know that with its one remaining eye, the bear was determined to watch the squirrel eat me alive.

"A queer dream, very queer, the sort one encounters when making the passage. Very vivid, but only a dream." He turned his tired face to Amélie and smiled a sad crooked smile. "What preceded the dream, though, was real, and I must record it, for such is my debt. So be a dear little owl, and fetch quill and ink and my journal. And then much more wood for the fire. It is mortal cold in the in-between passage. The very marrow of my bones is like ice."

As his little owl ran down the hall, crying out that her Pápi was awake, *awake*, Captain Cole raised himself in the bed and stacked pillows behind him. While he waited, shivering, he fingered a cuff of his fine green-and-gold-striped cotton garment. "So, a nightshirt," he remarked. "A nightshirt again, like a civilized man."

It was not Amélie but his wife Josephine that appeared with the writing materials. A tall gracious woman with gentle grey eyes, she set on the bed beside him the lacquered oriental tray that held the book, pen and ink jar, and bent and kissed her husband on the forehead and straightened his nightcap, that was colored the same as his nightshirt. With the straightening, the cap's golden tassel fell over his nose. A flicker of humor invaded the tear-streaked sadness of her long aristocratic features and as quickly was gone. She moved the tassel tenderly to one side.

"So, you are back," she said. "I was just wondering would I ever have my Oliver again, and if I did, could I keep him. As a captain he is more with the sea than with me, and then he is lost to the doctors, and then to a fever. So, love of my life, do you stay a while now, or will you be telling those stories again that will bring back the doctors?"

Cole took her hand and held the back of it lightly to his lips, meanwhile breathing deeply of the smell of her. It was not the smell of honey butter. There was no earthiness to it. He had left that behind. This was lilac water imbued with a body odor so light as to be almost indiscernible. This was his woman like a cloud, his Jo.

It was so hard, having two loves, and always leaving one behind.

"Jo, Jo, Jo," he said, still holding on to her hand, "Am I so old and infirm that you welcome me home with a kiss on the forehead? When we met in Marseilles, you threw yourself into my arms as if I were the last man on earth. And now I've been further from home than any sailor."

"It is not you who are so much older, Oliver," Jo said, "though your hair and your beard have gone white since the Bonne Chance went down, whiter even than all this shocking lot of snow. No, it is I who am no longer so young. I have missed you too much. But let us not speak of that."

"Jo," Cole said, "I must write. An account *must* be preserved of this doorway to the future and another life. But we will keep it under lock and key this time. I will not hawk it about again. The doctors may busy themselves with true madmen, and the newsmen with other news. My tale will be my legacy, and a later generation my heirs."

For a moment his mind wandered, and he looked vacantly about him. The events of his other life beckoned, but their voices were faint. He was forgetting again. His gaze fell on the guttering fire in the room's hearth.

"Now," he said, "will you please stoke that fire, dear, and feed me? My own vital spark has burned low, and is in danger of being extinguished entirely. And have Amélie bring the dorje and bell, so I can keep my wits about me. There is much to record, and already the details are slipping away."

"There is no bell, my darling," said Josephine. "You called for it at the height of your fever, when you were delirious and waving the little sceptre all about as if either to bless us or keep us at bay. I reminded you then. That was when you fell into the sleep no one could wake you from. I fear to remind you again, but I must. The bell was stolen. The little sceptre fell out of your purse as the pickpocket fled, or it would be lost too. The constabulary cannot find the man, and there is little hope that they will, for he is not a known thief, nor anyone known by the thieves. They say he might have been a sailorman, down on his luck, who has since shipped out. I am sorry. As for food, I was making a bouillabaisse for dinner, and have only to add the … how do you say, the *homard*."

"Lobster."

"Yes, lobster. I have only to add that, and I will bring you a bowl straightaway. And Oliver, will you receive a guest? Francis Stegman would like to see you. He said that as soon as you recovered—and he alone among all your friends never doubted you would—he would like to talk with you about another venture. Another ship."

"No bell?"

Cole went pale and slumped against his stack of pillows. She knelt at the bedside (with some difficulty, for the hoops of her dress interfered) and took his gaunt hand again. It was trembling now.

"Oliver," she said, "Please, please. Is a ship not more important than a bell? There are any number of bells, and they are not hard to come by."

"There is none like it in all the world, I fear."

"Dear, Francis wants you to go back to India. That is where they make them, is it not? You can get another one there."

Cole's head bent till his white beard was tucked into the collar of his nightshirt. The tassel of his nightcap fell forward again, and his eyes blinked shut.

"Oliver. Oliver! Do not leave us again!"

He shuddered and groaned. His back arched as if he had been stabbed and his whole body went stiff. Then he relaxed, and the hand she held squeezed back.

"Well," he said, opening his eyes again and forcing a smile, "He is a faithful loyal partner, our Francis, and I will be glad to entertain his proposition … tomorrow. But for now the dorje. At least the dorje. And soup and solitude and recollection. Above all, recollection. And a roaring fire. Roaring, my dear!"

She punched the fire up with the poker and brought more logs and laid them in. Before she left she gave him a different sort of kiss, a more amorous one, that even more than the newly stoked fire began to melt the frigid emptiness he felt inside.

Amélie came bearing the little double-headed golden scepter in both hands as if she were presenting it to a king. "Mama had it in her sewing basket," she said. "She has been using it for a spindle. She would have me hold it while she wound the thread onto it."

"Your mother has an unfailing sense of humor," said Cole. "Now away with you. You have discharged your onerous duties commendably, and are free to go. Never keep your friends waiting."

"Pápi, may I stay instead? And when you have done writing, may I hear the *story* of the bell and dorje?"

"If you are quiet as any mouse, you may stay, and I will tell you the story. But you must keep it to yourself now, and not repeat it any more to Gina or Lisbet or any of your other friends. Or anyone at all. It will just be our secret. Agreed? For I have promised your mother."

"I will just tell my dolls. They will never betr ... betr .."

"Never betray us? I am sure of it. Now come up here." He patted the bed beside him. "And remember—quiet as any mouse till I am done."

"May I hold the dorje?"

"You may, but do not wave it around, for it has magic that would make a wand weep for shame, so it would, and if you were to disappear as I did, your mother would never forgive me."

"No," Amélie said solemnly, for unlike her mother she believed her father's every word. "No, I will not wave it. I will just hold it. I promise."

So they sat, the dutiful daughter with the dorje in hand and the old sea captain with the dragon-decorated lacquer tray he had brought back from Shanghai in his lap. She did her best to be quiet as a mouse, only occasionally forgetting and humming or breaking into song or asking half a question before remembering her promise. He wrote feverishly, in spurts, first pondering and squinting and pursing his lips, then dipping the quill and attacking the pulped-rag pages of his journal.

The ink was running low when Cole's memory of his time as Raymond Kidd ran out. Setting the tray wearily to one side, he took his plump pink-clad Amélie into his lap and turned his mind to another story, one he never had trouble remembering. At least not in this life.

"Not too long ago, my dear, but very far away, on the far side of the world, the bold sea captain Oliver Cole brought his brig the Bonne Chance to the port of Calcutta in the state of Bengal in the country of India where the real Indians dwell, and he ordered the ship's anchor to be dropped into the black Calcutta mud, and he ordered his coxswain to row him ashore in the ship's spanking clean gig so he could get to his bargaining. For he had come to bargain—to buy for a little what he could sell for a lot on this side of the world.

"He was a sharp bargainer and a stubborn one, a stubborn man altogether and proud of it, a proud man altogether and stubbornly so. Therefore many days passed while he acquired the cargo he meant to carry back to England and there sell for a profit so handsome it would afford him the second ship that would be the start of his fleet, the seed of his empire, the key to the kingdom he would eventually leave to his little princess Amélie.

"He bargained for jute and bought two thousand bales, enough to hoist a mainsail to the moon. He bargained for flax and bought six thousand bales, of a fineness so fine the linen spun from it would be like a cloud, like the canopy over this bed, that gleams and shimmers in the firelight like a dream. He bargained for rice and bought nine thousand bags of a Basmati sweet and subtle as the perfume of the gods.

"A break came in the bargaining during a bout with a cowhide merchant sharp and stubborn as the captain himself. All morning they had sat on a tiled floor on embroidered cushions in a cloud of cloyingly sweet smoke from a hookah the merchant would not leave alone. Finally the captain excused himself and took a turn to stretch his legs and breathe some fresh air.

"Now it was not only an abominable smoke, little owl, but also one of strange propensities, for having gotten in the captain's lungs, it steered him wrong, threw him off course, deviated his compass, disturbed his powers of navigation. He had meant to go visit the stalls of the pashmina sellers, there to purchase for his wife the gorgeous French enchantress Josephine a shawl she would never forget, of that wool from the goats of the high Himalayas that is softer than silk. Instead he found himself wandering the banks of the foul-smelling Houghly. Having forgotten his hat at the cowhide merchant's, his head was bared to a sun that beat down like a hammer, so his brains rang again and his bewilderment grew.

"Now it was Durga Purja in Calcutta, the seventh and last day of that great festival, and the riverside was packed with revellers come to return their painted idols to the mud. The captain becoming caught up in their exceedingly close company was bumped and jostled right and left, left and right, from before and behind, till he scarcely knew if he was coming or going. The smother of drums and supplications from all sides only served to confuse him still further.

"They carried him along like a leaf on a stream. At first he resisted and called out in anger, but soon surrendered to the irresistible press. He found himself smiling, then laughing, then waving his arms and even shouting with glee like the rest.

"As they made their way into the shallows, the captain's boots sinking in the ooze and the brown water pouring over their tops, a machwa with its square sail furled was poled in among them and a body from it laid on the bank. The corpse lay face up, a rather handsome though pock-marked young man in a soggy red dhoti. With his eyes closed and his hands folded over his chest, he seemed merely asleep, and indeed the crowd ignored him and continued to dance, drum, chant, clap, splash and flourish its gawdy deities in an ecstasy of union that I am sad to report included even the captain.

"Later, in the stillness of dusk, when mud to mud had been returned and the floating paint rainbows from the drowned idols had swirled away and the rowdy worshippers and their awful hubbub had vanished, a sober captain sat alone by the corpse, deep in an unlikely mourning. While under the influence of the dream-inducing charas that his host the cowhide merchant had smoked in his hookah, he had come to see the dead man as a drowned divinity, a river god spit out by its own element, refused for some unfathomable reason by the river and cast out in the form of a human nobody. Such a death had seemed an awful tragedy, and the captain had wept. Then the tide of his intoxication had receded and he had realized it was only a man in the first place, a native heathen, of no significance whatsoever. His tears had dried, but the grief in his heart would not be hushed, no matter how he reasoned with himself.

While he grieved, and wondered at himself for doing so, a ragged beggar boy came and crouched by his side. At length, after observing the captain for a while at his vigil and listening with him in the silence to the distant lowing of cattle and the nearby chanting of peepers, the boy addressed him familiarly.

"'Didst know him, Maharaj? Was he thy cousin? Son? Nay, hold, the color of his skin is wrong. Thy debtor, then? Dost mourn the rupees that will not be thine? So I would were I you. Though how could I ever be you? Thy wealth exceeds mine as the sun does the moon.' He reached out and fingered the sleeve of the captain's fine coat. "Twould do thee more good, I am thinking, to share than to covet. A few coins for Ajay would lighten thy load and thy spirit, I swear it. Lakshmi not Alakshmi would thy deva be, and fortune not misfortune thy company.'

"At first the captain took little notice of the boy, but eventually, when it occurred to him that he must return soon or spend the night there, for the light was fading, he heaved himself to his feet and fished in his pockets for what change he might spare.

"As he turned to the boy to make his donation, he was startled to find someone else there. Standing almost directly behind him and only slightly higher up on the riverbank was a short stout shaven-headed man, who smiled a great gap-toothed smile at the look of alarm on the captain's face and then extracted from the folds of his dusty maroon robe two objects, a golden bell and a two-headed sceptre. Bowing, he held them out toward the captain while saying many strange words.

"Do you understand him, boy?" the captain inquired. "He does not speak Bengali, nor any strain of Hindi I have ever heard. Is he Chinese?"

"'Revered one, Protector of Wanderers,' the boy said, snatching the captain's coins before the captain should forget, 'It would be strange, stranger than moonrise in the morning, should I not understand, for is not Ajay beggar of the crossroads, doormat of the four directions? What language escapes him, so would that person's generosity. This is a man from Tibet, gentle master, from that remoteness they call Kham. He asks if you wish this drowned man's life returned. He says it is a bad idea, for *jumbies* ever make the poorest of servants. Their minds remain partly in darkness so they stumble and mumble and drop what they are given to carry. But he will do the deed if that is truly what you wish.'

"'Does he mock me?' said the captain. 'No one has that power.'

"'Each country has its faqirs, Wise One, who pretend to feats of magic. They are not honest beggars like Ajay. Come, let us leave him. I will take you back to town. I have a sister there who weaves a spell one may enjoy all night.'

"'Does he want money for this deed? I am curious. Ask him.'

"'Padma Bhusan, it is like asking a thief if he wants to rob you, but for thee I will.'

"So the boy asked the Tibetan, in the way of that strange language, what was the cost of death's defeat, and the Tibetan laughed. He laughed till he cried, till he could no longer stand, and then he sat down on the trampled ground and laughed. Unable to stop, he drew his robe over his head and sat shaking and quaking like a large maroon pudding. Finally he uncovered himself and replied to the boy.

"'The price, he says, is all you have or ever will, Maharaj. He is a madman, who frightens even fearless Ajay. Let us leave him now.'"

"'Tell him he shall have his price. Tell him, for he does not frighten me, and I will call his bluff.'

"In response to the child's translation, the madman stared hard at the captain, cocked his head and arched his eyebrows questioningly as if to give him one last chance to change his mind, and then nodded and lay down on the ground and closed his eyes and shortly began to snore.

"'Madman?' said the captain. 'I think not. He's but a halfwit. Lead me back, fearless Ajay. Lead me back to food and drink and lots of both, for though I am one man I hunger for ten. And then lead me to your sister and I will pay you her price. God forgive me.'.

"As they stepped around the Tibetan, who lay across the beaten path up the bank, the man turned on his back and called out, ringing the bell slowly and waving the scepter in an arc.

"'What now?' said the captain. "Does he curse us? Are we consigned to hell?'

"'O Destroyer of Illusion ...'

"'Enough of your names, boy. Call me Captain, only Captain. That is what I am, and all I am, and all I wish to be.'

"'O Captain, only captain, my captain, he mocks thee. Let us pay him no mind but think only of that which awaits us—food, music, my sister. Above all my sister.'

"'What does he say?' the captain said, firmly halting though the beggar boy tugged on his arm.

"'He says, for I will not lie,' said Ajay, 'that for one so wonderfully compassionate, willing to give his all for another and that other a dead man, thou art surprisingly dumb, like a dog with a butcher for a master who would stray for a mere meatless bone. And so he offers thee this bell and dorje as thy bone.'

"'Does he?' said the captain. 'And what are this bell and dorje, and how much does he want for them?'

"'What they are he will not say, but Ajay knows, o noble captain, and will tell thee as we walk, for thy feast and my sister beckon. Does not thy mouth water and thy loins ache? As for the price, it is just as it was.'

"'Tell him come to my ship, the Bonne Chance, and a purse will be waiting, for these are charming souvenirs and I will have them. Tell him I am a captain, Captain Oliver Crowe, and ask him his name.'

"'He says his name is also Dorje, and he will visit thy ship and thy purse, but he will not call thee captain. He names thee anew.'

"'Oh? And what is this new name?'

"'He mocks thee, my captain.'

"'Say, Ajay.'

"'Well then, he christens thee Emptiness Dog, or Howling Cur of Enlightenment.'

"Now, Amélie, my little sleeping beauty, a variety of things happened and did not happen.

"It did indeed happen (as your father I swear it) that as the madman rang the bell and waved the *dorje*, the drowned man in the red dhoti stood, staggered once to the left and once to the right, and then bowed deeply with joined palms in the direction of the astonished captain and the wide-eyed beggar boy.

"It also happened that the madman then put the bell and dorje in the captain's hands and patted him on the cheek and pressed a hand over his heart that stopped it beating till he removed it several seconds later, leaving a dusty stain on the cream-colored linen that would not wash out, and marking the skin underneath with a brown scar that is still there.

"It further happened that little Ajay then escorted the speechless captain away, with some haste and no goodbyes.

"It did *not* happen during their rapid return into town—for Ajay towed the captain at a shambling trot—that he remembered or bothered or dared to tell the captain what the bell and dorje were. He simply hurried him along till the lights of the town were around them and their food and drink nigh.

"It did happen, after a bowl of steaming curry had revived the captain's senses and a thrice-refilled glass of arrack had dispelled his astonishment, that he took into his lap the little beggar boy's sister, for she was indeed beautiful, if somewhat thin, and her great dark eyes enhanced with kohl did indeed weave a spell and her ready smile promise wonders.

"It did not happen, though he paid her price and more, that he made use of her. He held her through the night, but any quickening in his loins was as quickly extinguished by his tears, that came out of nowhere, for no particular reason, and would not be denied. Until the dusty dawn, he merely sat on the rickety dishevelled cot and held and rocked her with a grief keen as a razor.

"The next day he returned for his cowhides. Having no heart to resume bargaining, he offered the last price he remembered the merchant naming, and agreed without objection to the higher price that was immediately demanded, the wily native noting the captain's muddy boots, stained jacket, unshaven face and sunken eyes.

"Josephine's pashminas the captain bought without bargaining at all, which amazed the pashmina seller and left her talking to herself, for the captain's reputation preceded him and the seller had tripled her already high prices for foreigners so as not to be beaten down beyond what she considered fair.

"For a week the Bonne Chance waited, fully loaded. The monk never appeared, and the brig finally sailed. As the last line was tossed from its bollard, the captain threw onto the dock the payment purse he'd readied, and observed, as the purse burst open and the bright coins flew, how beggars and stevedores and respectable onlookers alike all scrambled for them, even diving into the water for the ones that rolled off or slipped through the boards.

"A beggar not among them was Ajay, for he had come aboard as the captain's new cabin boy, the other having passed puberty on the outbound voyage and joined the underpopulated afterguard. From the height of his new position and in the comfort of his new clothes, Ajay watched the melee on the dock, and listened to the captain's comments on greed the great equalizer, in a solemn stunned silence, and could not be persuaded away from the rail till long after his land and his sister had faded from view.

"They were in that settled stretch of weather between the northeast and southwest monsoon, and the fine days were many. The sailing of the ship was mostly left to Rune Jorgensen, the very capable first mate, while the captain sat aft on the quarterdeck with Ajay and the bell and dorje, going over what they knew about the objects, with which he had become obsessed. Not depending on Ajay's knowledge alone, he had sent the boy and his sister throughout Calcutta for information. They had returned with a number of pertinent tracts and a wizened old scholar in tow to decipher them, for with all his skill with spoken languages and a memory as long as the libraries of Nalanda, Takshasila, Vikramshila and Kanchipuram joined end to end, the skinny little outcast could not read a word.

"'Tell me again,' said the captain, six leagues south of Madagascar, holding up the dorje and marvelling at how the gold gleamed in the equatorial light even under the shade of the awning that sheltered them in their deck chairs. 'Tell me again.'

"Ajay sighed, for he could not understand the captain's pressing need to go over and over what he already knew. 'O avatar of Ganesh,' he said, and stopped himself, for the captain had stifled his native loquaciousness and limited him to a sailor's address, 'O *Sir*, it is the thunderbolt, it is the diamond sceptre. It is the symbol of awakened mind, indestructible and clear. It is wielded by those who would destroy deluded mind.'

"'Let us begin here in the center—*again*. This sphere here at the center, that is Shunyata, primordial nature of the universe, underlying unity of all things. From the sphere emerge these flowers, lotus flowers, one on either side, eight petals each. One flower represents Samsara, the other Nirvana—Hell and Heaven as the Christians understand, but here both as pure as the lotus, that grows from the mud without stain.'

"'Around the mouth of each lotus four *makaras*, half-fish and half-crocodile. These stand for the union of opposites. These prongs on each end of the sceptre, their tongues, enclose empty space as form encloses emptiness and emptiness gives rise to form.'

"'It is a symbol, sir, this dorje, of the way our minds create the universe, instant by instant, and so a powerful weapon with which to vanquish duality.'

"'Thus I have heard, O Insatiable ... *sir*.'

"'Yes, Ajay,' said the captain. 'You have heard, and I have heard, till we are sick of hearing. Yet we do not understand. Do you? Today, this time, do you?'

"'I understand one may feast and still hunger,' said Ajay, putting the dorje away in its soft leather bag. 'You are feeding me three times a day for a month, so this body has swollen as fat as a tick on the soft inner ear of an elephant, yet this mind still fixes on its dinner as the compass needle fixes on north. My only thought is ever when the next mealtime will be. Even now I hunger.'

"He took up another bag, and drew from it the golden bell with is figured handle. 'As for this dorje and drilbu, no doubt the Lord Vishnu in his wisdom understands, as will the lesser gods in their infinite patience after kalpas upon kalpas, but the words leave thy ignorant servant nowhere, as though stranded on a strand of drifting seaweed in the middle of this boundless sea.'

"'Now, *sir*, the drilbu.' He rang the bell and listened as the long resonance faded. 'Would that it could call the Lord Buddha as the Tibetans claim, for then The Omniscient One could explain all, and Ajay could go to his dinner.'

"Now the captain himself, little dreamer, though an educated man and a studious one, had no more idea what the words signified than did Ajay. No matter how often he heard them or at what length he pondered them, the teachings in the tracts remained foreign. Yet no matter how utterly frustrating he found them, he also found himself captivated by them. 'Boooooodha,' he would say to himself, and, 'Dooooooorjay,' drawing the syllables out as if they were taffy.

"From Good Hope to Liverpool, he availed himself increasingly of the privacy of his cabin, where he could focus without distraction on Ajay's explanations, and where he penned long ruminative letters to Josephine about nothing more than the two gifts he had so mysteriously been given, and what their significance might be, for he thought of nothing else.

"His crew commented among themselves on his reclusiveness, and on the rare occasions when he did emerge, as to take the noon sight with his sextant, they cast sidelong glances at him, some merely curious, others critical. All knew of his obsession with the drilbu and dorje. When they named the two religious instruments, which was rare, them being sailors and a naturally superstitious lot, they referred to them obliquely, as *his heathen toys* for instance, except for the two Chinese topmen known as

Hurly Burly and Heigh Ho who would not speak of the matter at all. A few of the more outspoken went so far as to take exception to even having the objects on board. 'Bad luck,' opined the cooper, speaking around his pipe in a circle of smokers in the forecastle. 'It stands to reason they will bring bad luck, for one is called a *thunderbolt*, and since when has a thunderbolt ever brought a ship *good* luck? No, mates, what a thunderbolt brings a ship is fire, and what fire does is burn, and what ships do as catch fire is go down, straight down to Davy Jones. He is askin' for trouble, and when he rings that other item, he is absolutely callin' for it. And trouble ever comes when called, you know as well as I. Mark my words.'

"There were times when even Ajay was excluded from the captain's company. On these occasions, the captain sat alone in his cabin with his chair turned to the wall, contemplating an exotic painting, framed in brocade cloth, that the boy had brought back with the tracts. The painting's subject was a single crowned figure in kingly robes on a lotus throne in an outline of flames. In his left hand, as if he were ringing it, was a drilbu like the captain's; in his right a golden dorje brandished like a weapon. His expression was forbidding, his attitude profound. Ajay had secured no explanation of the painting; none seemed necessary. Power radiated from it palpably. The captain began to feel that he might imitate what he could not understand. He took to aping the monarch, holding his own bell and sceptre in the same way and likewise frowning. He sat like this for minutes at a time, and then hours. The implements warmed in his hands with a warmth all their own. A sense of invincibility stole over him, a conviction that there was no need to understand, only to *be*. He *was* the ruler on the wall.

"When a French privateer attacked the Bonne Chance off the coast of Spain, he stood nonchalantly at the rail with his hands in his coat pockets, one on the dorje and the other on the bell, while the cannons roared and the balls crashed home around him. He met with disdain his first mate's appeals that they surrender, and when the British man-of-war was sighted that would come to their rescue, he was not surprised. He took it as his due and retired, leaving Jorgensen and the surgeon to deal with the wreckage and the dead and wounded.

"He had no idea how thoroughly deluded he was, and would not till the Bonne Chance reached Liverpool.

"Perhaps the jute had been loaded still damp. Two thousand bales of damp fiber stacked tight in the airless confines of a ship's hold for a hundred and twenty-one days, it could have set itself afire. I cannot explain it, my dear, but spontaneous combustion is ever so, as secret love may result in a fever if left too long undeclared. Any gate, it is true that the captain, in the throes of the anxiety with which he awaited the Tibetan, had for once disregarded the strictures of loading and not examined everything that was stowed. This haunted him afterward ... and now, even now ...

"Were you awake you would take me to task for that slip," Cole confided to his sleeping daughter, wiping away tears with the corner of his bedsheet. "For a storyteller is not to fall into his story. At least not with such a splash.

"What happened was the captain's luck ran out, hey? When the stevedores removed the lower hatches, clouds of black smoke billowed out. The Bonne Chance burned, Amélie. How she burned! We scuttled her to contain the blaze, but even as the Mersey poured into her and she settled in the dockside mud, her main and mizzen masts came down, crushing the dockside sheds and setting them afire.

"But that was not all. That was nothing, in fact, for the insurance covered the ship and the cargo. But it did not cover Ajay. My dear, had he lived, he'd have made a fine playmate for thee, perhaps even a brother, for he had so endeared himself to me that I thought of adopting him. The bell and dorje had come to me as if I were meant to be their owner, and he as if I were meant to be his father.

"I was on the dock at the pumps. There was a hose in my hand. I was spraying the flames. Ajay stood at the edge of the dock, looking down at the ship. Suddenly he looked up and called out, 'Oh my Captain, I have forgotten the drilbu and dorje!'

"I called back that he should let them stay forgotten, but it was too late. He jumped down onto that burning deck and straightway dashed into the cabin. When he came out, he was all on fire. His hair, his canvas shirt and trousers ... that the boatswain himself, that foul-mouthed old bully, had kindly fashioned for him from a scrap of worn-out sail, and of which he was so proud ... O Amélie, he was like a human torch.

"He jumped into the river, and that extinguished him. We pulled him out. He had the bell and dorje in his little fists. I had to pry them from his fingers, just like this." Cole worked the dorje from his daughter's grasp, that had not loosened as she slept.

"Yes, I thought to let him keep them, let him take his little medals to the grave, but in the end I could not. They are my curse. My burden. They were meant for me.

"So, on the mail packet that took the captain back to Halifax, word went round among the crew and the passengers that it was grief that kept the poor man to himself, morose and uncommunicative, but it was not. It was the bell and dorje. He shut himself up with them day after day as the sea miles flowed by. There was no monarch for him to contemplate now—the painting had burned with the Bonne Chance—but the image was burned in his mind. It haunted him, taunting him to realize what must be realized!

"It was also intimated that he secretly drank. This was said to account for his slurred speech when he did venture on deck. A natural mistake, yet Lord knows how many revelations of the universe we paper over in our haste to explain things away. The captain, you see, was not toping at all. His vocal irregularities and the facial tics that went with them were what will be called in the future *a technical problem*. The captain was *shorting out*, as we will say in our easy familiarity with the vagaries of electricity. His trips to otherwhen and otherwho had begun. The coachman, as it were, was at the door, wielding the brass knocker with a vengeance, and Oliver Cole's mind was the door.

"His first excursion was a short one. He rose from his chair. That is to say, he did not stand, but actually rose several inches into the air. When he came down, however, his chair had shifted with the roll of the ship, and so he landed on the arm of it and came crashing down on the floor, which rather let the air out of his grand moment.

"Nevertheless he resumed sitting with a feeling of great accomplishment, as if he were mastering the situation after all.

"The next time he did not rise but was flung, from the chair into the bulkhead before him, with such force that it bloodied his nose and left him lying on his back. Of course, being a seaman, he suspected the treachery as being the sea's, but when he stumbled out of his cabin to see what foul weather had overtaken them, it was a sunny day with gentle breezes and never a white horse in sight. No rogue wave had been his undoing. Only his roguish pride.

"Of that he felt so certain that he conducted the next session with his head bowed, in such humility and with his spirits so dashed that he ended by going to sleep. He woke a century and a half later as another man. But of that I have promised your mother not to speak again.

"The captain's body remained in the chair, as if in a drugged sleep. It was discovered, untenanted so to speak, after his continued absence from meals concerned the packet's captain and caused that worthy gentleman to send an attendant to check on his colleague.

"After a far from triumphal disembarcation at the dock where his wife and daughter waited—you will never forget that, now will you, my dear, your Pápi tied onto a stretcher and raving and straining at his bonds—after that, I say, those versed in such matters among medical men diagnosed him as having gone mad. They had some grasp of the electrical impulse, thanks to Galvani's pioneering treatise *De Viribus Electricitatis in motu musculari commentarius*, published some years before, and so correctly comprehended the captain's physical symptoms. They went on from there, however, to conclude that the shock of his loss was *merely* an electrical one, and that his tales of the future and a subsequent life were merely products of a mind disordered *as if by lightning, as if by the dreaded thunderbolt.*

"Now, he was an eminently respectable man, was our Captain, and counted among his cronies such notable Haligonians as brewmaster and sometime mayor Alexander Keith and shipping magnate Francis Stegman. In an effort to justify the confinement of a citizen of such prominence, the doctors paid for the publication of an article in the *Novascotian*. I have it by heart. Here is a passage:

> "The mad make all sorts of noise and utter astonishing remarks which lack recognizable or common meaning and the consistency demanded of ordinary logic. Worse, their expostulations strike listeners and observers as fantastic and absurd, having no bearing to a shared reality. Negative values are conferred. For madness lacks any heuristic power and communicative force that might contribute to a positive moral and social enterprise. It is a phenomena needing diagnosis, explanation, and treatment. It makes a dangerous gap in human efforts to establish relations through mutual

and rational understanding. Political downfalls and upheavals often emerge from those infected with madness. Ethical quandaries and moral disputes become irresolvable when participants take flight of their senses."

"And so Josephine Cole was deprived of her husband, and Amélie Cole of her father, a while longer than any of them had expected—one year for his voyage to the other side of the world, another for his voyages to another time, another life. And when he was released at last, having recanted his preposterous tales (though really merely ceasing to relate them), he fell victim to a treacherous thief, an experience which brought on a strange fever, so that more time passed before his loved ones knew his company again.

"My darling, darling girl," Oliver said, stroking his daughter's hair ever so lightly so as not to awaken her. "I will never forget that snowy street and your dear loving faces turned toward me—so close, so close again at last—and then slipping and falling, and then that vile scoundrel ripping my treasures from me as a ravening beast would tear the heart out of its prey.

"And now I have only the dorje, and must fathom the bell in its absence. *Must*, I say, for to wield a king's scepter without a king's wisdom, *that* is madness. That was my mistake and I fear has long been. The Tibetan was not a madman but a healer of madmen, a rescuer of lost souls. The bell … I read that it proclaims the truth of emptiness, and that by understanding this truth, nay, by *realizing* it with one's *whole* being, one gains compassion for *all* beings, all things, and thus defeats the lords of illusion that lead us astray into endless realms of suffering. And yet I have understood nothing, realized nothing. And now must listen for a missing bell. But I will listen, and I will hear. Though it kill me, though I be judged a madman a hundred times o'er, I *will* hear. For your sake, and for us all."

Josephine Cole returned with the bowl of steaming bouillabaisse on a tray to find her husband up and standing at the bedroom window, still in his nightshirt, holding back the heavy inner curtains and the lace undercurtains with both hands as he looked out. With the brighter natural light flooding in around him, he looked extremely pale and gaunt. And he stood with a slight stoop, like the older man he had come to resemble.

"Oliver! What are you doing out of bed, in your bare feet on the cold floor?"

"I am sore," he said to the patch of glass whose obscuring frost he had wiped clear with his hand, "stiff and sore. So I am stretching while I contemplate the snow. Our garden in the snow. Our garden wall in the snow. The street beyond, with people of *this* century on the sidewalks, the carriages no longer *horseless* carriages … and a pig, a pig in the gutter for all love … all in the snow, in that blank background of whiteness, so … so relieved of something. Perhaps of the clutter of too many details. Past, present or future, so many details. Any gate, I find it soothing—the view *and* my cold feet. On my own cold floor. *Our* own cold floor."

"You will please to lie back down now in your own warm bed," said Josephine. "*Our* own warm bed."

"I will not think of it as ours until I have lain in it with you again."

"It is ours. There is our daughter."

"So she is. So she is. Having been put to sleep by her boring prematurely ancient father, who is not really much of a storyteller after all, especially not for children. I absolutely heard myself say 'quickening of the loins'. How would I have explained that had she been awake to ask? A 'stirring of a man's imagination'?"

"It is good that she sleeps. She has missed you so much, so fearful for you been, that she has hardly slept at all. Not as a child should. She cries out in the dark. Sometimes she roams the halls without even a candle to light her way, poor thing. But come. Eat."

"This is good, this is fabulous," said Captain Cole, in bed again with the china bowl of bouillabaisse in one hand and a silver spoon in the other. "Ah, Jo, was it for love that I married you, or your French cooking, that can transport a man if not from one time to another then at least from the doldrums into bliss?"

"Enough of your flattery. Be quiet now and eat. And remember your promise. No more talk about another time. The only time we may discuss now is tomorrow, when, if you feel able, we might all go out together. Would you like that?"

"And have a picnic?" said the captain. "I would like a picnic. Our little sleeping beauty here would like a picnic too, I'll wager."

"Yes," said Josephine. She could not bear to point out that it was January and he had just been staring out at a chill landscape of inhospitable snow, "Yes, my love, and have a pic-a-nic. We three."

Chapter 6

Cat Comes Calling

Cat Kidd née McCallum was plunged into darkness.

Around her an anxious murmuring and agitated movements in the warm water that was up to her neck, and then the clear calm foreign voice of their instructor saying, "Do not panic youselves. Moon still in you hands. If dahk, if light, still hold. If dlop, no good. So, steady, steady. Dead, alive, hold moon and hold you mind. No ploblem heah."

And so Cat and her twelve classmates settled down and in the dark actually continued the exercise called Embracing the Moon in that slow motion aquatic ballet known as water Tai Chi in the swimming pool called the Centennial on Gottingen Street in downtown Halifax. They continued for five whole minutes, guided by the bad English but good attitude of their teacher Li Chang, until a pool employee with a flashlight came to say that the emergency generator could not be got working and so they could not get the building's lights back on, and since there was no telling when Scotia Power would restore the electricity, the pool was closing for the day.

By flashlight they dressed and departed. It was not till she was outside in her borrowed car in the late afternoon's waning daylight that Cat thought to check the cell phone in her bag for messages.

When she did, she got Raymond's several calls about his ghosts. No sooner had she listened to them, and frowning poured a cup of hot licorice tea from her thermos and peeled the wrapper from a tiny Chinese sesame cracker, than the phone rang with a live call.

It was Galen from the Brewery, calling to tell her that Raymond had disappeared.

"I know you two are separated, but I saw you on the tour today and … well, he told me about you giving him the keys to your apartment, and I thought I ought to call you. It's probably just a joke. Raymond's got a strange sense of humour. I mean, his costume was laid out on the chair as if he had just vanished right out of it, and there's this whole thing about ghosts in the Stag's Head, and he's heard the stories. Still, his bicycle's here, and his street clothes are still in his locker … I don't know. Nobody here wants to call the police, but …"

"Don't call the police," Cat interjected, instinctively, not knowing exactly why, "I think you're right and it's probably just his eccentric idea of a joke. He's probably at my apartment, waiting for me in the nude. I told him … well, we are still man and wife …"

"Understood. Enough said. I'll tell everyone it's taken care of. We've got enough on our hands as it is. We're in the dark here, and flooded with beer."

"Thank you, Galen."

"No problem."

But there was a problem. At her apartment on Clifford Street, no Raymond awaited her, nude or otherwise, and when she called him no one answered, not at either of his numbers, home or cell. She got back in the car and drove to the Rennekers' on Henry Street, where she knew Raymond parked when he went to work. His old pickup was still there in the big graveled lot.

"Dammit, Raymond!" She smacked the dashboard in frustration, "Why must you always, always, make up your own rules?"

She cried out with her window rolled down. A hand-holding elderly couple, who had started into the lot as a shortcut from Henry to Vernon Street, reversed course in alarm.

She listened to Raymond's messages again and then set out for Prospect. If she could not find Raymond, she thought, feeling crazy, she would talk to the ghosts that he said had turned into his guests. Who else could help her? But when she got to Prospect and 7 Lands End, no one answered the door no matter how insistently she knocked or called out that it was okay, that Raymond had told her about them.

"I'm an idiot," she said to herself, looking around furtively to see if any neighbours were watching. "The dead may hang around, in our minds or otherwise, who knows, but they definitely do not come back to life."

To give herself time to calm down and consider what she knew, she walked the mile out to the High Head and watched the sun in its approach to the horizon take on a hue of dusky orange and impart that same hue to the waves. It wasn't easy to be objective. Even looking out over the romantic Atlantic sunset brought back haunting memories, for she and Raymond had sailed there together in her namesake the yawl *Happy Cat*. Their trips together up and down the coast from Yarmouth to the saltwater lakes of the Bras d'Or in Cape Breton ranked highly in the handful of true glories in her life. No matter that they fought and argued terribly at times. Out on the waves under sail they were royalty fighting and arguing. Her mind wandered to whales they had seen, and dolphins sometimes by the hundreds, and the golden eagle that once landed in the upper spreaders of their mainmast while they were at anchor, that stayed there till the stars came out and for a short magical interval was silhouetted by a full golden moon. Then there was that September eleventh when their friends the Henkels in St. Margarets Bay had radioed that they would not be rafting up because the World Trade towers had been destroyed and they were too shocked to do anything but sit by the TV and watch the nightmare footage of the jets crashing into the two skyscrapers over and over again. The dead, Jen Henkel had said quaveringly over the on-deck speaker, might number more than fifty thousand. So the *Happy Cat* had anchored alone off Luke's Island, and its crew of two had rowed ashore with the big picnic dinner Cat had made for four, and they had sat in stunned silence on a driftwood log on the beach eating and drinking until after the champagne was finished when their hands finally touched, and then their lips.

They had made love on that blanket in the coarse pebbly sand, first as tenderly and sadly, and then as passionately and recklessly, as if they were the last two survivors on Earth.

Cat knew Raymond was gone now, as she had known he was coming before he ever arrived, before she had met him or even heard of him. The day his old pickup had pulled into the driveway of the vacant apartment across Lyon's Avenue in Spryfield, she had known she should abandon her dishwashing and go meet him immediately. When he had moved out to Prospect soon after, she had felt his absence acutely but had known he was still within reach, and had found him again and in a few years had married him. The day she left him and went back to the city, it was as if she had torn her heart out and left it on the dock. Yet she had always felt him near. When Raymond was not there, he had come to be even more there. But now there was nothing, no sense of him at all. And it wasn't as if he were dead. She would have sensed him dying. It was as if he had never been. As if he had simply stepped out of the picture and whisked his tracks away behind him.

She felt herself getting angry. She wanted to pound the granite beneath her into smithereens, to scream so the sea would evaporate. *How dare he?*

When the black rage came down, as it did now, it blinded Cat just as surely as if she had been staring into the sun, which indeed she had been doing there in that stony niche with the sea rumbling and shattering below and her thoughts running wild. There were dents in the walls of 7 Lands End where in such a state she had flung things at Raymond—cups, dishes, a telephone, their folk art carving of a great blue heron, whatever was at hand. The thought that he was gone now without even a trace made her so mad that *had* he been there, she would have thrown him off the cliff.

She would not call the police. She would find him herself. And when she did, he would wish another hurricane had found him instead.

"Mother, may I have a cup of cocoa?!" Shannon O'Keefe shouted as she tugged at her mother's apron. "And Mother, something strange at Booda Ray's again! It could be another terrist! Only it looks just like Mrs. Booda Ray!"

Dawn O'Keefe switched the vacuum cleaner off and as it whined to a halt said to her daughter, "Lord, child, how am I ever going to get my work done if you keep interrupting me? I still have dinner to finish and the table to set. No, you may not have a cup of cocoa. And you are not to call her Mrs. Booda Ray. She deserves our respect, the poor thing. You are to call her Mrs. Kidd. Though I wouldn't blame her if she took her own name back."

"Mother, Mrs. Kidd just smashed in their door with a log."

"She what?"

"She knocked a long time and no one came, and then she went all round the house trying to look in the windows, but the curtains are all drawn—I know 'cause I go round their house and the curtains haven't been open for days—and then she came back to the door and took a log from the wood crib and bashed the door open and went in."

"Oh. Well. Don't you worry about her, dear. It's probably just a question of something she left behind."

"Why doesn't she just use a key?"

"It's likely she's given it back. She doesn't live there anymore, you know."

"Doesn't she know there's a spare key on top of the wood crib?"

"Apparently not."

"But why not? It's easy to see. And why mayn't I have cocoa?"

Mrs. O'Keefe sighed. "As for the key, girl, you were looking down at it. With your father's binoculars, no doubt, which I have told you and told you you are *not* to be using. And how would Mrs. Kidd be seeing such a key and her not as tall as the crib? As for the cocoa, it would spoil your appetite. What you may do is help in the kitchen. You like peeling cucumbers. Take three of them out of the fridge and start peeling. I'll be in soon. Do a good job and don't make a mess and you can have your cocoa for dessert. As for Mrs. Kidd, we will leave her to take care of her own business. She isn't a terrorist. She's only a wife, God love her, and wives are far more terrorized than terrorizing."

"Mother, if she doesn't live there anymore, why is she still his wife?"

"Sweetheart, love is a mystery. One of those that doesn't bear much looking into, like our Lord's. Now run along. And put your father's binoculars back up on their hook!"

In the narrow tiled entryway of her old home, Cat stood clutching in both hands the stick of firewood that in her black rage she had used to bash open the door. To her left was the closet behind whose sliding doors her own outerwear had once hung, to the right the flimsy homemade shoe shelf that once housed her boots and shoes, and beyond that the old ha-track that had once held her many hats. In front of her, the door that led into the house proper had its glass panes covered with a pink and peach plaid curtain she herself had sewn.

That door was now jerked open by Octave Daggon.

"Who are *you*?" Cat demanded, cocking the stick of firewood for another blow. "And what are you doing in my house?"

"My name is Octavius," said Octave, jerking his head awkwardly in an abbreviated bow, "Octavius Daggon. Excuse me, Mrs. Kidd. You have just, as my brother would say, scared the *bejeezus* out of me."

"Octavius," said Cat. "Octave?"

"To my friends," said Octave.

"So, you're one of Raymond's ghosts."

"An unfortunate term, madam. As I told your husband, we were never ghosts but only lost souls. However, even that appellation would now seem incorrect, for we seem to be found. I am once again much as yourself. I bleed when I am stuck. I blush when I am stared at."

"Mr. Daggon, you're wearing one of my husband's robes. A robe I made for him. He's missing. You're here where he should be. I've never met you and yet you know my name. No wonder I'm staring."

"Raymond is missing?"

"Yes."

"I know your name, Mrs. Kidd, because I was here in this house when you were here, as Raymond must have told you. I watched the two of you whenever I felt like it. Forgive me for what must seem unforgivable, but there was little else to do. Now, what do you mean Raymond is missing? He was here just this morning."

"Mr. Daggon, if that's who you really are, my Raymond is a good man— at heart he's a very good man—but sometimes he can be very simple. He could swallow a story like yours. I don't know that I do. Tell me why I shouldn't call the police and tell them there are a couple of swindlers in my house who may have murdered my husband?"

"Oh, dear. You're quite incensed. I had forgotten how it feels to be the object of a woman's anger. It is a wonderful argument against reincarnation. Will you lower your weapon and come in? There are things I can tell you that might help you believe me. Things no one would know who hadn't lived here day in and day out since the house had a basement. And then we can talk about Raymond and how to go about finding him. For we must find him. He means everything to Angle and I. Without him, I'm not sure we can manage. Being alive again, I mean."

"Why don't you tell me what you need to tell me right here?"

"Because someone might happen by and see me if we stay out here. You may have noticed all the blinds are down and curtains drawn around the house. Raymond wants us to remain a secret—to *lie low*, as he put it—till we have a plan, an explanation for our presence here that doesn't involve revealing that we've come back from the dead."

"By the same token, if I go where I can't be seen, then you could do what you want with me and no one would know."

"Oh, dear. We have an impasse, a predicament, a standoff, a dilemma. Or as Angle would say, we're *in a fix*."

"No, *we're* not in a fix. *You're* in a fix," said Cat. "You have five seconds to start proving yourself before I walk out of here. And when I come back, you won't be a secret anymore."

"Oh, oh. Let's see … you wrote a poem once!"

"Yes?"

"It goes like this:

My heart is like a ship upon the seas.
I am easily moved.
Scolding will not improve me."

At the mention of the poem, one she had indeed written many years and three marriages ago, Cat was subjected to a rush of conflicting emotions. She was touched as she had been touched when the poem first appeared in her mind. She was no sort of writer at all. It had been a pure gift, a relief from the emotional battering her first husband had subjected her to, and she had always prized it and never tried to write another. She was perplexed that a total stranger was quoting it to her. And she was deeply suspicious. And though her black rage had mostly evaporated with the smashing of the door latch, traces of it lingered like a shadowy mist in the back of her mind. She had lowered the log. She raised it again now.

"Mister, that poem's hanging on the wall in the hall behind you. It's very short. You could have memorized it. If you're lying, if you're trying to con me, I will break your head. Don't think I won't. Don't think I can't!"

"Mrs. Kidd, I know you wrote the poem out on that napkin yourself, and that you gave it to Raymond as a wedding present, and that he held it so dear—not only the sentiment but the penmanship too - that he had it framed and hung it there so he would pass by it every day and never forget it."

"He could have told you that."

"I also know he found the very same poem in a book, a Japanese book even older than I am, one called The Tale of Genji, a book you claim never to have read."

"It's the truth."

"Raymond believes you. He loves the mystery of it, that perhaps you wrote the poem first in another life."

"Look, you, I don't know why my husband would have told you these very personal things, but they don't prove anything. Except maybe that he talks too much about things that he shouldn't. It certainly doesn't prove you were a ghost who was living in this house at the same time as me."

"Dear, dear, why is this word *ghost* so appealing? I've never threatened anyone. Look at me. Am I the sort of person anyone would find threatening, dead or alive? My father used to say my mother dressed me as a boy just to please him, because he only wanted sons, but he was never fooled. 'Slight and delicate as any slip of a girl', he used to say. I beg your pardon. I digress. I've never forgiven my father, I'm afraid, nor forgotten anything he said, though he got his comeuppance when they hung him, and I danced a little dance that fine day. But here we are now, and you still want convincing. How about this? I also know that when you moved out, while Raymond was away attending his grandmother's funeral, down in those United States so-called, you took your poem off the wall and packed it with your other things, and were almost out of the driveway when you changed your mind and brought it back and hung it up again. I know there were tears in your eyes when you did. Raymond couldn't know that. He still doesn't."

Whether it was due to the same shield-breaching solar storm that had triggered Raymond's disappearance, or some other vagary of the flaw in the fabric, or simply a wry sense of humour on the part of Victor Cooley, Angle Daggon and another boatload of monster cod, this time on being transported from nowhere to somewhere, missed the basement at 7 Lands End and instead made their landing on the stairs, which they descended in a slithering avalanche before fetching up with a resounding smack against the wall across the hall at the bottom, just behind the door to the entryway where Angle's brother Octave stood striving to bring home the truth of Raymond's story to Raymond's wife.

"And then," said Octave, shoving the pink-and-peach-plaid-curtain-covered door open through that helter-skelter heap of cod, with Angle naked in its midst, "there's this."

All that evening and into the night, as they cleaned and dressed the catch and sponged the bloody counter and mopped the slimy stairs and floor and afterward sat round the kitchen table eating cod croquettes and drinking tea, still bloody and slimy themselves, fish-fragrant and speckled with scales, too tired to bother with their own cleanliness, the three of them talked, and as they talked, about all that had happened and what to do next, they saw that they might help each other.

Angle, though humbled in his attitude toward others by his long sojourn in the in-between and the contemplation of the dagger-swallowing rose on his chest, still retained a certain valuable piratical attitude—what needed to be seized and could be seized should be seized (as long as no one was hurt in the bargain), and it should be seized now, for there was no time to be lost in the seizing of it. By which he meant the cod. "Although they come from there and then," he said, placing both hands palm down on the table and leaning forward to peer intently at his company, "there'll be no problem sellin' 'em here and now. The buggers are so big we'll have the buyers flocking to our door, for these days there's nothing like 'em. We can sell all we want, and we should, and we should start straightaway. For who knows how long we've got with Mr. Victor Cooley? And what do we need, mates, more'n funds?"

"Identities," said Octave, for he brought to the table an adaptive intelligence that fed like wildfire on the forest of his new world's information. Unlike his brother, he had not only watched Raymond and Cat through the walls during his time in their basement, he had studied and learned from what they did. He already knew how to use a computer, and had spent much of his short stay in his resolidified body sitting at Raymond's desk surfing the Internet, absorbing ideas and forming others at a break-neck pace. "We need new identities, you and me, Brother. Birth certifi-cates, drivers licences, social insurance numbers, health cards, *credit* cards. We'll have to break laws, but what other choice do we have? You can't do business as nobodies, and if we let on who we really are, they'll lock us up as lunatics."

"That's right," said Cat. "And if they do that, who'll help me find Ray-mond? Because that's your job. As far as I'm concerned, that's your only real job. My head tells me to call the police and report him as a missing person, but my heart tells me he's not where they can find him. I think he's gone out of this world. And since he's the one who invited you back into this world, and since you still seem to have some connections elsewhere, I think that makes finding him your responsibility. Don't you?"

"When first I come back from the other side," Angle said, absentmin-dely toying with a clump of scales in his beard, "when I was still *feelin'* it, you understand, the cord not bein' altogether cut, like, well, there I was at the Cap'n's bedside, and he was havin' a dream, and I could see into it. In his dream, he was a white-headed old man who had nearly got clipped by a buggy, and it made him fall down in the street. The man who helped him up picked his pocket. The Cap'n lost something so valuable, I'm thinkin' he never forgot it."

"I'm sorry," said Cat. "I have no idea what you're talking about. What does all that have to do with finding Raymond?"

"You were talkin' about responsibility. Well. That worn't really no dream. That was somethin' that once really happened. I know, because the thief was me."

"What?"

"What I'm sayin', *I robbed that old man back in my day*, just that way, and that old man, well, he's our Cap'n. Has to be. The Cap'n worn't drea-min'. He was more like rememberin'. Only it worn't even that. I think he was slippin' back to the past through that same flaw in the fabric that let Octave and me out of the in-between. That's why I could see it happen, like through the window of a stage goin' by. And now he's gone back al-together, I'm thinkin'. And so bringin' him back here, to this time, and to you, well, it's more up to me than you knew, innit?"

"This is getting weirder and weirder," said Cat, "Still, it makes some kind of sense. You and Raymond have unfinished business."

"So it seems. Only I've no idea how to go about finishin' it. It's not back to the past I've been able to go, only back into the in-between."

"Well, it's a start," said Cat, "and we've got to start somewhere." She ran her fingers through her hair and then saw blood on her fingers. "Oh, Lord," she groaned. "I've got fish blood in my hair. Yes, we've got to start somewhere, and all we've got is each other, and that's going to have to do. At least for now. Maybe in the morning, after we get some sleep, we'll think of something else. Right now I'm so tired I'm not even surprised I'm believing all this. Look, you're going to need an administrator, you boys. If you're going to sell fish, you need someone to sell them to, and I for one am not going to sit in a car by the side of the road with a hand-lettered sign doing it. We need to sell to a store on a regular basis. A chain like Sobey's or Superstore. I'll look into that. Also transportation. We'll need to haul the fish. We can go get Raymond's truck. I've got a key he forgot to take back. Right, and I'll have to teach you how to drive. Oh, Lord."

Later, with the cloth tape she always carried with her, a bleary-eyed Cat measured the two brothers for clothes. She meant to go home after their supper and planning session, but a maternal urge had arisen in her middle-aged bosom that would not be suppressed. The tenderness with which Octave had introduced her poem as evidence, and the slapstick silliness of Angle's appearance in the cascade of cod, spread-eagled nude with his long sailor's braid and his many tattoos, had brought back memories of her own three sons, all grown and off on their own. Whatever they had been, wherever they had come from, her two new accomplices needed clothes of their own. Raymond's ragged old robes were for Raymond. Continuing to wear them instead of consigning them to the rag bin was his eccentricity, and though it was one she was fond of, having made two of the robes herself, she did not want it visited upon anyone else. Especially not upon these two poor young newcomers. They were not babies, far from it, but still they had come into this world with nothing. And now they were under her wing.

For their part, the brothers did not want her to leave at all. They were touched by her mothering, and they trembled to think of her being so tired and yet trying to manage a self-powered vehicle that could travel at ungodly speeds.

"Boys, I know it must seem fast to you, who grew up when a man on a horse was the king of the road," she said to them there in the driveway, with the car window down and the engine idling, "but to me, even with a hundred horses under the hood, as we say, if I just go the speed limit, it's only creeping. I could do it with my eyes closed almost. And it's so late, there'll be hardly any traffic to worry about even if I should doze off and slip over the line for a second."

That left them gaping, even though they knew from her smile she was joshing them, yet they rallied as she drove away, and waved and called out their good nights until her car's red tail lights vanished behind the next house as she motored away up the road toward her apartment in the city.

"What a woman," said Angle, still looking in the direction she had gone, "stubborn as any mule and yet with looks any angel would trade her halo for. And the way she smells, no wonder the Cap'n can't get over her. Up to our necks in fish guts, and yet there was that sweetness o' her'n, holdin' its own. Lord, it's been so long, if'n she wasn't the Cap'n's, I wouldn't care how old she is."

"She reminds me of our mother," said Octave. "Spirit-wise, anyhow. Hard as a rock and then soft as a blanket, turn and turn about. A woman who would give everything and still go off on her own when the time came. I wonder if she has a rocking chair, and if she does, if she might let me sit in it, and it still warm with the warmth of her."

"You watch yer mouth, now, Octave Daggon. Don't you go too far."

"You know," the studious brother went on, undeterred, his heart over-flowing, "for the first time since we came alive again, I believe we can do it. With her help, I believe we can be human again. And entirely be free of … *you know who.*"

The seagoing brother looked up into the night sky with its vast spread of stars and breathed deep of the calm ocean coolness. "Well," he said, "God bless her. And God bless the Cap'n. God bless us all. Mayhap we can all come together again."

Chapter 7

Angle's Morning Outside

Morning found Angle outdoors again, this time in a lawn chair, a sort of rocking lawn chair that creaked as it rocked because the salt air had penetrated its special no-rust paint and rusted its joints. He was out by the cove on the remnants of Raymond's dock platform, that rested, tilted and askew, on the eroded pile of rocks that before the hurricane had served as the pad for both the dock and Raymond's boathouse. The boathouse still rested in the mud in the playground across the lane where the tidal surge had carried it. Angle had retrieved the chair from the boathouse in the dark and placed it as nearly as he could where Raymond and Cat once sat and rocked in the mornings, facing the sea and sipping steaming mugs of coffee, sometimes in conversation, sometimes in silence, sometimes holding hands, sometimes touching lips.

He had watched the sun rise, first over the village churchyard where he and Octave had been buried, and then over the church itself, silhouetting its high spire and cross. The early light filled the brimming breeze-wrinkled cove with a soft brilliance that moved him to tears. More than two hundred years had passed since he had witnessed the dawning of day and felt that first warmth on his face and that renewal in his heart.

Not that he had been far from tears anyway. It was grueling, he found, not only to need sleep again but to be unable to get it. To know now that he had once stolen from the Cap'n—even though that was another life and there was no way he could've known it was the Cap'n since he wasn't the Cap'n yet back then—the thought had kept him awake through the night. He closed his eyes and sat listening enthralled to the lonely cries of the seagulls, a serenade he dearly loved. A tear crept out over his cheek and down into his beard.

To be human again felt so good, yet demanded so damn much.

Unlike Octave, he was not sure he was up to it.

"Sir," said someone behind him, who turned out to be a tall solemn man in a priest's surplice and stole. "Sir, you are not where you belong."

Neither in life nor in death had Angle been so surprised. In his first life, the ambush and destruction of the *Queen Mab* and the hanging of his father had taken him all aback, but as a pirate it was in the way of things. His sword had been stained, after all, with the blood of the innocent. And realizing after his demise in the snowstorm that he was in the in-between had been a shock tempered with relief, for he had not landed in hell. And coming back to life, well, a pleasant surprise was always welcome. But this was a man of the cloth. The golden crosses on the violet band of his stole gleamed like polished weapons. He had the power of exorcism. He could banish you straight to the devil.

"So," said Angle Daggon son of William and Letitia Daggon who was no coward and would not quail, "My sins have found me out. Where is it I belong, then?"

"Please don't take offense, sir," said the priest. "It is simply that where you are, where your chair is, is where I need to stand. The bride and groom will stand here, facing the sunrise and myself, and all the guests will stand behind them. I take it you live here. You may join us. I'm sure no one will mind. Now if you please, we're running a little late. We were supposed to be doing the vows at first light. If you could just remove the chair. And there's no time to change out of your house robe, so you might want to stand in the rear where you won't be so noticeable."

The guests appeared as if on cue, driving into the lane in a long line, parking their vehicles up and down on both sides, and proceeding toward the dock from both directions. For the first time, Angle noticed the pink van across the lane behind the priest that had Sunrise Weddings on its side in large curlicued dusky rose lettering. The crowd in its formal finery soon overflowed the displaced dock and the space where the boathouse had been and the launching ramp alongside. A boy and two girls, one of them Shannon O'Keefe, stood on the whale's jawbone in the yard of 7 Lands End, craning their necks to see over their elders.

At a loss for words, Angle nodded to the priest, took the chair and retreated across the lane to the jawbone.

Shannon turned to him and stuck out her hand. "Hello again, Mr. Pirate. Remember me? My name is Shannon O'Keefe. Why aren't you in your Sunday clothes? Why do you wear your hair in a braid like a girl?

Where is Booda Ray's dinghy that you said you was going to bring back? What have you done with Booda Ray? And why *are* you a terrist anyway?"

"Shush, now," said Dawn O'Keefe, who was standing behind Shannon with her hands on her daughter's waist to keep her steady on the whalebone. "They've started the ceremony."

"I'll tell 'ee later, mate," said Angle. His natural good humor returned in a flash in the presence of Shannon's childish familiarity. He enveloped her little hand in his own hairy paw and gave her a conspiratorial wink. "We'll share a glass o' grog and I'll tell 'ee all about it."

Shannon's mother scowled at Angle, a very questionable addition to the company in her estimation, and might have rebuked him had not the moment come for vows to be exchanged. Afterward, as the newlyweds kissed and the formally kilted bagpiper perched on the seawall behind the priest began skirling away, she simply hastened her daughter away back across Raymond's yard to their house and indoors, not quite slamming the door behind her but shutting it with a pronounced emphasis.

The entire party melted away without anyone explaining the presumptuous event to Angle or even saying anything further at all. Who all these people were, what made them think they could use someone else's property without permission, as if it were a commons, he had no idea. The cars motored away up the road and he was left all alone in the yard. He felt strangely cheated, taken advantage of, used and abandoned. He stood there, in Raymond's ragged robe and rubber boots, stroking his beard and staring down at the whale's jawbone. The little succulents in the cavity had been crushed underfoot by the children into a gooey mess. He stood contemplating this crowning injustice and puzzling over the pain he felt. It wasn't his dock and they weren't his plants, yet his emotions writhed inside him like a ball of snakes, as if he'd been personally disrespected. He had not felt so unbearably disordered since having his bottom beaten with the flat of his father's sword.

To be human again, and wildly sensitive in the bargain, he definitely was not sure he was up to it.

On his dock in the outer harbor, Gordon Daggon had been too immersed in his morning routine and the usual cloud of noisy seagulls to notice the wedding at first. By the time the piper began piping, though, the morning's catch had been cleaned, packed and trucked away by his partner and the gear cleaned and stowed. When the martial cry of the pipes pierced the mere domestic squabbling of the gulls, Gordon heaved himself out of his comfortable chair, though he had only just settled down into it, and leaving his untasted toddy on the broad padded arm went to see what the occasion might be. He lit his pipe as he shuffled along off the stage, over the gangway, and onto the land.

He was a little disappointed, as he topped the low fissured rock dome where nets were laid to dry, to hear the piper's tune end in a last wailing shriek and to behold the hasty exodus of the wedding party. Then he saw that the man who remained, all alone in Raymond Kidd's yard, had a beard and a braid and wore one of Raymond's house robes—as had the self-declared old sea dog who Dawn O'Keefe said had made off with Raymond's dinghy. Gordon had seen the dinghy again that very morning. It was still anchored over the Cabbage Patch, bobbing and breasting the incoming swell.

The sight of a suspect perked the retired detective up and put a spring in his step. Damn the arthritis, he thought. From a hundred yards it was obvious that the man in Raymond's robe had something troubling on his mind, the way he stood looking down, stroking his beard and shaking his head to himself. It might not be guilt, but thirty years of experience told Gordon it was some sort of secret. And if there was one thing Gordon Daggon dearly loved, even more than his gulls and the bagpipes, it was ferreting out secrets. He would never be too old for that, he assured himself.

As he passed the woodshed and then the rosebush-bordered porch of the house of the widower Turner Charles and swung into the lane past the O'Keefe's house with its three-story turret, he kept his eye on the stranger, and so he missed Shannon O'Keefe watching him from the top floor of the turret with her father's binoculars.

When he came abreast of the whale's jawbone and the man still did not look up or acknowledge his presence, Gordon drew on his pipe, let the smoke trickle out, and then asked, "Was that the one that got away, then?"

"Eh?" said Angle Daggon.

"The bride," said Gordon Daggon. "Was she an old girlfriend—one you wish you had married? Is that why you're in such a study?"

"She's no one to me, mate. Just another stranger in a crew o' strangers. No idea where they came from, why they came here, where they went. They never asked *me* so much as a by your leave. Not even that bloody … not even the priest."

Now that they were eye to eye, Gordon was even more enthused. There was something in the other man's face, in the prominent cheekbones and Roman nose, in the shaggy thick eyebrows and challenging thrust of the chin that the beard exaggerated—something that tickled his memory.

"I got it," said Gordon. "Oh, that was too easy."

"Got what, mate?" said Angle, now thoroughly irritated, "A bad case of the piles?"

"You," Gordon said, pointing his pipestem at the man, "I thought I recognized you. You're an actor, right? You're here filming a movie, and you're staying in character. That's what this is all about—the beard, the braid, the earring, the nautical talk, I bet even the wedding. Another movie in scenic Prospect. Some kind of comedy this time with the past and the future all mixed up. Jeez, the stuff they come up with these days. So, where's the cameras and all? You must be rehearsing. I'll come up with your name in a minute. Say, tell production my house is available if they need another location besides Raymond's—I wouldn't mind a little extra income. And you left Raymond's dinghy anchored out there why? Oh, don't mind me. I used to be a detective. I know you can't talk too much about your show while you're still shooting. But listen, I got a boat over there too if you need one. Happy to help out and share the wealth. Well anyway, it's on the tip of my tongue but I can't spit it out—who *are* you? My name's Gordon Daggon."

Now Angle was staring hard. A latter day Daggon! He searched the other man's face. Slowly the likeness became apparent, only slightly muted by the many generations. He extended his open hand to meet Gordon's, in a rock-hard clasp in which they both tested each other, and he said, "Ang … Andrew … Dunevan. And mayhap you *could* render a service. That there dinghy … I'd like to go out and retrieve it. Would you mind ferryin' me out in your vessel?"

"Not at all, Ang Andrew," said Gordon, winking as he puffed, "And I won't even charge you for it. *This* time. I'll do it for the pleasure of your company. For I'm sure you're a star even though you won't break character and I can't come at your name. And a star gets the right treatment from Gordon Daggon."

"I'd be right obliged, Mr …. Daggon," said Angle.

"Call me Gordon, Ang Andrew."

"Mother!" Shannon O'Keefe called from the O'Keefe turret, keeping her eyes glued to her father's binoculars. "The terrist has taken Mr. Daggon prisoner. They're going out in Mr. Daggon's boat! He's going to do away with Mr. Daggon like he did with Booda Ray!"

"Shannon O'Keefe!" her mother called back to her. "You come down here right now. The bus will be here any minute, and you *are* going back to school today!"

At twenty-six feet, the *Severence* was among the smaller of the Cape Islanders of the recent generation. Having a homebuilt deckhouse and needing a new coat of powder blue on her peeling hull, she was also among the more quaint. But a man could stand and walk around on her back deck, and so Angle loved her. For the first time since the loss of the Queen Mab and his father's hanging and his own death by freezing and his long soul-searching sojourn in the shadows, he was back on a seagoing boat that let him stand, stand like a man and glory in the give in his knees as he and another Daggon rode the waves. The motion was jarring, he had to acknowledge. A motor-powered boat, he found, had no notion of going along with the rise and fall of the waves but instead bashed through the crests and crashed into the troughs in a headstrong, awkward and unsettling manner. Still the very posture, the standing and being carried along at his leisure instead of sitting and slaving away at an oar, roused his blood and made him recall when the sea was his highway, *his*, and the world his oyster. He had never pretended. He had captured, and he had killed.

"I ain't no actor," he growled.

In the deckhouse at the wheel, Gordon Daggon could hear his probably famous passenger talking, but the engine noise interfered with his understanding. "What's that?" he called back, his pipe clenched in his teeth.

Angle stumped forward in his borrowed black fisherman's boots, his sea legs not under him yet, and with his hands on his hips and his house-robe flapping open in the wind he bawled out, "I ain't no actor, you hear? I am what I am 'cause I done what I done. And here's what it is, mate—I ain't skeered o' what comes with the truth anymore. Ye say ye're a detector? Well, detect and be damned."

After a pause during which he tapped his pipe against the wheel to get the dottle out, Gordon chuckled and clapped. "Bravo," he cried as he turned his gaze back through the windshield to the plunging bow. "You're first rate, Ang Andrew. You stick with it like a dog with a bone. I hope you don't intend on rowing Raymond's dinghy back. If you don't mind, I'd rather tow it and let you keep on talking. In fact, I've got a little something here to wet your whistle while you do." He reached under the grey-painted plywood control panel to a net bag strung there and fished out an old mayonnaise jar full of amber liquid.

Angle stepped into the deckhouse out of the wind and took the bottle. Unscrewing the lid, he sniffed the contents and with a grim and disapproving look said, "Rum."

"Don't you like it?" Gordon said. "You're playing an old-time sailor, and you don't like rum?

"Which it ain't that," Angle said.

"Maybe you prefer the storebought version. This is a tad strong, being homemade, and maybe tastewise not up to your standards …"

"No, it ain't that neither."

"You could tell 'em back in Hollywood you went native, turned into a real Nova Scotian."

"Mister, I'm Nova Scotian already. Inside out. Never was a Nova Scotian more Nova Scotian than Ang … than yours truly."

"I believe you. I'm convinced. You're really good. So what is it? Got to work again today?"

"It ain't nothin' like that."

"Okay. No problem. I won't shove it down your throat. Here, I'll put it away again."

"No, no," Angle said, keeping his eyes fixed on the bottle and the bottle clear of Gordon's grasp, "No need to be hasty. It's just that, well, I made a promise. But it wouldn't do, would it, to say no on a day like today, with my new life on the slipway, all ready for launchin'? A fellow might give offense. No, that wouldn't do at all. So maybe just … just a taste then. Just a drop. To be 'micable, like."

"Good," Gordon said, fumbling a couple of plastic tumblers out of the net bag as the boat bucked under them, dusty tumblers that he proceeded to wipe clean with his shirttail. "And when we're done, maybe you wouldn't mind giving me your autograph. I got a marker here can write right on glass. You can sign the bottle."

"I can hardly believe what I'm writing," wrote Gordon Daggon, in the log which he normally carried on the *Severence* but which he now had in his lap as he sat in the chair on his dock. "And maybe it ought not be written at all, for the only thing anyone who reads it will believe is that I've lost my mind or I'm making it all up for a joke, both of which is what retired old farts like myself do in Prospect to pass the time on their way to the grave. But here it is anyway, for what it's worth, before I forget it or Doris calls me in for dinner, the testament of a former law officer. *And* a relative with a long overdue duty to carry out. *And* a fellow who's just met his match in the article of rum consumption. Given the latter, it may be hard to know who's talking at any one time, or if we're all talking at once. I can't help that. Here goes.

"Judging the suspect himself not to be of sound mind, I proceeded to bait him in an unorthodox manner, pretending I thought him an actor. Thus I was able to confuse and befriend him and get him out to what I thought might be the crime scene—the anchored dinghy. Not where I thought he might have killed Raymond Kidd but where he might have dumped the body. On the way I produced a bottle of bootleg rum which I had confiscated from Shorty Cornwall when we raided his waterside joint in east Dover. I had kept the bottle for years never drinking it because of its unusual potency—eighty-six point six six six percent it tested out in the lab—but always thinking it might come in handy one day. Had Shorty not got his throat cut in prison, I might have shared it with him when he got out. I knew his family. We all agreed a little detention might be good for Shorty. There were no hard feelings before he got his throat cut.

"Anyway, it was my intent to loosen the suspect's tongue with the over-proof liquor and then to induce him to confess by returning to the dinghy and asking him suddenly where was Raymond Kidd, what had he done with him, and what was he really doing in Raymond Kidd's house.

"Result: the suspect did indeed confess. Only not to the murder of Raymond Kidd. Not in fact to any murders at all for which he could be convicted, for he committed them almost two hundred years ago, and although there is no statute of limitations on murder, the murderer himself died not long after, and thus exceeded the reach of the law, at least as far as I can tell.

"What I am saying is—and I believe it to be true, God help me—is that the suspect is my ancestor the privateer and pirate Angus Daggon, who passed out drunk and froze to death on a rock on the High Head in the winter of 1843, and who has now come back to life, along with his brother Octavius, who died on the same day in the same way.

"The duty that I have is to help him now, for though he was never brought to justice for his crimes as a pirate, he seems to have served his time anyway, a sentence more severe than any court could have assessed him. It is *my* duty because it was my branch of the family who after his death took his house and belongings and made no effort at all to convey them to his mother Letty, who after her husband was hung moved to Halifax, and who later (and I know this from Doris's genealogical studies) died destitute there. In fact, she smothered herself in a snowbank on Barrack Street, now called Brunswick Street, after prostituting herself to a soldier.

"I did not tell Angus this about his mother, who was my great-great-great-great-great-aunt. That would not have been so great.

"Also I did not tell him I completely believed everything he said. I gave him a day to find Raymond, or at least to show proof he and Octave had not murdered him for his house, which once upon a time was theirs.

"What else could I do? The man has to be found, and if he really has gone back to the past, Lord preserve us, who better to go after him than someone who has just come from there?"

"You told him what?" said Octave.

"The bleedin' truth," said Angle, "That's what. Brother, there ain't room in my head for half that yarn you and the Cap'n's missus spun up. We ain't the Cap'n's nephews, and we ain't no Boodists, and we ain't been on no *retreat*. I don't even know what that means. Was someone to ask me, all I could say was we lost the damn fight, didn't we, and was runnin' away till we sorted things out."

"That wouldn't be so far wrong. I watched Raymond when he did retreats here, and I've been reading in his library," said Octave. "The Buddhists consider normal life, unexamined life, which they call *samsara*, to be like a battle nobody can win. So they retreat to examine things. To examine themselves. To see that the battle is just an illusion. That there is no one really there to be fighting, and so no fighting to be done."

"There you have it," said Angle. "I never could remember all that. And if I did, I could never explain it. What does it mean, *there's no one really there*? Here we are! And there the Queen Mab was, for that matter. And there our father was, a'danglin' from a yardarm of the gummint ship that blew her out of the water. And here he is under the house, though no longer a man ..."

"Hush, Brother, not even between us. Never speak of him ever again."

"I'm sorry. It's the rum talkin'. This here time we turned up in may be soft in some respects, but the rum's hard as ever."

"Oh, well done. You've let the cat out of the bag, you're drunk, and Mrs. Kidd is due back any minute. And now we have to tell her the whole world knows about us. Did you stop to think what this would mean in terms of finding *the Captain*? Hell itself will be a less popular stop than this village once the reporters get here with their cameras and put us on television. If he's gone where you say he has, a big fuss is the last thing we need. Peace and quiet is what we need if we're to figure out how to get him back. Plus not being in the bridewell, or a mental hospital, or ..."

"Ye're a deep old file, Octave, and ye've always kept up with the world. Reporters and cameras and tellyvision, I don't know about all that. But what *you* don't know, because ye won't stop talkin' long enough for me to get it out, is that this here Gordon Daggon, takin' his ancestry serious-like, feels a certain *family loyalty* toward us. He ain't goin' to tell no one about us right off, and mayhap not at all. All we got to do is find the Cap'n. He give us a day, either to *perduce* him, as he says in his policeman's lingo, or at least to show proof we ain't done away with him."

"Ah, well, that makes things all better, doesn't it? A whole day. To find someone who's not even here anymore—who hasn't even been born yet."

"Might ye not lower yer voice a bit, Brother? As if I were not at the masthead but lyin' here next to ye? It's punishment enough tryin' to wring sense out o' yer jabber, without ye drivin' me deef in the bargain."

"Oh, let *me* apologize. On the one hand, it seems to me that I'm speaking perfectly normally. On the other, all that liquor you swilled may have sharpened your hearing. Your brain may have swollen to the size of a peanut, which would bring it somewhere near your ears. What it is, Angus Daggon, I'm concerned. Here we are, to use *your* lingo, in an unknown sea without a star to steer by, and you're drinking hard liquor again. And looking a trifle transparent, if I may say so. I can almost see through you. It's as if you're going back on me. And I can't do this alone."

Octave had hitched himself up on one elbow to face Angle and make this emotional appeal eye to eye, but Angle's eyes had closed, and all he got in reply was the soft sort of snorting that was the usual precursor to his brother's full-fledged snoring. So he lay back on the cold concrete floor of the basement at Angle's side and tried drawing what comfort he could from their old haven, as Angle had mysteriously suggested they do, while waiting for Cat to return.

To be or not to be, Octave thought. That idiot Shakspeare had no idea what he was asking.

It seemed to Angle, with the room spinning around him and the warmth seeping out of him through the thin houserobe into the cold concrete floor, that he lay drowning in a whirlpool in a sea of troubles. Troubles that for a certainty were all of his own making.

He had thought himself lucky. All the blood he had let, all the wealth he had seized, all the trust he had betrayed, and what was his sentence? Not forever in the bonfires of Hell, but only an age in the shadows. With a brother there to help him see the error of his ways and guide his change of heart. Which was all that had ever changed in that unchanging place, and yet had been enough. Repentance had relieved him of the burden of his guilt. Or so he thought.

Now he saw that there was no escape. In the realm of the living, there was no getting around it. What you did found you out.

He wished no matter what it cost that he could bring the Cap'n back.

Chapter 8

The Simple

The secret life has its own protections. It hides and is hidden, and if threatened or attacked, or even too much loved, can vanish altogether, O, can pull back into nowhere—the eels into the eel grass, the corixidae into the pitcher plant, the brown owls into the drumlin woods, the drumlin woods into the maw of the earth movers—

O into nowhere, where the careless cannot follow.

As the new seasonal community of wealthy Germans appeared, lot by lot, spit by spit, and the barachois between the old village and Kelly Point was diminished to a nub, so the living spirits of the land took their leave. Of the few that remained, only one had the heart to respond to a summons, and that was the one that in life had been known as Simple Jenny, or Jenny the Simple, or just the Simple.

Her first words, on finding herself pulled together again, on two legs and breathing and seeing through eyes, were, "Sundew," and "Ditchweed," and "Sedge," And then more loudly, as she followed the narrow trail which once had been a road, where generations had trod and transported and now alder, willow and fir impeded passage, "Cinque foil! Periwinkle! Glasswort! Anemone! Killifish! Stickleback!", for the incantation, of all she had been summoned out of and was leaving behind, in a magical way brought it with her.

She was not as she had last seen herself in the pools and puddles that were Jenny the Simple's only mirrors, but as she had known herself in dreams. Her hair was not tangled and dirty and ragged, trimmed with a shard of broken window pane, but long and flowing and clean as creek water, as naturally arranged as the leaves on a tree, an autumn tree in glistening shades of gold and auburn. Her skin was not pocked, scarred and scratched but unmarred and unsullied, as fresh and radiant as sunlit fog. And she did not limp or hitch or falter, after her first several baby-like steps, but moved like the breeze through the bulrushes, easy and free, upright and unbowed—as if she had never been used, demeaned and cast aside, heavy with child, to lie alone in labour on the saltmarshy ground in the looncalling night, all afraid and forlorn, hoarse from screaming with pain, till the sky with its glittering greatcoat of stars had embraced her and taken her in.

What Cat saw as she came over the rise in Raymond's pickup, in addition to the descent to the village and the necklace of islands in the ocean beyond, was a tower of red hair in the road just ahead. A pillar of flame on two bare feet. Not until she drove past, veering into the opposite lane, could she see the naked woman beneath the mane.

She stopped and rolled down her window and waited as the woman approached. She was not offended. She herself in her youth had once stripped out of doors, in the mud and the magic and music of Woodstock, under the influence of mescaline. But there was no container here, no safety in numbers, no like-minded crowd. She feared for a woman alone and on the road in such an altered state of mind. When the woman stopped alongside, she said to her, "Honey, are you all right?"

The woman smiled but did not speak. Instead she kissed the tips of her fingers and touched Cat's cheeks with them.

The touch carried silence like a spell. It was in Cat's mind to ask the woman if she needed anything—a ride, clothes, someone to talk to, a place to go—but the question died before it reached her lips. A blissfulness flowed through her that exceeded any she had ever known. Gazing into the woman's gold-flecked green eyes, she was like a child filled with wonder looking into the clear depths of a pond. It was better than drugs or sex or anything she had experienced in thirty years of meditation. It was like nursing her first-born, only she was also the first-born.

She drove on. She could not stop watching the woman in the truck's rearview mirror. When a porcupine waddled into the road, she stopped so close to hitting it that its spines brushed the front bumper. She arrived at the driveway of 7 Lands End with her pulse high and her thoughts all astray. She forgot the bags of second-hand clothes beside her and the styrofoam chests full of ice for transporting the fish. She walked into the house empty-handed, with the pickup's alarm notifying the air that the driver had left the keys in the ignition and the door unshut.

The Simple walked into Prospect unnoticed by anyone else. The villagers who worked in the city had driven there earlier. Those who stayed home—the housewives and artists, the unemployed and retired, the one technical writer who sent in his assignments over the Internet, and a few notable others—were strangely all away from their windows at once. Oley Mullins was in his closet with a watering can trying to induce the growth of a new batch of marijuana plants from the half-dozen hydrangea seeds someone had slipped him for a joke. Of the five remaining fishermen, two were away selling their catch and two had settled in to watch television. Gordon Daggon had finished logging the details of his ancestor Angle's reappearance and was dozing again in his chair on his dock, dreaming moonshine-fueled dreams among the lobster traps and gulls. Shannon O'Keefe was in the bus on her way home from first grade. The two brothers were in their basement, with Angle snoring away on the floor and Octave, having unplugged it this time, once again exploring the mysteries of the damaged and dismantled pump.

There was little the Simple recognized but the course of the road and the unchanging sea. The road itself was different in its makeup, being uncomfortably hard asphalt instead of pleasantly soft dirt, and then painfully sharp gravel as she turned down the lane by the cove. The houses were different too, and there were no ships in the harbour. For all that, she knew exactly where she must go and she went there directly—to 27 Lands End, the last house on the lane, that had beyond it nothing but a short weedy field, the rocky shoreline and the sea, and that had the object in it she had come to retrieve.

Doris Daggon, with a tray of foil-covered dishes in her right hand, with her left was about to open the front door when the knob turned on its own and the door swung in against her, upsetting her and bringing the tray crashing down on the floor.

"Well, I never!" she cried, thinking it was Gordon and that it was his early unannounced return that had just resulted in the destruction of the special afternoon snack she had prepared for him. Without even looking to see who it was, she got down on her knees and started gathering the broken crockery and the larger chunks of sirloin and potato from the now splattered-everywhere stew.

The door pressed in against her. "Gordon, stop!" she said. "You've ruined everything. Don't push me over in the bargain."

"You have something," said the Simple from the other side of the door, "that must now be returned. It isn't yours and never was. And it is needed now." She sidled in through the opening. "I can find it. You don't need to help."

Skirting Doris in the close hall, her long red hair dragged over Doris's shoulder and her generous white thigh grazed Doris's arm, bringing Doris for an embarrassing instant eye to eye with her uncovered sex. Sweeping into the parlour, ignoring the talk show on the big flatscreen TV and the startled calico cat that sprang from the couch and dashed out of the room between her legs, she went straight to the mantle over the fireplace and took the bell from the bric-a-brac there—the same bell Angle Daggon had taken from Oliver Cole and that had in turn been removed from Angle's half-house with his other possessions by the respectable branch of the family after his death.

Looking into the mirror over the mantle, the Simple rang the bell once, said, "It's time to come home, sir", and departed, leaving Doris on the floor staring after her.

The cellphone in Gordon Daggon's shirt pocket, that he did not like but kept on his person because Doris had insisted, was set not to ring but only vibrate when there was a call, as Gordon did not like this modern business of being interruptible wherever you were and no matter what you were doing. When he felt the buzz at his breast, he would simply make a mental note that he had been called and then check for a message when he felt like it. Now, however, the buzzing had gone on to appear in his dream, in the form of the premonitory underwater warning of a serpent he had disturbed while hauling up a lobster trap, a giant serpent who then promptly burst out of the sea, its long scaly neck shooting up up and up into the sky, its horned head with spread jaws and dripping fangs then curling down to loom over himself on the deck of the Severence.

"Woman, you'll give me a heart attack," Gordon said, blinking, still barely awake in his chair on his dock, when he had grappled the device out of his pocket and got it open and pressed to his ear.

"I'm sorry, Gordie," said a sniffling Doris, "but we've just been robbed, by a nudist, and she's made me spill the stew!"

At 7 Lands End, the brothers didn't know whether to try on their new clothes or keep comforting Cat, who would not stop crying, although she was trying to smile at the same time.

"No, no, I'm okay," she was saying, "It's just that she was so, so beautiful. Inside and out. And when she touched me, I just melted. I can still feel it. And no matter what I think about, whether it's Raymond, or you two, or Gordon knowing the whole story, I just feel so full of love, I can't stand it. But try the clothes on. Do, please. If we keep going, I'll be all right. Please. You can let me go now."

She was sitting on the bed upstairs with Angle on one side and Octave on the other. Octave had her hands between his and was patting them. Angle had a hand on her shoulder and was patting her on the back. Both had troubled looks on their faces. Neither knew what to say, or even what to think.

Cat pulled her hands away and picked up the bags of clothes on the floor at her feet. "Here, go into the bathroom and get dressed. And hang Raymond's robes back on the hook. You're done wearing them. There's two changes of clothes for each of you. A pair of overalls, and a nice shirt and pants and a blazer, and rubber boots and some street shoes. Put on the overalls and boots so we can pack the fish. You can try on the other things later. You'll have to wear Raymond's socks and boxers. They don't sell underwear at Frenchy's or Canadian Tire."

She had stopped crying but was still dabbing at her eyes when the brothers came out of the bathroom in their faded denim overalls and black rubber boots.

"Well, that took a little figuring out," Octave said loudly. "A pair of trousers with a bib and braces. A first rate idea. Now Angle can splash away at his dinner and no napkin needed. He'll be the talk of the topers' ball—a man who wears his meals with pride. No, really, thank you, Mrs. Kidd. It makes me feel more at home, having clothes of my own again. A sign that I am really here, and not just visiting. Say, what is that ringing? Sounds like our old town crier."

"Ye don't hear no one cryin' *Oyez, oyez,* do ye?" Angle said crossly. "No. Because why? Because the only town crier that's left around here is Octave Daggon, who won't quit punishin' a feller even when he's said he's sorry. Can't you pipe down a mite?"

"We'll go out to eat once we've dropped off the fish," Cat said to him. "You'll feel better with food in your stomach. And don't worry about Gordon. If we can't find Raymond by tomorrow, and you're really trying, I'll talk to Gordon. I won't let him turn you in. And by the way, after you have brought Raymond back, we should get you a haircut. The braid has to go if you want to fit in."

"Cut my braid, what took me seven years to grow, and has been with me to the grave and back? Well, I don't know. I'm that used to it, I wouldn't know who I was without it."

"We all have to move on." Cat sniffled, and her eyes were still shining with tears, but she was smiling more easily now. She felt as if she were advising one of her sons. "Whoever's ringing that bell sounds like they've stopped outside our door. If I were a child, I'd say the ice cream truck was here."

"My God," said Octave, who had taken off his boots and gotten on the bed and was standing looking out the open skylight. "It's Simple Jenny. At the front door. With never a stitch on her and looking like a goddess! And she's ringing that strange golden-handled bell you stole, brother, the one you promised her and never gave her."

When rightly wielded, and the Simple in her purified form was the perfect wielder, the emptiness bell as empowered by the mad monk Dorje had the power to cut through the illusions of time and space and even different realms. Not only could the reduced-in-the-daytime human population of the village hear the ringing no matter where they were, but also an ever-increasing population that was no longer human but had never completely forgotten the experience, for Prospect was filled with all sorts of lost souls who were so attached to the wild wonder of the place that they had never been able to abandon it.

All the sailors that had come back as seagulls, some over and over through a number of lifetimes, were completely stunned. Their feathered forms fell from the sky as abruptly as if they had been shot. This flustered an already discombobulated Gordon Daggon, on and around whose dock and in one case in whose lap the seagulls fell. He opened his mouth in amazement and his pipe fell out. The pipe bounced off his knee and down through a gap in the planking into the water, where it hissed and went out as it sank and came to rest atop a tiny china angel, one that had been consigned to its watery grave sixty-three years before by a sad young Paula Christian after she had stepped on her favourite keepsake and broken off its wings.

The angel, inhabited by a very small retiring spirit, was moved by the ringing and the impact of the pipe to turn over in the muck so that its face would be turned to the sky. Paula Christian herself, who had died in her fifty-fourth year of a ruptured aortic aneurysm, turned over also, in her grave in the cemetery by the road to the city, but so she lay face down. The sadness of her mistake had never left her, and was still so strong she could abide no consolation even now.

Victor Cooley, in his yellow dory, on hearing the bell three miles out by Betty's Island, shipped his oars and began to cry. As the tears dodged their way down his whiskery cheeks, he remembered how as a schoolboy he had crossed the village's iced-over back bay against the rules as a shortcut to the convent because he was late, how his satchel had bucked against his back as he dashed breathlessly from the shore to the door, and how the bell-ringing nun had detained him as he entered, saying, "Victor, a shortcut has saved you today, but it is a dangerous one and you must not take it anymore. You must learn to leave in time and go the long way like everyone else. If you had broken through the ice, you would have gone where nobody could find you. I want you to stay for a while at your desk after school, and I want you to think about that, how it would feel to be somewhere where no one could find you, and where you could not find your way back on your own, and then I want you to pray to the Lord for forgiveness, that He may always be with you to guide you back home."

Just off Saul's Island, that sheltered Prospect Harbour from the sea, a fin whale raised its head not far beyond the breakers and with its grapefruit-sized eye looked nostalgically on the familiar spire of the village church before reversing course to continue along on its migratory passage further out.

Back in the village, a deer dashed around disoriented among the houses, knocking at doors with its antlers.

An ancient blue-black moss-backed thirty-pound lobster scuttled up from the shadowed water under the government wharf into the sunlit shallows by the shore and waved a freakishly large claw above the surface as if signalling for help.

The mink that had taken up residence in Raymond's displaced boathouse stood on its hind feet behind the snow tire where it had been defecating and did a hornpipe.

A pheasant waited by the roadside for a car to come, and then threw itself into the onrushing windshield.

Along the coast for miles either way, throughout the granite outcropping and the tundra-like meadows behind, there ensued a general rustling, sighing, creaking, grinding and clattering, and on the High Head in particular a chameleon-like blushing of the lichen on all the standing stones.

Under 7 Lands End, a demon screamed.

Eldridge Kidd was a deliberate and determined man. After finding, in his wife's emails, his son Raymond's purportedly nonfictional account about a couple of ghosts coming back to life in his house, he gave a good deal of thought to the matter and to whether it was his parental duty to visit and assess his son's sanity.

He did not take time from his daily pursuits to consider the matter. While patrolling his vineyard, overseeing the harvest that was underway, his attention was single-minded, because it was his firm opinion that the itinerant Mexican pickers would do their job well only if closely supervised. Making the rounds of his silvery olive trees higher on the slope, he gave himself up to the simple pleasure of being a man who had risen from humble origins to be able in his old age to afford the luxury of pressing his own olive oil. And when he rode his four-wheeler up the steep dusty trail to the top of Lion Mountain and looked out over the vista of golden hills receding into the distance sixty miles to a Pacific Ocean visible as a thin bluish line, he thought of nothing but his beloved bedridden Angelina, who would never again accompany him to that scenic summit for a picnic, to share a glass of their own wine together under the sun.

It was in his bedroom, where he slept apart from his wife and the interruptions of her nurse's nightly ministrations, that he attended to the question of Raymond. There he lay in the dark in the wee hours and asked himself whether his presence was required at all. His son was now middle-aged, and it seemed to Eldridge a reasonable thing that a statute of limitations should exist with regard to a parent's responsibility for his children. How long, he asked himself, like a lawyer addressing a jury, was he bound to bail the boy out of his difficulties? When should he have to grow up and take care of his life on his own? When should the natural law of the survival of the fittest be allowed to hold sway?

Then again, he argued back, Raymond did carry the Kidd name. If he made a spectacle of himself, the family name would be dragged down. Thinking of the long labor he had put into the uplifting of that name, of the stupefying second bankruptcy and the absolute exhaustion that accompanied the third recovery, an exhaustion he feared had brought on Angelina's dementia, it was all he could do not to get up at once and buckle on his trousers and head out into the night like a marauding vigilante.

He did get up, at length, but only to pace his room by the faint illumination of the night light plugged in low on the wall by his bed. He paced in anger till the anger wore off, and then he paced in sadness and memory. Finally he fished a flashlight from the top drawer of the built-in drawers in his walk-in closet, and shone it on that narrow strip of wall by the curtained picture window where his selection of family photos resided.

The framed five-by-seven black-and-white of Raymond showed the two of them together. His son sat on his shoulder, a plump boy of six, his eyes wide and his mouth open with laughter. He was pooching out his little belly against the trick western belt buckle Eldridge had bought him for his birthday, and the toy pearl-handled derringer concealed inside the buckle had sprung open and fired its cap. A wisp of smoke was just visible above the hammer.

The father in the old-fashioned suit who held his son was laughing too, laughing with him and for him and because of him.

The next morning Eldridge put the grape harvest in the hands of his Mexican foreman and bought a first-class fare to Halifax, the connecting flight of which left from Santa Rosa for San Francisco that very afternoon.

The first thing he heard when with a bone-weary arm he opened his rental car's door in the driveway of 7 Lands End on the other side of the continent was the ringing of the emptiness bell. In his fatigue he took it for the village church bell and wondered why it did not ring more loudly and voluminously. He tried clearing with his finger the hairy ear he had turned toward the ringing.

"If that's the best you can do," he said in a tired rasp in the direction of the church, whose spire topped the intervening houses further along the village road, "you'll be lucky if anyone comes to the service."

To Raymond's displaced boathouse in the playground next door beyond the swings, Eldridge said nothing but only frowned and shook his head. It irked him no end that his son left his things where they lay—his toys and his clothes when he was younger, and now this. Wouldn't he ever grow up? Seeing the symbol for the Tibetan seed syllable HUM painted in scarlet on a turquoise-stained panel of plywood nailed to the frame of the wood crib by the door, this distaste for his firstborn son's incorrigible childishness grew till it exceeded all bounds. He entered the turquoise house as if it were Raymond's room long ago, not bothering to knock, disregarding any social norms of privacy, regarding the damage above the knob where Cat had bashed the door in with the stick of firewood as just another sign of a juvenile delinquency absurdly long-lived and absolutely intolerable but not at all surprising.

Throwing open the curtained inner door, he called out, "Now, Raymond Montpelier, what's all this nonsense about ghosts?"

"And that's Raymond's father!" said Cat, upstairs in the master bedroom, on the heels of Octave's revelation of the identity of the bell ringer at the seaside door. "And he's in the house!"

"Between the devil and the deep sea," said Angle, who had jumped up beside Octave on the bed and was staring moonstruck out the skylight at Jenny the Simple down below, who for her part, in all her natural glory, was now looking up at the brothers and in particular, and with a look that pierced his heart and soul, at Angle. "Lord," he said, turning away and clapping a hand over his heart, "What do we do now?"

"I never heard you call on the Lord before," said Octave, "except to take his name in vain. Why start now? It was once your heart's desire to be a captain. Take it on yourself, man. Give orders. Lead the way. We'll *board her in the smoke.*"

Angle grabbed his brother by the bib of his new used overalls and pulled him nose to nose. "Octavius, do not put a mock on me now. Them was different times, and the man I was then is not the man I am now. Of all people, you should know that."

The ringing stopped as the one called the Simple stilled the bell between her breasts and called up to them, "Angus Daggon, it is time now to put matters right."

"Oh, oh," Angle said, breathlessly.

"Perhaps it's her who's made captain," said Octave, still grappled to his brother. "She's calling out orders already, and she's only just arrived on deck."

"Raymond, where are you?" Eldridge called out from below, "And why is there a naked woman at your front door?"

"I'm going down," Cat said. "You heroes do what you like. I'm coming, Mr. Kidd! Listen, I don't know who she is, or why she's here, but as human beings, I'd have to say that you two make really good ghosts."

"Reckon we'd better go down," Angle said.

"Reckon you better let go of me," Octave replied. "Courage, brother. Take my hand. We'll go down together."

"Wish I'd never been born," Angle said. "Either time."

"Not to worry," said Octave, giving his hesitant brother his hand, "The worst that can happen is you'll get your wish. She could be here to pass judgment on you, and play the executioner too."

Cat McCallum had never been one to suffer the ill temper of others easily or for long, so when she reached the bottom of the stairs and Raymond's gaunt old father greeted her with a scowl and said, "You? What are you doing here?", she was inclined not only to turn the rough side of her tongue on him but to let it run wild. She knew, however, that Raymond's father was like his son at least in this, that he could be charmed by a charming woman in a heartbeat, and so, exceeding herself in response to her excessive situation, like a train changing tracks she cried, "Eldridge! How wonderful to see you! I'm so glad you're here!" and embraced him warmly.

Suspicious still, but with the thrill of her touch going through him like a wildfire through a drought-afflicted wood, the old man extricated himself and said, "I thought you two were separated."

"God works in mysterious ways, Eldridge."

"Oh, so you believe in God now?"

"I believe you're here for a reason."

The tears were genuine that sprang to her eyes. She really was so alone in all this—Raymond separated from her not only by miles now but apparently by lifetimes, a couple of contentious ex-ghosts on her hands, not enough money to support herself let alone fund anyone's return to the living—and Eldridge had appeared as if in answer to her prayers.

She squeezed his frail person against her again and said, "I need your help. I can't ... I just can't do this by myself."

"Do ... what?" Eldridge murmured, overwhelmed with the contact and the sight of the Simple at the glass-panelled front door.

As if in answer, Octave and Angle appeared around the turn in the stairwell.

"And who are you?" Eldridge cried.

"Octavius Daggon," said Octave, descending and extending his hand. "At your service." And over his shoulder to Angle, "Brother, do go on and let Jenny in, please, and drape something over her, for heaven's sake."

"What, *me*?" said Angle.

"*You* are Octave Daggon?" said Eldridge. "One of the ghosts from the basement?"

"We are not, sir, and have never been ghosts. I assure you. Neither in basement nor out. Yes, you, brother. She was your paramour. And jump to it. We'll have the whole village down on our heads."

"There was a ghost in my son's story called Octave."

"Raymond wrote a story about them?" said Cat.

"He did, and emailed it to his mother. A true story, so he claimed. That's why I'm here—to sort out his foolishness and put an end to it. Now where is he? Where is my son, and what's going on here?"

"He is neither here nor now," announced Jenny the Simple, having let herself in. She swept toward them with her mane of red hair trailing behind her and the emptiness bell held to her breast. "Nor will he ever be again, unless he is called so that he listens, and listening hears, and hearing remembers, and remembering chooses, and choosing chooses well."

"And just who in the devil ..." said Eldridge, his gaze going up and down her and coming to an uneasy rest on her full and freckled bosom. "... are you?"

"In no devil but only near one," she replied enigmatically, shrugging away the blanket Angle had grabbed from the guestroom bed and was trying to wrap around her. "My time for shame is past, husband."

"*Husband*?" said Cat, Octave and Angle all at once.

"Wed in the woods," she nodded, looking only at Angle, "by the ground where we lay, and the joy that we shared, and the witnessing sky."

"Excuse me." Eldridge raised a hand to shield his eyes from her nudity and flattened himself against the wall to keep from touching any of it as he slipped by her in the crowded hallway. "I have to sit." Taking a chair at the kitchen table, he called hoarsely back to them, "Nine one one is the emergency number in Canada too, isn't it?"

"It is," said Cat, going instantly to him. "Why? What's the matter, Eldridge? Is it your heart? Is there a problem with your pacemaker?"

"No," he said, waving her off and pulling a cellphone from his inside coat pocket. "I'm calling the police. Whatever you bunch of lunatics are up to, you're not getting away with it."

"Wait!" called Gordon Daggon from the front doorway. He had come at a run from his dock and now stood with his hands on his knees, bent over, trying to catch his breath. "In the name of the ... law ... please ... wait up a ... minute there. There's ... no need to call ... call the police. I ... am ... was one." Then, straightening and holding the hitch in his side, he caught sight of Jenny the Simple, with his family's heirloom clutched to her chest, its golden handle rising out of her cleavage, and he concluded, "Oh, my. Oh, dear."

"I don't need a *former* policeman," said Eldridge. "I need one that can arrest these four fakers right here and now."

"Arrest us? For what?" said Cat.

"Fraud, kidnapping, indecent exposure … I don't know. Impersonating ghosts."

"We are not ghosts," Octave said, renewing his objection. "We *were* lost souls. But now we're just human. Or at least trying to be."

"Any gate," put in Angle, "since when would impersonatin' a ghost be a crime?"

"Since you did it to try to extort money from me," Eldridge said.

"Since we what?" exclaimed Cat.

Jenny the Simple rang the bell, sharply, three times. "Let there be no ill will!" she announced. "We are here for the sole purpose of putting things right. All of us, that is, but for the demon beneath, and he can do no more than cast his evil thoughts abroad and hope they take root in our minds. So be on guard for what suggests itself to you. And let you sit, and hear what I am called to say."

Despite her nudity, or perhaps because of her complete lack of self-consciousness about it, the power of her presence enforced itself on them. They all sat down, all round the table, quite like chastised children. Their chastiser moved the chair back from the head of the table and stood there instead. To keep all their eyes where she wanted them, which was on hers, because the men would stare and become inattentive, she crossed the long falls of her red hair in front of her to conceal her charms.

"First, I am Jenny the Simple no more, but only the Simple. The girl Jenny was called simple as you might say fool, or idiot, and so she was, perhaps, with flowers of the field in her hair, yes, and briars too, and an old flour sack for a dress and no room in her mind for the learning from books. Simple Jenny. Moonstruck Jenny. Ragamuffin Jenny. Pitied and despised. A nuisance, a joke, *and …*" She moved along the table till she came to Angle, and stopping behind him put a hand on his shoulder and her lips to his ear. "… a lover no handsome sailor wanted any to discover."

When Angle flinched at her touch and looked down at his lap, she straightened. "No, never look down, Angle Daggon! It's not enough in your exile to have foresworn your brutishness, not enough that you finally feel shame. Now you must face your peers and hear the tale told.

"'Tis not only your tale, and not the whole tale, for we live but one life at a time, and the whole tale would take several. Yet you are in it, as is this bell, and we will tell enough of it to bring us to your friend, who has slipped through the flaw, as Octave puts it, so we may try to bring him back."

"How can you know how I put it?" said Octave. "You have only just arrived!"

"How are we three alive again at all? Because the flaw has spread. More holes have opened, and many boundaries vanished. Much is not as it was, Octave Daggon. Your thoughts are not foreign to me. Nor are yours, Angus … my love." She put the bell on the table, and with her hands thus freed began to undo the suspenders of Angle's overalls.

Angle reached up to stop her but let go immediately, having received what amounted to a moderate electric shock. "No, my love," she continued, freeing the suspenders from their buttons and folding the bib of his overalls down over his hairy chest. "There is no holding back now. You must bare your heart. There was a time when this rose did not swallow its dagger but the dagger rent the rose. No quarter asked and none given. You have blood on your hands, Angus Daggon. Not only the blood of your child and the woman who bore it, but also of those that you slew. Did you think that repentance alone would scrub the stain away? No, not in two hundred years nor a thousand. Hold your head high, now, and show them your pain."

What Angle showed them was a tear, only a single tear, but one so filled with pain that it scored his cheek as it travelled, and smoked and sizzled on the table where it dropped, and left a black spot when it boiled away.

"*What* was *that*?" blurted Eldridge.

"That was proof he is more than you think," said the Simple. "As for himself, however, he is only what he thinks, and what he thinks he is, deep down where he conceals it like a pirate's treasure never to be shared, is a vile murderer like his father, a soul not only lost but ever damned."

"He's not bleeding, either. That … tear, it sliced open his face, and he's not bleeding," said Cat.

"He's not human after all," said Gordon. "Come back from the dead, maybe, but not human. No human does that."

"He is simply," said the Simple, "in the process of becoming completely human."

"Angle," said Cat, "Are you all right?"

Looking at her, Angle's other eye twitched and began to brim, but he did not answer, and his profoundly sad expression did not change.

"He is in a hell of his own making," said the Simple, "and so his tears burn like fire. But you make it worse. 'Twould be best if you let me continue."

"For the table, too," said Octave, snorting and giggling, overwhelmed for an instant with a merriment he knew was unforgivably inappropriate but that for the life of him he could not contain.

Angle himself at this point took the bell up from the table and gave it a single sharp admonitory ring. Complete silence reigned as the vibration endured.

"This bell," said the Simple, "has an effect, does it not? It communicates where words fall short. Even animals get the message." She looked pointedly at Octave, then said to Angle, "You stole this bell, my love, but never rang it. You merely left it on your mantel, an oddity you could not turn to coin, a stolen bit of goods that was no good to you, a laughable mistake. For generations, Daggons kept it on their mantels. For a while it reminded them of you, a laughable mistake in the Daggon line, a drunk who sawed his house in half and froze to death in a snowstorm, passed out on a rock by the sea. Latterly, though, it was just a curious heirloom, with no tale attached at all, rung by chance if at all. Your wife never told you, Gordon Daggon, that the mirror over your mantelpiece broke because she rang the bell while dusting it one day. She told you the crack had appeared on its own, and that the house must have shifted.

"So far can I see, but no further. Where the bell came from, why the deep magic is in it, what its deepest meaning is, I cannot tell. I know it can bring Raymond back, and that he must be brought back. And I know of the demon, that hides in the lake that is there and not there. His mind is strong, and can influence you—Angus and Octavius most of all—so you must watch what you think, and beware what is suspect.

"So. We have been called, and now it is us who must do the calling. But before we can begin, I need one more tear from Angus, one just for myself and our baby, who came to us out of all the souls wandering, who depended on us, and whose reward was a bed of cold moss for a manger, and a hole I scratched out of the ground for a grave." She put the tips of her fingers to his cheekbones just above his beard. They smelled of earth. "And who came to lay me to rest? The creatures of the woods and the worms in the ground. Not Angle Daggon, no, not even then. Oh, Ang, how could you not have come!"

Now a second tear dropped by the first, the table smoked again, and there were two black spots. And one more wound on Angle's face.

"Oh!" said Cat, and would have gone to him, but was stilled by a gesture from the Simple.

"Keep your seat," said the Simple. "It is good. He is better for it."

"But his poor face!"

"It will heal." She lifted her fingers from Angle's cheeks, leaving muddy fingerprints behind. Yet when she turned her palms outwards to the company, her hands were not only clean but so brilliantly spotless that they actually glowed. She could feel with those hands, as if they were roots registering tremors in the earth, the racing hearts of all those round the table. She looked long into each of their faces, all except that of Angle who sat before her, and saw more alarm now than amazement. "You think I am here for revenge," she said to them. "Octavius even imagines hitting me—anything to spare his brother, that same brother who once in a drunken rage would have killed him had not there been a house to saw in half instead. But it is healing I am here for and only that. It is what we are all here for. The call has come suddenly and summoned me from nowhere. The brothers Daggon were delivered from the in-between for it, this latter Daggon from drifting away in an old age of sea dreams and toddies. As for you, Cat McCallum, for this you were simply called home. And you, Eldridge Kidd, to greater love.

"Let you brew something warm and soothing now, not black tea but the chamomile there in the back of the cabinet where it's been since you left, and serve Father Kidd first, for he is old and his journey has taken a toll. Then let you all join hands, and I will ring, and we will call on Raymond to return."

Chapter 9

Picnic At Point Pleasant

Smoke from the neighbourhood chimneys and steam from the nostrils of the team of horses at the curb and the huddled couple on the doorstep rose into the clear air of a cold winter morning in Halifax, accentuating rather than disturbing the overall stillness.

The wheel horse on the curb side of the four-horse team stamped and pawed at the paving stones through the light snow on the street. The driver admonished the animal for its impatience, and Francis Stegman swung open the coach's hinged window so he could wave at his friends on the step.

"I thought you said just the three of us," Oliver Cole complained to his wife as he stood rubbing his sore ear.

"So I did, Oliver," said Josephine, "but you did say you would speak with Francis about business today, and our accounts are in such a bad way. Oh, do not push such a long face. It will not be all business. He has planned a … a fête, a treat, a surprise in your honour."

"That is why you have no picnic basket?"

"That is why."

"Then, if Amélie has not gone back for the basket, what has she gone back for?"

"For your precious trinket. Your *dorje*. She said you would want it."

"So I would. Its presence comforts me."

"Here she is now."

"Here you are, Pápi. Here is your magic. Now we will be *invincible*."

"What a good girl you are, Amélie. Thank you."

"Are you warm enough, Oliver?"

"A snowman would be warm in all this gear."

"Then we will go. And you will be gracious with Francis," said Josephine, turning up the collar of his long coat, snugging his muffler and resettling his beaver felt top hat, which he had contrived to tilt sideways while rubbing his ear so it was almost falling off. "Please, Oliver?"

"Stop your fussing. I am neither a child nor any longer an invalid. And I do not need to be told how to behave."

"He is your oldest friend," she said, gathering her flounced skirt so it would not drag in the snow on the walk. "And most loyal. Please remember that. No one else is so determined, nor so able, to assist us." She began her descent of the steps, being very careful, as they were also snowy. "You see? The new gardener has not cleaned the walk or the steps. This is how it is when you cannot afford to pay proper help. Now, away to our wintertime picnic. May your earache and your grumpiness disappear, and may we all enjoy!"

As the coach rattled them down to the wharves, the captain on his first excursion out of doors in more than a month kept mostly to himself, returning his old friend's discreet but concerned inquiries about his health and thinly veiled allusions to the surprise in store with a civil smile but little response of any substance and no curiosity at all. This was not so much due to indifference as to the ringing in his ears, that kept him rubbing at them, and to his insatiable appetite for everything he saw, which kept him gazing out the stage window or fondly at his wife and daughter as if every aspect of this older world might cement him in his former identity—every horse-drawn conveyance and old-fashioned street lamp that would have to be lit by hand every evening, every hand-painted advertisement on the brick walls along the way, every mast of every sailing ship at the wharves at which they halted, every panel of red leather in the coach that enclosed them, every hair of the two buffalo blankets from America that covered their laps, and most of all every fiber of fabric in the two bonnets whose wearers had missed him so much they did not mind a picnic in the snow.

On seeing, however, that he was spoiling things for Francis, Oliver roused himself to ask where indeed they had come to. "For we have passed the Commons, and here is no park-like setting but only ships. I did not think to picnic on a ship."

"My dear Ollie," Francis said with a revived smile, "on such a ship as I am about to show you, you might never have expected to set foot at all, much less picnic."

They alighted from the coach, the men handing the women down, and proceeded along the waterfront past barrels and bollards and under several nodding bowsprits towering high over their heads till they came to a particular pier jutting out into the harbour.

"She is called the *Great Northern*," said Francis, leading them to the gangway of an enormous ship, one that dwarfed all the others, "but she is great in all directions, for north, east, south, or west her match does not exist. Come, let us ascend."

It was a longer ascent for Francis and Oliver, since they did not stop at the deck like Josephine and Amélie, who were taken in hand by the ship's steward for a warmer tour of the ladies' grand saloon belowdecks, but continued on up a set of narrow iron stairs beside the housing of the ship's portside paddlewheel to the bridge at the top that spanned the ship's width and connected to the starboard wheel housing. Here Francis indicated with a gesture of his hand the long sweep of the ship forward, past the orange-painted smokestack and massive foremast to the bow, a distance that in itself was more than the entire length of most ships. "Three hundred and sixty feet long overall, thirty-four hundred tons, iron-hulled. Over a thousand horsepower at your beck and call. Thirteen knots no matter if there's wind or not. The largest, strongest, fastest ship on all the seven seas. What do you think of her, Oliver?"

"What do I think?" said Oliver. "Why, she's a bloody great *steam*ship, that's what I think."

"Listen," said Francis. "I know you are a dyed-in-the-wool ragman, but consider. I hold the contract for the London-Boston mail. In addition, I am granted by the Admiralty a yearly subsidy of almost a hundred and seventy-five thousand pounds. Where could you do better?"

"Better than what, Francis? What are you talking about? I'm happy for you. I don't have to like your monstrosity."

"The thing is, Oliver, I think that you could come to like her. As her captain, I believe you might. She is a ship of the future and needs a man of the future to guide her. I am not making light of your tales or the time they have cost you. You were ever a forward-thinking creature. And besides there is Josephine and Amélie to think of. Will you do it?"

"Will I do what?"

"For God's sake, Ollie, must I spell it out? I want you for her captain. But stay, make no answer now, for there is more. Let me show you round her briefly, and then hey for Fiddler's Green and our picnic, and 'tween-times I will tell you the rest, and you can consider and we can consider specifics. And then with some good food and fine wine in your hold, and a bit of a campfire to warm your old bones, perhaps this dark mood will subside, and you will see your way clearly."

Oliver grimaced and gripped the rail of the bridge, looking up and around at the mastheads and smokestacks fore and aft, and down and around at the vast deck and the sailors. The sweepers were almost done with the snow. A contingent on the forecastle sat or stood in a ring smoking and chatting and driving home points of emphasis with their pipes. "Perhaps I will," he said. "And perhaps I won't. But I tell you this, Francis. I don't encourage idlers, especially such loud ones, and I don't understand why the damned engines are running, and throbbing so infernally, while the ship sits here at rest. Or how they can run and no smoke issue from her chimneys."

"Why, they are *not* running, Oliver. And as for those sailors, they are not idle but merely waiting. They are the crew of the ship's pinnace that will take us to our picnic. And I cannot hear them at all from this distance. Are you all right?"

"Yes, yes. I have a headache is all," Oliver said, shaking his head to clear it. "A thumping great ongoing broadside of a headache." He rubbed his eyes with a gloved hand and his right ear again, again knocking his top hat askew. "It must have me imagining things. Carry on. Let us rejoin the womenfolk and accomplish this tour of yours. I shall rally directly, no doubt."

Although the ringing and another sound as if of distant voices calling out continued, the headache they were causing gradually vanished. Despite his reservations, Cole was moved by the spanking new ship. Powered by steam though she was, she still had two impressive masts—he had been to a future where ships had none. And she was well-found—best manila for the rigging, best poldavy for the sails, no expense spared anywhere to get the best that Pilcher's yard in Northfleet had to offer. And she was in her vastness undeniably spectacular. He began to feel larger himself, so much larger that it was as if the great ship's grandeur moved the heart of another man, a smaller one who stood slightly behind him and in his shadow. The complimentary remarks of this smaller man, as they toured and inspected, seemed to this new larger self to ring false, to lack substance. He was fairly certain his friend was not deceived either, for Francis Stegman was no fool and had not amassed his fortune by being one. And so Oliver was glad when Amélie interrupted, in a high state of excitement, to ask if she could indeed be taken up to the foretop on the back of Samson Savage, middle-aged forecastleman and father of three, who had already given in and agreed to do so. He was glad because from that point on, after he gave his own consent, the attention was shifted from him to Amélie, first by Josephine, who could not help voicing her concern for her daughter's safety, and then by all on board as a hundred feet above them Amélie in the giddiness of her delight began to sing and wave her mittened hands in the air, visibly troubling and slowing her carrier in his ascent. Even the boatswain, a sour-faced man whose eternal sour pleasure it was to remind the seamen of their duty, forgot himself and stared upward with his hand over his heart as if he were saluting.

The company's concern did not extend to Oliver. In his sudden largeness of being, a swelling that extended to all his senses, he knew Samson Savage would not slip, nor his daughter's legs lose their grip. He could see the diminutive figures far up the mast as if they were right before his eyes, and feel the lack of danger around them. He rose past them, into the scattered clouds in the blue sky behind them. He reached out toward the sun.

Underway on the pinnace, where his smaller self took him when the tour of the steamship was done, he could feel the rolling Atlantic beneath them as if he swam in its icy depths, and yet he was deeply bathed in the warmth of the springtime he felt approaching in the gentle southwest breeze.

He saw what no one else was seeing and felt what no one else was feeling. Then it dawned on him that he could hear what no one else was hearing. Beyond the whispering of the breeze in the pinnace's rigging, beyond the whispering of the high clouds in their passage, he could hear another whispering, one beyond them not only in space but in time, one that had a name in it that was not his but that sounded almost as familiar.

The voices were not in his head, nor was the ringing. He was, he realized, being summoned.

"Oliver, here, be a good fellow and take the helm," said Francis, taking him by the elbow. "Return a while from your reveries." And then in his ear so only he would hear, "At least long enough for me to go to the head."

"Hey? The helm? Oh, yes, certainly. But wait, you have six hand-picked seamen on board. Are they here just for ballast? Why not ask one of them? Am I not on a picnic? Is this not a holiday?"

"Well … I am proud of my new pinnace. She is part of her parent, the Great Northern. Who would be captain of the one would be captain of the other. You should get to know her."

"I very much doubt …"

"Humour me, Oliver. Please."

"Very well, then. What course? Where are we headed? Shall I take soundings for you too? And paint the cabin and grease the mast?"

Francis nodded and smiled, the first time he had done so on their outing, being so concerned for his old friend's well-being. He patted him on the back. "Yes, that is quite enough. That is more like the old Oliver. Good. The course is as you have her till the harbour and the high sea meet. When you get that feeling, when you really get it, then back to Point Pleasant, where we'll anchor off, row in, and have our picnic."

Oliver left the rail and took the long tiller of the pinnace in hand, leaving Francis free to go below. As he stood steering, just under the long mainsail boom, he noticed his wife and daughter looking up at him expectantly from their seats along the uptilted windward side of the cockpit. They sat close together, a blanket over their laps, mugs of steaming cocoa in their hands, the steam whipping away in the breeze. On the lower lee side of the cockpit, two of Francis's younger seamen sat grinning up at him.

"What? What is it? Have I broken out in spots? Has a seagull done its business on my hat? Why do you all stare?"

"Oh, Oliver," sighed Josephine. "It is nothing, really. Only that we speak, we say your name, not once but many times, and still you do not hear."

"Mr. Stegman says the helm is what you need," chirped Amélie. "It will *put you right*, he says."

"He does, does he? Well, I dare say it will. Look, I grip it firmly. I am the grave, brave seafarer once again. And I attend. Speak, my darlings, and forgive me. And you two," he said to the sailors, "stow those grins and go join your mates on the foredeck."

And so he ignored the summons and attended to the little craft and the observations of his loved ones. Josephine was glad to see the snow melting on the land around them, to larboard the low-lying McNab's Island and to starboard the ridged peninsula that terminated in Chebucto Head farther out at the southwestern limit of the long harbour. She liked the dappled effect the brown land made, where clearings existed in the mostly bare winter woods, against the remaining white drifts. Amélie said it looked much like a herd of spotted cows. She then, while looking further into the situation with the compact brass telescope that Francis had lent her, fired question after question about the dozen or so vessels around them. What kinds were they? Why were those ones called fishing *smacks*? Were the men aboard them that hungry, that they smacked their lips as they fished? And why was that one called a *man* o' war and not a *ship* o' war? And did they all have names and why, and what were all their names and why? And where had they come from and where were they going? And did they all have captains like her Pápi?

"Captains they all may have," said Francis, emerging from the cabin, rubbing his bottom that was numb from sitting on the bucket that served as the head, "but like your Pápi? Well, few if any, and fortunate them that do. For your Pápi is a captain to guide men's destinies as well as his ship. Look at him now. Born to the helm and the horizon in his heart always calling. Hey? Hey? So here it is, Oliver," he said as he sat. He lit a cigar in cupped hands and then, as he threw the match overboard, shook off a bit of burning phosphorus that had exploded onto one finger. "Ow! Damn lucifers. Handy as hell but always liable to bite. Pardon my Saxon, please, dear Josephine and Amélie. Any gate, Oliver … what it is, it isn't just a captaincy I'm offering. I know you aimed for a fleet of your own. It's partnership. Full partnership. Cole and Stegman, if you like. With you sole overseer of all we move by sea, and I of all by land, for it's the railroads and overland freight I'm keen to turn my hand to now. What say you? You have always been one to think large, Olly, so think empire, one to rival the East India Company, nay, surpass them, for they are in their dotage and we in our prime."

Josephine gasped.

"Ready about!" cried Oliver.

The pinnace came around in a long graceful curve like a swan on a pond. As the sails swung over, Amélie with her telescope spotted the cannon high on the bluff of York Redoubt, and remarked her discovery with a squeal of delight.

"But we have not gone nearly far enough," Francis objected. "I had pictured us right off Chebucto Head, with nothing but a clean sweep of ocean before us."

"I have the picture, Francis," replied Oliver as he steadied them on their course back toward Point Pleasant. "I need go no further. The *horizon in my heart*, as you put it, in your feeble attempt at manipulating me, is indeed *always calling*. The only question is, how shall I answer it? And the only answer is, in my own way, in my own time."

The gruff tone of her husband's response interrupted the intense feelings of amazement, relief and gratitude that Stegman's offer generated in Josephine. She very nearly choked on the sip of cocoa she was swallowing. The cigar in Francis' hand stopped just short of his mouth as his pleasure too received a check. Of the four of them, only Amélie was unaffected. Oblivious to the the grown-ups, she began to laugh as with her scope she spied an osprey gulping a mackerel in the blighted top of a hemlock tree.

"Truly," Francis said finally, "I hesitate to ask what you mean, Oliver. But I must."

"Of course you must," said Oliver. "And I will answer, as plainly as I can, once we get to our picnic. Till then let us dwell in the space between things, silently, speaking only to accommodate a child's curiosity. Let us in mere company be, simply be. Then round the fire and with some food and wine in us, I will open my mind to you. Will you indulge me till then?"

Josephine managed a wan smile. "Of course we will, my love."

Francis, unable to mask his disappointment, merely nodded his agreement and called forward, "Mr. Savage! Hoist the signal, if you please."

Immediately four small flags—each with some vivid two-coloured combination of yellow, black, red or white in various geometrical shapes, arrayed one above the other on their halyard—rose in jerks to the masthead and fluttered there.

"What are those for, Uncle Francis?" said Amélie.

"They spell out 'fire', my dear, and are for getting one started. The army is clearing the point for a gun emplacement. The commander has agreed to let the burning of what has been cleared coincide with our picnic. The signal is one we agreed upon previously, to let him know we are ready and are coming in. We are early, however, and he may not be ready."

143

The commander was ready, however, and shortly a column of smoke was seen to arise from the point of land that was their destination.

Freed from having to reply, Oliver again gave himself up to his listening while at the same time resisting any impulse to respond. He clung to the tiller as to a bit of wreckage in mid-ocean, striving to put his thoughts in order. He wanted to satisfy everyone, and he knew he could not.

"It's not working," said Cat.

They had been chanting for what seemed like hours, calling Raymond back home, while the Simple stood ringing the bell, slowly and rhythmically.

"Of course it's not working," said Eldridge, whose hoarse old man's voice had grown even more thin and shaky. "This is crazy. We're all a bunch of lunatics. Myself included. People don't disappear back in time, into other lives, and if they did, you couldn't call them back just by chanting and ringing a bell. You'd need some scientific help."

Around the table all ten hands unclasped. The Simple, whose place was still behind Angle, silenced the bell and said, "He is on the water and so hears us only faintly. It is in the nature of that unstable element and his passion for it. But soon he will come to the land, and there we will be as a trumpet unto him. So let us rest and refresh ourselves, and continue anew with undiminished fervor and resolve."

Eldridge Kidd unfolded himself slowly from his chair and went to the glass doors to the patio and put his hands to the draw cord of the vertical blinds there.

"Wait," said the Simple, "What do you mean to do?"

"I mean to draw these blinds," snapped the tired testy elder. "There's a little girl behind the woodshed next door with a pair of binoculars turned on us."

"Let her watch," said the Simple. "Let all who are watching see all they can see."

He sat back down, grumbling inarticulately.

"And who else would be watching?" said Octave.

"It's hard to know," said the Simple. "Did Cat and Raymond ever know you and Angle were watching? Here, be useful. Bring us something to drink. Not tea this time, but ale. It will bolster our spirits."

When they had rested and drunk, they continued.

Raymond, this is your home now. We need you. Come home.

Raymond, this is your home now. We need you. Come home.

Raymond, this is your home now. We need you. Come home.

The five cavorting sailors had not been allowed much to drink—a glass of bumboo each, with the rum nicely flavoured with sugar and nutmeg yet excessively diluted with water—but they did not mind it. The long winter was winding down and they had plush berths in a worldbeater of a new ship with an amiable employer. Also they had been picked for this duty because they were the crew's best dancers, and they loved to show off. They were quite willing to run through their repertoire of jigs, reels, strathspeys and individualized hornpipes to the fiddle of their mate Albert Benbow beside a blazing bonfire for the entertainment of Mr. Stegman and his guests, and they did not mind the smirks and occasional disparaging remarks of the soldiers laboring at their gun emplacement. *Didn't the lubbers wish they had the luck?* So although the diminutive Albert was not perched upon a capstan head as was their custom, and though dancing in shoes and their shoregoing best on the motionless land rather than barefoot in loose working clothes on a gently heaving foredeck did leave somewhat to be desired, they were mainly content, and that contentment showed on their sweating, bobbing and turning faces.

"That's the same satisfaction I have seen on you, Oliver, aboard the Bonne Chance with a contract in hand and a cargo awaiting across the sea somewhere. That look of fulfillment that suits you so well. Why don't you take up my offer? You have earned it. It is not charity," said Francis Stegman.

They had finished their turkey sandwiches and were eating quince pie, the quinces of which had been boiled in wine and seasoned with cinnamon and nutmeg inside the crust. They sat at a table improvised from a board laid across two taller stumps cut to height and with leveled tops for the purpose. Amélie, disdaining the folding chairs of the grownups, sat on a stump with a cloth thrown over it against the sap, munching her second piece of pie from her hand and pitching crumbs to a squirrel. She pitched carefully, having found that if the crumbs landed too far away, the squirrel, whether from slowness or timidity, would be robbed of its treat by the pair of sharp-eyed craning seagulls also in attendance.

Francis produced a second bottle of wine from the hamper beside him on the wet leafy ground and refilled their glasses. The bonfire of felled trees roared and crackled behind and downwind of them, with the smoke drifting away toward the city.

"If I have earned anything, Francis," said Oliver, "it is this." From a side pocket of his coat he extracted the dorje and displayed it in his open palm. The gold shone warmly in the combined light of the fire and the afternoon sun. "I see Amélie has been polishing it."

Since it seemed to be offered for his examination, Francis reached for the little double-headed sceptre but Oliver pulled it back, folding his hand over it. To cover his embarrassment at this denial, Francis said quickly, "Oh, one of those barbarian baubles from the East. I have seen them. Well, gold or not, if that is all your long labour and hard losses have amounted to, I must say it seems a negligible return."

"Perhaps," said Oliver, opening his hand again, "if the worth of its metal or its value as a collectible were all, but it is more than that. Much more."

"Oliver?" said Josephine, in a cautioning tone, dabbing at her lips with her napkin. "Please. Remember your promise."

"Nay, do not muzzle me, Jo," he replied, "and do not fear, for I speak only of the here and now. Francis, we all owe a debt to our fellow man. You know that. Some of us pay it and some do not. You yourself are one who does. You belong to the Poor Man's Society and make your donations. I am a member of the same society and have made mine. When the church bells of Halifax ring of a Sunday, I should find satisfaction that two of them were bought by me. But it's a hollow sound, I find. I do not slight your contributions, Francis. They come from a good heart with the best of intentions. The problem is they do not strike the vital point. We do not suffer because we are poor—I have known a rich man put a pistol to his ear—or because we are sick or oppressed or alone or unloved. Or because we are said to be mad. These are just circumstances. In themselves they hold nothing of suffering. Yet the suffering in this world is nowhere absent. It rises from each of us like the smoke from that bonfire till it blots out the sun. Throwing money at it without understanding it merely feeds the conflagration. We need to understand it! We need to understand *why* we suffer.

"I grow passionate. Forgive me. I will take a drink of wine. Now listen. Could I, I would take passage tomorrow for Calcutta, and from there make my way overland to the Himalayas, to the land of Tibet, and indeed never stop travelling till I found the man who gave me this bauble, for he has the understanding I seek." He smiled at Josephine, who had gone very pale, and taking her hand he looked fondly across the clearing with its bustle of load-toting soldiers at Amélie, who having finished her pie had gone to dance with the sailors. "But I cannot leave now. The queen and princess of my heart must be provided for. What I propose is this: to be the Cole of Cole and Stegman for ten years, and at the end of that time to end our partnership and start my pilgrimage. With you, my darling Jo, and Amélie, if you will come. If you choose rather to stay—and I do not blame you if you do—I'll settle all my fortune on you, give you the freedom to remarry if you wish, and leave alone.

"There. There you have it, both of you. All of you," he said, looking up at the sky, "for although I am called, this is the call I must heed. And one other, for you must excuse me now while I heed the call of nature."

He left them staring and went down to the seashore, away out of their sight, and unbuttoned his trousers.

"But they're asleep," complained Octave.

"Let them sleep," said the Simple. "They have done all they can. Only keep all hands joined and the circle unbroken."

The two older men, Eldridge and Gordon, nodded in their places at the table. As their grips slackened, so the others tightened theirs, except for Angle, whose right hand, extended across the table for Eldridge's left hand, had gone mostly numb. To keep the circle together, he concentrated mightily on willing his scarcely responsive fingers not to lose the totally limp ones of Raymond's father; mightily, indeed, for his attention would keep wandering in a very warm way to the presence of the Simple at his back. Although her breasts did not actually touch him, being blanketed by her long red hair, he felt, as his long dormant libido reawakened, as if they were boring into him, and as if they were all on fire. He remembered the last time he had tumbled her, there in the gritty sand of a salt water pond by the sea, and he wished that his hands could be holding her now.

"I think we should call it a day," opined Octave, who felt his brother's left hand heating up in his right one. "We've been at this mumbo jumbo for hours. Raymond's not coming back. Let him be who he was. We can go on without him."

"Octave Daggon, you hold on or you'll go on without me too," said Cat. "And without this house I'm still half-owner of. What's the matter with you? First you ridicule your poor brother, and now you want to abandon the man who let you out of the basement. Your benefactor. My husband. This isn't the sensitive Octave that won me over with poetry. This is some heartless idiot that belongs back underground."

"It's true," said Octave, looking alarmed. "This isn't like me. It's as if I'm being worn thin, and something else is reaching through me, trying to take over. I'm talking like my father used to talk to my mother."

"It is certainly the demon. Keep all hands joined," warned the Simple. "And if you have not put all your heart into your voices before, then do so now. We have come to a crucial pass. We tire, and my sense of Raymond wavers and grows faint. If we do not bring him back now, I think we will not bring him back at all."

She resumed ringing, again holding the bell by its handle with only the tips of her thumb and two fingers, as if she were a living metronome. Only four voices joined her in the chanting, however, since the two old men slept.

"This won't do," Angle said. "If'n he couldn't hear all of us, how's he going to hear less of us? We should chant louder. We should shout, in fact, I'm thinkin'."

"The volume makes no difference," said the Simple. "If we cry out, it will only alarm him. He must hear us like the voice of his own innermost longing."

"I ain't no kind o' hand at this *séance* stuff," Angle said, pronouncing it *see-ants*. What I long to do is spread a little more canvas, 'fore the wind dies altogether."

"There is one other thing you can do," said the Simple, "you alone of us all. I have not told you it, for it is a desperate measure. You might win, and then be lost again."

"I ain't no hand at riddles neither. Tell me plain. If it can bring the Captain back, then I will, and be damned to being lost again."

She pressed herself more closely against him, ever so slightly. "You might be lost to *me* again. Dare you risk that, now that you know what you forswore the time before?"

The words stuck in his throat at the pressure of her body. He had to spit out his conviction bit by bit. "Were you not ... somehow called," he said, "to bring ... the Captain back?"

"I was, somehow, but now that I am here ..."

"Then that is what we must do. Tell me how."

"But my love ..."

"Tell me how!"

She pushed herself back from him, closed her eyes, and put the bell to her brow. The black thing below was affecting her too, and she strayed from her course. The cool metal calmed her and cast off the veil that was settling over her, of her own longing and desire.

"Of course," she said, as softly as a dying breeze. "Of course. Yes. What it is, you must go back and bring him yourself."

"And how am I to do that?"

"You have a power that the living should not have. You can go to a place just by imagining yourself there. Usually only the dead can do this, because their bodies are imaginary anyway, and usually they do it uncontrollably, because they are terrified or fooled, and so for better or worse they move on and keep moving till they land in other lives. You yourself remained here, stuck like lichen to a rock, because you love this place so much. Yet you can mind travel now, because the boundaries are broken, and the fault line runs through you."

"He can do it, all right, but it's anyone's guess where we land," Octave said. "And we always get there mother naked. Power my arse. It's more like slipping on a peel."

"Octave, hush," Cat said. "If you can't be positive, then just keep quiet."

"He's right," agreed Angle. "I can do it, but I ain't much good at it. And anyway I don't see how that would bring the Cap'n back. Sure, I've done it for me and Octave, but we was both *here* already, and it was *now*. The Cap'n is back *then*, and somewhere else that I don't even know where he's at."

"You did not know what you *could* do till you did it. You do not know what you *can* do till you try. Time is not what it was. Space is not what it was. Wherever and whenever he is, if you imagine yourself with him, I believe you will go there."

"Then I just imagine us both back here? Why all this ringin' and chantin' then? We could have done this to begin with."

"Because, as I said, you might get lost. You might send the Captain back and stay yourself where you were in your prime. And so return to your old ways."

"I will not," he said, turning to look up at her. "I'm done with all that. Can't you see?"

"I see what I see," she said, smiling sadly down at him.

"Then come wi' me. I won't return to my old ways, and I will take you for my wife, and you can have another child, many children, and we'll raise 'em together."

"I cannot."

"But you said …"

"I do not say I *would* not, only that I *cannot*."

"How can you know that?"

"I know what I know."

"You cannot go."

"No, I cannot."

"Then I cannot, either."

"Oh, for Christ's sake!" cried Octave. "What is happening here? Your doxy shows up, and suddenly your precious captain and your baby brother can go hang."

"OCTAVE!" Cat said, striking the table and waking both Gordon and Eldridge with a start.

"Then I will ring," the Simple said. "And let us chant with all our hearts, for we are all in dire peril. We are not the only ones calling. He calls who is below."

Angle turned back to the table and stared down at the scars of his tears. And then it came to him—strongly, like an order—what it was he must do. He had the power. She would not be blown away like dust. And so he snatched the bell from her and began his imagining.

Chapter 10

The Man Who Came Out of the Sea

The late afternoon sun cast a band of blinding brilliance across the small expiring waves at the seaward end of Point Pleasant, where Captain Oliver Cole stood pumping ship. Looking into that light, for it delivered itself to the shore at his feet like a path, he saw a hand, and in that hand a bell, and a voice in the light spoke to him, saying, "Sir, it's me, old Angle, come to bring yer bleedin' bell back. Take it, won't you, and forgive me what I done."

Without bothering to put it away and button up, the captain let go of what he himself was holding, wiped that hand absentmindedly on his trousers, and staggered out into the water with both hands outstretched to take back what had been stolen from him, the other half of the key to his mystery, that he believed would unlock time and space and even death itself.

As his one hand closed around the golden handle, and the other round the body of the bell, he saw two faces, one of the man who had robbed him, whose name sounded strangely familiar, and one of a woman he had never seen before, a wild beauty whose mane of red hair seemed on fire in the light. As he took the bell back from the thief, the thief and the wild beauty kissed.

The brilliance that bathed the three flared. The captain slipped and fell forward with a splash and went under. Soon the small expiring waves were alone along the shore, and the captain's footprints in the sand began to disappear too.

Little Amélie, who had tired of dancing with the sailors and gone off wandering again with her telescope, had been contemplating the unique ability of men to relieve themselves standing as she observed carefully and with a good deal of concern the very odd appendage that enabled such behaviour. Now she sprang from behind the rock on which she had been steadying her telescope and went running toward her mother and Francis Stegman.

"Do not worry," Francis was saying to Josephine, holding her hand under the food-laden trestle between them. "You have me. Whatever happens, I'll be here."

"Mamá, Uncle Francis!" Amélie cried, "Pápi has fallen into the sea!"

The attendant had no idea how he had come to be an attendant. And yet he knew exactly what to do. At the sound of the bell, he hurried to the little door beneath the stairs, gave a quick double rap, and then stooped and went in.

Inside, in a vast cavern lit by torches, he was not overly large but relatively small. Even the crowned couple at the head table of the feasting assembly dwarfed him, and they were children.

"Ollie Ray," said the boy, who was robed all in blue and whose crown was blue too. "It is time we were wed. You may perform the ceremony now."

"At last!" said the red-robed red-crowned girl, jumping to her feet.

The one hundred and eight other guests at the feast applauded loudly.

"Hear her! Hear the Queen!" they cried.

The attendant approached the head table along the aisle between the two columns of tables and, after bowing deeply to the couple three times, stepped onto the palm of the boy king's lowered hand and was lifted and placed on the snowy white tablecloth.

"Watch your step, Ollie Ray," said the boy king. "Do not detour through the soup. Now, how shall we begin?"

"I am very sad to say that we shall not begin at all, your Majesty," the very diminutive attendant said, gravely. "The two of you are too young to be husband and wife, and besides that you are brother and sister."

"Indeed?" said the boy. "Why are you here, then?"

"To serve, and to learn," said the attendant.

"Is that so?" Turning to the assembly, the boy cried, "We are *not* to be married! He is here but to serve and to learn."

Now hissing and boos filled the cavern.

The boy raised a blue-ringed forefinger for silence. "However ... however, I remember now, he is also here to fix the flaw, so we can all go home."

Again applause, an assortment of flashes as photos were snapped, and more than a few cries of, "Hear, hear! Now that's our Ollie Ray!"

"He's going to write a book," the boy said, as the applause subsided.

"A book?" said a guest in the front row, where all the most important guests sat. "A mere book, to fix the flaw?"

"Oh, it will be no mere book," said the boy, with a singularly sweet smile. "It will look quite monumental on a coffee table."

Laughter now, more applause, and even some stomping from the drunks in the rows toward the rear.

"What's its name? What's this masterpiece to be called?" barked someone from the furthermost table of all, back in the flickering shadows.

"Its name? Oh, my goodness. I'm afraid I don't know. What's the book to be called, Ollie Ray?"

"Forgive me, your Highness," said the tiny attendant, who had taken a seat on the gilded edge of the king's plate. "I didn't know I was writing a book."

The girl in red leaned over, her jeweled red earrings swaying, and whispered in the boy's ear.

"Oh, how fitting, how fine, and how perfectly fun. The Queen says we will call it A Traveller's Guide for Lost Souls!"

The girl leaned again, her red crown clinking this time against her companion's blue one as she leaned a little too far. "I see. Oh, jolly good," said the boy. "The queen says he will write it in the form of a song, and that all lost souls who sing it will definitely find their way home." He raised his goblet. "To the lost souls!"

"The lost souls!" the assembly echoed.

The queen leaned once more, this time to sniff the attendant.

"What is it, my precious?" the king said, observing her frown. He listened as she answered behind her hand, and then to the assembly he cried, "Ah! The queen says our hero stinks of wood smoke and a lack of vision and needs a purifying bath! What say you? Shall we bathe him?"

A general roar of approval ensued. Several tables in the rear were overturned. A rhythmic clapping and demand began. "Bathe him, bathe him, bathe him!" The ring of torches in the cavern flickered with the force of the clapping. A few lonely timid and insubstantial beings who had been lingering around the perimeter of the cavern now retreated fearfully into the rock.

"Olly Ray," said His Most Youthful Majesty, "The consensus is, you should be bathed. Remove your clothes."

"I ask the Queen and Yourself to forgive me," the attendant replied, getting up from the lip of the plate, "and will retire and attend to the matter myself if only Your Majesty will help me down from the table as you helped me up."

"The consensus was not that you should bathe yourself, Olly Ray, but that you should be bathed. Take off your clothes, and since you are small as a bird, we will give you a bird bath."

When the attendant had grudgingly removed his clothes, which consisted now of no more than a top hat and an overcoat, the king picked him up, presented him in his nakedness to the assembly, and then dumped him unceremoniously into his goblet.

"Flap your wings, little bird!"

The attendant, however, heard never a word, being entirely submerged.

At the far end of the public parking lot between Stegman's shipyard and Point Pleasant Park was a low brick wall that marked the end of the lot and the beginning of Halifax harbour. Beyond the wall, at the top of the riprap that sloped down to the water, a black cat prowled among the wild rose bushes, ever so slowly, like a statue that every minute or so came to life, extending a paw, retracting a paw, gliding forward a foot and then freezing again, its gaze fixed on the gulls at the water's edge, some bobbing in the small waves for tossed crumbs, others scrabbling among the rocks for the crumbs that fell short. The crumb tossers were two expansive crewcut women who sat on the flat top of the wall and at the same time flowed down from it in circumferential cascades of tattooed flesh that shorts and halter tops did little to contain or cover. While they held hands between them, one tossed with her left hand, the other with her right. Each had a bag of sliced bread at her side from which she pinched the crumbs. When they were not pinching or tossing they were billing and cooing and chatting.

"It's so good to get out," said the one.

"I love the sun," said the other. "I thought winter would never be over. It just kept coming back."

"If it wasn't for you, I couldn't have stood it."

"If it wasn't for me, you wouldn't have been on your back half the time."

"Oh, you."

The carpenter in the pickup parked nearby felt strangely moved and won over by the lingering kiss the two exchanged—strangely because a moment before he had been thinking how gross they were, and how they ought to be arrested for indecent exposure. He ate another forkful of imitation crab salad from the plastic tub on the passenger seat beside him and washed it down with more beer.

"I got to stop drinkin' alone," he said to himself, running hammer-battered fingers through his thinning saw-dusty hair.

The man who came out of the water did so slowly, millimetre by millimetre, so slowly and gradually that no one but the cat in the roses noticed him till his nose and mouth broke the surface and he took a great long gasping breath and let it out with a roar, shaking his seaweed-saddled head from side to side with a vengeance.

The seagulls took wing on the instant, their shadows fleeing inland over the cat. The cat stretched its eyes to the limit, flattened itself to the ground, and sped away like a shadow. The two women dropped their crumbs and grabbed and held each other closely, cheek to cheek, bosom to bosom, in one great gelatinous trembling.

"Oh ... my ... God!" said the one.

"Oh my," said the other, as the man's privates emerged.

The carpenter started his truck and backed into the car passing behind him, spilling his crab salad and beer onto the plaid upholstery of the passenger seat.

The man who came out of the sea blinked and stared, clawed the seaweed out of his hair, and staggered ashore towards the two women.

"Excuse me," he said. "That is bread in those bags, is it not? Will you share?"

The one woman surrendered her entire bag to him. The other just stared.

Stuffing his mouth with stale bread, the naked man wandered inland, past the heated exchange of the carpenter and the driver whose car he had backed into, along the perimeter of the high barbed-wire-topped chain link fence of the shipyard. As he walked, he marvelled at the mammoth orange-and-white cranes that stories above him moved boxcars through the sky like small packages.

"Forget something, buddy?"

Other vehicles had passed him, some speeding up, some slowing down. The blue and white one with the official seal on the side was the first to slow down to his pace.

He smiled at the uniformed woman who had spoken. "That is possible," he replied. "In fact very likely. But why do you ask?"

"Last I heard, it was still against the law to leave your clothes at home."

He stopped and regarded himself. "So I have," he said thoughtfully, "Perhaps you could direct me to a tailor."

"Sure. In fact, why don't you let us take you?"

"I'd be obliged, if it isn't out of your way."

"That's what we're here for."

"You wouldn't have anything to drink, would you?" he said as they drove on together.

The uniformed man in the driver's seat laughed. "I'd say you've probably had enough to drink already. I can smell you from here."

"I believe that's because I was bathed in a goblet of wine. The passage can be very chaotic, and more than a little whimsical. But I didn't drink any, and I don't want any. All I want is water."

"Sir," said the woman on the passenger side, "it's my duty to inform you of your right to remain silent. But I'm curious. Just exactly what is this passage, and where all have you been?"

"I'm sorry," he said. "If I remember correctly, I believe I promised not to tell. By the by, I'm very sorry for the smell. One has so little say in these matters."

After the attempt to retrieve Raymond had failed, and in the bargain Angle and Octave and the Simple had disappeared in a blinding flash of light and Gordon had gone off stunned and incommunicative and Eldridge in the same state of bewilderment had returned to California, Cat McCallum with the help of her friends had moved out of the city and home to the house on Lands End.

Her friends, every one, disapproved of the move, and why wouldn't they, she thought as she sat at her sewing machine, feeding fabric under the needle. The reason she gave for the move was a lie. She said that Raymond had called her from California where he was staying with his parents, and had asked her to be waiting for him when he returned. It wasn't a good lie, she wasn't used to lying, and the questions had come at her too thick and fast.

Why was he with his parents? If his mother was dying and Cat really meant that much to him, why hadn't he asked her to come be with him? How long was he going to be there, till his mother died? When did the doctors think that would be? She had agreed to move back after only a telephone call? Had she forgotten how she felt when they helped her leave him in the first place? The grief? The weeks of tears? Her absolute conviction that he was a man who absolutely could not love?

She had spent the long winter alone, for there was no one she felt she could confide in who would believe the truth, and it was not in her to keep spinning a fabric of lies. This morning she had found herself awake at four o'clock, awake with a wakefulness she strained to deny but could not, so she had gotten up and gone to work on Bitsy Murran's prom dress, laid out in its fitted muslin pattern pieces on her cutting table, that had replaced the turquoise couch and its coffee table when the living room area reverted to her sewing space.

It was an important dress for an important dance for an important person, she kept telling herself, to make herself attend. She had known Bitsy all her life, had delivered her back in her days as a midwife, had watched her grow from a howling baby to an attractive young woman. Standing at her table, talking to herself about the quality of dress Bitsy deserved, that it was her responsibility to make, she began cutting the fabric, silk taffeta for the full skirt, China silk for the lining, a sequined and beaded dupioni for the bodice, all of a light jade colour somewhere between sea green and turquoise. Since they were the easiest to sew by artificial light, she put the lining together and all the panels for the skirt. When sunlight lit the windows, she raised the shades and undertook the making of the bodice, the most difficult and exacting part of the dress, a strapless, fitted, boned article in six pieces with a zipper to go under the left arm.

At her sewing machine now, where Raymond's desk had been, she sat with the coveside window open beside her and the sunlight and the birdsong and a cool breeze off the ocean for company. She felt a tugging at her heart to be happy simply because it was spring, spring at last, but the mere thought of being happy unleashed the memory of that fall day of their failure, and the smile on its way to her lips was detained.

She tried to fend off the memory by increasing her concentration. Not only did the bodice have six pieces, but each of those six pieces had a matching piece of cotton batiste she had to join to form the interlining between the bodice and the lining. After that, she had to make little sheaths of seam tape to hold the plastic bones that would stiffen the bodice, bones that once would have been whalebone but were now plastic.

The thought of whalebone stopped her again. Raymond had gone back to another wife, according to Angle. Cat couldn't help thinking that her bodices would have used whalebone, and that Raymond might be feeling her stiffeners even now as she pressed up against him.

She laughed aloud—it was silly to make up a woman to be jealous about, especially a woman whose own bones would be dust now. Yet she *was* jealous, with a jealousy that made her hands tremble. She had been oppressed like this all winter long. She remembered the Simple warning them against letting the demon below affect their thoughts. Was there really a demon below? Were there demons at all? She had asked the latter question of a visiting Tibetan guru at a program in Halifax that February, and he had laughed too, and readjusted his robes, and advised her to keep meditating, and when thoughts of demons arose, to just let them go. "Your skies here are grey," he had chirped, in his halting English. "This is their colour most often. And so your mind becomes grey too. But it is only the weather. Sun is always here, outside, inside, no?"

She had been meditating for thirty years, and he had treated her like a novice. Men. She wished there were more women gurus. She walked across the big open room past the divider with its mantel on one side and woodstove on the other till she came to the kitchen table where they had all sat, and where the Simple had warned them so straightforwardly and stood ringing that bell on and on, hour after hour, as if an entire population had perished from plague and she were ringing to bring them all out. That was a woman for you. Practical, acknowledging the problems and getting the work done. Cat had admired her for that.

She went back to her cutting table and bent again to her work. Once built, the boned interlining of the bodice stood up on its own. She set it aside and turning to the six outer panels began with her seam ripper to pick off the sequins and pearl beading in the seam allowances, so the needle of her machine would not hit them and break and send a piece of needle flying into her face, something that had never happened to her in fifty years of sewing but that she always feared would. And then, slowly and methodically to overcome her weariness and wandering thoughts, she changed the regular foot of the needle for a zipper foot, which held the needle not in the middle but on one side, so the foot would not be obstructed by the sequins and pearls outside the allowance.

Still memory worked in her, and she went back to their failure. All that ringing and chanting, yes it was very practical, but where had it gotten them? In her mind's eye she saw Raymond's gaunt old father Eldridge asleep in his chair, upright as a ramrod, and the old fisherman Gordon slumped over and snoring with his chin on his chest. Both with their arms still outstretched as if they had died on a cross and their hands clutched in the hands of their neighbours as if death would not part them. Cat had held those limp hands. So had Angle and Octave. The ghosts. Dreamers in the hands of ghosts. The blind leading the blind. Of course, they had not *liked* to be called ghosts. No, they had their *dignity*. *Lost souls*, they preferred. Lost? Found in her life, anyway. Who was lost was her husband—that asshole, that self-serving lamebrain, that … love of her life.

She grabbed a tissue and dabbed at her eyes. If she cried on the silk, it would stain. And it wouldn't do to have a prom dress pre-stained with tears. In the ordinary way of things, Bitsy Murran would probably add her own tears.

The ordinary way of things. What had happened to it? She missed it, and she wanted it back. She took two outer panels of the bodice in hand. It was ordinary to worry about one's work, so she did that. Would the bead-ed and sequined silk act anything like the muslin of the pattern? Would the curves be the same? It was so very fitted, this sort of construction, so very tricky. The curves had to be exactly right so they would fit young Bitsy's bosom perfectly.

She brought herself to a fine point of attention—even with glasses, this sort of fine work was no longer easy—and did not relax until the princess seam was done. Then she pondered the heart-shaped cleavage-revealing neckline. How would she finish it, how pipe it? She had a scrap of lamé that would pick up on some of the colours of the pearl beading. Were those the colours she wanted to accentuate? Was the remnant long enough to minimize the bias piecing?

Raymond, this is your home now. We need you. Come home.

The chant pierced through the shield of her workaday thoughts. If they had just gone on a little longer, she was sure it would have worked. She had felt he was hearing them, turning their way. A little more chanting, a little more ringing. Hadn't the Simple come from nowhere just to bring him back?

It had all turned into someone else's love story. An ex-pirate with a se-cret guilt surfacing as tears of fire, GIVE ME A BREAK, turning to the woman he had wronged in another lifetime, in another world, breaking the circle of hands to take her in one arm and snatch the bell with the other, saying, saying …

WHAT WAS HE THINKING? THE SIMPLE HAD SAID WHAT TO DO. IT WAS A SACRIFICE. YOU DON'T COMPROMISE WITH SAC-RIFICES. SACRIFICES ARE ALL OR NOTHING.

… saying, "I will give him the bell. And you will pull me back. And we will all go on from here together."

And he had kissed her. And she had kissed him back. And in the end it had all been about the two of them. The sacrifice was compromised and had not worked. Not only had it not worked, they were gone, the Simple and both brothers, and she had no idea where. And Raymond Kidd was still gone. And Cat McCallum was all alone.

She wrenched her mind back to the bodice and Bitsy. And suddenly she was uncertain. Had Bitsy worn a bra when she had measured her? Had she? Usually when making a boned bodice, she would measure the customer in her bra, as the bodice would substitute for the bra in the event, and then the dimensions would be as they should. But now when she pictured it, she saw herself stretching her worn old cloth measuring tape from Bitsy's left shoulder to her left nipple, then from her left nipple to her right nipple. And then the breasts became fuller, and paler, and freckles appeared on them, and it was the Simple in her mind, smiling down at her with those gold-flecked green eyes, saying, "Am I not beautiful? Does not everyone want me?"

Cat sat frozen, with the unfinished bodice forgotten before her. Through the open window came the song of a single mourning dove, that called and called from its perch on the telephone wire beside the sparkling cove, and got no answer.

The seagulls cried in discontent at a Severence that had not budged from its dock and was dispensing no fish guts. They likewise got no answer, for Gordon Daggon and the outdoors were quits that fine morning. With the blinds drawn to keep the reflection off the television screen, he could not even see how fine it was. Nor did he want to. It would only have made him more miserable.

He tried to suppress the next sneeze but failed and felt his sore throat tear with the eruption. He tried not to swallow, but he had run out of tissues to spit in. A drop from his nose trickled into his silver mustache.

"Jus' murder me," he moaned from his recliner. "jus' kill me. No more bloody torture."

"Seventy years on God's earth," said his wife Doris, bringing in a tray with a teapot and a steaming cup of tea, "and you still haven't learned how to be a good patient."

He pulled the brown shawl tighter that she had draped around his shoulders. "Tea?" he murmured with disgust. "I don't want no more tea. Want a *toddy*. Need a *toddy*."

"And I need a husband who's not an old fool. *No rum for a year from the day it deceived you.* That's the promise you made, and that's the promise you'll keep. There's no use playing on my sympathy." She handed him the cup. "Here. You want to be out again checking your traps, you'll drink this right down. And stop snivelling. I'll bring you more tissues."

"'S'not … even … real … tea. And you'd ha' been fooled too."

"Real my foot. What has real got to do with it? It's flannel leaf tea. I picked it and dried it and brewed it. All you have to do is drink it. And how would I have been fooled, who don't drink rum of any kind, homemade or storebought? I don't hallucinate! I don't see ghosts!"

He made a face as he choked down a sip. "Oh, *bitter.* At least put honey in it, can't you? Or lemon juice. Or something. Well, you saw the Simple, didn't you?"

"I saw a nut case. No, it works best pure. And you should have arrested her."

He swallowed again and rasped out, "Oh, who cares. Won't be much in the traps, anyway. We only got five last time out. Five lobsters out of fifty traps. And Doris, get it through your head—I can't arrest anyone. Not anymore."

"You could have made a citizen's arrest. She stole our bell. Instead it was her as arrested you, you nasty old man. Couldn't keep your eyes off of her, could you? No, you're no news to me, Gordon Daggon. And speaking of news, haven't you had enough? You've been watching that channel all morning, and they just keep reporting the same things over and over."

"I can't change it, Doris. The batteries in the channel changer are dead."

"Ah, the poor invalid. Stuck in his chair. Well, I'm going into town this afternoon. I'll get you more batteries then. For now, what channel would you like? I'll change it."

"No. Leave it be. The poor invalid likes the same news. With any luck, it will put him to sleep, and out of his misery."

"Sometimes I wonder," she said, shaking her head at the screen, "There must be a reason they do it. Maybe they're *trying* to put us to sleep."

Gordon groaned as he forced another bitter sip down his throat.

"Anyway, you big baby, before you nod off, try to drink the whole pot. And tell me now if you're going to need anything else. I'll be upstairs cleaning and won't be able to hear your mumbling and whispering. Oh, and here's some more same old news. Maybe this will help send you to dreamland. *You can't ring for me either. We don't have a bell anymore. Some drunk ex-detective let it walk off with a crazy nudist!*"

"That settles it," Gordon whispered to himself as she stomped off up the stairs, "there *is* a hell."

He settled back into his vigil and waited for his eyes to grow heavy. There was breaking news, however, news he hadn't seen, and suddenly his eyes were as wide open as they could be.

"They're calling him The Man Who Came Out of the Sea," the anchorwoman was saying.

The call of the single mourning dove, haunting and unanswered, made Cat think, *Raymond would have answered. He liked to imitate doves.*

She had tried to escape into her work, but her thoughts about Raymond had found her and like an iron hand around her neck were choking her, slowly but surely. Abandoning the bodice, she stood up so suddenly that the inflatable cushion she sat on to spare her aching hips was knocked off her swivel chair and onto the scrap-littered floor.

It was her one untidiness, leaving her sewing area strewn with the detritus of her cuttings. Raymond had often pointed out the bits of thread and fabric that her feet carried into the rest of the house and left for him to unsnarl from the vacuum cleaner when they clogged it. He found this one messy habit of hers confusing, since she *never* failed, from his point of view, to remind him of the least thing that *he* left out of place.

"Oh, Raymond," she said out loud. "You were so easily confused."

She left the cushion where it lay. Her hips ached anyway, and she was not about to aggravate the pain by bending over to pick up a cushion that had not done its job. She needed a break. What would it be, meditation or coffee? Meditation would help settle her thoughts, but it required more sitting. She had been working for five hours straight. Her hips hurt already from sitting. She opted for coffee.

She walked out of her sewing area and into the kitchen, where she ground the beans in their loud little grinder and loaded the espresso machine with the grounds. Then she discovered she was out of bottled water and so filled the filter pitcher from the tap. Here was another unpleasant thought. She did not like using water from the cistern. Gulls did their business on the roof, and that business washed with the rain right down into the cistern, and all the filters in the world, whether charcoal or ultraviolet like the one down in the basement, could not in her mind take the essence of that business out of the water. It was an unpleasant thought, yes, but it would have to get in line with all the other unpleasant thoughts that were plaguing her. She needed her coffee. She poured in the questionable water while mentally daring it to do its worst.

While she waited for the drink to brew, she looked out the kitchen window over the cove. She could not account for her anxiety. There were no new problems. The monthly check from Raymond's father had come in the day before, right on time, so the mortgage and the other major bills were covered. Eldridge had not spoken to her since their failure to bring his son home. He had left in his rental car the next morning without a word of farewell, and he did not respond to her letters or emails and would not answer when she tried to reach him by phone. But the checks had started arriving immediately. And really, though she still tried to contact him from time to time when she was lonely and missing Raymond the most, she understood. He had seen, and he had believed, and he was doing what he could. What he could not do was talk about it or even admit it had happened. Who in their right mind would?

She imagined the frail old man at Angelina's bedside, wanting to tell her about it, that their son's ghosts were real after all, that he had sat among them holding hands and chanting while another ghost with a fetching bosom rang a bell, all to bring their son back from another life.

She imagined him trying but never succeeding, instead simply massaging her limp wasted hand and nodding at her as she stared into space, as Cat was staring out the window at the high tide in the cove.

"They call him The Man Who Came Out of The Sea," the anchorwoman said. Her smile blended earnestness and mirth in what training and instinct advised her was just the right measure. "Witnesses at Point Pleasant Park say the man, white, middle-aged and … unclothed … just walked up out of the sea, out of nowhere. Eva Woodhead and her … wife … Joanne Woodhead say they were at the scene feeding the gulls when it happened. We have them with us in the studio now. What was it like, you two? Were you frightened?"

The camera switched to the crewcut tattooed couple, who sat together holding hands, still in their skimpy shorts and halter tops, occupying most of the studio couch. Eva Woodhead said, "I'll say. It was like, you know, in one of those monster movies where the zombie comes out of the grave? And you just happen to be there and you're its first victim? But then he was a real gentleman, and just asked if we would share our bread with him."

"He was handsome, too," said Joanne Woodhead.

"Handsomely hung, anyhoo!" roared Eva. The camera stayed on her while she quaked with laughter. Her vast unstayed bosom in its rolling accompaniment threatened to overwhelm the straining halter top entirely. Then the picture jerked back to the anchorwoman who, struggling to stifle the inclination to join in and laugh too, was another long moment in proceeding.

"Police say," she managed finally, with a wild look in her eye, "Police say the man, whom they have taken into custody, seems to suffer from amnesia. He's perfectly alert, they say, even, even *distinguished*, but cannot provide them with an identity. Tests showed an insignificant amount of alcohol in the man's system. Investigating detective Darryl Burnhardt said it's possible the man became temporarily deranged while diving and tore off his diving gear. We have this police photo. If you recognize this man, please contact Halifax police.

"Now to the weather with Alexander Dupree. Alex, summertime fog along the coast. It doesn't seem to be happening. What on earth is up with that?"

"Well, Teresa," said Weatherman Alex as the scene turned to him and his map, "as we all know—or should know—not everyone believes it— what on earth is up is that the earth is *warming* up, and in particular its seas. Our question today: Has the north Atlantic lost so much of its cool that the warm southwest wind blowing over it no longer causes fog? Let's join oceanographer Arshia Sarasvati and the crew of the research vessel Neptune III off the Grand Banks, normally at this time of the year one of the foggiest places in the world, today so clear it's almost like the song." He mimed holding a microphone with one hand and made a sweeping gesture with the other as if to indicate the sky beyond BTV studios. "*On a clear day,*" he sang, "*you can see forever. Dr. Sarasvati?*"

On the deck of Neptune III, Dr. Arshia Sarasvati awaited her cue. The cameraman with her assured her it was only a minor technical problem and would soon be resolved. Oddly enough the doctor, usually keen for public recognition, was relieved by the delay and rather hoped the problem might remain unresolved. To be the bearer of bad news was one thing. A good reputation could be forged from bad news. The ranks of authors achieving worldwide notoriety as global warming doomsayers were swelling every day. But she did not relish having to admit ignorance. And admit it she must. Off the Grand Banks, the water was still quite cold enough to form sea fog. The fog simply was not happening. The fishing vessels around them and in the distance were all plainly visible, and their captains, a number of whom spoke with her daily by radio, were uneasy about it. Sarasvati was uneasy too. Beyond her failure to account for the phenomenon scientifically, with a fortune in government-funded instrumentation at her disposal, she was uneasy in her bones. She could feel something creeping up on her in broad daylight, over the unveiled sweep of waves, something profoundly malevolent and insatiable, and she could do nothing about it. She could say nothing about it. She would just have to play dumb.

Out the kitchen window, Cat could see the turquoise boathouse, restored more or less to its former position overlooking the cove. Eldridge had paid for the moving. She had been very clear about the positioning of the building, but when she had returned from the city and her shopping, she found the movers and their heavy equipment gone and the inland end of the structure so close to the wild-rosebush-muffled telephone pole there that its wide double doors lacked the clearance to open. The good news was it didn't really matter, since there was no boat to be put in or taken out of the boathouse, and anything or anyone else could go in through the door at the side. Well, maybe. The door at the side hung from one rusted hinge at the top since the hinge at the bottom had rusted all the way through and had broken in half.

She went outside with her coffee and sat where she had always loved to sit, by the boathouse at the edge of the cove with the morning sun full in her face. It was different now, of course. The two chairs were rotten in places, loose in their joints and missing much of their paint, hers its red and Raymond's its blue; and the dock platform had been shattered and bowed by two hurricanes so the chairs sat a little unevenly. Also the flower box at the back of the platform was gone and weeds stood chest-high in its place, tall curly dock enlaced with purple flowering vetch. Still, it was better than it might be. How many people had the time and place to have their morning coffee by the sea? She imagined herself enjoying the experience for the billions who didn't, and sending at least that little happiness out to them all.

That little happiness. She touched the arm of Raymond's empty chair. Raymond had never enjoyed sitting out there that much, not in the morning anyway. The morning breeze was too chill, the sun painfully bright in his eyes (and he rejected the idea of wearing a hat and sunshades before breakfast). Still he would come out and sit with her and hold hands and sip coffee. And the neighbours would greet them as they passed along the lane, out for their morning constitutionals, or to the mailboxes up by the church, or on their way into town. Raymond had remarked more than once how the lane in dividing their property also invaded their privacy, but Cat had never cared about that. She liked seeing people and didn't care if they gossiped about the fact that she and Raymond sat outside in their house robes.

She was considering the weeds, and why it was she let them grow here by the sea when she had so meticulously eliminated them from the other side of the road, when she heard Gordon Daggon wheezing and sneezing and muttering to himself, walking along bundled up and bent over with one hand to his throat.

"Good morning, Gordon," Cat called to him. "You sound terrible. What are you doing outdoors? You sound like you ought to be tucked up in bed."

Gordon raised in greeting the hand that was not held to his throat, but he did not look up or venture an answer till his slow march had brought him abreast of the dock, when he stopped in the lane and, rounding slowly toward Cat, said in a scratchy whisper. "Which I … AACHOOOO … Which I … AACHOOOO. Oh, bless my soul, that hurts."

"Gordon, if you're going to talk to me, come sit. It's not neighbourly to be so standoffish. Come sit down and I'll go make you a cup of tea."

"Aaaaaaaaaaaaaa. Tea! No tea, please. What it is … AACHOOOO … God damn and blast!"

"What is it, Gordon? You haven't been over to see me since the night we … since we tried to bring Raymond back home."

"Which it's Raymond," rasped Gordon. "He *is* home. I just saw him on the telly. On the *news*."

She knew her reaction should have been one of gratitude. She should have thanked Gordon for telling her. And she should have driven immediately to the police station in Halifax to collect her miraculously returned husband. Instead she had rushed back into the house like a crazy person, slamming the door behind her and leaving him standing there alone and amazed in the lane, holding the coffee cup she had thrust into his gnarled arthritic hands.

She had managed to make a pitcher of saffron water and get it up to the shrine room without sloshing more than a few drops on every stair, and into the offering bowls on the shrine without spilling too much on the glass top. And now with the still steaming golden liquid in the bowls and the candles and incense lit and the room lights on, she sat cross-legged on her cushion behind the long low black puja table. She had sat there some over the winter, but never with the lights on or the offerings renewed. She had practiced in the grey mornings as if mourning at a grave, with the thermostat still turned low for the night, shivering a little even under her shawl, with her breath clouding in front of her. The photo of Raymond she had placed on the shrine had a tiny cloisonnéd Chinese saucer in front of it that held the ashes of his name, that she had written on a slip of paper and burned, and beside it his wire-rimmed glasses, that had been left behind at Keith's when he had disappeared. She had meant to burn the picture too, to let go of him entirely, but had failed at the last instant, after scorching only one corner, because it had been like touching the match to her own flesh. And now he was back.

She sat and hyperventilated till she fainted, and when she came to, aroused by the ringing of her cell phone, she cried and cried through all the calls from her friends in Halifax who had watched the mystery man story and had recognized Raymond from the police photo.

"There's something different about him. I can't put my finger on it. But it's him all right," said Inge Holland. "I thought you said he was in California."

They all had said much the same thing, and they all had offered to go with her to the police station to *confront* Raymond.

She did not stop crying till the police themselves called, in the person of Detective Darryl Burnhardt, to inform her that they had an unidentified man in custody that callers were saying was her husband.

"He doesn't seem to know who he is, Mrs. Kidd. Or even care. So this may not be easy for you. But I'd like you to come on down. Perhaps you'd like to bring a friend."

What friend could she bring? She had lied to them all. And Gordon, well, poor old Gordon with his flu and his disapproving wife was better left out of it. She would have to go alone.

She sat for another hour. In that time, the old grievances welled up. Raymond and the rum and the bad temper and arrogance it brought out of nowhere to an otherwise gentle and manageable soul. Raymond and his unbelievable unwillingness to deal with financial affairs, and his tendency to disappear for days on his costly big sailboat, and his blaming of her accounting skills for the failure of their bookstore. Raymond and the day she pulled up in the driveway to discover her belongings piled out on the lawn.

Scene after scene accosted her, but as she continued to sit, the virtue of thirty years of meditation practice came to her aid. Her anger arose and subsided in a succession of storm waves, but in the end the ocean was calm and she was still in love.

Cat McCallum, veteran of storms.

She smiled at herself and wiped her last tear away. She did have one friend she could bring, anyway, one she had always told the truth. On Raymond's cushion beside her, her old grey stuffed bunny sat meditating too, its stuffed orange carrot still between its paws, as uneaten as ever.

In the red brick building on Bilby in north Halifax, where homes and businesses and trees intermingled and only the trees were more than two stories high, BTV news director Tom Lutz, anchorwoman Julia Barnes, and relay technician Abernathy Crumb sat together in Lutz's office discussing the Man from the Sea story over coffee.

"Well, that was a shambles, wasn't it?" Lutz was saying. He was a tall slender man in a powder-blue long-sleeved shirt with white stripes and white cuffs and a white collar he wore buttoned but tieless, and he had the kind of piercing blue eyes and intensity you only wanted trained on you when he was smiling. And he wasn't smiling.

"You wanted a boost in the ratings," said Julia Barnes.

"I want a team that is always, *always* professional, Jules. We may not be CBC, but we have to have the same professionalism. And that professionalism includes not laughing on a live news broadcast at someone in the news who is neither a clown nor a comedian but a man obviously suffering from some sort of mental disorder. A man who probably has family, and whose family has feelings. And access to lawyers. And the ability to bring lawsuits."

"I didn't laugh, Tom. I couldn't help wanting to, but I didn't actually laugh."

"It was obvious that you wanted to, and were trying not to, and that's just as bad. And you, Ab, we have an eight-second cutoff, do we not? How did that gross woman's comment on the proportions of the man's genitalia escape you? How was it that you did not catch that and *cut … it … off?*"

Ab returned his employer's angry stare with a vacant one while he tried to come up with some sort of defense. "I, I … she didn't curse, boss. The rule is for curse words."

Lutz gave his technician and anchorwoman five more seconds of hard-faced disapproving scrutiny and then cracked a thin smile. *"Cut it off—* don't you get it? The man's geni…? Oh, never mind. Listen, you two. You went with your gut, and maybe you followed it over the line just a little. But I'm not going to can you. In fact, I may decorate you. The phones haven't stopped ringing since the story aired. And the kudos outnumber the complaints ten to one. *The Man Who Came Out of the Sea*—people loved it. They want to know more.

"Jules, I want an interview with our mystery man. I don't care how you get it, just get it. And be quick. He could be only a diver with a unique survival story. Or he could be someone important. He could be a crime figure that survived a hit. I don't know. My hunch is he's news, and that we won't be the only ones checking him out. Unless I miss my guess, CBC will go after him and maybe even CNN and the BBC. You could find yourself running with the big dogs on this one. Now go."

Still Cat did not hurry, but prepared herself well. The shower was important, for freshness of mind as well as cleanliness of body. The hair, the teeth, the face, the blouse, the skirt, she put them all together carefully, as if they were her armor and she were going into a battle. Even her underwear was important, whether or not it came to Raymond seeing it. Taking a last look in the mirror, she corrected the pencilling of her lips, zipped on the knee-length Italian boots she had bought in an earlier marriage to a successful young lawyer and had reheeled three times, and then marched out the door to Raymond's down-at-heel, dusty old pickup.

Beside her, buckled into the passenger seat, rode her sidekick, the button-eyed grey bunny with its everlasting carrot.

He was wearing beige prison clothes. His escort to the interrogation room had been the same officer who had brought him the clothes, a heavy-set black woman with close-cropped greying hair who looked tough and formidable in her uniform but spoke gently. There was a kindness about her that could light up the universe. Greatly moved, he had put a hand out to caress her cheek. She had pushed his hand away, but not roughly or too suddenly. Even her verbal rejection of his gesture—*No sir can't have none of that*—had been made with a smile. She would be born again in better circumstances, he thought. She would not have to wear a gun then or make her living amid violence.

She had said that a doctor would be coming to talk to him, to maybe help him with his memory, but he would have to be patient, as it might take a while. Later she had looked in again, to say the doctor would not be coming, but not to worry.

"A woman we think may be your wife is on her way instead."

So. He might have a wife. And his name might be? *Raymond Kidd*. And hers? *Catriona*. And she might take him home.

"Ain't you glad?"

"If she's as nice as you," he had replied, "of course."

"He hasn't been charged, Ms. Kidd," said Detective Burnhardt, as he escorted her to the room where Raymond waited. "We could charge him with public nudity. We could hold him for psychiatric observation. But he seems to be clear in his mind. He just can't remember what happened to him. If he really is your husband, we'd like to release him into your custody. Likely he's just had a knock on the head, hit a rock down there or something, and will be fine in the morning."

"They say he was found naked," said Cat. "Is that right?"

The detective nodded. "We're assuming he was diving, and that he tore off his wetsuit on becoming disoriented. Have you ever known him to be claustrophobic?"

"I never knew he could dive." She was remembering Angle appearing naked with the cod, and Octave's explanation that your clothes did not come with you when you travelled in between.

"Well, it's probably nothing we need to investigate. If he's yours, sooner or later you two can have a heart to heart, and you can ask him what all he's been up to. And hope it's only diving you didn't know about."

The detective opened a door. On the inside was her Raymond, dressed like a prisoner.

"Hello," he said, cheerfully, from the interrogation table. "Is it me?"

Chapter 11

The Lightning that Went the Wrong Way

The funeral for Captain Oliver Cole was famously well attended, by many because they had known him, by others because he was well known, and by a certain contingent because, uncertain what the turnout would be and wanting to please Josephine, Francis Stegman had paid them. And then there were those who were there only for the food and drink, the unstinting availability of which had been advertised at Stegman's behest in the Novascotian, their mutual friend Joseph Howe's newspaper, and pasted up in bills throughout the city. The numbers of this latter sort of guests exceeded all the rest.

The twenty plank tables of food were ranged around the Cole backyard, inside walls whose gates had been thrown open for the affair. The food itself—platefuls of sliced bread, cheeses and plum cake, bottles of wine and jugs of beer—was as constantly replenished by a swarm of servants as it was devoured by the ravening crowd.

"How long does the carnage continue before we proceed to the grave?" said Captain Piper Handy, a former shipmate of Cole's, who stood with Stegman his employer and two other black-gloved black-hatbanded men on a balcony of the Cole home.

"According to Oliver's native Yorkshire traditions, which he asked in his will be observed, until enough liquor has been consumed to *kill his sins*," said Stegman. "With every drop accounting for a sin, a single jug should have done. Yet Oliver imagined himself a great sinner, with many lifetimes of sins to account for, and his widow asked that we respect that. So we have to get through ten kegs of Mr. Keith's fine ale and forty cases of wine from all the cellars of his friends. When that is consumed, the coffin comes out and is laid on a table and opened for a last look. Then we go."

"They will be drunk as lords by then," Handy said.

"They will have eaten and refreshed themselves well in the name of the deceased," said Alexander Keith, himself from Scotland and fond of the old ways. "And that is the point."

"Bless him," said Joseph Howe. "He may have lost his mind, our Oliver, but never his heart. Hello there, you, Curly Ford!" Howe called down from the balcony railing. "You disgrace of an Irishman, put that silverware back! Ah, but Ollie, he would have loved to have seen all of them here," he went on, returning his attention to his friends. "Even Ford and the rest of the roughs and their slatterns from Barrack Street. There's that black whitewasher Hank Kellum, always up for charges of something or other. Ha ha ha, I can never think of his occupation and keep a straight face."

"It's fair like Calcutta for all the types," said Captain Handy. "Indians in their blankets, dandies and dollies, solid citizens, soldiers, sailors … there's that hulking idiot from my afterguard, Absent Andrews. He has trod on that poor whore's foot and I daresay crippled her. And now she has frightened him with her howling and he has backed up and fallen across a table and broken it. Dear me. I shall have to attend to this. Gentlemen."

With the departure of the captain, the three remaining gentlemen stood silent, lost in thoughts of mortality. Stegman passed cigars to his companions and lit one of his own.

"The fog will overtake us," Howe observed. "It has entered the outer harbour and has already obscured Maugher's Beach on McNab's Island."

"I will not mind it," said Stegman. "Our friend is enshrouded. Let the whole world be so in his honour."

"Tell me, Francis," said Howe, in a fog of his own cigar smoke. "Was it really a shark? I must ask."

"Of course you must. You are a newspaperman. I can see your headline now, 'Mad Captain Drowns Himself'. No, sir. He did not. It was a shark."

"I have never known sharks come so far into Halifax harbour. And to have one snare Oliver while he waded? Well, I can scarcely credit it, sir. Nor, I'm afraid, will my readers."

"If they read it is so, they will believe it. And since it is so, then they should. Say it is so, man. Think of Josephine. This is hard enough for her already."

"I hear he was so mauled and dismembered that the undertaker could not render him presentable, and so only Josephine will be allowed the last look."

"She wishes he may not be remembered in his ravaged state. At least not by the public. You will not be so ghoulish as to ask to join her, will you, Joe?"

Alexander Keith came to Howe's side, putting an arm around him and resting a black glove on his shoulder. "We have long supported each other, Joseph Howe, and raised many a glass together. Would you really taint our dear Oliver's memory with the suggestion of self-murder? Would you? For the mere notoriety?"

Howe sidled out from under Keith's hand. "Sir, our friendship is founded on self-interest, and you know it," he said. "We make a formidable triumvirate. But the truth is my love, and lovers may come between friends. Even the best of friends."

"Yes," said Francis Stegman, "It's a pity. But true."

Resting his elbows on the iron railing, he looked out through the trees to the harbour and the fast-approaching fog, and tapped his cigar on the railing so the ash fell among the feasters below.

No less a figure than Anglican bishop John Inglis himself, in black cassock, white collar and purple Canterbury cap, said the last words over the open grave on the fogged-in slope of Camp Hill Cemetery.

The renowned cleric spoke with mixed feelings. The circumstances of Oliver Cole's death were questionable and he had admitted him into hallowed ground nevertheless. The sum that Francis Stegman had placed at the disposal of the bishopric would indeed allow for the renovation of the entire cathedral on Argyle, and Captain Cole himself had been a substantial benefactor and buyer of bells, but he was John Inglis, and he should not have been persuaded.

He channeled the strength of his misgivings into praise for the dead.

"He was a man who dared greatly, and a man who shared greatly. Let us hold him in our hearts."

Now began the ceremonial offerings. Each attendee had received a spray of box and yew to toss onto the coffin. The line that formed stretched away into the fog, so that its end could not be seen. This made it seem to little Amélie, standing beside her mother, after she had counted no fewer than forty-seven sprays being tossed, that the line was endless.

"They will not have to fill the hole with dirt," she said to her mother. "It will be filled with greenery."

Private Angus Walmsley, out of a lightness of heart brought about by a full belly of beer, chose that moment to give just the right shove to his friend Private Peter Waite, so that Private Waite lost his balance, which had been none too steady in the first place, and delivered himself into the hole along with his offering.

During the ensuing confusion of the extraction of the soldier, and under the cover of the reproachful murmuring and remarks from those close enough in the fog to make out what had happened, Francis Stegman leaned close to the bereaved widow and whispered in her ear, "Mrs. *Stegman,* then? You know it would be best."

To which Josephine, turning her head slightly but keeping her eyes cast down, whispered in return, "You are a … an eminently practical man, Francis. Sane and, and sound. And we need that now. Especially Amélie. So …" She paused to collect herself and to arrest with her lace handkerchief a tear that would insist on escaping its confines. "So … so yes. But there must be proper mourning."

"Of course."

"Oh, I see," said Amélie, oblivious to their whispering, "they just press the pile down from time to time with drunken soldiers."

A smattering of drops fell from the clouds which had crept up on them masked by the fog, and then the rain fell thick and sudden. The line to the graveside dissolved and the assembly of mourners dispersed in all directions.

"Here, throw your offering now," Josephine said to Amélie, and turning to Stegman she said, "And you, you should throw this."

Stegman dropped the spray he had been carrying and took from the widow the long-stemmed rose she extended. It was a hothouse rose, the same as she and Amélie carried, only theirs were bright red and his a pure white. He added his own color, however, when a thorn caught in his glove and pricked his thumb, so that a drop of blood welled up through the tear in the black fabric and onto the branch.

He shook the branch free from his hand with an oath and kicked it into the grave.

And then they were running through the driving rain and rolling fog, the three of them together, holding hands so as not to become separated or lost.

By gaslight that evening, Joseph Howe finished his account of the funeral. Putting his pen down on the desk, he lit his pipe and reviewed what he had written. Over and over he perused the part about the lightning bolt that had struck as the crowd fled for shelter, struck right into the open grave as the gravediggers were hurriedly shoveling in the dirt.

"Killed by a shark while wading at a picnic," he reflected aloud between puffs, "and his coffin struck by lightning. No, it was the Lord's own sign, I'm thinking, that consecrated ground is not for madmen who drown themselves. But enough, Oliver," he said as he lifted the lamp of the gaslight and set fire to his report. "It is not up to me to second the Lord's motion. Rest in peace."

In the Hardest Heart tavern, the full name of which was Even The Hardest Heart Softens Here, one of the gravediggers from the Cole funeral was saying to his cronies, over a dented pewter mug he held with still-muddied fingers, "Yar, yar, but that lightnin', it never strook into that hole, it coom out of it, I'm tellin' ya. It coom *out* of the hole ..." Ale slopped on the table as he flourished his mug to illustrate. "... and what got strook was jus' the fookin' clouds, gennulmen. And when it strook the clouds, gennulmen, didn't they and the downpour part for a flash, like the waves of the iverlastin' Red Sea did for Moses, to show the sun itself? Didn't I see it up there with me own two eyes, all bright and shinin' in a clear blue sky? Now, this all happened in an instant, sure, no longer than it takes to snap yer fingers. But I seen it. I yam a *witness*. It were a right miracle and no mistake, and I'll niver stop raisin' me glass to the bold cap'n, who had the last say after all."

Chapter 12

A Prescription Renewed

Cat asked the detective if she and Raymond could have a moment alone together, and now the couple sat contemplating each other across the cigarette-burned and coffee-stained interrogation table.

Raymond saw the tears in her eyes and wondered what else he might say to her, but at the moment, although there was something familiar about her, he did not recognize her and could not place her. He had only the policewoman's word that she was his wife.

"You could ask how I am. You could start out like that," Cat said to him. It was no trick to her, reading his mind. She had had years of practice. His thoughts at the moment were as obvious as if they had been inscribed on his forehead. "Or you could just put your hand out, like you want to hold mine."

"How are you?" he said, putting out his hand.

"Not so good," she said, taking it. "Since you disappeared, I haven't slept well, I don't eat well, and I can't concentrate on much of anything. You haven't been off my mind for more than moments at a time. And you don't even remember me."

"I would like to remember you," he said. "You're very beautiful. And I don't want you to cry."

She smiled and began to cry at the same time. "'Tears are the rain from heaven that lets us grow up truly human'. Do you remember who said that?"

"It sounds familiar. There's something familiar about you altogether. Even the way you smell. But no, I don't know who said it."

"The Khenpo. Your teacher. You came home from his program at Ear of the Elephant in New Brunswick and told me that yourself. We hadn't known each other long. You'd only moved here from America three months before. But you cried when you saw me again, and said you'd missed me that much." Her hand tightened around his. "Don't you remember?"

"No," he said. "I'm sorry. I don't."

She let go of his hand and rummaged in the gaily-coloured jute bag she had laid on the floor by the chair. "Okay. I have something here. When you disappeared from the Brewery, your clothes stayed behind. This did too." She took a glossy red paper sack from the bag, and from the sack a small black-velvet-covered box. She opened the hinged lid of the box to reveal a gold ring. "It's your wedding ring. Would you like it back?"

Her eyes pled with him to say yes. Feeling overwhelmed, he responded mutely by holding up the hand that was still on the table and offering it to her with the fingers spread.

"No, not that hand, you dummy." She went around the table and took his left hand. At first the ring would not go past the knuckle of his ring finger. She moistened the ring with her tongue and tried again and with a shove and a twist heaved it over the knuckle and into place. "There. That's the second time I've put it on you. The first was at our wedding. Does it bring back anything?"

He held the hand close to his face and examined the ring front and back. "What are the figures on it? I can't make them out."

She reached again into the jute bag and took out a brown glasses case and handed it to him. "Here. You left these behind too."

He took the pair of wire-rimmed glasses from the case but hesitated to put them on.

"What are you waiting for?" said Cat.

"I don't know," he said, frowning. "There's something about them. Are you sure they're mine?"

"I was with you when you bought them, Raymond."

"Well … if you say so."

He made to put the glasses on, but had no more than touched the frames to his temples when they popped out of his hands and slid into place on their own. Both he and Cat heard the soft sucking sound that accompanied this inexplicable occurrence, and were both amazed, but only Raymond felt the rush in his mind as of a wave crashing. When that was over, it was as if he were just coming out of the ocean again, purified and renewed, only this time without a completely clean slate.

He looked at Cat closely through the glasses, and filled his lungs with the honey butter smell of her.

"Sweetheart," he said. "Where are we? What am I doing in these clothes?"

"You know me?"

"Know you? Of course I know you." He looked around the room, at the interrogation table, and again at his prison uniform with consternation. "What's going on?"

"I'll explain it in a minute," Cat said, putting her arms around him. "First just hold me. And then be still while I kiss your face off."

It seemed he had returned to her completely. He remembered himself as Raymond Kidd, he looked like himself now that he was out of the prison uniform and into the clothes she had brought him from home, and he was as happy to have her with him as he had been in the first year of their marriage. Her cup, she thought as they walked hand in hand out of the police station into a bright sunny day, was overflowing.

The first check to her perfect good fortune came in the parking lot when Raymond balked at putting the key into the ignition of his old pickup.

"What's wrong?" she said from her seat on the passenger side as he sat there with the key in his hand and his hand in his lap, staring at the steering wheel. "I thought you'd like to be the one to drive us home."

"I don't know if I can do this," he said.

"Why not? Don't you remember how?"

"Technically, yes." He put the keys down on the console between them and held his hands up before him. "It's just that when I look at the wheel, all I can imagine holding in my hands are reins. As if I need a carriage, not a car, and horses, not horsepower."

She told him not to worry about it. They changed places and she drove. He was very quiet and kept rolling the window up and down. This she would have found irritating anyway, but especially so now. What she wanted was for him to talk to her and tell her where he had been all these months. Had he really gone back and become someone else? Was he really ready to be himself again? Not only that but her husband and *her* husband only? She wanted his complete attention, and he was spellbound by a stupid window.

"Raymond, stop that and talk to me!" she blurted out finally, after she had become so flustered that on their way out of town she had driven around the Rotary twice before getting off onto St. Margaret's Bay Road. "What on earth are you doing, anyway?"

"I'm sorry," he said, frowning slightly as he clasped his hands in his lap. "I was just thinking what a great idea. I suppose it's been patented."

"What, window winders?"

"Yes."

"Raymond, window winders have been around forever. Even automatic windows aren't new. You know, the ones where you just click a button and they go up and down on their own? Hello?"

"Right, right. Of course. Love, please forgive me. It's like I'm flickering back and forth in my mind. One minute I'm Raymond and the next ..."

"Yes?" said Cat. "And the next?"

"The next I'm Oliver. Captain Oliver Cole." He looked out the window as they passed a woman walking along hand in hand with a young girl, both in flowered bathing suits with beach towels draped over their shoulders. As he watched, he felt a pulsing at his temples as if a current were running through the frames of his glasses. The faces of the two swimmers for an instant took on the features of two other faces he had known. He pressed his hand against the glass as if to reach out to them. His voice quavered. "Who had a daughter named Amélie. And a wife named Josephine."

Cat was having trouble steering. She wanted to pull over and leave the truck on the side of the road and walk into the woods and keep walking. She wanted to swerve into the other lane and hit the first thing that offered. She wanted to shift into reverse just to see what would happen.

"Raymond," she said, after a supreme effort brought them safely to rest inside the yellow outlines of a parking space at the Bayer's Lake Superstore, "we have a lot to talk about. I don't know where you've been, exactly, or what's happened to you. Angle told me a little. But I can't talk about it now. I have to calm down. I have an ordinary life again, and ordinary things to do. Right now we've got groceries to get, and a good bottle of wine, and some fabric from Fabricville. Tonight we'll have a special dinner to celebrate your homecoming. After that we'll catch up. Till then just be Raymond as much as you can. When you can't, I don't want to hear about it. Okay?"

"Angle," Raymond mused. "I remember an Angle. And Octave, his brother. Two ghosts from my basement …"

"*Lost souls,*" Cat snapped, cutting him off. "Not ghosts. Lost souls. But let's not talk about them either. Not till later. Now roll your window down just a little, so it doesn't get so hot in here, and let's go shopping."

In his confusion of identities, he seemed childlike to her. Her instinct was to keep him close, so he would not wander away and disappear again. But she remembered he liked shopping, had been better than her, in fact, at reading labels to find out the ingredients of things, and in comparing prices and finding bargains. Doing it on his own again, she reasoned, might help settle him back into himself. She sent him off to get steaks. Told him not to worry if he could not find her afterwards—she would wait for him at the checkout counter. But he was not long at all in catching up with her again. She was still in produce when he dropped two plastic-wrapped t-bones into the cart.

"Here, honey" he said. "It's hard to see the marbling the way they spread the labelling all over the whole package now, but I think these should do. I know you like tenderloin, but that was forty dollars a kilogram, and these are on sale for fifteen."

The easy intimacy in his voice pleased and disarmed her. This was how it had been when they were good together. She didn't mind if he never remembered how it had been when they weren't.

"They'll do fine," she said. "Honey."

At the liquor store he did fine too. They went together this time because they had only one thing to get, but he led, and checked the sections by country, and completely on his own chose a three-year-old pinot noir that they had tried before and loved, the grapes of which came from his parents' vineyard in Mendocino.

At Fabricville, feeling confident and relaxed and knowing he was completely out of his element, she cut him loose completely and left him to wander the aisles as had always been his habit when they visited the store together.

With his knowledge no longer being called on, Raymond's mind ticked back to neutral. The curiosity that took over was that of a child. He roamed among the bolts and swatches and swathed dummies with an outstretched hand, feeling the different textures, marvelling at the myriad colours and patterns.

He had stopped at a print of sailing ships on a blue background and pulled out a length to admire when Julia Barnes spotted him and made straight for him.

"Hello," she said. "That's very pretty, isn't it? What does it make you think of?"

She was appealing to look at—the gold chain that dipped into the cleavage of her low-cut blouse was particularly inviting—but there was a false quality to her inquiry, an assumed friendliness, that called forth a lingering memory in Raymond of a time when he was restrained and accosted by doctors speaking to him in the same manner. It tripped a switch. He answered as Oliver Cole.

"Why do you ask?" he said. "Do you mock me? Have you read that I am mad? Do you expect me to say it makes me think of another lifetime to which I have travelled? If you refer to my incarceration, has it not occurred to you that you run the risk of my biting your nose off, or doing some other mad thing?"

"I'm sorry," Julia said. "I didn't mean to offend you. I'm Julia Barnes from BTV News. And you are?"

She held out a hand. He ignored it. He rolled the ship-printed fabric back up and turned to her. "Why do you ask?" he said again.

"I need to know," she said with an easy smile, shrugging. "You're the Man Who Came Out of the Sea. I told your story on my show and now people are talking about you. You're the mystery of the hour. I need the rest of your story—who you are, what you do, what happened to you. You say you were … incarcerated?"

The switch tripped again and he was Raymond. He rubbed his hands together that sported Raymond's wedding ring. He rubbed his beardless cheeks and looked down at his black tee shirt that had the red stag of Keith's Brewery for a logo. "I'm sorry," he said. "That was a long time ago.

A very long time ago. I'd rather not talk about it. Now if you'll excuse me, I have to get back to my wife."

"Look," Julia said, "I'm not mocking you, and you don't have to talk to me. But you're going to have to talk to someone. You can't do what you did in broad daylight in public and not talk about it."

"What did I do? I went swimming. No big deal."

"You didn't just go swimming. You came out of nowhere from under the sea, in only your birthday suit, and then went strolling down the avenue letting it all hang out till the cops picked you up. You didn't know who you were, what had happened, or where you were going. You're with your wife now so it all must have come back to you. If it's really no big deal, why don't you just tell me about it?"

"I can't," Raymond said. "I made a promise." He pushed past her and headed for the sales counter, where he could see Cat paying.

"Look," Julia called after him, "I'll find out who you are. That's no problem for me. But it might be a problem for you to have reporters from all over camped outside your house, which is what's going to happen, I guarantee you. But I can keep it from happening if you give me an exclusive."

As he and Cat drove away, with Cat's purchases in a plastic bag in his lap, the news woman ran into the parking lot, hampered by her tight skirt and stumbling on her high heels. "Please!" she shouted. "Think it over and call me!"

"Who is that?" Cat asked.

Raymond was watching to see what car the woman went to. He watched in the rearview mirror and then out the window as they turned onto the street. He saw her hobble to a BTV van and get in. He looked ahead at the traffic light at the end of the block. "Could you go a little faster," he said, "so we can get through that light? She's a reporter. I don't want her following us."

"A reporter? She looked more like a fashion model." Cat looked at herself in the rearview mirror, at the grey in her brown hair and the wrinkles around her eyes and the sagging skin under her chin. "Is it some young thing you got pregnant? Is that where you've really been?"

The light turned yellow. Cat took her foot off the accelerator and downshifted.

"Please go on through."

"Raymond, answer me."

Raymond's mind was like a TV with the channels being flipped through. He saw Josephine, Amélie, the reporter, his sometime lover Mimi. He saw himself as Oliver Cole being restrained with leather straps across his body and a gag in his mouth, his reward for insisting he had lived in the future. Again an electric sensation raced through his glasses and into his temples. He clapped his hands to the sides of his head. He looked at Cat and saw her as a skeleton behind the wheel.

"I love you," he said. "I think I may throw up."

She stepped on the gas and sped through the red light just as the cross traffic started into the intersection. Horns blared behind them.

"Should I pull over?" she said.

"No. Just take me home. I'll be okay once we're alone." He forced the last words out though he could not look at her again. At least not at the moment. He waited for the surging in his glasses to stop. He had tried to take them off and when they would not budge he had remembered they would not come off. He took a deep breath and put his hands down and then with a further effort reached over and gave Cat a reassuring squeeze on the thigh. "I'll be all right," he said. "Nothing happens, eh?"

She wanted things to be ordinary. It was ordinary for Raymond to shrug off painful situations with Buddhist sayings, this one so popular it had been a bumper sticker. The sexy sea green Italian sports car had worn one that had rolled into Halifax with him as a newly landed immigrant. So she was inclined to agree. In their time together she had hated it when he squashed her complaints with such sayings. Now it was like a lifeline back to the ordinary. And he did want to be with her.

A sedan sped around them with its horn honking furiously and three arms extended out the windows all shooting them the finger. The vehicle veered close, almost sideswiping them. Startled, Cat swerved onto the gravel shoulder and then back to the highway. The truck fishtailed and then straightened.

"Right," she said to Raymond. "Nothing much. But you should still put on your seat belt. How many times do I have to tell you? You should always put on your seat belt. And you never do."

They made the long curving turn onto the coast highway that would take them almost all the twenty-five kilometres to the village through a stretch of sparsely inhabited countryside uninterrupted by traffic lights or stop signs. Twenty-four and a half kilometres later, on the peninsula road with the village just over the rise, they drove into the fog.

Raymond rolled down his window and sighed at the inrush of cool salt air and the age-old melody of gulls crying and surf crashing. "Jiggity jig," he said wearily. "Home at last. And isn't that curious? Now the glasses let up."

Although they still would not come off, the glasses had indeed let up. They rested dormant on Raymond's face, the searing energy gone that had emanated from them and penetrated him from ear to ear, and they functioned again seemingly as ordinary glasses. Cat was Cat and not a skeleton any longer. He exchanged waves with Nettie McEachern leaving the village for her early evening walk, and as they drove past her she did not rot and wither but maintained her upright and wiry old woman's body with its cloud-white hair and wrinkled tan and thin-lipped smile that exposed no teeth and eyes of inner mirthfulness that betrayed no surprise. Nor did his next-door neighbour Durlyn O'Keefe deteriorate as he welcomed Raymond home across their yards, the carpenter getting into his red pickup as Raymond got out of his green one. And did he bring back any California wine?

The glasses, however, were not inactive altogether. Their presence was felt like a tweak or a slap or a gouge or a bite by every ghost and lost soul in the vicinity, and these were many, one at least to every house and a slew of others outdoors, under the little bridge through which the cove flowed to the back bay, under the government wharf, in the jungles of Japanese knotweed, among the granite outcroppings that buffered the village from the relentless sea, in certain seagulls, deer, seals, whales and lobsters, in the porcelain angel that hollow and headless lay half in the mire on the floor of the harbour under Gordon Daggon's dock.

In the nearby barachois, the natural spirits rustled and murmured like the leaves on the low trees in the stiff onshore breeze.

Under the basement of 7 Lands End, a demon growled with a sound like a rock splitting, and hugged its prey more closely.

Raymond set the groceries on the kitchen's wooden countertop, so familiar with its knife scars and skillet burns and coffee and beet stains, and stood gazing over the sacks and out the kitchen window at the cove with its rocks, boats, docks and stages just so, a view he had seen swept with rain and cloaked with snow and mesmerizingly brilliant under the sun and hauntingly obscure as it was now in the blowing fog. Then he turned and took Cat in his arms and held her so tightly she complained, and out of an overpowering emotion that was half thankfulness and half unrequitable longing he whispered, "Please, never leave me again, and never let me leave," not giving a damn how unrealistic and corny it sounded.

Of the two who were back in the basement, one said, "There's your captain." And the other, "Aye, if you're meaning the one I went back for. The one underneath is no cap'n o' mine, may his black heart be damned. I wish he had never been born."

"Then you wish we had never been born," Octave said.

"I don't wish it," said Angle. "But I wouldn't mind it. Forgive me, brother."

Even after she had begun to disbelieve in it, Cat had bought things for Raymond's homecoming. Over the months of his absence she had accumulated candles, incense, lingerie, gifts, romantic music, scented bath oil, everything that caught her eye she thought might heighten that first evening of their reunion and remind him she was the love of his life.

Now he was really here and her loyalty had paid off. She lit the pair of crème-coloured tapers that stood in silver candlesticks her mother had left her, and turned off the room lights. A salad of kale and red cabbage with sunflower seeds was already on the table. She served it in shallow gilt-edged china bowls. In the softer light, the chips and cracks along the rims were subsumed in the glow of the gold. The matching plates on which Raymond was serving the grilled steaks were likewise transformed. She felt radiant herself in a new cotton yukata with cranes flying over a full moon, and thought Raymond in his new yukata with its pattern of elegant white knots on an indigo background had never looked more handsome.

She switched off the cello sonata with its dignified deep sadness that was so uplifting, and asked Raymond to pour their wine from its crystal decanter. Outside in the evening doves were calling and could be heard clearly through the sliding screen door to the deck, where Raymond had been barbecuing. A slight stirring of the night air made the candle flames flicker. Raymond moved to slide shut the glass door but Cat stopped him.

"Let them flicker," she said. "I want to hear the doves."

They ate their way through the salad and steaks and were poring over brandy-filled chocolates when Cat's sense of what was necessary finally broke the spell. She had waited for him to be forthcoming with his story, but he seemed content to simply sit and chew and gaze at her, so she told him her story to get things going. She started with Angle and Octave and her first encounter with them, and finished with the failed summoning and the disappearance of the brothers along with the Simple.

"There was a flash and an awful smell like something shorting out, and they were gone and the bell was gone. I got Gordon out the door and put your father to bed."

"Tears of fire, eh?" said Raymond. He shook his head and chuckled.

"You don't believe me?"

"It's not that I don't believe you. It's just so much like something in a dream."

She pushed his plate aside to reveal the blackened burn marks underneath. "There. Is that a dream? That's where they fell. I watched them smoke and sizzle. And you, you went back to another life, didn't you? You had another wife. And a child. Was that a dream?"

"No, it wasn't. I'm just saying … I don't know what I'm saying. It's like some sort of cosmic joke."

He looked handsome, even younger, more like the man still in his thirties that he was when they met. But there was a tiredness in his eyes. She had watched him all through dinner trying to rub them, trying to get the glasses off or at least lift them up so he could get his fingers underneath. She wanted to ask him about the glasses but was afraid to. Instead she said, "You must be tired. You've had a long trip. Two hundred years long, from what I can gather. Why don't you tell me *your* story now? Then we can go up and have a bath and get on with this celebration."

He tried. He was best with the story within a story that was Captain Cole's recounting to Amélie of the voyage to Calcutta and the destruction by fire of the Bonne Chance. He was particularly convincing during the part about the mad Tibetan monk and the gift of the bell and dorje. She could smell the hashish in the cowhide merchant's hookah, feel the heavy heat of the Indian summer, see the madman ring the bell and wave the dorje, and the dead man stand and bow. He became so involved himself that at the Tibetan's stopping of the Captain's heart with the mere laying on of his small brown pink-palmed hand, he gasped and pulled back his yukata to see if the impression of the fingers was still there. But when it came to the Captain's time with his other family in Halifax, he faltered.

"I'm sorry," he said. "Not much comes back to me here. I think … I think I remember Calcutta because of the monk, and because I told the story. But other than the *fact* of Amélie and Josephine, the rest of it's gone like a dream. I feel the memory. I just can't open it up."

"The Simple said you could hear us ringing and calling. Could you? Did you see Angle at all when he went back for you?"

"I don't remember. The last thing I saw was the sun in my eyes and a hand with a bell coming out of the air. I remember reaching out for it. Then I fell and kept falling. I couldn't see anything. It was all in the dark."

"It was six months ago that we summoned you. That's a long time to fall."

"Yes, it was."

He stopped chewing the chocolate that was in his mouth. His eyes blinked shut and his head nodded forward. Then he looked up and swallowed. He tried to rub his eyes again, encountered the glasses, and cursed under his breath.

Cat got up. "Come on," she said, taking his hand. "Let's take our bath. I don't want you falling asleep on me."

But he did. Upstairs, in the master bedroom, he fell asleep on top of her as he was telling her how much he loved her. He knew the hurt it caused her, knowing that he had another wife. In his passion, he felt he knew that Josephine had never loved him like this, so intensely and completely. He tried to explain. He said, "Josephine … Josephine", and then collapsed, with his glasses pressed into Cat's breast.

The silver in his once-dark wavy hair reminded her of whitecaps on the sea. She stroked the waves and whispered to him, "Raymond, this is your home now. I need you. Come home." She let him lie while the tears came, and then she rolled him off. She saw he had not drunk his wine. She tried drinking it for him, but choked in her sorrow. Then she put out the candles around them and turned on her bedside lamp and made a list of things to do, of ordinary things to do.

The muttering in the basement began again, and again Raymond lay listening.

He found Angle and Octave sitting on the deep freeze, in a glow of their own making, dressed as they had been that winter night when they froze to death. Both their bodies and their pipes glowed. Even the smoke had a faint luminescence.

"Well, if it isn't the prodigal son," Octave said.

"What's that? What are you saying?" demanded Raymond.

"Which he can't hear us," said Angle. "He don't even know who we are." He cupped a hand to his mouth and bellowed as if from ship to ship at sea. "Sir, it's Angle and Octave, reportin' for duty!"

All Raymond heard was more static, though with the volume turned up.

"This return through the flaw, it has *shivered his timbers,*" said Octave. "And were he not wearing the glasses, he would not even see us, I think."

Raymond himself suspected the glasses. And not only of revealing the two apparitions. His own hands were glowing, from the tips of his fingers to just past his wrists. He held them up and made fists and then opened them again.

"Now what's he a'doin' of?" inquired Angle. "Has he gone moonstruck in the bargain?"

"His glasses were repaired by a lost soul with power. There's no telling what all he sees."

"Would that I had the power," said Angle, suddenly eloquent. "To undo what I have done, and to cast into a farther hell the one who has profited."

Octave laid his pipe aside on the lid of the freezer. "Let us reintroduce our captain to our devil. Mayhap that will recall him to his duty."

"Aye? And should that fail, then what?"

"Then we are lost. But that is nothing new."

The brothers got down from the freezer and motioned for Raymond to follow them.

"Yes, and why should I follow?" Raymond wanted to know.

For an answer, Angle crossed himself.

"That means nothing to me, spirit."

"For Christ's sake," Octave said, "That won't help. He's a Boodhist. You have to kowtow to Boodists to show you're sincere."

"Get down on my knees? I won't do it."

"It's for Jenny, brother."

"Any gate, I don't know how it's done."

"Yes, you do. We've watched Raymond up there in his shrine room. Here, like this." He backed up to the workbench along the far wall, put his hands together as if in prayer, touched them to his forehead, throat and heart, and then dropped to the concrete floor and slid himself out flat, face down, hands stretched out in front of him as far as they would go. Angle copied him. Octave said, "Now, a couple more times."

Raymond watched the two spooks prostrate to him. It was not right that they should—he was not someone to prostrate to—but he was moved by it, and when Angle gestured to him with a palm scratched and bleeding from sliding on the rough concrete, this time he followed.

"Now, that was a masterful touch," said Octave, as they proceeded on hands and knees through the square opening into the crawlspace.

"What was?" said Angle.

"The bloody hand."

"That just happened. I didn't plan it."

"It would never have occurred to me."

"In course it wouldn't."

Under the water pipes and wiring and ventilation ducts they went, Raymond having to actually crawl on his belly to get under the ducts. He felt extremely apprehensive. There was something reptilian about crawling that threatened the humanness he had just regained. Or thought he had regained. His glowing hands suggested otherwise—that he was not back altogether. Also his memory was stirring again. The last time he was here, he had a flashlight in his mouth, and he was swimming at this point.

"Where are you taking me? And why am I doing this?" he mused aloud.

"Which we're a'takin' you to see what's what," Angle said, as if he could be heard. "And you're a'doin' of it because you're the cap'n."

The hum of the sump pump was loud, yet it had not drained the long narrow pool that led between folds of the polyethylene away into the dark. They crawled close to the edge of the water. The pump switched itself off. Angle said, "She's in there, Cap'n, and it's you as has to help us get her out, though it was me as put her in. For I can't go there, though I have tried. Lord knows."

Able to hear Angle again suddenly and not realizing it, Raymond thought to himself there was no way the pool could be that deep. It was just a shallow skim of water from the frequent flooding that stayed trapped in the polyethylene.

"Can you see her?" said Angle.

A light shone from far down in the pool.

"I see a light," said Raymond. "But it can't be."

"It can be, and it is. And now you can hear me again, sir, and thank Heaven for that, may I beseech you not to waste a minute but go and see what you can do."

"You want me to go down to that light?"

"Aye, yer Honour, and sort things out, and bring my Jenny back."

"What makes you think … wait, you are Angle. Angle Daggon. And you're Octave. And Jenny is …"

"The Simple, that Cat was a'tellin' you of. Who ought to ha' been my wife. I was holdin' on to her when I went to bring you back."

"Angle, what's happening to your face?"

"His tears burn," said Octave. "They actually burn. And so they leave a trail. Now that he can cry again, which he hasn't since he was a boy, it happens every time. Picturesque, don't you think? Like something from the South Sea Islands, tattoo-wise."

"Shut your gob, would you? Sir, keep yer eye on the light, please. I meant well. I did. It fair tears my heart, to think I meant well and yet this is what happened."

"Exactly what *did* happen, Angle, and what am I supposed to do about it? I can't go down there. I'd need diving gear."

"Just keep yer eye on the light. You can make it, yer Honour, and when you do, just bring her back. I'll tell you all about what happened later."

Raymond kept his eye on the light, and as he did so, it grew in brilliance. It was not as if it grew toward him, but as if he grew toward it, as if without moving he were being plunged fathom after fathom face first toward the distant source. And as he came nearer, much later, after it seemed like he must have descended halfway to China, the light resolved itself into the luminous nakedness of the Simple. She lay on her back, half sunk in a roiling blackness that seethed around her on the pool's bottom. An inky arm had extended itself up by her floating red hair and bent at the elbow was buried in her mouth. The gross thickness of that black arm had stretched her lips beyond all limits. The horror in her distended eyes that Raymond first beheld from the outside, he experienced firsthand from the inside as helplessly he kept going right into her.

Time in the in-between is an erratic thing, sometimes the same as normal time, sometimes not. Sometimes a stroll there eats up months, as was the case with Raymond's return from his other life. Sometimes it is just the reverse, and an eternity there is no more than a minute in the world of the living, and so it was with Raymond in the Simple in the demon.

The demon's absorption of the Simple was infernally slow mainly because the demon liked it that way. Her purity was more delicious than German marzipan made with rosewater; the demon's way of taking her in was like having a lick at a time. She was an unlooked-for treat, delivered by Angle's mistake and the flaw in the fabric. Raymond's presence was another effect of the flaw; he had not altogether come out of the in-between, as witnessed by his glowing hands, and so he had easily slipped back in, and now he was subjected to her hellish devouring, enduring every agonizing instant, on an on for what seemed like centuries.

Bodily this felt as if acid were eating him, mentally as if all of his fears multiplied tenfold had their fingers in a crack in the very essence of his being and were slowly but surely prying him apart.

In what consciousness he could muster, he called for help, first as an adult, naming his Buddhist teachers in this life and visualizing them and pleading with them to give him the strength that he needed, but latterly as a child. The pain was so crushing that all he could remember was the prayer his mother taught him as a boy:

Now I lay me down to sleep
I pray the Lord my soul to keep
If I should die before I wake
I pray the Lord my soul to take

Finally he was nothing but a layer of dust, completely pulverised and speechless.

He heard a familiar voice then. "O Dog. My master says, you have not called *his* name."

"Ajay?"

"Ajay no more. Now Thunder's Reach, o luckless one. But my master's name is still the same. He says you are not seeing clearly, that you must find what you need to see clearly."

"What must I find?"

"You must do the thing properly. Call on my master. "

"I don't remember his name."

"He gave you two gifts. He was named after one. I am named after him."

"Please, just tell me."

"No, you must exert yourself. If I am Thunder's Reach, then he is …?

"Thunder."

"He is Tibetan, not English."

"Please …"

"Think. He rang the bell. He waved the …"

"I don't know. He was mad. You said not to trust him."

"What did he wave to bring the dead man back to life?"

"A … *dorje*. His name is Dorje."

"I'm afraid I am doing your work. Still, he may come."

She woke to the stale smell of his unfinished wine in its glass by the bed, and remembered him saying at dinner that although it was good, he found it difficult to drink. In his transit between lives, he had dreamed a strange dream, one in which he was dropped in a giant goblet of wine. It was from the sensation of drowning that he had awakened as Raymond Kidd again and staggered out onto Point Pleasant Beach wreathed in seaweed.

Although the dream wine was more than excellent, the sensation of drowning in it, he said, had been more than horrid.

She took the coaster from under his glass and put it over the top and got up and switched on the vent fan in the bathroom to get rid of the smell. Then she went looking for him.

The night was still and clear, the fog having retreated offshore. The stars shone as they do in skies undiluted by city light, breathtaking in their endless layers and their illumination of the vast expanse. By their light, standing at the glass doors by the kitchen table, she could just make out Raymond down on all fours in the backyard, his unbelted bathrobe hanging loose around him, groaning AH AH AH.

For a moment she thought he had gotten drunk anyway, and terrible memories and then anger welled up. Her hand went to the switch on the wall that would turn the porch light on and expose him, let him see himself in his humiliating state. Then she changed her mind. He had been through a lot, and she didn't want the O'Keefes next door seeing him like that. She took a flashlight from a cupboard and went out.

He was not being sick. He was licking the lawn.

"What on earth are you doing?" she said. "Are you out of your mind?"

He looked up at her with his wet face glistening but his glasses untouched. "Yes, a little," he said, "but it's getting better now. I'm taking the antidote. And then we have to gather it, a lot of it."

"The antidote?"

"The dew, which is perfectly pure."

"Which I have heard some strange things in my time," said Angle, who was on his knees near Raymond, trying to brush the condensation into the palm of his hand, "but this bears the bell away, so to speak."

Octave had found a spider web between two dandelions and was flicking it to make the droplets release into his own outstretched palm. "Well, we are out of the basement again, and that is a blessing," he said. "And perhaps it will serve." He stopped to moon at Cat. "She is a rare beauty, is she not?"

"One, you cain't hardly see her behind that there torch. Two, she is a little past her prime for me. And three, stop your jawin' and pay attention to what you're a'doin'. It's Jenny is the beauty that's a'needin' of us now."

From her vantage point in the turret across the way, Shannon O'Keefe watched the scene through her father's binoculars. "I wish I could read lips," she said. "I bet what they're saying is important. They're probably planning a terrist piracy. Conspiracy."

"I wish my binoculars worked as well as yours," said Julia Barnes, who sat beside her at the window. "I can barely make them out."

"These are special," said Shannon. "My daddy got them for sailing at night. Here, you look through them."

As she took the glasses, the reporter gave silent thanks. She had certainly done the work to get here, getting Raymond's name from the fabric store clerk and his address from the store's phone book, tracking him to his house with her cellphone and the internet's mapping resources, knocking on doors and asking questions of his neighbours along the lane, but it was certainly something very like divine providence that led her to the very person who made it her business to keep a close eye on 7 Lands End, and at the same time let the girl's parents be away overnight with the girl's grandmother at a hospital in Halifax.

In the greenish illumination of the night glasses, she could see Raymond and Cat perfectly. There was something else, however, that she could not quite make out. Off to one side of the couple, further into the yard, a disturbance in the air seemed at moments to define in highlighted outlines two other persons kneeling or crouching in the grass. And then the outlines would dissolve and she would think she was imagining things. And then a village cat in its pursuit of some nocturnal prey stopped suddenly right between where the two outlines had been, and peered from side to side, and pawed the air and hissed.

"The monk's leathery old face came to mind and I began to weep," Raymond was saying. "His lips were moving but I couldn't hear him. All I could hear was Ajay's translation. He said Dorje agreed to take me as his student. I said but I hadn't asked. He said it was because I was too dumb to ask and only knew how to weep, that if we were to wait until I finished weeping, we would be there for another thousand years. I said but I already have a teacher in this life. Ajay said to see Dorje as no different than him but only a reverse emanation. Then I was told to stop talking and listen. I was not really stuck but only *a prisoner of my own compassion*. To really engage the demon and free the Simple, I have to gather enough in-between juice to make a looking glass into the past, where I will see what I need to overcome the demon. Whatever it is, I have to find it in the world of the living, and then properly enter the in-between again and actually go down in the pool instead of only imagining myself there. And then he snapped his fingers, Dorje did that is, and I was back in the crawlspace with Octave and Angle, as if no time at all had elapsed, and Angle was in my face saying *"Well, if you can see the bloody light, why don't you go on down there?"*

Raymond stopped talking and took several more vigorous licks of the lawn. When he looked up again, Cat shone the flashlight in his face and said, "Your eyes are bloodshot. It couldn't have been the wine. You didn't even finish yours. You've been off drinking rum, haven't you? Well, I'll forgive you this one time. After all you've been through, I guess it was to be expected. Please stop licking the grass. You look demented. I'll get you a glass of water."

"It won't work," Raymond said. "It has to be pure."

"I'm not getting it from the cistern. I meant the bottled water. That's purified."

"No, you don't understand. It gave me the black megrims, being down there so long, what we now call a migraine, I think, but one so arcane that the only thing for it is in-between juice—morning dew, that forms in the dark and is perfectly pure on its own and not from some treatment."

"Your mad monk told you that too?"

"Yes," he said, and took another lick, "And it also makes the mirror. Catriona, I'm not drunk, and I can't go back to bed. There's no time to lose. You have to believe me. Now, be an angel and help in the gathering."

❀

Remembering his shipboard days when he was Captain Daggon, but having been reduced to a sludge-like form with limited vocal abilities, he called himself *Capaggon*. He was a brutish demon, being of the rock variety, but not a stupid one. He had a very good idea of what was going on— the intruder had been in the mind of his prey, and his prey had no secrets from him. There was a plan afoot to rob him of her.

He was also, despite his reduction, someone still to be reckoned with. Early on, after his hanging and at the outset of his residence in the underlying rock, he had driven his son Angus to saw the family home in half to keep from sharing it with his brother Octavius. Then through the years, as the half that stayed there was sold out of the family and rebuilt and inhabited by strangers, he had affected them one after the other, radiating negativity like a dark hidden star. That radiation had inspired Norris LeClerq to burn his fishing boat rather than sell it when he was too old and stove up to use it anymore, vowing he would rather *see her in Hell than have another at her wheel*. It had cast a pall over the planned happiness of the Mikmaq lawyer Nora Lee, who bought the house from the demented LeClerq's relatives. And it had poisoned the marriage of Raymond Kidd and Cat McCallum.

When the flaw in the fabric visited 7 Lands End in the guise of a hurricane and flooded the basement, Capaggon had almost consumed Kidd himself. Now he had something better, a morsel pure as crystal and sweet as candy. She made him strong. He was not about to give her up.

In his strength, he was able to more than broadcast his negativity. He found he could direct it, even pinpoint it. It had no effect any longer on Angus, who had contemplated too long and too effectively on the dagger and rose, and Kidd seemed to have some protection. Instead he looked to Octavius, who was weak in his pride of never having behaved badly, and to Cat McCallum, who was tired and who wanted so badly for things to return to normal and for Kidd to once more be the man of her dreams. He focused on these two, and he shone toward them through the space, trying to ignite as if through a magnifying glass small dark fires in their hearts. It drained him and slowed almost to a standstill his ingestion of the Simple, but certain it would assure him of her in the end, he put up with the delay.

"Honey, would you stop shining that light in my face?"

"I *don't* believe you. Gather dew for a mirror? You'd need a bowlful. How are you going to get it, lick it up and spit it in?"

"I'll stop licking in a minute and start gathering."

"You and what army?"

"I've got Angle and Octave here helping."

"I thought they were confined to the basement again."

"I escorted them out again. I seem to be able to. I don't know why. Now, please, you're blinding me, and it's making my head hurt again." He held up a hand palm outward against the beam of her flashlight.

She switched the flashlight off. "There's nobody here, and no monk, and no demon. Just a drunk. You make me sick. I'm going back to bed. You can sleep out here."

"Sweetheart, please." He got up on his knees and reached out to her.

"Squeeze your in-between juice out of your robe. It ought to be wet enough."

He caught her robe as she turned to leave. She swung and slapped him so hard it knocked him onto his back. She saw that his glasses not only stayed on but were not knocked askew in the least, but she could not have cared less. If they were magic, he could have them. If they were cursed, he deserved them. She stood over him and said, "I'm leaving in the morning. I hate you."

Chapter 13

Mr. In-Between

They were a peculiar small herd of cattle on their elbows and knees on the lawn, foraging with china cups and butter knives in their hands, finding their way by starlight and the dim phosphorescence of their own bodies, scraping the dew into the cups drop by drop.

They had migrated to the deep grass over the septic field. The air smelled of the sea and the wild mint they had crushed under them and of a damp earthiness tinged ever so slightly with excrement.

Raymond sighed and set his cup down and stabbed his knife into the ground. "This is ridiculous," he said. "We've been at it for at least an hour, I'm soaked to the skin, and we haven't got enough dew between us to drown a fly, much less see visions in."

"Which a fly could die o' thirst for all I'm gettin'," Angle grumbled.

"There must be a better way," said Octave, whose thinning hair hung down damp over his eyes.

"It's even more ridiculous for you to look soaked too," Raymond said. "You're still in between. You can't get soaked."

Octave shoved his wet hair back over his scalp. "You have no idea, Mr. Kidd," he said, "no idea at all what it's like to be us. You skimmed through here, and maybe you do have one hand that's still in here, but we've been here a hundred percent for a hundred and fifty years, and I assure you, it would be just as easy for you not to be soaked as for me."

"Belay there," Angle growled. *"Not enough dew to drown a fly,* you say. You know what drowns a fly? A pitcher plant. Because why? Because they hold water, that's why. And if they hold water, it's bound to be pure. And you know where they grow? Why, in the barachois, that's where. I seen 'em eye to eye more'n once when I was lyin' there with Jenny. And if that's where they grow, why then, that's where we ought to be lookin'."

"You're a marvel of reasoning, brother," said Octave.

"It's worth a try," Raymond agreed. "We're certainly not getting anywhere here."

"All right, then. Let's go. You go first, sir, so as we can follow behind."

"Gentlemen," said Octave, "you go. Escort or no, I am done for the night. I feel strangely drained. I believe I must go back inside."

"But we need you, brother. It is all hands on deck now. For Jenny. Can't you push on?"

Octave rose unsteadily, leaving his cup and knife in the grass. "It's always you needing me, isn't it?" he said, glaring at Angle. "You get drunk and go off in a snowstorm, and it's me that comes after you. You cry because you killed us, and you lament and moan for all the evil things you've done, and it's me that has to comfort you and turn your mind around. And now your selfishness strikes again, and sends your lover to a devil, and it's *me* you take to task. *My* steadfastness you question. Well, to hell with you. You and your *captain* can go have your adventure. It's time I looked after myself."

He turned and stumbled into the house through the nearest wall, leaving Raymond and Angle agape.

"Wow. Mrs. Booda Ray has laid him out. He's flat on his back," said Shannon O'Keefe, having gotten her father's night vision binoculars back from the reporter.

"Yes, and that's not all," said Julia Barnes. She didn't need her listening device to hear Cat tell Raymond she hated him and was leaving—the whole neighbourhood could have heard—but she kept the dish on its pistol grip aimed at them through the open window anyway. It had been very useful in letting her hear Raymond's recounting of his encounter with the demon, and because of its recording function she now had twelve seconds of Raymond's own voice as testimony for any story she might write.

She didn't think it likely there would be any story, of course. The man was either crazy drunk, as his wife maintained, or simply crazy. Nevertheless she had taken the whole tale of the demon down in shorthand on her steno pad as she listened.

Later she was glad she had. The little girl saw it first. Raymond went into the house and came out with three china cups and three butter knives. But Julia too saw him hand two of the cups into the air, because each time the hand holding the cup became luminous, and the whole of the figure that was taking the cup also glowed. Then, though all was barely visible again in the dim starlight with no moon, the two cups could be made out floating over the lawn by themselves.

"It's the pirate!" said Shannon. "I couldn't reckanize the other, but the one with the braid down his back was the pirate that stole Booda Ray's dinghy."

Shannon told her all about the pirate and the dinghy and the wedding, and she made eager notes with a growing conviction that she had a story after all, and later when Raymond walked away up the road with one of the floating cups alongside, she did not hesitate to follow.

"Can I come too?" Shannon said, as Julia stuffed her listening device and headphones into her duffel bag and zipped it up and hefted it.

"It's a free country," Julia said. "You'll have to keep up, though. I can't wait for you."

"Oh, you won't have to wait for me. I won the hundred yard dash at my school. I'm fast."

"Well, come on, then. We've got to hurry or we'll lose them."

The two went down the turret ladder quick as firemen down a pole, and rushed into the night in pursuit.

The barachois was neither here nor there, a place where land and sea intermingled. Most of the time, the sand bar in the village's back bay was boundary enough, but at high tide the bar was topped and the connecting bogs that reached inland received their twice daily infusion of salt water. And something more. The spirits of the barachois had something of the ocean in them. They were easily moved and unpredictable, and where tamer spirits might simply have moved on, they resented the increasing and increasingly destructive incursions of humans into their habitat. The bulldozers were chewing up their home at the edges and spitting it out as lots for new oceanside subdivisions. When the Simple was among them and part of them, her compassion had served as a restraint, but she was gone now. Worse, they missed her, and wanted her back, and knew her absence had something to do with the humans. They were afoot in the fog now, sensing a

different sort of high tide, one that might carry them over the bar between their realm and that of the intruders, and this was an effect of the flaw in the fabric, that in Prospect had not been knit up.

They let the first two pass that came among them this night—one glowed and one had a glowing hand and this made them questionable—but the second two had no suggestion of protection, and them they led astray.

Angle and Raymond had filled their cups and were heading home. Raymond had some doubts about the pitcher plant liquid being pure enough. Weren't insects digested by the stuff? Might this not have an adverse effect on any vision seen in it? Could any vision at all be seen in it? But he was not about to mention these doubts to Angle, who was plowing ahead so he could hardly keep up. There was only one thing on the former pirate's mind and that was rescuing the Simple. His look of fierce grimness testified to it, and persuaded Raymond to at least have a go with what they had.

It was all he could do anyway to keep the juice in the cup at the rate they were going, splashing along through the boggy stretches with his rubber boots getting stuck in the mud, ducking under half-fallen firs, pushing through thick growths of willow, all in the foggy dawn with only the spectral radiance from Angus and his own hand to guide them.

The cries for help stopped them. Angus crashed on for a few steps but brought himself up with a string of nautical curses.

"And who would be here besides us?" he cried, turning.

"I don't know," Raymond said. "Can't you see them? You're in between again."

"In between or out, cain't see through fog."

"You've been taking us through it fast enough."

"It's 'cause I know the path. It's the one Jenny always used when we came in here to … well, it's a little growed-up now, but I could never mistake it."

Raymond could guess why the Simple and Angle had come into the barachois. The words *lie down together* were clearly the ones Angle had omitted. He placed his cup carefully in the rotten top of an old stump. "I'm sorry," he said. "But whoever this is, we have to help them too."

"Damn my eyes, don't I know it? And there's two on 'em, and they're not in the same place."

"We'll have to split up."

"And they're women."

"A woman and a young girl, I'd say. They must have strayed off the path."

Angle stuck his cup in the rot beside Raymond's. "Why they was *on* the path is what I'd like to know. And why it's *always women?* Can you answer me that?"

"I don't know," Raymond said. "I don't think I'll ever know that."

Julia Barnes was not a tall woman. This was not obvious on television where she was either sitting down or standing in high heels and having her height further enhanced by he camera angle. But it was quite obvious to *her* now that she had wandered off the trail, out of the bog and into the even soggier marsh nearer the sea, into water that was suddenly to her waist and among a growth of rushes that was higher than her head.

The blowing fog not only blanketed the landscape, effectively blinding her and rendering her flashlight useless, but also seemed to buffet and bully her physically. In fact it was less as if she had wandered and more as if she had been shepherded away from the path and from the little girl with her. The swirling smother had shapes in it now, nebulous fingers that urged and caressed her, and silvery vague faces that sighed and sung and kissed her all over, as if her jeans and tee shirt and zipped-up wind-break-er were not there, as if she were not dressed at all.

Her flashlight was plucked from her hand, and then her video camera from her waist, the case tearing free from her belt like wet paper.

She screamed once and the soft soothing voices said *sister don't worry, it's all right, we love you, we're bringing you home, welcome home, welcome home.*

She screamed a second time as she began to be laid down, and then the brackish water filled her mouth.

Little Shannon O'Keefe, though lost too, was having a different experience, one she didn't mind at all.

In the first place, she hadn't been too concerned at being separated from her new friend the TV star. Grownups were always wandering off, but they always turned up sooner or later. It seemed to be a point of honour with them. So she had responded to Julia's first few calls, saying, of course, that she was *over here*, and then, no, over *here*. After that it was as if someone had put cotton in her ears, the world became so quiet. It wasn't alarming to her to be lost, not in the barachois. She had played there often and knew you always came out somewhere. She didn't even think of it as being lost, really. She was where she was, and everywhere was worth being. There was always something to discover, like how on one rock, of a size you could climb on, there was both orange and green lichen, and if you looked long enough you could see faces in the differing patterns of colours; or how a mouse, venturing out of the tall grass in her presence, unafraid of her as anything, could be nosing and darting around bold as you please, almost at her feet, when suddenly out of nowhere, with no more warning than a spot blooming into a shadow, a seagull could swoop down and carry the mouse and its newly found confidence away and away and away in a curved yellow beak.

She was only slightly more amazed when she found herself surrounded by a band of children who appeared out of the fog, or rather detached themselves from it, for they were of the same substance only illuminated from within, with features that changed as you watched and could not quite be pinned down. But anyhow there was no time for watching. They wanted her to run and play with them. They danced around her in circles, one going one way and one going the other, mouthing her name in a way she heard inside her head without it ever coming in through her ears. And then they peeled out of the circles and took off in a line that was like a string of Christmas lights, and called for her to come after.

There were a few splashing steps as they took her into a creek and around its bend, but then they were out and racing uphill, up a steep hill at the top of which stood a single bent tree in the early light, with the fog stretching away down below in a broad unbroken sea. It was a stunted old hemlock with a cleft in its trunk that the lightning had made, and long branches that swept back as if being gathered to make a ponytail, having been blown that way since their inception by the winds from the sea.

When her new playmates danced into the tree one by one, Shannon followed them, laughing like them, like any maniac.

There was no question of choosing who to help. With the screams, Raymond saw Julia Barnes in his mind as he had seen her at the fabric store, provocative, with the gold chain dipping into her cleavage, and before he could even remark it to Angle he was gone, whipped away with a force that would have left him gasping had he not been underwater staring into the faraway eyes of the sinking reporter.

When he rose with her in his arms, in the pale light that preceded the morning, the fog spirits closed around them immediately, flowing, sliding, sighing, singing, kissing. One licked his hear and whispered, "You are naked. She is naked. That is nice. So very nice."

Looking down, he saw that this was true, that his clothes had not accompanied him (though he still wore the cursed glasses) and that hers were floating away, worn by a fog spirit doing a slow backstroke.

"Nice?" he said dazedly. "I think she's dead."

"No, no," said the multitude. "Sleeping. Only sleeping. Sleeping towards us. Coming home."

He looked down at the reporter. It was nice to look down at her. "Home? I don't think so. This can't be her home."

"Oh yes! It is! Oh yes! She left to go get us a human, and now she is back, and she has brought us one."

He thought they were lying. He thought it might help to ignore them. He slogged out of the water and laid his comely burden on the damp mossy ground and tried mouth-to-mouth resuscitation. After several tries, her bosom heaved slightly and her breath came faintly. Still she did not open her eyes.

"You cannot take her back. She is with us now."

The host of spirits parted to reveal a vapour among them that took on the disrobed form of Julia Barnes. Her features, though, like those of the others, seethed and smoked and slipped away in a silvery haze. The shape moaned with pleasure and beckoned to Raymond.

"She wants you to come too. See?" said the many.

They surrounded him in a slowly turning wheel, with their shadowy fingers pointing at him where he kneeled.

The captain had vanished, and Angle had guessed how he had gone and where, the woman having screamed only an instant before. He could guess why the woman was screaming, too, for though he could not see through the fog he could feel the presence of the barachois spirits and sense their threatening demeanor. He had meant to warn the captain of them, but had not been sure how to explain them, and he had taken too long.

As Angle was still in between, the clothes of his long-ago life did not leave him this time, and he landed where he meant to precisely, beside the sweptback hemlock where the call for help came, on his feet and only slightly unsteady.

Only the little girl was not there whose face he had envisioned, the little girl from the wedding, who had stood on the whale's jawbone and whose voice he had recognized when she called out from the fog.

He found to his surprise that he had a flintlock pistol in one hand and a cutlass in the other. He dropped them both. The cutlass clanged off a stone.

"Will I slash? Will I rage?" he said, shocked. "And for who, and against what?"

He looked around him in the daybreak at the sea of fog below that made the hilltop a lone island. At the foot of the hemlock was a little pile of clothing topped by a pair of diminutive pink tennis shoes.

"Where are you, Shannon O'Keefe?" he cried. "Didn't we have a glass o' grog to share?"

A fiery tear scored his cheek. "Oh Lord," he said, "not again. Where *is* she?"

"Mr. Pirate?"

The voice was muffled and faint and he could not make out the source at first.

"Mr. Pirate?"

"Child, I have *not* got all day. There's another as needs me. Speak up!"

"The tree. I'm in the tree!"

He stooped at the cleft in the trunk of the hemlock and peered in. As if from a distance, he saw her, retreating and growing smaller all the while. He touched the cleft and immediately shrank to the size of it, which was no bigger than his forearm had been, and stood there perched on the gnarled lip of the opening.

"Dear me," he said. And then he was gone, and it was less as if he had stepped in and more as if he had been sucked in, beard first.

Cat scribbled furiously in her gold-embossed green-leathered daybook that for the first time ever was doing double duty as a diary. Early on in her life, things to do had eclipsed in importance things already done, and she had let the daily record lapse. Now she felt she must express her feelings or explode. Yet the more furiously she wrote, the more explosive she felt. She shoved the pillows behind her into place for the umpteenth time. She was on Raymond's side of the bed. She had locked all the doors in the house and latched the windows.

She slashed her way down the page.

"Will I be able to read this later? I DON'T CARE! I won't have time! I'm two days behind schedule already! I haven't even started framing the Vajrakilaya thangka for Stephen Berlioz, haven't even rolled it out on the table because I don't want some wrathful deity staring at me like he wants to eat me alive. There've been too many spirits in this house already. But it has to be done, because is my husband working? No! And is the money his dad sends enough? No! And will I get paid if I don't do my work? NO! And I forgot to wish Johanna Cason a cheerful birthday, when I know how that will hurt her feelings. And that propane bill has to be questioned. There's no way I used that much gas when I kept the thermostat down all through the winter, let myself freeze half the time just because I was so low in my spirits. SPIRITS! OH GOD! Him and his spirits and his time travelling. Well, he can go on travelling for all I care. Why should I always be the one that leaves? The homeless one? He can leave this time. I'm his wife. This house is half mine. More than half! He ought to be committed. It ought to be all mine! All mine!"

In the bed beside Cat, though unbeknownst to her, lay Octave. He had been highly tempted to watch her change into her nightdress, but had averted his eyes at the last. She reminded him that much of his mother. Nor did he try to insinuate himself under the covers. He simply lay close, feeling the heat of her anger and being warmed by it, as he had lain by his mother as a child and been warmed on the nights when his father was away on the Queen Mab and she in her loneliness and disappointment had given vent to her hatred of her husband's murderous ways and cursed him till the walls rang.

These walls. Oh yes, the house had been divided and rebuilt and generations had come and gone through it, but they were essentially the same walls. His walls. All of them. Not a one should have ever been Angle's. The house should have gone to the sober, the dutiful, the law-abiding son. The son with the name of an emperor, *Octavius.*

He read Cat's last words with a thrill. Her last exclamation point had pierced right through the page. An emperor needed an empress, and here was one after his own heart, who knew what was hers and was ready to take it. Fierce, beautiful, capable of poetry if only as an unconscious channel, and when it came right down to it … not his mother. A little older than him, conventionally speaking, but what was twenty or thirty years really in the grand scheme of things? She was a kindred spirit and she would be his companion. And if he could not have her in the flesh, he would have her in the spirit. He would roam the house at her side and he would love her, and perhaps she would feel his presence through the intensity of his love. And perhaps some day the flaw would let him cross again and take her in his actual arms and make her his. All his!

In the form he had assumed, he had no mouth to smile, but the one who had once been Octave's father was very pleased with himself. On the deck of the Queen Mab he would have been laughing so hard they could have heard him in the maintop in a gale. He would never be rooted out of his rock. When it was time, when he had finished feeding, he would emerge on his own. He would be very powerful then, for the Simple in her purity was supernaturally nutritious food. He would roam, and he would forage, far and wide.

Till then, he would continue as he had begun, sending out like a heartbeat his anthem, his pith instruction, MINE MINE MINE, to the two who were so close now as to be almost one in his sight.

Nets, nets, nets. There were always nets to be sorted and dried out and patched, and these were one's own nets, and it was just as well that the work was endless because what else was there to do in a place where one was really no more than an afterthought.

But there was another net, and Victor Cooley though a lost soul was no fool. He checked it too. It did not contain sea creatures. It was a net of awareness, and its harvest was less tangible. It linked the population of the in-between in Prospect, and provided all the communication there was. You could not see or speak to anyone, or otherwise breach your solitude with messages of any length or detail, but you could sense who was there, and where they were, and how long they had been there. It was mostly the newly lost who made the noise. The rest tended to settle for some flavor of insensibility that made the pain of their particular dead end bearable. The most notable exceptions to this rule were the brothers Daggon, who were forever chattering to each other, and the demon Capaggon, who brooded and flared and who tainted the net with his seeping stinking sticky negativity.

This morning it was neither the newly lost or the long lost who were making the fuss, but the not-quite-lost, and this was something new and amusing. Victor had tuned in as he might have to a new radio program when he was alive and still an excitable young boy. For change was in the air. There was nothing you could do for established residents of the realm. Their suffering was unassailable. Even the newly arrived like the little girl under the government wharf who had drowned there while swimming, or the boy in the tree fort on Moon Island in the back bay who had been killed by a speeding motorist outside his home at the edge of the village— the ones his heart went out to—their transition was complete and beyond Victor's influence. But the not-quite-lost were a transient population. They popped in without properly dying and with a little help could be popped out again. He had discovered this with Octave and Angle during their brief sojourn among the living, and now he was getting a reading from two other accidental tourists who were less than pleased with where their turnings had taken them.

No, the land of shadows was not what it had been. There were leaks. He did not know how or why they occurred, but he intended to investigate them whenever they did. His constraints were less than those of other in-betweeners. He was stuck not in a particular spot but in a general area, that island-studded stretch of ocean around Prospect that he had fished for a living and had loved beyond anything.

Two of the new not-quite-lost, being in the barachois where he had often gone for eels, were just within his boundaries.

He cackled with glee as he rowed through the fog over the sandbar and into the salt marsh where Raymond and the reporter were being inducted by the enraged and out-of-control protector spirits of the barachois. And then he cast a net that was of his own making, and he cackled again.

Raymond felt himself called upon, not only by the spirits in their turning wheel but also by his teachers. Or his teacher. For they all became one in the mad monk, who was not laughing now but only watching through a peephole in his heart, to see if he had learned anything or would still be a fool.

He did his best. He raised his glowing hand to ward the spirits off and opened his mouth to pronounce the truth of their insubstantiality and so dissolve them back into the fog, but his hand froze in mid-gesture and the power of speech abandoned him.

He was fading. The wheel around him was turning and he was turning too, coming apart, blowing away. He was a dream person in a dream that was disintegrating. Was this dying again? Whoever he was, whoever he had come to be, he was no longer afraid of the process, but he was deeply discouraged that, given what he knew about the nature of things, he was unable to help anyone. Not the stranger beside him or the red-headed woman that the demon was devouring or the here-again-gone-again brothers Daggon. And he had left Josephine and his daughter Amélie without a word and now he was leaving Cat the same way.

Her honey butter smell filled what was left of his being unbearably. He did not care how angry she had ever been or what she had thrown at him or how she had criticized him. He loved her more than anything.

Still and always a fool. And so what?

He did not feel the net that was thrown over himself and the reporter Julia Barnes. It was a very light net, weighted only at its ends, and there was no more sensation in his flesh.

Reversing course through the wetland, Victor Cooley in his phantom dory slowly pulled back out to sea through the fog with a load of eels that squirmed and wriggled almost up to his knees, their bronze-black backs harmonizing with his black rubber boots, their silver bellies contrasting.

"Well, well, well. The livin' brung back by the dead," the old man said around his pipe, chuckling at his rare catch. "Blowed if we ain't all lost."

There was a wind inside Octave like the hurricane that had accompanied his rebirth. He had stewed and he had simmered, and now with the morning light in the windows he wanted to shake Cat awake and shout out to her that there was *no time to lose*. He would be born yet again and he would do it *now*. He wanted breakfast with its mouth-watering aroma of frying bacon and the chewing and the swallowing and the fine stupor of a full stomach. He wanted to change his antique clothes for modern ones, and not castoffs but something stylish that would turn Cat's head and make her look at him as someone she could love. *Should* love, for wasn't he the one who could give her what her current fool excuse for a spouse never could and never would?

He would shake the world and catch its riches as they fell out. If by accident he and Angle had brought enormous fish back from the in-between, creatures of an earlier time, what was there to prevent him from establishing a link to the past that would give him whatever he wanted? He could imagine himself into the vaults of a bank, into a jeweler's closed shop, into the hold of the *Queen Mab* itself where he could steal the booty from under his father's nose for an added relish. *And he could let it be known that this power was his.* Wouldn't the nabobs of all continents come calling?

And if he could reverse the link and yet keep it open, couldn't he go back and stay back and enjoy all the fruits of his future knowledge? He would know exactly what to buy and what to sell and what to invest in. He could predict the outcome of wars. He could become the single most important man on the planet. And he could share it all with Cat, whom he would take back too. She would never have to slave anymore over her sewing machine, straining her eyes and ruining her temper. She would be his queen, his good luck, his brightest ornament.

She would have a rocking chair inlaid with gold and encrusted with emeralds, and books bound in the finest leather, and he would sit and watch her rock and read, and there would never be a happier fellow.

And he would take them back and forth and each time make them young again, so they would never die.

All he needed was the emptiness bell. He had seen it dissolve boundaries in the hands of the Simple. Angle had misused and lost it, the snivelling ninny, but they both knew where it was. He had but to go down there and get it, down into the pool that was not really there, to his father—yes his father, for they both knew who it was though they refused to acknowledge it—to his father who owed him and knew it and would not mind yielding what could be of no use to a degenerate demon, a being of black sludge at the bottom of nowhere, who needed only to feed, and would be happy to feed undisturbed.

He could feel the wind welling within him, the heaven-sent wind. He resolved to go down there and not be afraid.

Although it was only for a couple of hours, Cat slept, and in that time, because she was so tired and her sleep so deep and dreamless, she was out of reach and could not be affected by the demon. When she woke therefore, although her body still ached for more rest, her mind was fresh and clear. Spying her open daybook on the floor, she retrieved it and reread what she had written in the night, and was appalled. She tore the sheet out, and the next one, and the next, till not even an indentation in the blank sheets remained. How she must have pressed with her pen! As if it were a sword she were stabbing him with, her Raymond, who had come back to her through the ages and whom she had denounced in a black mindless rage. She lay her head back on her pillow and let the tears flow.

She was thinking she had to get up and go find him, no matter how tired, when a familiar sound reached her, one she had heard only once but would never forget, a slithering great squelch of a sound like the one that had accompanied Angle's arrival on the stairs with the boatload of cod.

She grabbed her robe and ran to the stairs and was still tying the sash when she saw what had arrived this time—not cod but eels, and in the flipping roiling pile at the foot of the stairs, instead of Angle, lay Raymond and the reporter Julia Barnes, both as entangled with each other as eels, and neither with any more clothes.

Raymond looked up the stairwell at Cat looking down at him, and then became conscious of his compromising appearance, and smiled sheepishly up at her. At the same time, Julia Barnes saw that she was lying naked in a heap of eels, cheek to cheek and wool to wool as it were with Raymond Kidd, with his wife watching, and found it impossible not to scream.

The only spot of colour on the grey and glassy sea was Victor Cooley's yellow dory and his red and black plaid jacket as he rowed out beyond the islands. The load of eels was gone and he had sponged the planking clean where they had lain, for though all was imaginary, he imagined it very vividly. The rank odor of the land—of the marsh and the mud and the plant matter rotting—was still thick in his nostrils, puff away at his pipe as he might. So he was going further out where the sea air was freshest and freest. He wondered if he might not keep going, to the Grand Banks and beyond. The boundaries of his in-between world were now breachable. Of course, there was his unofficial duty as protector of the village, but he had done what he could and it was time he be relieved.

He rowed strong like a young man, so the boat leaped ahead, till in the distance behind only the spire of the old church remained. He rested on his oars and took a long last look. Then he rowed even more strongly, till there was nothing but ocean all around.

Angle found himself in a hall that stretched as far as he could see, a very sumptuous passage with ornate candelabra along the panelled walls and Persian-style carpeting down the middle of the marble floor and at intervals big windows revealing fabulously lush gardens with statuary that turned to smile and wink at him, and topiary animals that each according to its form managed some sort of modest bow.

So far along the hall that she was very small indeed, Shannon O'Keefe called to him, but he could not make out what she was saying. He walked toward her but the distance between them stayed the same. He ran till his labouring breath tasted of blood and still the gap was undiminished.

He stopped and stood with his hands on his knees, gasping. "All right," he called out. "What's yer game? Who's in charge and what's the ransom?"

The woman that stepped from a doorway to confront him was a queenly figure dressed in a smorgasbord of styles that had vanished long before Angle was born. Her gown had an English opulence of gold filigree against a Spanish severity of black and silver, was plumped out with a French farthingale, and with an Italian reticella lace ruff served up her head with its elaborate coiffure and powder-pale face and cherry-red lips like an exotic dish on a plate.

A white rat with a gold collar hung upside down from one puffed sleeve. She chucked it under the chin and cooed to it. "Ah!" she said. "The pirate. At last. Well, you have certainly taken your time. Stop your bellowing and we will show you your place."

"Place?" said Angle, eyeing her suspiciously. "I didn't come for no visit. I come for her." He nodded toward little Shannon, who was waving at him and dancing with impatience.

"So," said the woman, "you are a lover of little girls. How would you like her? In the garden? Perhaps under a tree? As you ravished our Jenny?"

The rat scampered up on her collar and hissed at Angle.

Angle frowned. "I'm tryin' to make amends for that."

The woman eyed him up and down and with her ring-laden fist cupped to her chin walked around him several times, so that the train of her gown wound around his ankles.

"I'm afraid we cannot let you have our new girl," she said. "But if you are going to the aid of our old girl, we can free you to do that. Or you can take the new girl's place, and we will try *you* out. But we cannot let you both go, oh no. Too much has been taken away, and nothing at all given back."

"So that's how it is, then," said Angle, finding himself paralyzed where her garment encircled him.

"Yes, that's how it is. Make your choice. And by the way, you should address us as Your Majesty."

"I can cry tears of fire, you know. I can burn up your dress, there. *Yer Majesty.*"

"It will not help you, I'm afraid. You can go nowhere till you make up your mind."

"You're a hard-hearted soul, to require this of me."

"We are no soul at all. We have never been human, that we can recall. So, which will it be?"

"All right, all right. The girl."

"What's that? You are murmuring into your beard. We can't hear you."

"The little girl, then. Let her go, and I'll take her place. But lemme tell her somethin' first."

"You may not speak with her. Tell me, and I will tell her for you."

"There's two cups on a stump on the path on the way back, two china cups—tell her to take 'em to her neighbour Raymond. And to be careful not to spill 'em. They've got that in 'em that he needs to get our Jenny back. *My* Jenny, damn your eyes."

"What was that last thing?"

"I said … *please,* Yer Majesty."

"Very well." She made her way back around him till he was free of her train, and then looking him up and down again she clapped her hands and squealed with delight, scaring the rat so it jumped to the floor. "Oooh! A real pirate! What fun! And how would you like to be added, as a statue or as topiary? It *will* be nice, you know. You will not have to cry tears of fire anymore. Or tears of any kind. You will not even have to move except once in a great while, to greet newcomers."

Capaggon brooded. Cat and Octave were out of his reach, in a state of astonishment through which his radiation passed like so many bullets through thin air. The arrival of the eels with Julia Barnes and Raymond had coincided with Octave's descent to the basement, knocking him down and burying him. He had arisen spluttering and spitting without a thought in his head. And the spectacle of Raymond and the screaming reporter in a nude embrace, and Octave miraculously emerging from nowhere again, had stopped Cat's mind entirely.

Capaggon needed thoughts to twist. Without them, he was powerless. He waited for more to arise among the company he watched from his lair, impatiently because his meal was in his grasp and he was ravenous. And yet he could not feed while danger threatened. So he waited and brooded and watched for an opening.

"And then I was outside myself and among the fog people, and I was one of them, looking back at my body in Raymond Kidd's arms. This is not about me, of course, and much can be edited later, but I am a reporter and although it makes me blush, I have to admit that I was beckoning him to us, as seductively and provocatively as a fog person could.

"The next thing I knew, I had lost even the shape of a person. I was in a boat rowed by an old man, and I was surrounded by eels, and as my body was nowhere among them, I must assume I had become one. It was an old dory-style boat and the old man was grizzled and hook-nosed and smoking a pipe as he rowed. He laughed and said around the pipe, 'Well, the living brung back by the dead.' I had no thought about that at the time, probably because I was an eel, but now it makes me think I had crossed over into what Raymond Kidd calls the *in-between*.

"Mr. Kidd must have been an eel too, because he was nowhere in evidence either, and yet there I was in his arms when the scene changed again and we were back in our bodies in his house, having slid down a short flight of stairs into a wall. We were naked, except that Raymond still had his glasses, which seemed strange.

"I am a woman, and it was disgusting to find myself embracing a naked stranger in a pile of eels, so I screamed, yes, and kept on screaming, for that and for everything else that had been done to me. But I'm also a reporter, so even as I screamed I was noting the dynamics in the room, how Mr. Kidd was torn between comforting me and trying to think what to say to his wife, who was standing there in her houserobe staring at us.

I could tell she was torn between jealousy and a natural feminine urge to comfort me in my panic, because her husband was obviously not up to the job. In fact, he made me scream even louder. He kept trying to assure me that everything was all right, and I knew it wasn't.

"As if that weren't enough, another man came out of the heap of eels on his hands and knees, a little sandy-haired balding fellow who was also naked, and seeing where he was and that he had no clothes began slapping himself on the forehead and crying out, "Not like this! Not again!"

"I guess that was what decided Mrs. Kidd. She shook her head and said, "That's it then. Ordinary's out the window. Make way for the new ordinary," and came marching down the stairs kicking eels aside right and left with her bare feet.

"'Raymond,' she said, shaking him by the shoulders, 'You take care of Octave. Get him some clothes, and yourself some too, and clean and put away these eels. I'll take care of her.'

"Having made up her mind, she was kindness itself. The first thing she did, seeing I was not only hysterical but shivering with cold, was take me upstairs for a bath.

"It was a fabulous tub, made for two, and I could have lain there much longer, with the hot water up to my neck and the underwater jets whirling it around me and Mrs. Kidd washing my hair and massaging my shoulders and listening to my story and telling me hers, but we were interrupted by her husband knocking on the door and telling us to come to the shrine room as soon as we could.

"I've been to the temple and seen the shrine room of the Buddhist community in Halifax, but I had never seen one in a private home and had never imagined the soothing and peaceful effect it could have. The only light was from a pair of candles on the shrine itself, that burnt with a steady flame and illuminated more than anything the seven clear bowls of water beneath them and the small bronze Buddha above and behind on a dais. The incense smoke from the bronze censer on the shrine curled and turned like the sensuous gestures of a flamenco dancer in slow motion, and imparted to the air the scent of sandalwood, clove and cinnamon.

"Along the wall opposite the shrine was a long low black table covered with texts and religious instruments on brocade cloth, and seated behind it, cross-legged on cushions and all facing the shrine, were Mr. Kidd, the other man who came out of the eels (whose name is Octave and who according to Mrs. Kidd is a lost soul come back to life), and little Shannon O'Keefe.

"I cannot tell you the relief I experienced at finding the little girl there. I did not stop to see if I was interrupting anything, or to bow as Mrs. Kidd had after passing through the curtain, but rushed across the room to Shannon and picked her up and hugged her to me as if she were my own lost daughter. I hardly heard what she was saying to me—something about being tricked into a tree that was really a mystery palace where her old friend the pirate had come to her rescue—because I was too busy raining tears and endearments on her and telling her how sorry I was for having lost her and that no story I could ever broadcast mattered as much as her.

"Mr. Kidd asked rather irritably if I would mind sitting down, because Shannon and myself were *not the only ones who needed rescuing,* and if instead of hindering the process I might make myself useful by writing down what was to happen next, as a record that might be of use to others.

"I had avoided looking at him because of our embarrassing encounter among the eels. Now I saw that, in spite of the peaceful atmosphere, he seemed far from at peace. The hand trembled that handed me an orange notebook and a pen and indicated that my place was at his side between himself and Shannon. When I was seated beside him, he bent over and stared into a wineglass half full of a clear liquid on the low table before him. Sweat showed on his forehead in the candle light.

"Meanwhile Octave was explaining to Mrs. Kidd that the eels had been no problem at all because the moment the first ray of the rising sun hit them, coming through the clearing fog and the hall window, they had all gone up in smoke.

"'And the smoke,' he said, 'Well, it didn't keep rising but swooped over and went out of the house through the cracks under the doors. And I swear I saw something like eyes in the cloud that formed outside, that gave us a look like a cat contemplating goldfish in a bowl. And then the cloud moved away toward the barachois. Where Angle is trapped. Because I didn't go with him.'

He was interrupted by Mr. Kidd, who shouted for him to be quiet, and then went on to shout at us all, 'I can't see if you won't stop talking!' He clapped his hands down on the low table so the wine glass jumped and almost spilled. 'Let me do what I'm supposed to do, okay?!'

The thoughts Capaggon twisted were Kidd's now and Kidd's alone. He had to twist them more subtly, for not only did the man have protection but he was also in a powerful room of protection, one whose every symbol made Capaggon nauseous. If the man's fear of failure had not been so strong, he could not have touched him at all. As it was, he had to alter his approach. It was still MINE MINE MINE, but instead of material possessions, the object was now responsibility. He gave Kidd to think it was all up to him, and to doubt he was up to the job. He slipped into the man's mind sideways, as if he were really aiming somewhere else. His negativity became less like a meteor shower and more like a shadowy mist.

"Mr. Kidd's behaviour frightened me, but I was more concerned for Shannon than myself. I didn't want to say anything for fear of provoking another outburst, so I wrote in the orange notebook and laid it down and caught her eye and pointed to it.

"I had written, 'Are you all right? Aren't you hungry or sleepy after being up all night? Wouldn't you like to go home?'

"When Shannon read it, instead of writing me back she stood up in her corner, which made her about as tall as the rest of us sitting, and announced to everyone, 'I'm fine. I'm not sleepy, because I napped in the tree. And I'm not hungry because they fed me there too. All the ice cream I could eat. And I don't want to go home because I would miss Booda Ray's vision. But I am wondering something. Why do they call a person *Booda Ray* who is not acting like a Booda at all? I looked it up on my mama's computer. The Booda was always a very nice person. He didn't scare people. He wanted all the beings to be happy.'

"Octave blinked and stared at the child. Mrs. Kidd put a hand over her heart and gasped. Mr. Kidd buried his face in his hands.

"'They call him Booda Ray, sweetheart,' Mrs. Kidd said then, 'Because he wants to be like that. He just forgets sometimes. We all do.

"'I think what we forgot this time is that we ought to have begun with a little meditation. If you have a question, and you need to see things clearly, it helps to settle your mind first. Let's try doing that now. Raymond knows how. Shannon, if you and Octave and Ms. Barnes will let me lead you in a little guided meditation, we can all sit quietly for five minutes or so.'

"I don't know how it was for the others, but for me, that five minutes was hell. Mrs. Kidd said to let our thoughts come and go, but mine just came and came, till it seemed like my head would explode. And they were all of what the fog creatures had done to me—pawing me, kissing me, drowning me. Stealing me away.

"I must have shut my eyes. I opened them to find Shannon's hand on my hand where it lay on my thigh. She had pushed her cushion against mine and was comforting me. I took heart from her innocence.

"Mrs. Kidd had begun the meditation by striking a gong in the form of a small brass bowl. She struck it again at the end.

"'Okay,' said Mr. Kidd, 'I'm sorry everybody. Shall we try it again?'

The meditation must have worked for him, because his voice was calm and steady now and his face was serene. He looked over the wineglass again and said, 'If there is anything to be seen, let it appear. For the sake of the Simple, please, let it appear. For the good of this household, and beyond that all beings, please, let it appear.'

Chapter 14

The New Ordinary

"Wait, let me guess," said Tom Lutz, leaning back and flourishing his cigarette in the air. "It appears now. Five minutes of meditation and the vision appears and the girl in the basement gets rescued from the demon." He stuck the cigarette between his teeth and snapped his fingers. "Boom, just like that. It's a miracle. You've brought me a Buddhist miracle story."

"Maybe it's not a miracle," said Julia Barnes, from the other side of his desk. "A miracle is an *interruption* of the laws of nature. Maybe it's what Mrs. Kidd called it. The New Ordinary. Maybe that's what this story's about, and why it's big. Maybe the laws of nature are changing.

"Anyway, you're wrong. The meditation didn't do it. Nothing happened. He stared and stared at the wine glass, and still couldn't see anything.

"Finally he saw something, and then he started laughing. He picked something out of the liquid in the glass with his fingers and put it on the palm of his other hand and held that palm up for everyone to see and really started to roar.

"He laughed and laughed, and didn't stop laughing even when his wife asked him what it was, because in the candle light there didn't seem to be anything there.

"'It's a fruit fly!' he said. 'A fruit fly!' He could barely get the words out, he was laughing so hard. He put his hand to his mouth, licked it and swallowed. 'My dinner!' he said. And then he just sat there laughing, with the tears rolling down his face.

"I still don't know what was funny. I thought he had lost it. But then Octave joined in. Just a giggle at first, and he tried to hold it back, but couldn't. After that it was Mrs. Kidd. And then Shannon joined in. And finally me too.

"I couldn't help it. It didn't matter what he was laughing about. It was just too funny. Everything. Being alive. Being there. Sitting cross-legged. Breathing. Having thoughts about anything. I almost fell off my cushion. It was like we had all lost our minds.

"That's when the wine glass lit up.

"It wasn't a bright but a cool light, like a television makes, and as it switched on, our laughter switched off. We sat up straight and still, as if the next guest on the talk show were going to be God.

"I never saw anything but the light, and I don't know what the others saw, but Raymond Kidd saw plenty, and I wrote it all down. It's right here in this notebook."

The first image in the wine glass was the emptiness bell. By all rights, it should have been very tiny. But for Raymond it was as big as if he were at a movie and sitting in the front row. At first he saw only details, the four prongs at the handle's end curved around a central prong, symbolizing the five Buddha families. And then it shrank just enough so that he could see the thing entire.. And then the picture went black.

He was wondering if that was it and the bell were the answer, *which was no answer because where was the bell now that Angle had lost it,* when the shrinkage continued and the bell appeared within the blackness that was the sludge of the demon with the Simple half-absorbed and her red hair floating up and her terrified eyes looking right into his.

The bell was in the demon then. *Great,* he thought. *Now how is that supposed to help?*

Then he was whirled away, up and out of his house and over the village rooftops and along the road to Halifax—so fast that the cars on the road blurred and the police car among them was only apparent because of its siren and flashing red lights.

And then he was in Halifax. Only not twenty-first century Halifax. When the furious transference ended and a normal pace resumed, he was in Camp Hill Cemetery, in the fog, at the funeral of Captain Oliver Cole, witnessing Josephine's graveside promise to become Francis Stegman's wife. He knew it was the right thing for her to do and that Francis would take care of her, but even though he was not Captain Cole anymore, he felt such a wrenching in his guts at her prompt leave-taking that the dew in the wineglass shivered and the vision for a moment was obscured.

When it steadied again, what appeared was the face of Cole's daughter Amélie. Josephine was telling her that it was time to throw her offering of box and yew onto the casket.

What Josephine did not see was that Amélie threw something else besides her spray into the grave. She threw Captain Cole's dorje, the one the mad old monk had given him. It tumbled end over end down into the hole as slowly as if it were falling through water, the gold radiant with its own inner light. The sprays piled on the casket parted as if blown by a gust of wind. The little sceptre struck and bounced high off the lid, with a report like that of rolling thunder, and the lid cracked.

"Goodbye, Pápi," said Amélie.

A few seconds later, a sudden downpour sent the entire funeral party scurrying for cover, and just as one of the gravediggers was hefting a streaming shovelful of dirt to throw in, a lightning bolt issued from the grave.

It came out slowly at first, like the growth of a tree shown with time-lapse photography, the branches lengthening and forking in slow motion. The gravedigger slipped in the mud and fell flat on his back with all the urgency of a falling leaf. The shovel, having parted company with his hand, was floating away with its muddy contents intact when with a burst and a terrible blast the tree of light shattered the storm and shot into the shrineroom through the wineglass and obliterated the room with luminosity.

Afterwards there was no light at all. The candles had been extinguished, and the dew in the wineglass had gone dark.

"After a while we got up, except for Mr. Kidd, who stayed on his cushion. My legs were numb from sitting cross-legged so long. I suspect it was the same for the others. I know it was for little Shannon. It tickled her that she couldn't feel her left foot. She kept giggling and stomping on the floor with it and kicking it against the wall and the bookshelf.

"'It's like a block of wood,' she said. 'Or a paperweight. Or an anchor. I can't feel it at all. But it's a good thing I have it, because if I didn't, I would just drift away.'

"I think she was a little over-excited. We were all dazed. You can't imagine how bright a lightning bolt is till you're in a room with one. Mr. Kidd had been staring right into the glass, relating his vision as fast as it happened, like a sports announcer, and caught it square in the face. He hadn't said a word since. I was the first to speak up, I guess because I'm a reporter and it's my job to keep asking questions no matter what, right? So I wondered out loud why the wineglass went dark. It wasn't just that the light inside it had gone out. The liquid itself had gone dark and was black as ink.

"'I believe,' said Octave, and several seconds went by before he finished his sentence, 'I believe that would be from the enzyme that the pitcher plants secrete, that digests their prey, the flies and ants and other insects so ignorant as to be lured in. We must have exhausted the enzyme, having all been lured in and being somewhat more substantial, and so it has lost its transparency.'

"That seemed to lead nowhere. Mr. Kidd was unresponsive. I decided to leave. I tucked the orange notebook into the robe I was wearing, told Shannon it was time we went, and started out of the room. Mrs. Kidd stopped me at the curtain that serves as the door.

"'I need your help,' she said. 'Won't you help me? We need to get him to bed. I can't do it alone. He's too heavy.'

"She meant her husband. I did what she asked. We took him between us. She talked to him all the way to the bedroom, calling him pet names, telling him it would all be all right and urging him forward in a soft coaxing voice like you would use with a child. He never answered. It was like he was blind drunk. He moved like a zombie.

"I turned away when she took off his robe. She said, 'Why does it bother you now?'

"Once we had maneuvered him under the covers, he let her pry his hands from his face. When he still wouldn't open his eyes, she kissed him on both lenses of his glasses. I wondered why she didn't take the glasses off. To me, she said, 'You'll be careful, won't you? We'll need you later, at the cemetery. Give us a call when you've rested.'

"Shannon was waiting at the top of the stairs. When we went out, we found a police car at her house. I didn't go over with her. I picked her up

226

and hugged her and told her she was the bravest and best companion I had ever had, and I meant it. She asked if I would mention her in my story. I said I would if she wanted me too. I was looking worriedly at the police car when I answered. She said, 'You don't have to be afraid, you know. You didn't do anything wrong. I asked to go.'

"It was as if our roles had been switched and she had suddenly become the grownup.

"She said, 'I'm going home now. You should go home too.'

"She skipped away up the lane singing, 'Amélie, Amélie, she's just like family!'

"I went home too, but I didn't get out of the car. I sat in the driveway with the motor running. I needed to rest. I still do. But I decided it was more important to see you first. So here I am. And that's my story."

Cat was afraid Raymond was in shock. He would not answer her, he would not open his eyes, and he was trembling all over. She slipped out of her robe and got under the covers and spooned herself into him from behind. Soon the trembling stopped.

"Honey," she said, "I couldn't see what you saw, but I believe you. And I'm going to stay with you and help you find what you need, even if it means robbing a grave. And after that I'm going to stay with you too. New ordinary or old, I'll never leave you again, and we'll figure out how to live with each other. And if you disappear again, I'll find you, bell or no bell, so don't think you can get rid of me like that."

She lay with her arm around him for a while, and then turned on her back and watched the daylight cavort in a patch on the orange ceiling, thinking it was no mean trick that let sun rays bounce off the wavelets in the cove and then bend through the air till they could enter the house through the skylight.

She thought Raymond had fallen asleep, and was about to do the same, daylight or no, when she heard him say something. He was still turned away and his words were unclear.

"What did you say, my love?" She put a hand on his hip under the covers.

"I said, it's these glasses. You can't see what I see 'cause you don't have cursed glasses. I'm glad you believe me anyway, and I'm glad you can see what we have to do next. Most of all, I'm really glad you can stay."

When the full weight of what had happened descended upon Octave, he felt crushed. All his life and death he had been with his brother, and though their brief life together had been a trial, the long isolation of their death had been bearable only because of Angle. With his endless supply of jokes and stories, a sailor's full repertoire, he had helped keep Octave sane, away from the howling mad realm of the ghosts. But what had really bound him to his brother was the change that had come over Angle as his contrition exorcised the demons that had owned him as a pirate, when he could cut a man's throat without batting an eye. He had, over the course of nearly two hundred years, become a very good soul and a very loving brother.

And now he was gone. The little girl had told him all about it. And Cat was off taking care of Raymond, after taking it totally for granted that he Octave had crossed over again and not even asking him how it had happened or congratulating him or giving him a welcome-back kiss.

Alone in the shrineroom, abandoned and forgotten, besieged by negativity and giving into it entirely, he reached out for the wineglass and began sipping the murky liquid inside, rather hoping it would kill him again.

Inside the hemlock, the process of Angle's undoing had begun. It figured to be a long drawn-out process, since his character was a strong one and furthermore had been defined for what would have been several lifetimes in the realm of the living. He had given himself up now, however—that was part of the bargain—and was suffering a tugging apart at the edges that he knew would go on until he and the statue he had opted to become were no longer two separate things.

He still could see through boundaries a little. He saw the little girl climb down outside, and turn and hesitantly kiss the hemlock's bark before she left.

He hoped she would remember the cups on the stump. Otherwise, what would become of his Jenny?

And what would become of Octave, who needed him too?

His heart swelled till he thought it must burst the strict confines of the statue.

His next thought (and his last one with any coherence, one that would have made him smile in his beard if his lips had not been turned to plaster) was, *Well, that would make a mess in Her Majesty's garden.*

Raymond was snoring, and Cat was entertaining thoughts of how she might frame the Vajrakilaya thangka for Stephen Berlioz, thoughts that were on the threshold of becoming a dream in which she was clasped to the bosom of that black and wrathful deity, when an insistent knocking on the front door brought her back fully awake.

The policeman at the door, seeing she was in her houserobe, apologized for the bother but wondered if she would mind answering a question or two. He had been called to the village on a missing person report, only to have the missing person, little Shannon O'Keefe, appear as he stood talking to her parents. That would have been that, of course, had she not accounted for her absence with a wild story that involved being tricked into a tree by a bunch of fog spirits and rescued by a pirate.

"I was about to put it all down to an overactive imagination and let her parents deal with it," said Detective Darryl Burnhardt, after Cat had let him in and sat him down on the turquoise couch. "After all, she was safe and unharmed and what more can you ask? But then she said, how dumb could she be, that when she had first seen her gallant pirate, coming out of *Booda Ray's*, she had thought he was a terrorist. Her mother then volunteered the information that Booda Ray is Raymond Kidd. Also known as The Man Who Came Out of The Sea. So that's why I'm here. I'm sorry we have to meet again under these circumstances, but I'm sure you'll understand that as a detective this is the sort of coincidence I really have to look into.

"Mrs. Kidd, I can ask you a whole lot of questions, or you can answer just one. What is going on here?"

Cat scarcely hesitated. If the New Ordinary was here for her, it was here for everyone, and this uniformed busybody with his cleancut good looks and apologetic smile would just have to make what he could of it. "I'll tell you," she said, "but I need a cup of coffee first. It's a long story, and I haven't had much sleep. In fact, I was just nodding off when you knocked."

"I'm sorry." He looked at his watch. "It's nine o'clock. Most folks are finished sleeping by now."

"Of course. Would you like a cup too?"

He had a notepad out and a pencil ready when she returned. "Well, that's old-fashioned," she remarked. "I would have thought you'd be using a pocket recorder, or maybe texting direct to headquarters so the SWAT team could be getting its swat gear together."

Burnhardt took a sip from his cup. The coffee was strong and black, as he had asked for, and as excellent as he could have hoped for, but there was no gratitude in his voice when he replied, "We don't have SWAT teams in Canada, Mrs. Kidd. We have Emergency Task Forces. Are you thinking we'll be needing one here?"

"Oh, I was just kidding, detective."

"I think you had better take this seriously."

"Well," Cat said, sitting beside him and adjusting her robe to be as prim and proper as possible, "I can if you can. Let's start off with the ghosts."

"Ghosts?" said Burnhardt, as he began to write.

"After he was a pirate, sometime around the mid-nineteenth century, Angle Daggon died in a snow storm, along with his brother Octave, and they both became ghosts. I'm sorry. I mean lost souls. They prefer to be called lost souls…"

And so Cat recounted as much as she knew of what was going on at 7 Lands End. She included what the brothers had told her and all Raymond had told her and what she had experienced herself. She recounted the re-incarnation of the brothers, revealed that the Man Who Came Out Of The Sea had actually come back from another life into this one and now had a demon to defeat, and led the busily scribbling detective through the details of Raymond's vision, up to and including the lightning bolt that had bridged the gap into reality through the medium of the in-between juice in the wineglass.

She kept to herself their intention to retrieve the dorje from the spurious grave in Camp Hill Cemetery. She was and always had been a fierce ally of the truth, but Jenny the Simple had to be rescued, and that could not happen if they were arrested.

"There," she said, taking a last sip of cold coffee. "That about does it for the details. The big picture, I think, is that the way things are is changing. The new reality, soon to come to theatres everywhere, has border crossings between then and now and here and there, between the natural and the supernatural. We're up against more than global warming, detective. Octave calls it a flaw in the fabric. I think we might be due for a more extensive unravelling. Is that serious enough for you?"

"Mrs. Kidd," Burnhardt said, erasing and making a last emendation, "It's my duty to point out that what you've just told me might be used against you. Whether it's serious, or a lie, or an indication of unsound mind, you gave it to an officer of the law. If it's the truth, then you've no need to worry. Now, if you'll just read all this back to make sure I've gotten it right, and then indicate in your own writing that you've spoken voluntarily and not under duress, and sign your name after it, I'll let you get back to bed.

"And thank you for the coffee. It was just right."

In another room, with other cups of coffee by them, Tom Lutz was giving Julia Barnes his assessment of her story.

"Well," said Lutz, stubbing his cigarette out, "it's an orange notebook all right, and you did come into my office during working hours wearing a houserobe, one that's obviously not your own. As for the rest of it, where's your proof? I mean, it's a doozy of a story. It's got everything. Ghosts, abduction by spirits, a vision in a wineglass, and out of nowhere a lightning bolt to top it all off. I love the eels, by the way. I can just imagine how that would have felt. And how you would have looked. But Julia, sweetheart, you've got nothing to show. No footage. Some words you recorded. Some words you wrote down. For Christ's sake, I ought to be calling in the boys in the white coats. Tell me why I shouldn't. Tell me it's a joke. Tell me you need some time off, and I'll give it to you. Tell me something. You know I'm all for you. You're in line for my job."

"There's more to come, Tom," said Julia. "I just need another camcorder and a little more time. I'm going to get the footage. And I guarantee you it *will* jack our ratings through the ceiling."

"Sell me on it. If it's just intuition, the answer is no. And make it something I can swallow. You're walking a very thin line here."

"Okay. That grave. That grave is here in Halifax, in Camp Hill Cemetery. And the thing the little girl threw in that caused the lightning bolt, the *dorje*, is in that grave. Raymond Kidd has to go for that dorje. He needs it. It's what the whole show was about. He had to find out *what he needed*. He sees himself as some sort of saviour, with this dorje being what he needs to carry out his mission. It doesn't matter if it's true or not. If he goes after the dorje, it means digging up the grave. And when he digs up the grave, legally or illegally, that's a story. And I'll be there to shoot it. His wife say they needed me there at the cemetery. They'll be calling me to tell me when to be there."

"Jules, number one, you're guessing. Number two, even if your guess is right, how long before he does it? You're my anchor. When you stay out in the field, someone has to fill in for you. Now, that's no problem for me. Nikki Mazell does a great job and I don't mind grooming her for the position. She's quick, I can send her out and she'll come back with a story and still be ready for All The News And Then Some. The problem is a problem for you. Your viewers *like* Nikki Mazell. They like her a lot. They're younger and she's younger and she's got an edge that appeals to them. She could be up for your job before you're up for director. You want to chance that?"

Julia took a cigarette from the pack that lay open on the desk, a horribly strong Russian brand that Tom special-ordered from a local tobacco store. She lit the short thick filterless slightly oval-shaped cylinder with Tom's maple-leaf-embossed lighter and coughed out the smoke. "You say," she said, when she could speak again, "that you don't care if these vile things do shorten your life, because every year since they released you from that North Vietnamese prison camp has been a bonus. You also say that while you were in there, it was only your life you were afraid for, never your job. You knew you would have a job if you ever got out, because you had a story. Well, I have a story too, Tom."

"It's like that, is it?"

"I guarantee you, it's just like that."

The tall thin man who was her boss, who had not always been so thin, took out another of his special cigarettes and lit it and leaned back in his chair and drew deep and blew two smoke rings, one through the other, and then laughed a long eerie laugh that ended up in the higher registers before disappearing altogether.

When he leaned forward again, there was something like death in his face. "Well," he said, smiling, "Go get your story then. But if you don't get it, don't come back.

"It's like that."

Cat lay with her back to her husband, so dissatisfied with herself that she could have screamed. The glass of water at her bedside—she wanted to throw it at the wall. What had she done? Spilling her guts to a policeman. Now they were exposed to the law. She had signed a paper. Whatever possessed her? The law was the law. It didn't understand. It had no imagination. She could be confined. If Raymond was interrogated, they would definitely both be confined.

Her brother Franklin in Boston was a lawyer. She thought of calling him. But they hadn't spoken in seven years, since the death of their mother. How would she begin, and how would it end? Franklin had been quite content to have their mother institutionalized when her memory went. Would it bother him to have his sister institutionalized when her sanity went? What made her think he would believe her?

What made her think anyone would believe her?

She could almost hear the demon laughing. The thought made her so mad that she fell into one of her black rages as if into a hole, and thence into a tortured sleep.

When she awoke it was evening and Raymond was gone.

She looked for him all through the house, and then in the boathouse, where it had once been his habit to drink secretly. On top of the shelves, the ranks of empty wine bottles were still there, having miraculously survived two displacements by hurricane. But no Raymond. Also not there were the oars for the dinghy, that he usually left leaning against the wall by the door. She realized she had not noticed if the dinghy were in its usual place on the ramp. She ran outside and saw to her dismay that it was not, and then to her relief that it was tied to the end of the dock and had only floated around the corner out of sight. The oars, however, rested akimbo in their oarlocks, ready for use.

The fog had rolled back in and she could not see far. The tide was back in too, lapping at the weeds near the top of the ramp.

"Raymond!" she shouted. "Raymond, where are you?"

The widower Turner Charles had a rump roast of moose in the oven and while he waited to baste it again was outside on his elevated porch clipping the tops of his hedge of wild rosebushes. "I think you'll find him in your gardening shed," Turner said, calling to her across the cove, pointing with his shears. "I asked him what he was up to when I saw him standing there staring into the fog instead of pushing off, and he said he had changed his mind and that it was shovels he needed for exercise, not oars."

"Oh, thank God," Cat said.

"Is anything wrong?" Turner said. "I heard about Shannon, and the police going to your house."

"Wrong?" she said as she headed back across the lane. "Oh, no. It's just the new ordinary."

The door of the gardening shed was open and Raymond was inside, scratching his head and regarding with a wry smile the three long-handled tools leaning against the wall between a worn-out snow tire and an inverted stack of rusty tomato cages.

"Look at that, would you?" he said. "A shovel with a broken scoop, a pick with a loose head, and a spade with a cracked handle. I've let things slide, I guess. It'll be a miracle if we get anywhere with those."

Cat stood at the doorway. The shed smelled of fertilizer and potting soil and weed killer. "We don't have to use those. We can buy what we need on the way in. Raymond, where were you going in the dinghy?"

"Can we? What time is it?"

"I don't know, but I meant tomorrow. Surely you're not thinking of doing it tonight. We've got to plan. I've got to see if there's any way of doing this legally."

"It can't wait. We've got to go now."

"Raymond, look at me. Come out of there. I know you're thinking of Jenny, and I know it's horrible what's happening to her, but if we make a hash of this, it's not going to help her at all. Come out and sit down and let's talk."

"There's nothing to talk about," he said, coming out with the spade, pick and shovel. "If you're coming, you need to get dressed. You can't go grave robbing in your houserobe."

She stopped him as he tried to walk past. "Raymond, what's going on? You're in a big hurry now, but a few minutes ago you were ready to go rowing. What was that all about? Sit down and talk to me."

He didn't answer but he didn't push past her either. He was pale and breathing hard. She relieved him of the tools and sat him down in the shed doorway, which was about as high off the ground as a footstool and just wide enough for her to fit there beside him. She took hold of his hands. They were trembling and clammy.

"Why, you're afraid," she said. "That's what it is, isn't it? You're terrified. And you were running away. That's what it was with the dinghy."

"I wasn't asleep," he said finally. "I heard you talking to the cop. I got out of bed and put my ear to the grate in the floor. I heard every word. I didn't hear him believing you. I heard him say *unsound mind*.

"When I was Oliver Cole, they put me away me for telling my story. I lay there thinking of it happening again, and my heartbeat went weird. Slow, fast, slow, fast—so slow it's like it's stopped, so fast it's like the governor's busted. I waited till you were asleep and then I couldn't stand it. I came out to get in the dinghy and row till I couldn't row any more."

When he didn't go on, but just sat there with his head drooping and his breathing getting faster, Cat said, "What made you change your mind? Raymond?"

"I'm sorry," he said, sitting up straighter and blinking. "What made me change my mind? You. You see your old garden plot there?"

"I can now. I won't be able to in a minute, with the fog eating it up and the light going. Why?"

"Remember the trouble we went to? Having good dirt hauled in, building that brush fence as a windbreak, putting a rain gutter and a rain barrel in back of the shed so you'd have water for the plants? Getting that exotic garlic from Tom Mays over in Lunenburg for your first crop?"

"Yes, and the dirt turned out to be no better than what was already there, and the garlic failed, and so did everything else I tried planting. So what?"

"So now it's just an overgrown mound, no sign there ever was a garden or a fence. And the rain barrel burst because I forgot to open the spigot and empty it last winter."

"Are you trying to make me cry, Raymond?"

"No, I'm trying to tell you I gave up too soon. I could have tried harder to make it work, spent the money to bring in more dirt, done more homework on how to grow things out here. I could have tried harder to make us work too. I let things go a lot, is what I'm trying to say. Somewhere along the line, I got into the habit of thinking that whatever needed to live would live, and whatever needed to die would die. I can't do that anymore. I've got to learn to take more care of things. Of people. Of you. Now would you excuse me for a minute? I've got to lie down."

He stood up and started toward the house, then stumbled and fell forward onto his face in the grass.

"I'll just be a minute," he mumbled, his mouth turned to one side. "Then we've got to get going."

"You've been here before. Don't you remember? It's arrhythmia," said the skeleton in the doctor's outfit, "and yes, it's quite dangerous. The heart is misfiring, so you've got blood pooling in the ventricles instead of moving on. While it's pooled, it can clot. If it does, and the clot gets into the bloodstream, you can have a stroke. You can die. It could happen while we're talking."

Raymond managed a ghost of a smile. "I've been here before, eh?"

"There's three options. The first is not to do anything. It's possible that your heart could resume beating regularly all on its own. It happens. The second is drugs. The third is electroshock. Each of the latter two options has its advantages and its drawbacks. Shall I describe them to you? The last time you chose electroshock."

Flat on his back on the operating table, Raymond looked up at the skeletal medic. "If you don't mind," he said weakly, "I'd just as soon skip the descriptions and get on with it. Do what you think is best."

The doctor nodded. "That's what you said the last time. I'm glad to hear you still believe in me, even if you don't remember me." He gave instructions to the skeletal nurse, who went out.

"We'll give you a shot of morphine so you won't feel anything. The shock will stop your heart. That should let it reset and start beating again regularly. But you will be dead for a moment. I hope you don't mind. You didn't last time."

Cat heard Raymond say, "Oh, I don't mind too much. I'm kind of used to it. Do you mind, honey?" But the only answer she could give was to strengthen her hold on his hand. She wanted to smile and be strong for him, and was afraid if she spoke she would lose her composure.

She smiled as if in appreciation of the witticism he made about the two defibrillating paddles the nurses attached with a gooey substance to his chest, though she didn't catch the gist. She smiled as she explained to the incredulous doctor that Raymond's glasses could not be removed because of his religious beliefs. She did not smile when they turned on the juice and Raymond flopped like a fish on the operating table. She did not smile when his pulse disappeared and he lay there like a fish on a counter ready to be dressed. She did not smile when the moments became forever and he lay there still.

Raymond was plunged in the wineglass again, and again found that the depths of the wineglass were as the depths of the sea. Only in this case the depths remained dark, and he did not emerge on any shore. He could not tell down from up, or whether he were sinking or rising. He was too tired to figure it out. He thought, *what difference does it make,* and prepared to drift off.

"What art thou thinking, Noble One? This is no time for drifting," said the little Indian beggar boy Ajay, as he swam into view close alongside, lit from within by his own luminosity. He wore gold bathing trunks patterned with red knots of eternity. His lips did not open, but his words came clear to Raymond.

"You have to get yourself another man," said Raymond, also with his mouth closed. "I'm not up to the job."

"There is no other man. *You* are the man," said the beggar boy, now eye to eye.

"Where is Dorje? Why does he send you?"

"The king sends his messenger. The dorje is in the false grave. How many times must you be told?" The boy lingered a moment longer then darted away, more like a fish than a human.

"But how do I get back? I can't tell which way is up!" Raymond called after him.

"That is a common problem!" was the distant reply.

The doctor knew by the monitor. Cat knew because she was holding his hand again, and suddenly he was returning the pressure. He was back. His eyes fluttered open and shut, and he said a few words.

"He wants to know if *I'm* okay," she announced to the emergency room team.

The doctor applauded softly, and the nurses joined in. "Well, that's a relief," said the doctor. "I believe he's set a record. I've never known anyone take that long."

She leaned closer to hear Raymond's next words. "Honey butter," he whispered. "Thank you. I just followed my nose."

While an attendant carted him to the curb in a wheelchair, Cat went to get the truck. Octave, who had followed from the waiting room, helped Raymond out of the chair. "I would have come in if they had let me," he said.

"What are *you* doing here?" Raymond said.

The truck came alongside and Octave handed him into it, saying to Cat at the wheel, "He wants to know what I'm doing here."

She waited till he had shut the door and they were all three in the cab, and then she said, "Raymond, you asked me to bring him. You *insisted* he come."

"Right. We need him. We need you," he said, turning to Octave. "So, where are the tools?"

"Don't you remember anything?" said Cat. "You rode here in the back of the pickup with the tools lying right by you. You had the shovel handle in your hand. But what does it matter? We're not going to use them. It's past midnight. You just had your heart stopped, and it nearly stopped mine as well. We're going home."

"I feel like I've been kicked by a horse," Raymond said, rubbing his chest. "And this gunk they put on me, why didn't they clean that off? It's sticking my shirt to me. No, we're not going home. This was just a pit stop. We can't put it off any longer. We may be too late already."

"You want to go to the cemetery? Now?" she said, looking out at their headlights slicing into the fog.

"We've got to," he said. "I'm the man."

Newsgatherers keep a lookout for odd, whimsical, humorous stories that help leaven the sad, serious, usual stuff that is the staple offering of news outlets everywhere. The story of the Man Who Came Out of the Sea, therefore, reached people near and far, in some cases along with a cellphone-taken photo of the naked man emerging from the waves.

In the hills of Mendocino, Eldridge Kidd sat under a sun umbrella on his balcony, sipping a cabernet made of his own grapes, the vines of which he could see below him in their ordered rows on the lower slopes. Both the story and the photo of his son were displayed on his laptop on the table under the umbrella. His good friend Doctor Sam Weller had emailed him the link. To his wife, who sat in her wheelchair facing the valley, in a stylish wide-brimmed zebra-striped sun hat and dark glasses, Eldridge said, "Angie, Raymond's back. Of course, he makes his appearance with his usual flair. And sooner or later they'll identify him and make a big deal of him being our son. But you know what? I don't care. I'm just happy he's back. You like that, don't you? You always said I was too hard on him. I wish I could go visit him. I'll call him later on. Maricela, would you come out and scratch my left foot again?"

It bothered him, being illogical, that his left foot would itch when there was no feeling at all in the rest of his legs. That he couldn't bend over far enough in his wheelchair to do the scratching himself was even more of a trial. Life altogether since the stroke he had suffered on his return from Nova Scotia was a trial, his worst since dementia had robbed him of his Angelina. Walking his land and drinking his own wine had sustained him somewhat. But now he was housebound and losing his taste for the wine. Still, they had Maricela. She was young and a good helper and her English was improving. He was a little tired of Mexican cuisine, but she had recently discovered Angelina's book of handwritten recipes and was trying them out, and that pleased him. She would never be a cook of Angelina's caliber, but she was not bad, and it distracted him to look at her. When she knelt to scratch his foot, the sunlight in her long black glossy hair made him forget that there were things that he would never understand, such as where his eldest son had gone, and where his wife had gone, and how it was that he himself the strongest one of all was going nowhere.

In an outdoor cafe by the zócalo in Oaxaca, Blanco Sanchez, who was reading the story in El Imparcial, exhaled and said, "Cool." He passed the half-smoked *churro* to his new girlfriend, Estrella, and showed her the photo. "Look, my father. He is famous now. I should tell them who he is."

Estrella said, "Cool. Good thing, to have a father. When are we going to visit him?"

"When the moon kisses the sun," he said, kissing her.

"What does that mean?" she said.

"Nunca," he said. "It's not likely to happen. He was just with my mother one night. He lives a long way away. He sends me things from time to time."

"We should go then. You should get to know each other better. It isn't enough that he should send you things. Things are not like a father. They are very different, in fact."

"Oh, there's no hurry. What needs to happen happens. *Es la onda, no?*"

"La onda, sí, pues. The flow. Yes, we go with the flow, *mi amor."* She made to pass back the nub of the *churro,* but Raymond said "No, no, here come the soldiers again. Put it into your pocket, and let's go."

In this life, Raymond had a teacher who was also Tibetan and wore robes. Unlike Dorje, however, he no longer travelled on foot and was therefore not dusty. His students kept his clothes new and clean, because it mattered to them, and he took cars and trains and boats and planes because otherwise he would never be able to visit them all. They lived too far apart, all over the world, in countries separated by oceans. Presently he was in Nepal, in the taxi from Kathmandu airport, contemplating Raymond's image as it appeared on the screen of the cellphone held out by his coat-and-tie-wearing American secretary. The taxi bucked and swayed and swerved in the busy traffic on the bumpy road in the smog-hazy valley, now narrowly avoiding a bicyclist, now tail-gating an exhaust-spouting bus. The teacher steadied the secretary's pale wrist with a brown hand. After several minutes the secretary, a tall stooping vulture-like young Jewish man from Manhattan, asked the teacher in Tibetan if he had seen enough and if the phone might be put away. "You are still very impatient," replied the teacher. "Halifax Ray, he is travelling in a very dangerous manner, even worse than we are in this taxi. He needs my blessing. Shall I give it?"

"Of course, Rinpoche," said the secretary.

"Then give me the phone." The teacher held the phone to his mouth and breathed on it, fogging the screen. "There. That should do. Do you think that will do?"

"Of course, Rinpoche," said the secretary. "Then you are still very gullible," said the teacher, handing the phone back and folding his hands over his ample belly. "But who knows? It might do, after all."

"I wish you would fasten your seat belt," the secretary grumbled.

"Of course you do," said the teacher.

"You are a good boy, and that is a good wish."

In Halifax, others had recognized Raymond from the cellphone photo, among them Mommy NoGood. Mommy was a street person who had been a street walker till age and overeating had taken their toll. Sometimes she remembered being attractive and having a proper place to live. Tonight was not one of those times. Tonight she had been beaten again for being a fat woman with a mustache who still panhandled with the suggestive manner of a hooker. All she could think of was finding her way to that space between buildings where there was a concrete stairwell down to an unused basement with a forceable door. Once in her nest of old newspapers, with her candle stubs lit, she sat rocking on her haunches and patting and consoling herself while the tears had their way with her. She never cried for long anymore though, and as soon as the tears dried, her imagination kicked in. *Imagination is your friend,* her mother once told her. *Keep it with you and you'll never be alone.* Tonight she imagined the Man Who Came Out of the Sea. She had seen his picture in a paper at the library, and had known who he was right away. He had owned a bookstore on Barrington, and for a while had let her come there and read. She had stayed in the back room and tried not to be a bother, but she found it more comfortable to read lying down, and one day he had come to her and said it would not do, he ran a store not a library, and she was scaring his customers away and making his employees uneasy. She remembered his apologetic smile and the kind manner with which he had escorted her out. She had not gone back, but she had thought about him and the feel of his hands on her for some time after, and with a certain heightening of the senses she rarely felt anymore, she made up a new story about him there in the flickering shadows. When the story was ripe and complete in her mind, she struggled up out of her nest and went out to a pay phone and called the police.

Burnhardt woke his chief with the call and was just getting an earful of abuse for it. When he got an opening, he said, "She's a call girl who says she was with Raymond Kidd a week before he turned up as the Man Who Came Out of the Sea … She wouldn't give me her name. She doesn't want to be arrested. Says it's bad for her level of business. She's expensive. I knew that statement from Kidd's wife was just spit in my eye, and this is proof … I'm glad you remember, sir, and yes, I was somewhat vocal about it. You've got to speak up if you want to be heard … I'll find the hooker, sir, don't you worry. Halifax doesn't have that many high-priced ones. Anyway, he takes her out for a night on the town, starting with dinner at daMaurizio. He goes the whole hog, four-hundred-dollar bottle of champagne, says it's a celebration, won't say why. Later on in this ritzy apartment on the water-front … I'll find out where it is, sir. Let me finish, please. Well, with a buzz on him from a few lines of cocaine—she swears she didn't do any—and a couple of glasses of brandy the likes of which she'd never tasted—*it must have cost as much as the champagne, she only had a half a glass to his two though, professional ethics*—lord she was sexy, had a voice just like velvet, I can't do it justice—anyway, she takes him around the world and he tells her everything … Yes sir, around the world in bed … No sir, she didn't get any more specific than that. Anyway, he says his ship is coming in, and on that ship are six containers with enough of the white stuff to bury Halifax like a blizzard. She figures his deal went bad and he got dumped in the harbour ... No sir, I know there wasn't a mark on him, but there could be another explanation ... No sir, she didn't say she was calling us out of her sense of civic duty. She says he got nasty at the last and said things she didn't want to repeat, things that offended her deeply and that she was not going to let go unanswered. She didn't realize she had the courage till she heard what had happened to him, and that he'd lost his memory, but *now the tables are turned and it's his turn to cry* ... Yes sir, those were her exact words ... I'd like to pick Kidd up tonight, sir. I had a hunch it was drugs from the very beginning ... I know I've pulled a double shift, sir, but I'm not that tired ... If it doesn't check out, there's no harm done, and if it does then we've got him and he doesn't get away, that's what the hell I'm think-ing ... Yes, sir. Of course I value my job, sir ... Right. We'll talk about it tomorrow." The line went dead before Burnhardt had finished. He then said a few things that would have offended his chief deeply.

They were there at last, at the curb by the main entrance to Camp Hill Cemetery, having stopped on the way at a late-night pizza joint. Cat switched off the lights and the engine. In his anxiety, Raymond began talking before he had quite finished swallowing a last dry bite of crust.

"Before we start out," he said, choking a little, "let me tell you what I'm thinking, so it'll stop circling around in my head like it's waiting for something to die. I've had enough of all this. I'd like to go home and lie down and forget all about it a while. I'm pretty wasted. And there may be no magic weapon in this grave we're going to desecrate. But what else can we do? You both know the Simple is real. As real as we are. And she's down there in hell getting stuffed like a trophy fish. She's not getting time off.

"You both saw the lightning come out of the wineglass. You know I'm not crazy. It's like the song: *Strange days have found us. Strange days have tracked us down.* Forgive me, but you're living proof of that, Octave."

"So why are we wasting more time?" said Cat. "We don't need convinc-ing. We're ready to go."

"As ready as I'll ever be without Angle," Octave added, somewhat listlessly. "I don't even know why I'm back. It must have been something to do with those damn eels."

Raymond pressed on. "What it is … I just want us all to hold hands for a minute. I'm embarrassed to ask, but I'm no hero, and I'm feeling a little shaky. Can we do that? Can we spend a few moments just being human together?"

They held hands and Raymond shut his eyes and saw the three of them sitting on the edge of a precipice and looking over, and being drawn by the very act of looking ever closer to the edge.

They got out of the truck and got the shovel, spade and pick, only to find the cemetery locked. The spear point finials of the wrought iron fence made climbing over impossible. Raymond solved the dilemma by finding a tree with an overhanging limb, having Octave boost him up to the limb, and then lying full-length on it and reaching down to swing the others over, but it cost him. The weight pulled his bruised chest down hard against the rough bark. The pain shot through him almost like another defibrillation. After transferring Cat, who was no lightweight, he almost lost his grip on Octave and for a horrifying instant thought he would drop him to be impaled.

Shouldering their tools again, that they had passed through the gaps in the fence, they faced into the cemetery. Its foremost headstones were illuminated by the streetlights, but those in the next row were mere silhouettes. The ones after that were lost completely, for there were no lights in the cemetery, and their flashlights could not breach the fog.

It was then that Raymond revealed, ruefully, that he had no idea where the grave was that they were supposed to excavate.

"There weren't so many graves in the vision," said Raymond. "The cemetery was brand new back then. We'll have to go stone by stone till we see if there's any logic in the way they're arranged."

They advanced into the shadows, using their flashlights only briefly at first to read the names on the markers, then leaving them on when they were far enough away from the street for the beams to go unseen by passersby.

"I don't see any logic," Cat said, rows later. "The names are all over the alphabet, and someone who died in 1942 is right next to someone who died in 1836 is right next to someone who died in 1985."

"We'll just have to get lucky, then," said Raymond.

"Lucky? How lucky have we been lately? You just had your heart re-started, Angle's trapped in a tree, and the woman who rescued you is being eaten by a demon. I think we ought to skip the luck and go for what's practical. And what's practical is to go home and rest and find out tomorrow from the cemetery records exactly where the grave is. We could be out here all night and not find it this way. You can't even read the names on some of the older graves. We could go right past it and not know it."

"We had a vision."

"*You* had a vision."

"All right. *I* had a vision. But you both saw the lightning. And the power of it's with us. I can feel it. Let's split up and spread out—Octave to the left, you straight ahead, me to the right—and if after an hour or so we haven't found it we'll call it a night. There's a road in from each entrance and they all cross in the middle. We'll meet there. If you do find it, hoot like an owl. In sequences of three till the others get there. How's that? Can we agree to that? We're already here. We ought to do something."

They did as Raymond suggested and before long had lost sight of each other. Each roamed alone among the patternless collection of variously fashioned and colored headstones, horizontal tablets, crypts, and obelisks. Tiny water droplets of fog danced in their flashlight beams. They peered closely, moved as quickly as they could through the cluttered dark, and at last came to a halt separately, by graves none of which were the so-called final resting place of Captain Oliver Cole.

What stopped Cat were three chalky headstones in a row, so small they were like baby teeth, ranged next to a mossy-sided normal-sized marker that leaned backwards obliquely. Frank, Lewis, and Henry Blackadar had all been sons of Emmeline Blackadar, were born in 1858, 1860, and 1862 respectively, and had each lived for one year.

The enormity of Emmeline Blackadar's loss leapfrogged from those numbers into Cat's heart of a midwife and mother of three sons herself.

"You tried so hard," she said. "So hard. And had no luck at all." As the grief worked inside her, her flashlight went out.

"I'm sorry," a voice said behind her. "I'm afraid your device is undone. It had yet to be invented back then, in the time into which your great empathy has transported you. Nay, do not run. I am here not to harm but to help."

The figure that stepped from the gloom carried a lantern and wore a three-cornered hat. "Here," he said. "This light is not as bright, and it stinks to high heaven, but it gets me around, and perhaps it will serve for you too."

"Who are you?"

"I am Burton Latimer, steward of these grounds. You were trespassing, you know, it being long after curfew, so you deserve what you get. But my duty, notwithstanding, is to care for all who enter here. So, let us see what can be done."

Octave was detained by an eroded tablet of pale limestone on which at first no name could be discerned at all. But this marker, of all he had happened upon, for some reason appealed to him, and as he gazed, it changed before his eyes. The stone became as if newly hewn, and the epitaph reappeared letter by letter, as if in the act of being chiseled. Finished, it read:

Letitia Daggon 1798 – 1858
Mother of Angus and Octavius

His flashlight went out as had Cat's. He dropped it and sat heavily down and ran his fingers over the inscription. Then he hugged the stone and wept.

"She had what amounted to a pauper's funeral," said Burton Latimer, approaching with his lantern. "No one attended but another old crone, one who had given her all and then stolen some more to buy the headstone."

Having spent his own time in between, Octave recognized an apparition when he saw one and was neither frightened nor amazed but remained sunk in his sadness. "I would have accompanied her here to the city," he said, "but she forbade it. Said I could not follow where she had to go. Still, I'd have come in the spring. But I myself died in the winter."

"Her life in the city was hard," Latimer said. "From her friend's lamentations, I gathered they spent time together in the bridewell on Spring Garden Road. More than one winter. They would get caught a'purpose for some petty crime they made sure would be noticed. The cells were cold, but the streets were colder, and the lodgings they made use of with men were not theirs to call home. So, you knew her intimately, did you? Loved her dearly, perhaps? Were one of those men who nevertheless would not keep her?"

"I was her son, damn and blast you."

"Ah. And how might it be that you died, and yet are here once again in the flesh to discover and mourn her?"

"Does it matter? I was where you are, in the world between worlds, and I never knew why. Such things happen. And now I am back, such a thing as should never have happened. Who cares? The devil's work? The natural order of things wearing out? I only wish I had followed my mother, and were nowhere to be found."

"You truly wish that, do you?"

Raymond had stumbled onto one of the cemetery roads, and crossing the twin graveled tracks had encountered the monument of Alexander Keith. Although he could not see even to the top of the monument's spire through the murk, he recognized it at once, before even reading the name, by the cans and bottles of Keith's ale ranged round the base, left as offerings by the wandering inebriated.

He had been introduced to the spot in broad daylight as a new brewery tour guide in training, so he knew exactly where he was. His problem was that he could not move on. Keith's grave brought back a memory that had stopped him in his tracks. It began with that time between tours when he sat down as an actor in apron and boots who pretended to be from an earlier century and assistant to the famous brewmaster, but just as he had been transported from that chair, so his recollection now shifted to that of Captain Oliver Cole, waking to find himself back with Josephine and Amélie, both overjoyed to have him out of his coma and back with them, both so alive in his mind that he held out his arms there in the cemetery as if to hug them and gather them in and never let them go again ever.

"Was I to paint you grey," said Burton Latimer, "you would make a prime headstone. The women would swoon." He spoke companionably, as if he had been there all along, and gesturing to one side with his lantern and a nod of his three-cornered hat, he continued, "But come, do not injure yourself with an empty embrace. Let me show you what you seek."

"How would you know what I seek?" replied Raymond, with some heat when he saw who it was that had surprised and made light of him in his moment of tenderness. "And what makes you think I would trust you to show me anything after what you did to my glasses?"

"Your glasses? I repaired them, as you asked."

"I never asked you to stick them to my head so they wouldn't come off. I never asked to see skeletons where there ought to be people, and ghosts where there ought to be nothing."

"Ah, well. *Caveat emptor*, and all that. Anyway, you should be grateful. Now you are less likely to be fooled by illusions. The burden of seeing things truly, however, is that you can never go back. So the glasses are yours for this lifetime. Now stop whining and come along. Otherwise I must leave you. You are not alone in needing my services tonight."

"I don't need anything from you."

"Very well."

Latimer strode off decisively and was no more than an obscure silhouette in the fading glow of his lantern when Raymond changed his mind and hurried after. Increase his pace as he might, though, he could not catch up. Soon in his haste he was tripping over the smaller markers. At one point he caromed off a slender indistinct tree. Yet he could not close the distance to the mere firefly-like spark that Latimer's lamp had become.

The moment he gave up and quit running, his flashlight came on again. Swinging the beam onto the inscribed lid of the crypt in his path, he found himself staring at the epitaph of Captain Cole's friend Francis Stegman:

Man of vision, mover of millions
Who lies here with his beloved family
His wife Josephine
& his daughter Amélie

At his request, and because she felt strangely compelled, Cat related her story to Burton Latimer. She was not sure he was there through the telling, because she avoided looking at him. There was something in his eyes that made her fearful. Nevertheless, the flickering light of his lantern remained, and so it was to the dancing shadows of the graves of Emmeline Blackadar and her three short-lived sons that she poured out her tale, beginning with her two failed marriages and the three sons resulting, continuing with the difficulties with Raymond that had led to their separation, and ending with her experiences since Raymond's disappearance and return.

"I never wanted ghosts and time traveling and grave robbing. Just one good companion. One father and home for my children. A husband strong enough to let me be however angry I am. And an ordinary life with only ordinary magic. The sweetness of tomatoes from my own garden, the way a lawn smells after you mow it, the way the right clothes make you good to look at."

The aspect of the light changed as a shadow slanted across the graves of the three infants. "So," said Burton Latimer, "It all boils down to—you're unhappy and you want to be happy. A common tale after all, despite the supernatural frippery toward the end. It falls within my powers, therefore, to offer you a choice. You can choose to be happy, or I can guide you to the grave you mean to rob, and you can risk the consequences of that ever ill-fated deed. Time is of the essence. What say you?"

Octave had likewise been asked for his story and like Cat had exposed himself fully. He did not mean to at first, for Latimer's revelation that his mother had been reduced to prostitution had stung him to the quick, but by the time he reached the sinking of the Queen Mab and the hanging of his father, he almost sang with gratitude at the chance to unburden himself. He spoke to his mother's headstone rather than to the apparition. Because the lantern light remained, he assumed that Latimer was there, but really he did not even care.

"You might say I've been blessed, to come back and all," he concluded. "But you'd be wrong. When I lost my mother, my life ended. The rest has been an empty show, alive or dead. Had I it all to do over, I would follow her no matter what, and if she would not let me live with her, I would find lodgings nearby, and never ever let her come to such an end."

"Again I must ask," said Burton Latimer, "if that is truly what you wish. For I may grant that wish. There is no time to lose, for business is pressing, so steel yourself and say it formally, beginning with the words, *I wish,* and the wagon with your mother will have just disappeared over the rise, and you will be afoot in Prospect to follow after."

No story was desired of Raymond. When Burton Latimer reappeared for him, the steward of Camp Hill Cemetery wasted no time in making an offer tailored to his situation.

"Ah, Mr. Kidd," said the lantern bearer, "Or should I say Mr. Cole? I see you have found what you sought on your own. Now perhaps you will be more disposed to accept a helping hand. For you, because your dilemma is unusual, I will also offer my advice. You have a choice of identities. I will recommend one. Excuse me." He stepped between Raymond and the Stegman family crypt and tapped the stone lid with his lantern three times, at which the lid dissolved and a blinding light poured out. The light moderated to a luminous blue-green glow that revealed a stone stairway leading out of sight down into the earth. "My recommendation is that you choose the life of a successful man. Here your life is a failure. You had a business and you lost it. You had a job at a minimum wage as a pitiful sort of actor, an aging man among a cast of mere children scarcely starting out on their careers. You are unemployed now, with no prospects, and instead of seeking work you are off after the pot of gold at the end of the rainbow. How long do you think your reunion with Catriona will endure under these circumstances? At the bottom of these stairs, on the other hand, you will find yourself again in the bedroom of Captain Oliver Cole, a successful and accomplished master mariner, in the company not only of a precious wife but a precious child. Francis Stegman will again make his offer, and this time you will accept it, make a name as the first captain of the largest ship ever built, renew your fortunes, and live out your life as a beloved husband and father.

"You have only to be my guest and enter here. Do so now, for the entrance is unstable and will not remain open for long."

Three choices were made that night in Camp Hill Cemetery. After the third, a double thunderclap sounded, and a light rain began to fall through the fog.

Three owls hooted almost simultaneously.

Cat, Raymond and Octave stood in the rain regarding each other speechlessly. Each had been led to the grave of Captain Oliver Cole—which they would never have identified had they come upon it on their own, for the shattered monument had fallen forward and hidden its epitaph—and as Burton Latimer their guide had vanished, each had given the agreed-upon signal to bring the others, only to find themselves standing there together already.

Astonishment kept them silent at first, then the regret like a punch in the gut each still felt from refusing the offer of Burton Latimer—the offer of happiness. They shone their flashlights on each other, then at the ground, then at the fallen marker with its Celtic cross, that lay there and obviously had lain there for some time, for the grass grew untrimmed around its several fragments and curled over and held it in a familiar embrace. In quiet consent, they lay down their tools, positioned their flashlights on the ground so the beams criss-crossed the grave, and began lifting the marble chunks aside, so they could dig.

The sweat of their exertions wet their clothes from within, for the chunks were dense and heavy and imbedded in the earth, while the misting rain that made the marble slippery also wet them from without. When they had done, Raymond lifted his head, wiped his streaming face, and said, "So, you were visited too? What did you turn down?"

"I don't want to talk about it," said Cat. She picked up the shovel and shoved its broken scoop into the ground and levered up her first clod.

Octave shouldered the pick with the loose head. "I turned down the chance to let my mother know I really loved her," he said.

"Why did you do that?" Raymond said as he inserted the spade, sunk it further with his foot and his weight, and gave a measured tug to see if the taped handle would hold.

Octave buried the head of the pick and it stuck. As he struggled to retract it, he said, "Because, I'm an idiot, and I prefer the company of idiots."

Dee Divine, arrested for the third time in a month and on her way to the station, said, "Say, they shootin' a movie downtown?"

"What do you care? You plannin' on auditionin'?"

"You such an effin' smart ass, Gordy. Naw, I saw folks climbin' into the graveyard on my way to work. Thought they had to be actors. Who else would bust into a graveyard?"

The tear in the top of her stocking, that should have been hidden by the hem of her dress, was in evidence again. She sent it back into hiding with a quick yank of the shiny fabric.

"I thought maybe they shootin' a horror movie or suthin'. Thass all."

"Graveyard? What graveyard was that, Miss Divine?" said the other officer.

"You know, the one where all they famous folks buried."

"Camp Hill?"

"I don't know. Yeah, I think so."

"She definitely wants an audition. Hookers and horror movies go together like flies on shit."

"You payin' double next time, Gordy. You ain't got no respeck."

The other officer, because it was a boring evening and there was nothing else to do, called in to report suspicious activity observed at Camp Hill cemetery.

"Your partner now, she got respeck. She know we all jus' workin'."

The prostitute spoke with genuine censure in her voice. It was a damp dreary evening, though, and she was not unhappy at the prospect of a warm dry cell. Gordy was just being Gordy. She *would* charge him double next time, but since nothing times nothing equals nothing, it would still be for free.

Farther offshore, the waves had grown to terrifying heights, and now the yellow dory was more like a car on a roller coaster. The little craft fairly flew, heaving clear of the water at the crests of the waves and racing down their backsides as if gathering way to take off on the upswing. The rower plied the oars with such strength that they bent with the strain to their breaking point.

His hair was no longer white nor his limbs wasted, and he had flung off the plaid wool jacket of his never-warm-enough old age. He was young again, with shiny black hair like oil fresh from the ground, and white teeth and full muscles, and he laughed like a maniac as he reached and pulled.

"Victor Cooley, almost gone!" he cried to a whale going the other way, its grey back passing him not ten feet away.

As his senses along with his aspects of body became magnified profoundly, he heard clearly the scrape of metal on stone that was Cat Mc-Callum's blunt-headed half-shovel hitting another rock, and the splendid wretched cursing that was Angle Daggon's gritted-teeth response to being turned into statuary, inch by agonizing inch.

The Simple's mute horror fairly scalded his awareness.

For all that, though his laughter left off, he never missed a stroke nor slowed nor varied a point of the compass from his course to the northeast.

"Yer on yer own now, baeys and girls," he said. "Good luck. And may the Lard have mercy."

They were not soldiers and he was no leader, yet he felt they had just won a battle, and he was proud of them. They frowned and were uncommunicative, but their ranks had not been broken, and they dug. Lord, how they dug. They attacked the barrier between them and their goal as if they had a grudge. In half an hour, with the sparks flying from Octave's pick and though Cat's broken shovel made small mouthfuls, they had excised a rectangle roughly seven feet long by four feet wide, using Raymond's foot as the measure, and were already a foot down in the stony ground.

For his part, though he was the largest and normally would have been the strongest, Raymond lagged behind the other two. He felt horribly bruised in the middle of himself where the two paddles had jolted him, and the steady light rain, that did not seem to bother Cat or Octave, weighed him down as it soaked through his clothes, and the wet earth that stuck increasingly to his spade made each removal a struggle. He noticed but disregarded a slight resentment that his wife did not sense his discomfiture or suggest that he rest.

Spurred on by his own vexation at the choice he had had to make, between the loves of two lives, he determined to dig till something broke. Whether it was the taped handle of his spade or himself made no difference. He knew that before long, as the hole deepened, one of them would have to get out and leave off. He did not mean for it to be him.

He did not reckon with his cell phone interrupting with O Canada, his ringtone for strangers. Grudgingly, wondering who the hell it could be, he stabbed his spade into the mud beside him and answered. And found himself talking to Julia Barnes, the reporter.

"You're in the cemetery, aren't you," she said. "Why didn't you call me?"

"I didn't know I was supposed to."

"Your wife didn't tell you? She said you'd need my help, and that you'd call to let me know when you were going."

"I'm sorry. We had an emergency. She must have forgot."

"Never mind. I'll be there in a minute. I'm already parked outside behind your car."

"You'll have to find your way in on your own. I can't send anyone after you, and I can't tell you how to get to where we are."

"It's okay. The gizmo I put on your car led me here, and I got the location of Cole's grave from the Camp Hill website. I know what I'm doing. I can get there."

They were saps, out of touch and clueless. Julia suppressed the urge to tell them, but it was true. They weren't dressed for the weather, and their tools were a joke. The first thing she saw when she found them was Octave's pickaxe losing its head. Away in the dark a ringing impact suggested the flying metal had struck a headstone. She had qualms about pitching in with losers, but she stifled that too. She had come to help as well as to report, and she was ready from head to foot. She wore rubber boots, gloves, brown overalls, a baseball cap with her blonde hair tucked through the back in a ponytail, and a full-length raincoat with a hood. She brought to the task a brand new shovel and a BTV video camera in a waterproof camera jacket.

"How'd you get in?" Raymond asked, suspiciously.

"Bolt cutters. Ever hear of 'em? I cut the old lock off the gate chain and put a new one on, one I have the key to. I put the bolt cutters back in the car. Simple, eh?"

"She's got gloves," said Cat. "Why didn't we think of that? I'm getting blisters already."

"That's a proper shovel, too," said Octave. "But what's that other thing?"

"It's a camera, Mr. Daggon. You have to have one to shoot stories for television."

"Who said anything about shooting a story?" said Raymond.

"I'm a reporter, Mr. Kidd. That's what I do. I'm going to help you dig, and then I'm going to shoot the story. Don't worry. I'll wait till we find what you're looking for. Then you can throw a few shovelfuls back on and I'll shoot while you find it again. I'll only have the light on for a few minutes. I doubt anyone will see it, not in these conditions."

"I'm not worried about the light," said Raymond. "I'm worried about your making this a story. I don't think it's a good idea."

"Mr. Kidd, according to your vision, there's no one buried here, so you can't be arrested for grave robbing. At most it would be a misdemeanor for digging a hole on public property. The attention you'll get from my story will more than make up for any penalty. Beyond that, people have a right to know. They need to know."

"I saved your life there in the barachois. You owe me."

"The old man in the dory saved my life. If I remember correctly, you weren't quite up to it. I appreciate your effort, and I appreciate what you're trying to do now. But this is bigger than you, and my career's on the line. It's not up for debate. If you find that thing that caused lightning from a vision to jump into your house, the event is going down in history. Otherwise, you go home empty-handed, and we all go home unhappy."

She felt fresh and invincible in her appropriate outfit with her appropriate gear. The three of them looked wilted and tired in their dripping clothes with their drooping postures. "What's it going to be?" she pressed on, sensing they would cave.

Cat sighed and shook her head and went back to her hard labor with the broken-headed shovel. "Let her do what she's going to do," she said. "We haven't got time for a standoff."

"Go ahead, missy," Octave said to Julia Barnes. "But you should know, this has nothing to do with happiness. It's about misery, and trying to end that for somebody. I turned down happiness already."

He turned his back on them all and went off in the murk with his flashlight to recover the missing head of his pickaxe from among the leering headstones.

The trio had grown to a quartet, but the same elemental music prevailed, a steady if ragged melody of chucking and sliding as the earth was levered up and thrown out, set to the omnipresent percussion of the rain.

The lack of conversation resumed after Raymond added his grudging consent to the inclusion of Julia Barnes with her camera. Each digger was fiercely concerned with the effort and the thoughts that went into the effort and the timing that kept all the efforts in harmony, so that no one struck the other as they dug.

In the end they were lucky the reporter had joined them. Though Octave had repaired the pick by driving a thin sliver of stone with another stone into the top of the handle, eventually the head loosened again and finally sailed off where it could not be found. The shovel with the broken scoop broke further, so that Cat suddenly found herself digging with only a handle. The crack in the handle of Raymond's spade matured into a full break, tearing through the duct tape, making further repair impossible. The brand new shovel of Julia Barnes alone remained serviceable.

They were all filthy dirty and themselves strained to the breaking point. Cat lay couched in a heap of mud from their displacements. The blisters on her hands had opened and her sciatica had hit a pitch of pain that she had never experienced before, one she would not have believed possible. Octave sat cross-legged by Cat with his head in his hands, watching rain drops trickle off the tip of his nose. Raymond sat on the lip of the hole watching Julia Barnes work. His chest hurt almost too much to breathe.

"There's really only room for one of us anymore anyway," she had said. "You and the Reborn can take a turn when you've rested."

"How about you?" he had said. "You've been going all out too."

Hood or no hood, her eyeliner had streaked in the rain, giving her a ghoulish look. Still, and feeling no disloyalty to Cat, he found it pleasant to look down at her by the weakening beam of the flashlight. She had unzipped her raincoat in the heat of her exertions in the close space, and her wet clothes had gradually made her youthful form more apparent. He rested his weary mind on the topographical revelations of her clinging tee shirt.

"It's almost dawn. I can't quit now," she had said stoutly if a little breathlessly. "We've got to be almost there, don't we?"

And then her shovel thumped against something hard, something hollow. "Okay," she said, "Help me up. It's your turn now. I want you to be the one who finds it, whatever it is."

Burnhardt had been wandering the cemetery for an hour in the fog and the drizzle and was cursing the hunch that had brought him—that Raymond Kidd was there somewhere. Twice he thought he saw someone, once behind a tree and once behind a monument, and twice that someone seemed to run away. Each time he had given chase. The second time he had slipped on a marker that had fallen and sunk into the ground till only its wet polished face showed, and had taken a tumble that muddied his uniform and bruised his knee.

"No, I'm all right," he said into his walkie-talkie as he limped along after his fall. "Probably just some kid. Stay in the car. I'll give it fifteen more minutes, then we'll call it a night. Drinks on me later. Sorry to have dragged you out … hello?"

The walkie-talkie crackled with static, though he still had his thumb on the send button, and a raspy voice that was not the voice of his partner said, "Hello, detective. Have you seen the light? If you haven't, press on till you do. Never say die."

While climbing back down into the hole to be the one who made the discovery, Raymond slipped and sprawled on his face at the bottom. He rose dripping mud like a swamp creature. On his forehead was a bloody patch where a root stub had caught him as he fell.

He took the shovel from Julia Barnes, who was concerned at the cut but at the same time unable not to point and laugh at his appearance. He laced his hands and boosted her out of the hole.

"Get the camera. Let's get this done and get out of here," he said.

The bright light of Julia's camera blinded them after their long stint with nothing but the gradually dimming flashlights. They didn't the see the addition to their company, and no one heard his footsteps because Julia had started her commentary.

Raymond nodded into the light and said what he was asked to say. When the reporter was satisfied, he bent back to his task. The shovel pierced the rotten wood of the casket easily. He went down on his knees and groped around inside, and then stood stunned with his find in his grasp.

"There," Julia Barnes cried triumphantly. "You've got it! And I've got my story!"

"And I've got what I came for too," said the stranger in their midst. "Mr. Kidd, please step out of the grave."

Raymond ignored the inconsequential talk overhead. He had wiped the object with his shirttail, and the rain was spattering off red and amber gems embedded in heavy silver. Of what was not his dorje but a Christian crucifix.

Not knowing who was there with Raymond Kidd but judging they might be dangerous—mob or drug cartel members or who knew—Burnhardt had drawn his gun. Julia Barnes noticed this, but in the heady flush of her success kept filming anyway and simply included the policeman in her commentary.

"A new development. It looks like our would-be hero is about to be arrested. Good evening, officer. Julia Barnes for BTV News. Can you tell our audience why you are arresting Raymond Kidd?"

With the camera turned on him, Burnhardt froze. "Julia Barnes? The anchorwoman? This is for TV?"

"Yes it is. And for an audience that will probably ultimately reach around the world. Now, what can you tell us? What are the charges?"

"Ms. Barnes, I'm not arresting him. I'm just taking him in for questioning. We got an anonymous tip that he's involved in drug smuggling. What, he has a permit for this?"

She turned the light away from the detective and directed it back down into the grave at Raymond. "Mr. Kidd, the officer was apparently not informed about your permit. Can you produce it for him, please?"

With the uniformed man's entire attention on Raymond, Octave tugged at Cat's arm and with a nod of his head indicated they should withdraw. She took a few steps back with him into the fog and whispered, "They know who I am. Besides, we can't just leave Raymond."

Down in the hole, Raymond looked up into the blinding light. To the skeleton with the badge and the cap and the firearm, whom he could just make out with his hand shielding his eyes, he said over the sound of the rain, that had grown louder now, "This isn't what I came for. It's valuable, probably. But not to me." He knelt and laid the jeweled cross down in the mud on the uncovered lid of the coffin and thrust an arm all the way to the shoulder back into the breach he had made and groped around desperately.

"He hasn't had a good look at you," Octave said. "Anyway, if we're all taken in, who's going to get Raymond out? Come on, we've got to go."

Cat gave a fearful look back. "Oh, Raymond."

"Okay, that's it," Burnhardt said. "Mr. Kidd, come up out of there, or I'm coming in after you."

"It's for the best," Octave said. "Don't worry. I'll be with you."

The detective stepped on the same spot where Raymond had slipped and himself went sprawling into the hole. As he hit, taking Raymond down with him, the gun in his hand went off with a reverberating roar.

"Oh my God!" Cat cried. "Raymond!" She ran back to the hole and looked in, retreated again, went back a few steps, retreated another few steps, then panicked. "Okay," she said to Octave. "Okay! Okay, let's go!"

They ran off in the fog and the dark with the rain pelting down hard.

Julia Barnes kept on filming.

At least, and at last, he could rest. Or so Raymond thought as he was locked in his cell. As stark as it looked bolted into the wall, the steel tray with its minimal mattress constituted a bed, and he had nothing to do but lie down and for a while take an allowed leave of his senses.

He did not disturb the clean tautly tucked sheet but simply fell onto it on his back with his muddy clothes still on. Later he lifted his feet with their even muddier boots and transferred them onto the bed too.

He closed his eyes with the hope, almost a prayer, that he would slip off into sleep as he had slipped into Captain Cole's grave, suddenly and effortlessly. But as if they were on a spring and had not been properly secured, his eyelids swung right back open. The light in the cell was still on, and the light in the corridor was still on. And they could not be turned off. Not by him. And he could not sleep in the light. He looked all around his spartan quarters, at the bars, the bare walls, the stainless steel toilet with no tank, and could find no rest anywhere.

He had done all he could and still failed. And he had turned down his chance to go back.

He looked at the camera on the ceiling outside. He was on display now, another creature in the most exotic of zoos.

"Give it up," Cromwell said. "You got him. Like an idiot, you managed to shoot yourself in the process, but you got him. He's not going anywhere. Watching that monitor is not going to convict him of anything, and he can't see you staring daggers. Go home. Draw the curtains. We got curtains. He doesn't. Get some sleep."

Burnhardt cradled his bandaged hand but did not take his eyes off Raymond Kidd. "I'll find out what he's up to. And I'll get his gang too. Demons, my ass."

"I never seen you like this, Darryl. You think the man's some kind of master criminal? He's just a nut case. And you're turning into one."

"You like being made a fool of? That's what he's doing to us, all of us. He thinks we're a bunch of smalltown flatfeet, and he can pull this Joker stuff on us and get away with it. But I'm going to see he reads his comic books in prison from now on. I'm gonna smoke his real deal. You watch me."

"I'm watching you," Cromwell said. "And I don't like what I see."

Raymond blinked, and out of nowhere Burton Latimer was there in the cell beside him.

"No wonder you can't sleep," Latimer said. "You would have to be something less than human. I'll wager you can feel the metal underneath this excuse for a mattress. And they've issued you no pyjamas. Are you satisfied now?"

With the slim hope that he was hallucinating, and that the apparition might disappear, Raymond closed his eyes.

"Come, come. You cannot ignore me," Latimer said. "It isn't polite, and anyway it won't answer. I'm here and will not go away."

Raymond looked up into the blue eyes that were like sadness's own lighthouse. "But how can you be here? This isn't the cemetery."

"Mr. Kidd, in my real life, so-called, I was a button maker. Shank buttons, sew-through buttons, covered, cloth and frogs, I made them all. I made things to hold other things together. When I died, I found myself at my wife's grave, unable to move on. She herself, God rest her soul, had not waited for me. Yet I was stuck. And so I became steward, or guardian if you will, of the burying ground called Camp Hill. These three hundred years, I have greeted every tenant, and whenever I could, I tried to reunite them with their happiness."

He smiled his kind smile in which his eyes were unable to participate. "Mostly I failed. I seem never to have quite gotten the knack of it. So it was with your spectacles, and so it was with the choices I offered last night. Not one of you chose happiness. Yet I do not despair. I've come today to give you one more chance. I have with me what you sought and failed to find." From the pocket of his leather vest, he produced the golden dorje. "Will you take it from me?"

Raymond reached and then withdrew his hand. "What's the drawback?"

"Drawback?"

"I suspect all your offers come with strings attached. Why's it glowing. Why's the dorje glowing?"

"Because it floats, Mr. Kidd, right where life and death meet. Actually a trifle under the surface. This is not a bad thing but an added value, for to accept your barbarian charm you must re-enter the in-between, which will free you from this bridewell. You may come out as I came in, with an amused disregard for your captors and their solemn penalties."

As well as he could, which was not very well, since his consciousness seemed to be ebbing, Raymond contemplated Latimer's offer. "I have to die to get it?"

"You are going to die anyway. I suspect sometime today." The apparition reached into Raymond's side with a phantom hand. "Yes, I'm afraid you overreached yourself fatally with last night's exertions. Your heart is like an overwound clock, with the spring at the breaking point."

Raymond felt a coldness in his chest. "I don't trust you," he said. "You're trying to trick me again. Why wasn't the dorje in the coffin? Why was that crucifix there? And what's in this for you? You still haven't told me how you got here, past the confines of the cemetery. I know ghosts don't wander freely."

"Tut, tut, tut. Tick, tick, tick. Where will you go? Who will you be next time? It's uncertain. The only certainty is that you will have unfinished business, and it will weigh on your mind, and you won't even know why. The ignorance will gnaw and undermine you all your days. Meanwhile, you will have left the Simple in hell. Yes, I know your story now. I have it from your wife, Catriona. You are a man who claims to give his all, but always holds something back. Which is worse, Mr. Kidd, a trickster, or a coward? This is the only pertinent question. The questions you ask have no bearing. You're wasting time. Take the dorje and meet the demon. It's dead simple. Tick, tick, tick, Mr. Kidd."

Raymond's heartbeat accelerated even as the button maker challenged him. The cold around his heart spread through his body. The sweat under his wet clothes was cold. Why had his jailers not given him dry clothes and let him change? His head throbbed where he had cut it falling into the grave, his hands where they were blistered from the digging. How could he choose when the offer might be a hoax? And yet how could he not?

The idea of death, even as a mere postponement, he found suddenly appealing, as he had while his body lay on the operating table with its heart stopped and his spirit drifting in the void. Anyway, it was death either way. He thought of the mad monk, and opened his fist like a flower.

"I'll take it," he said.

Chapter 15

Full Power Stall

Because the body stays behind, and the mind is wild and untamed, entering the in-between is rarely as straightforward as stepping over a line between one territory and the next. A blacking out happens first, and what comes next could be anything, a bed of roses or hot coals or insubstantial vapor. This is only the first station, but it can seem like the be-all and end-all.

Raymond had meditated for twenty years and would have sworn that his mind had been tamed. Nevertheless, he awoke to find himself falling through a cloud.

It was his first solo, and he had followed all the instructions that had served him so well with the instructor aboard. But when he engaged in the maneuver called the full power stall, something went wrong. He had pointed the two-seater Cessna straight up while giving it full throttle as he was supposed to, and when the engine had stalled, he had maneuvered the controls to come back straight and level and under power again, exactly as he had been taught.

He had not expected to go into a tailspin when the Cessna nosed over and dropped.

He fought the wheel and worked the two rudders as well as he could with the plane being buffeted and himself pinned by centrifugal forces. As the turning ground rushed up at him, he saw a green pasture with black cows. And then the little country airport with its single cross of runways. And then his instructor on the terminal tarmac, a big leather-jacketed man in mirrored aviation glasses, signalling frantically to him. And finally, alongside the instructor, his mom and dad, holding hands and staring up with stricken faces at the crash to come.

Then he fell without an aircraft and it was white all around him.
He fell forever where there was no end to falling.
And then he hit anyway and everything went black.

Burton Latimer idled his way along Spring Garden Road, a changed man in a changed time.

His leather vest and homespun blouse had been exchanged for a polo shirt and a nylon windbreaker, his homespun trousers for designer jeans, and his leather boots for hi-tech tennis shoes. Instead of a three-cornered hat, he sported a Halifax Rainmen baseball cap. For a few blocks he doffed the cap to everyone he passed on the busy sidewalk, excited as a little boy that he could once again remove his head covering and replace it at will. He desisted when no one returned the courtesy, seeing it apparently was no longer the custom and wanting to blend in. To help resist this habit of his former life, he thrust his hands in his pockets and held them there. This also served as a delightful reminder that he no longer had a lantern he was forced to carry. Soon the hand that for so long had been wed to the lantern relaxed and stopped clutching at a handle that was no longer there.

At a corner by a restaurant with outdoor tables, he slid a handful of coins whose issue spanned three centuries into the battered guitar case of a street musician, and then, in higher than high spirits at his long-sought liberation, as a joke he asked if he might hear a rendition of A Canadian Boat Song, that had been popular with the generation after his in the time after his death. He had heard it sung at the funeral of a well-liked local actress and had repeated it often during his nightly rounds of Camp Hill. When asked by the startled busker if he might sing a few bars to bring the piece to mind, he responded with genuine feeling,

From the lone shieling of the misty island
Mountains divide us, and the waste of seas
Yet still the blood is strong, the heart is Highland,
And we in dreams behold the Hebrides.

Fair these broad meads, these hoary woods are grand
But we are exiles from our fathers' land.

"Sorry, I don't do Celtic," said the busker. "Everybody around here does Celtic. How about some Paul Simon?"

As the shaggy man strummed the first chords of Bridge Over Troubled Waters, the newly minted man laughed and continued his promenade.

At the public library, he shared a bench with a woman who was feeding the pigeons. For a time, too elated for words, he marvelled in silence at the ten-foot statue of a striding and serious Winston Churchill that graced the library grounds, and smiled at the white pigeon droppings on the weather-darkened bronze that seemed to make light of the great statesman's weighty deliberations. Yet when the woman asked if he might spare the price of a meal, he found himself more than ready to speak up and further engage with his new fellow citizens. Though she was no beauty and indeed somewhat repulsive with her faint mustache and whiskery double chin and an odor that rivalled that of his old fish-oil lantern, he told her she might be his guest at any eating establishment she chose, as long as he might tell her his story.

The maitre d' of the Marlinspike hurried to them as they came through the door. "Mais no, Mami!" he said, addressing Latimer's guest with some urgency, "You must come to the back. But even so it is too early. I will have you something later, something nice, okay?"

"It's okay, Jockstrap, I've got a date," said Mommy NoGood. She ushered Latimer forward by the elbow. "The meal's on him."

With his chin on his knuckles and his little finger patting his upper lip, Jacques deliberated. He raised his eyebrows questioningly. The man responded by bowing summarily with his Rainmen cap pressed to his chest. "Yes," said Latimer. "The lady is with me. Are we not welcome?"

"You are paying for her meal?"

"I am."

"You have money?"

"You are impertinent, sir," said Latimer. From the cap he took a ten dollar bill.

"This is all your money?"

"No, this is just for you. For finding us a table somewhat apart from the others. We would like to be as alone as possible. *Je me faire comprendre?*"

Jacques palmed the money quickly and unobtrusively and complied. It was early and there was no one upstairs yet at all. Even should the man prove a runner, he had a good tip and the sweet but awfully smelly home-less woman was out of sight and therefore out of his hair. He took them up and seated them by a window overlooking the street and asked perfunctorily if they would like wine, expecting a reply in the negative.

"It isn't necessary to trust me," said Latimer. "But I will trust you. Here is a hundred dollars. Bring us a wine that is worth it."

Jacques again stretched his eyes. "But your food … you have not ordered."

"Bring the wine, and you can help us match the food to it."

Mommy NoGood overruled this strategy by daring to order everything on the limited lunch menu. Latimer sipped at his expensive chardonnay and was silent at first, as content with her cackling abandon as he fancied she must have been with the cooing concentration of her pigeons. Her first glass of wine she knocked back as if it were water, and she devoured her appetizers as if they were made of air—a spicy beef salad, an organic crimson oak leaf salad with cherry tomatoes, a local sunchoke and soy soup with white truffle oil, and two fresh vegetable spring rolls with peanut sauce. After a swipe at her chin with the cloth napkin, she downed another glass of wine and with a wild-eyed smile asked if he might consider ponying up for another bottle.

"Yes," he said easily, "and while we are waiting for it and the main course, or main courses, you will repay me by beginning to listen.

"My name is Burton Latimer. I died nearly two hundred years ago."

Though he was weak when he passed, Raymond's intention never faltered, and it guided him unerringly through the hallucinatory labyrinth of the in-between. The blackness at the end of his infinitely long fall was the crawl space in the basement of 7 Lands End.

The golden dorje in his hand shone like a torch. By its light he saw clearly that the pool in the folds of the polythene ground tarp had shrunk to a puddle only an inch or so deep, yet as he ventured in head first, once again he was swallowed entirely.

As he plunged, he saw that above him in the master bedroom Cat and Octave lay facing each other, awake and struggling but as incapable of escape as two flies in a web, for Capaggon's negativity had burst its bonds and become tangible. Their muddy clothes were peeled away and their bodies being shoved slowly together, two pieces of a puzzle that did not fit and so were being forced to fit.

The pool thickened around him the deeper he sank. His progress began to seem negligible. Nevertheless he saw where he was going. The unquenched light of the dorje penetrated to all the way to the bottom and the demon far below.

All that showed now of the Simple was her eyes, that were now void of expression, and a seaweedlike upwaft of her long red hair. The rest was inside the black tar.

Raymond wanted to scream.

He was too late after all.

"… and now I am here," concluded Latimer.

The table was cluttered with dishes that Mommy NoGood had not let the waiter remove because each had some scraps of food left and she was reluctant to finish her incredible meal and her incredible interlude with the crazy rich man. In a lazy inebriated satiated haze she stirred in small circles with her fork a last gobbet of duck that was more fat than flesh, and said coyly, "So, you made a deal with the devil and got out of it at last. Ain't you the cheese? I bet the next thing you'll be wanting is a little loving."

The button maker felt an inexplicable affection for the ridiculous old whale—truly, he loved everyone at the moment—and so he resisted the urge to be cruel. He said instead, "The next thing I'll be wanting is to make another deal. I don't know with whom yet, or quite how to do it, but if Raymond Kidd could go back to the past and come forward again, it's at least possible. He seems to have done it in a rather helter-skelter fashion, to no benefit. But think of this, Mommy. If a man could go back to the past and use his knowledge of the future, he could do almost anything. Make the right investments, take the winning side in wars, become the ruler who is never wrong."

He held his glass with its last golden sip up to the light from the window. "You think this costly wine a rare treat. You want the bottles for souvenirs. You call this *living high on the hog*. But this is nothing. What's been buried with the dead, and what I have taken unseen over time from those who mourn, is more than you can imagine, and will keep me for a while, but I want a grander game."

Mommy nodded as if she understood completely. "If you was to take me back with you," she said, making eyes at him that were slightly teary, "I'd be young again. I was beautiful when I was young. You wouldn't be sorry."

The beam from above stung Capaggon. He looked up through the helpless eyes of the Simple and saw Raymond and felt his hatred and frustration and was pleased in spite of the pain. He willed the water to thin so the man could descend. He would extinguish the nasty light and then enjoy the delicious emotions, and the man, undisturbed. As he had muffled the deafening bell and ingested the woman and her judgment-clouding passion that was sweet as syrup.

In a dream, Raymond knew, you can do anything, as long as you know you are dreaming. You can fly or walk through fire or stop a bullet in midair. As a tantric Buddhist he had practiced this without much luck. He had hovered once, a few inches off the ground. Yet he believed the possibilities were unlimited, and he knew the in-between to be much like a dream. So now he imagined the thick waters thinning and himself still in time to save the Simple. The dorje would be a lightning bolt in his hand and he would cleave the demon at a stroke and get the bell back too. And then he would free Cat and Octave. And then wake and be back in Cat's arms.

It seemed to work. The water thinned till it was thinner than air. He came down fast, somersaulting to get his feet under him, and raised a cloud of sediment when he hit. Through the cloud he struck the demon a tremendous blow that sunk his arm in all the way to the elbow.

It did not cleave the creature, however. Instead the dorje and his hand disappeared inside the amorphous mass and stuck there, and pull as he might, he could not extract them. He imagined the dorje vibrating and shattering the demon. Nothing happened. He racked his brains for another solution. He imagined a spinning dorje that would slice the demon to shreds. The little sceptre remained completely inert. If it still glowed, the light was no longer visible. Nothing occurred to him but that the demon was not fighting fairly and ought to be reported to the authorities. But who were the authorities? He fetched the demon a hearty clout with his other hand, his weaponless one, and that hand disappeared to the wrist and stuck too.

He was in a story from his childhood, an Uncle Remus tale, in which Br'er Rabbit was fooled into attacking the tar baby constructed by his enemy Br'er Fox. "Tu'n me loose," he hollered, the words escaping in bubbles, "fo' I kicks de nachal stuffin' outten you."

He knew the demon was manipulating him, turning his own thoughts and memories against him, but the part of him that knew was no match for the furious rabbit that was the rest of him, that kicked away according to the story and was then stuck hand and foot, and that unhesitatingly followed up with a head butt that sank him in to his ears, thus rendering him completely helpless.

"Har, har, har." The laughter creaked like a door on rusty hinges slowly opening inside his own skull. "Yezzz, an' where are yer furren friends now?" The voice had suffered from long disuse, and was thick and slurred, barely comprehensible. "A-ban-doned ye, 'ave they? Left ye alllllll on yer own? Poor laaaad. Wellllll, niver ye mind. Divil take 'em. Come to table now and join the par-teeeeee. Yer damzel in diztrezzz awaitz! Har, har."

The demon pulsated and percolated and began to draw Raymond in alongside the Simple. The voice cleared.

"Think 'ee I haven't loved? I had two sons. The one a useless mama's boy. T'other, 'e could cut a throat as well as any, but 'e gawked like a ninny from the bushes while his father were jerked to the yardarm. And that vile bitch their mother, didn't she turn informer, elsewise how was my Queen Mab found out? I cursed them all as the life were choked out o' me. And then I who were Cap'n Will Daggon were biled down to a gibbering wraith, chained to the bedrock beneath me own house.

"So much fer love."

Wherever he was immersed in Capaggon, Raymond felt himself draining away and knew the horror he had witnessed in the Simple's eyes. He would not be returning to Cat or going on to a next life or awakening in a Buddha field or even carrying on in the in-between as an aid to lost souls. He was food for a demon, the father of Angle and Octave. Had they known? Why hadn't they said? He couldn't pursue the line of questioning. He was being sucked into hell and it hurt as though a million fat needles had been shoved into him all over and were doing the sucking, withdrawing his essence, destroying his soul. He waited for Ajay to intervene somehow and tell him what came next, but it seemed to be true what the demon had said. He was on his own now, his mind going, unable to summon even an image of his teacher the mad monk.

"And now fer you, who were a captain too, and have yerself only to blame."

The voice refined further till it became his own, fed by his own thoughts, saying, "Remember what you were, and what you could have been again, and despair."

When he did, when he remembered what he had been, it whisked him away from the demon to the deck of the Bonne Chance. A bonny breeze was blowing on a sunny day and the ship with all its sails abroad from mains to moonrakers was tearing through the waves throwing a grand wake high and wide. He was homeward bound from Liverpool, with Chebucto Head in sight. Josephine and Amélie had met the ship offshore, brought there by the mail packet outward bound for London, and were there with him, the three of them under an awning on the aft deck, Amélie in his lap and Josephine beside him in a second chair. He was bringing forth gifts from a bag for them both. Josephine had draped over her shoulders the intricately worked bright red and gold shawl he had handed her, and was exclaiming over it. For Amélie … he opened his hand and there in his palm lay a dorje.

Seeing his daughter's look of uncomprehending disappointment, he wondered at himself for having brought her such a ridiculous souvenir, and the scene changed.

Josephine and Amélie were gone, and he was in the cockpit of the Happy Cat fighting the wheel of the yawl in a gale. They were running before the wind, he and Catriona, and in the trough of each towering wave the boat jerked hard to starboard as if to head them back into the steep onrushing sea. If that happened, if he let them get sideways, they would broach and be swallowed. Slowing them down would have helped. Though heavy and deep-keeled, the hard-driven yawl was breaking free and surfing down the foaming crests, attaining impossible speeds. But he could not shorten sail.

The twenty-year-old mechanism of the roller-furling headsail had failed, so the great billowing genoa could not be reeled in. The main could not be dropped or even reefed because the old wooden masthead had cracked, causing the halyard sheave to twist and the line through it to jam. The little mizzen sail behind him was the worst culprit. It gave the wind a grip on the stern of the yawl and put the brute force in the slewing motion that after eight hours had worn Raymond out in his struggle to hold their course. Dousing the mizzen would have been key; he could not let go the wheel to turn and tend to it. Had Cat been younger or stronger or more experienced, she might have taken the helm or gotten the sail down, but she was braced with all her might not to tumble out of her seat by the cabin door, and looked terrified, and he could not ask it of her.

He fixed his eye and his hopes on the speck on the horizon fifteen miles ahead that was the steeple of the village church. He could see it, therefore they were in reach, therefore he roused himself time after time and held on.

He knew something else too. The Happy Cat had not been made for seas like these. Her undersized ribs were breaking. He could feel the stiffness going out of her, and he could hear the electric pump running nonstop as the water leaked into her and rose in the bilge.

He forced a smile for Cat and yelled, "It won't be long now!"

"You son of a bitch!" she screamed back over the shrieking wind. "How could you let this happen?"

The blessing line for Lama Dorje was long, winding around the entire perimeter of the converted warehouse in which the teaching had been given. One by one the practitioners approached the elevated throne, bowed, and received the robed and crowned lama's black hand on the tops of their heads as he chanted. Now and again he would recognize and greet a student personally. Raymond hoped the lama would recognize him, but he was after all not the man he had been when they met on the banks of the Hooghly, and he was also at the end of the line. Hundreds would pass before him, the lama would surely tire of the ceremony, and his pat on the head would be a perfunctory one.

A black Ajay in a blue blazer with a monogrammed tie picked at his sleeve. "O Howling Cur, of course the lama knows you. Come with me and he will bless you now."

The boy inserted Raymond in his wheelchair at the head of the line, and even announced him. "Dorje-la," he said, "I have found him. Your heart son is here."

The lama motioned for Raymond to approach.

"A fortunate day," he said, in excellent English, leaning forward from the large brocade pillow on which he sat cross-legged to gaze down at Raymond. "Fortunate indeed. When an accomplished master and a truly devoted student meet again across lifetimes."

Raymond basked in the lama's benevolent smile, while at the same time marvelling at his extreme blackness. He remembered him as being brown, Ajay too, yet they were both now like chiselled and polished obsidian.

"You have given up much, Raymond Kidd who was Oliver Cole. From riches you have descended to rags, from prominence to obscurity, from love to solitude. All in pursuit of the genuine Dharma. And now you are crippled and dying. Stand, and let me bless and release you from these earthly bonds."

Even as he willed his wasted legs to support him, and with amazement found them answering the call as he pushed himself out of the wheelchair to his feet, somewhere Raymond knew that something wasn't right.

The lama's hand was an electric can opener, about to relieve him of the top of his skull.

He reached up to grab the black wrist, and found himself back in the demon Capaggon, his hand on the emptiness bell.

With all the strength he had left, with every fiber of his being, he imagined the bell ringing. And it did.

Flushed with fullness and with more prey awaiting in the bedroom overhead, prepared and waiting like trussed capons on a dish, Capaggon tested his boundaries and found them yielding. It was as his son Octave had said, not knowing his father could hear. There indeed was a flaw in the fabric. He extended himself further, and felt a tearing, as of his invisible chains pulling free from the rock that had held him so long.

He gathered himself for a greater effort. He might do as his sons and become human again. He would need a human form. He could be William Daggon again, but why not be someone known already in this time, whose credentials he could carry unsuspected into the flesh fields that awaited, where he would feed right and left?

This was *his* house. Always had been. What better form than that of the alleged owner?

He imagined himself as Raymond Kidd. And became so.

The pool vanished in a roaring vortex into the bowels of the earth. Not a single drop remained. The new man made his way on hands and knees from the dark to the light over a dry and dusty polyethylene ground covering. Where the crawlspace opened into the basement, he got out and stood and stretched and lost his balance and fell on the concrete floor and stood again and held onto the shop table till the dizziness passed.

He was weak from the exertion of his liberation, hungry as any lion, and there was an unfamiliarity to having arms and legs again and being in the upright position that he had not expected.

He managed the stairs keeping a strong grip on the rail. He knelt unsteadily by the bed that was his first destination, and with his eyes closed breathed deep of the aroma of the wide-eyed couple sandwiched there so unwillingly. The smell of their fear was like ambrosia to him. A growl of anticipation rumbled in his throat. He leaned toward the woman. Of the two, her scent was stronger and stirred him most. He stroked her muddy tear-streaked cheek with the pads of his fingers and felt her tremble, and rested his lips on her neck and inhaled her heady fragrance till he almost swooned.

He was not quite either of the beings he had been, but an unprecedented and unstable merger, and now it was a simple smell that tipped the balance. He said to himself, "Honey butter," and remembered her as his wife Cat, and that memory finished what the dorje and bell had begun, for more than hunger or even desire what was aroused in him was love, a love that ran deeper than anything.

The darkness in him vanished as if the sun had just risen.

He did not bare his teeth to resume the feeding that would have sustained his materialization but instead kissed the soft hairs at the nape of her neck and whispered, "It's all right. You're free now. I'm going."

He was there, and then he was not there. Cat saw him come, and knew him by his features but not by the look in his eyes, which was that of a predator, fierce and hypnotic. When he bent to her neck, she was certain he meant to rip out her throat. Instead he kissed her and spoke to her with Raymond's voice. At that moment, a whiteness like a cloud escaped him and darted upward and out through the skylight above the bed, and a greasy blackness like the smoke from an oil fire drained out of him into the floor, and he himself faded and disappeared.

Released from the hold that had bound them, Octave rolled away from Cat and gathered the clothes that had been stripped from him and dressed hastily with his eyes turned to the wall.

Cat went quickly to the bathroom and threw on her robe. "Did you see him?" she said, across the room. "Did you see Raymond?"

"I saw something like him," Octave said, "But the eyes were wrong. I thought it was the demon, come to finish us."

"I thought so too. And then something changed."

"Yes. Something did." Octave sat on the far side of the bed, still facing the wall. "Mrs. Kidd," he said, and hesitated, clearing his throat. "Mrs. Kidd, I've been dead before. It doesn't frighten me. What oppresses me is that you were almost killed, and that I could do nothing about it. And it shames me no end that I could not help myself, that when we were forced into the posture of lovers, I reacted as one."

"Something has changed about the house too," Cat said, putting her hands out as if she were feeling the air. "Can you tell?"

"Mrs. Kidd, did you hear me?"

"Yes, I heard you, Octavius. And I understand. You reacted as any man would. But it didn't go anywhere. Nothing happened. Leave it. Who cares?"

"Don't you care that I love you?"

She considered the half-strangled declaration and slumped shoulders of the woebegone younger man in his mud-crusted shirt with his prematurely receding hairline and his way of squinting as if he were always looking into the sun—stuck into a strange life, robbed of the brother that was all the family he had left, tempted by Burton Latimer with the mother who had left him—and shook her head in disbelief that such a predicament as theirs had ever arisen in the world.

She called him to her then and held him and assured him that she did care and that she loved him too, but as a mother would love a son, as his own mother had loved him.

"She cared for you no end. I'm sure she did. But she was broken, Octave. I know how it feels. Forgive her for leaving you. And be my friend now and help me find Raymond."

"Good evening, Canada," said the anchorwoman, "I'm Julia Barnes, and this is All the News and Then Some.

"You may remember our story The Man Who Came Out of the Sea. Well, this evening we've got the Man Who Came Out of the Grave, and the Man Who Disappeared from His Cell.

"As it turns out, all three men are the same.

"Fifty-two-year-old Raymond Kidd, the subject of our initial story, was apprehended by Halifax Police late last night in historical Camp Hill Cemetery in downtown Halifax. Police detective Darryl Burnhardt found Kidd six feet down in the grave of one Oliver Cole, nineteenth century merchantman captain. The first footage you will see shows Kidd digging away, explaining why he's doing what he's doing, and discovering a silver crucifix inlaid with rubies and imperial Brazilian topaz just as Officer Burnhardt arrives on the scene.

"Next we have an interview conducted just this afternoon with Burnhardt in which he reveals that Kidd has vanished from the cell in which he was being held, leaving behind a pair of shattered eyeglasses, a tricorne hat, and—get this—a fish-oil lantern. He had the eyeglasses with him—intact—at the time of his capture. The other two items appeared as if from nowhere. How did they get there? What was he doing in the grave. How did he disappear? Is there a method to his madness? You can judge for yourself based on Kidd's explanation and the rantings of Detective Burnhardt, who was relieved of duty after his reaction to the escape was deemed excessive. BTV News taped the interview in Burnhardt's Dartmouth home after being called by him from there.

"At the risk of my job, as the detective has risked his, I have an experience of my own I'd like to share with you afterwards, one that happened to me while I was with Raymond Kidd before he went grave robbing. It will either help you understand all this, or make you think I'm nuts too.

"Here we go. Hold on to your seats, folks. This reporter's trying to."

Nettie McEachern rested on the Spelling Rock for a longer spell than usual on her way up Mile Stump Hill. Her breath came shorter these days, persevere as she might, and she could see the day coming when her daily walking would end and the indoors would claim her. She was determined to push that day back, but was discovering that even determination had its limits. Twice already this morning she had tripped on the pavement on something that wasn't even there. She tried to take her thoughts off mortality by listening to the gadget her nephew had given her. It made her feel excessively modern and at the same time in the swing of things to wear earphones on her walks. Right now the news was on and she was listening to the story about Booda Ray. Even that had to do with the grave. Goodness gracious. Booda Ray a grave robber. She missed all the rest of the story just thinking about that. Finally you merit a rest and then someone comes digging up your bones. She would give that young man a choice piece of her mind, see if she didn't. Next time she went to clean his house. Whenever that was. He hadn't asked her yet this year. Well, if he didn't soon, she would go over there anyway. She filed that task for future reference and put her mind on the portrait of herself that hung in the hall upstairs, as she had been painted so long ago by that other American who came to vacation on Saul's Island. As a raven-haired beauty with a winning smile and no dentures and so much vitality visitors said they could feel the warmth of her radiating off the canvas. And then she set her sights on attaining the top of the hill and got up off the rock and walked on.

Tyler Robb, watching the story on a different sort of pocket gadget, got no further than Raymond's arrest and disappearance from his cell before it was time for the next tour.

He led the group through the ingredients room, the brewing room, the barrel-making room, and finally down to the bar.

Inside the bar, after the singing and dancing and joking and drinking and gaming were over and the guests had been led out through the long stone corridor down which ale by the cask was once rolled, he went by himself to the room they called Mr. Keith's private sitting room and sat down in the chair from which Raymond had disappeared the year before.

Whatever was going on with that old man, Tyler wished he knew the disappearing trick. If he did, he would disappear from this job where he had to say the same things over and over thousands of times every season or get docked for improvising. He would disappear for a living and become famous.

He took off his apprentice brewmaster's apron and twirled it in the air and threw it down and said, "Ta da!"

But he did not disappear and he did not walk down the corridor and out the doors onto Lower Water Street forever and away. Because although it was only ten dollars an hour, it was a job. And you had to start somewhere. And the next tour was in five minutes.

He tightened his boot laces, got up from the chair, tossed down a forbidden glass of ale at the bar, and retraced his steps to the beginning point.

It was Gordon Daggon's birthday and he was spending it babysitting. Doris was upstairs in bed with a cold, and little Shannon O'Keefe was in his lap. The television was on but at the moment he was ignoring it while he explained something to Shannon, who was holding, one in each hand, two homemade birthday cards with stick figures on the front drawn in crayon.

"Yes, they both say 'Happy Birthday, Uncle Gordon'. They do *say* that. But just saying it doesn't make it so. I'm not really your uncle, dear. Our families live close, and are close, and you've taken to calling me that, and that's all right. But this other card was from my kid sister Margaret's son Geoffrey. He was really my nephew. You're not really my niece. We've no blood ties between us."

"If you're *really* his uncle and *not* really mine," Shannon pouted, "why am I here for your birthday and he's not? He just sent a card. I came myself. That means I love you better."

Gordon took Geoffrey's card from her, gently, and rubbed the crayon on the paper lightly and fondly with his thumb, as if he could feel something through it beyond the texture of the coloured wax. The figure on the card had a magnifying glass in one hand and was examining a stick fish it had caught with the fishing pole in the other hand. "He loved me well enough," Gordon said. "He was smart, too. He knew I was a detective before I retired."

"Then why isn't he here?"

"Oh, he'd be here if he could. But he can't anymore, you know? He grew up a little bit, and got to be a lifeguard over to Lawrencetown Beach, and one day he had a problem. A young boy and his sister, not much older than you, got swept out to sea by the rip tide, and Geoffrey went out to rescue them. He brought in the girl and went back for the boy. But he got tired, eh? And he didn't make it. And he didn't make it back, either. He drowned."

Both the sandy-haired sprite of a girl and the ash-whiskered seventy-six-year-old birthday boy fell silent then as any room there might have been to say anything else was all filled up by what had been said already. By and by they began to watch the television again, and the story about Raymond came on.

When the story was over, Gordon switched the sound off with the remote control. Shannon said, "I guess it's a dangerous place, where we live. Geoffrey drownded, and Julia almost got drownded by those spirits in the barachois, and I got tricked into a tree, and my friend the pirate who rescued me never came back, and now Booda Ray, he's gone too."

Gordon, who had been steadily fortifying himself during the story with generous sips from a cut crystal glass on the coffee table that held more rum than water, said he guessed so too, that not coming back was sort of a tradition for people who lived by the sea. "And yet it might be that we never leave at all. Your friend the pirate, who is my ancestor Angus Daggon, he died here a long time ago. Froze to death up on the Head. Turns out he never really left, though. He was here all along as a spook. I'm sorry." He stopped to toast the air in apology. "I meant *lost soul.* And really was no longer a pirate but the best sort of gentleman. Who knows? He came back once. He might do it again.

"And maybe Geoffrey, maybe he's still around too. Sometimes I think I feel him. And Booda Ray, he seems to come and go and then show up again.

"Who knows? Maybe we love this crazy coast too much. Maybe we all ought to up anchor and move into safe little boxes in the city, away from the sea and its surges. Away from far horizons that get to be like a uniform, like a badge. Maybe we ought to learn to let go and move on when we die.

"But I'll tell you one thing. When I was a detective, I never behaved like that fellow on the TV. You don't lose your temper and start making accusations right and left. That Raymond, for instance, if he's a drug smuggler, I'll eat my hat. No, he doesn't ask enough questions, this Mr. Burned Heart. He looks into things with his eyes closed. They did right to send him home. They'll do better to cut him loose altogether. He's a disgrace to the force."

"You sure are drinking a lot," said Shannon. She settled back against his chest. Uncle Gordon's sweater smelled of rum and pipe tobacco, and she liked it. "When my father drinks a lot, he talks like you're talking. It's a little hard to understand."

"It's my birthday," said Gordon. "A man's got a right to be a little hard to understand on his birthday. And besides, it's just cold medicine. Doris is sick, and this keeps me from getting what she's got."

"Should I have some? I'm good at taking medicine."

"No, my dear. You don't need any. You just snuggle up there, and in a minute I'll go get you some more cake."

Julia Barnes sat in front of the desk of Tom Lutz, in a cold sweat, and Lutz just sat there letting her soak in it while he smoked.

"You went out on a limb," he said finally. "And then you jumped."

The way he looked at her, with his hard eyes and his thin lips compressed, was so snakelike she shuddered in spite of her determination not to be cowed. She believed in her story, and if she was going to be sacked, she thought *bring it*. But the whip-thin station manager was a formidable presence. She couldn't help feeling like a naughty schoolgirl called in by an unforgiving principal.

"I had to," she said. "It's all true. It all happened."

Lutz nodded and breathed smoke. "Sure it did. But you only had proof of the grave robbing. The rest could be gospel, but you didn't have footage."

"No, but I had Burnhardt."

"That was hearsay. Sensational—you got the guy to really come un-glued—but still hearsay. So far the police haven't confirmed that they ever held Raymond Kidd, much less let him be *spirited* away. And then off you went with your swamp spirits and your vision and your lightning bolt."

"You kept your hands off, Tom. You told me to do it my way."

"I did."

He stubbed out his cigarette and opened a drawer. She was sure she was about to hand her her walking papers. Instead what he set down hard on the desktop like a declaration was a bottle of champagne.

"There," he said. "That ought to make the cork pop all the way to Ar-mdale, like that anchor in the Halifax Explosion. Which would be fitting, since you're another kind of explosion.

"Julia, what you did, it's not the kind of journalism I was taught. But it's good. It's new, and it's good. It's just the different kind of news a different kind of world is looking for. You've put us on the map, girl. Calls are com-ing in from everywhere. What I want to do next, after we finish this bottle, is talk about keeping you here. Because you're going to get offers from everywhere. Toronto. New York. If the Devil has a broadcasting company, he'll be looking for you. You're about to be a hot commodity, Julia Barnes." He placed two stained BTV coffee mugs alongside the bottle. "I've had this on ice since before the program. I knew you wouldn't let me down. And I apologize for being so hard on you. I just wanted to make sure that when you did get yourself out there, on the end of that limb, that there would be no way back, and that all you could do was to jump.

"You did it in grand style, I must say. You're more than a hell of a re-porter. You're supernatural."

"You asshole," said Julia, her eyes gleaming with tears and the armpits of her blouse damp with sweat. "Give me that bottle. I'll be the one to pop the cork."

In the dark in the bedroom of Angelina and Eldridge, that was punctuated by night lights and dimly pervaded by moon and star light from the picture windows, one word was said, by a voice that had not spoken in years, and that was, "Raymond?"

Eldridge heard his wife speak, because as usual he lay unsleeping beside her, and he waited for her to say something else. But she did not, and she did not respond to him when he called, "Angelina?" in the dark or when he turned the bedside lamp on and said it again.

He did not watch the news that morning because his heart and head were fully occupied with Angelina's one word, and he spoke no more to Maricela during breakfast than to ask for more soft-boiled eggs, though he had not eaten the ones she had brought him already.

At noon he requested that Angelina and he be taken down to the lake that was nestled in a fold of the vineyard. There he had the two vineyard workers put them both on the barge he kept there for excursions on sunny days. So many sunny days, however, had passed without the barge being used that it was in a sad state of disrepair. The faded awning was ripped where the branch of a live oak had fallen on it, and the motor had to be taken apart and cleaned and oiled and reassembled before it would run. Finally they were in the middle of the lake. Eldridge told Aureliano to drop the anchor, fold back the torn awning, and swim back to shore. Aureliano, normally a very willing young worker, asked Eldridge to repeat the last instruction, thinking it due to his employer's bad Spanish. He could not imagine that the incapacitated old man would want to be left alone with his helpless wife out there on the water with no one to attend. But it was so, and after hearing the instruction again, accompanied by specific emphatic gestures, he took off his shoes, threw them the twenty yards or so to shore, and jumped in with his clothes on.

When he swam back that evening, against his instructions, which were not to come till he was called by Eldridge on his cell phone, he found the old couple both dead in their deck chairs, holding hands and smiling, their eyes closed as if they were merely sunning themselves.

Estrella was a waitress in an upstairs restaurant that overlooked the central square of Oaxaca. Her boyfriend Blanco Sanchez liked to come on Fridays when there was live music from the bandstand in the square. He liked a seat by an open window, and a large bowl of tomato soup, and he liked to talk to Estrella as if with his pale skin he were a foreign tourist with a wandering eye whose Spanish when he ventured into it was ridiculous.

"This soup, how you say, *supa,* it is *muy soberoso.* In my country, *en mi payaso, los Estados Refritos,* all the *supa* comes in cans, *canos* you know, but here you make from *tomatos muy freshos.* Will you come closer, *acércame* more close, so I can *tocar* your *fresho tomatos?*"

And then she would come closer and he would raise his hands as if to touch her chest but instead would clap them to his cheeks and exclaim with a horrified look, *"Dios mio,* what was I *thinkando? El infierno* must be full of *sinneros* like me!"

It was always something like that, innocent and fun, and at the end of the meal he would loudly offer to increase her tip if she would accompany him afterwards, and she would haughtily refuse and slap away his money-filled hand. And afterwards of course she would indeed accompany him and they would sing and dance and laugh and love the night away.

Today was only Thursday and she was not expecting him. When she came to the window he was looking out at the empty bandstand in the dying light and at first did not acknowledge her presence. Then he took her hand and kissed it and said somberly and formally, *"Amorcita,* my father has problems and I must go to him. Will you come with me?"

"To Canada?" she said. "All the way to Canada? What about my job?"

"About your job, well, nothing," he replied. "We are going further into our lives. You must bet on our luck."

"What kind of problems does your father have?"

"I will tell you on the road. The *micro* is parked outside."

She had some further astonishment to express, regarding passports and clothes and commitments and goodbyes, but already the butterfly wings of her heart were in motion and she knew she would go with her untamed mestizo and follow his lead if it led to the ends of the earth.

❀

Cat felt a great weight had been lifted from the house, and knew beyond doubt that the demon and his negativity had indeed vanished from 7 Lands End. She wanted to celebrate with Raymond and tell him their marriage was golden—gold, silver and diamonds all wrapped up in one—because it had survived and the dark times were behind them. She went room to room searching for him and calling his name. She was sure she would know when she found him. If there was no appearance, she was so full of love she was certain she would feel his incorporeal presence. She checked upstairs and downstairs and even in the basement. The second time around she opened all the closets and drawers and peered into the crawlspace with a flashlight. Finally, feeling foolish and exhilarated and anxious all at once, she opened the door of the woodstove and rummaged through last winter's ashes.

It was only when she stood at the kitchen window looking out at the cove, where the tide had receded and the seagulls were stalking the mud for stray crabs, that she realized she had not checked in the shrine room. Each time she had passed it, it was as if the fierce warrior noren at the entrance had warded her off. Now she went back determined.

She passed through the noren to find the shrine room lit with candles and fragrant with incense and with her cushion and Raymond's arranged side by side as they had been before she left. She sat down on her cushion and whispered, "Raymond?"

She felt nothing but the sense that she should meditate.

After a while doing that, without calling his name again, she could feel him on the cushion beside her. She put her hand out and felt him take it in his own, as lightly as if she were touching dust in the sunlight.

So they celebrated, hour after hour, while the candles turned into puddles and the incense to ash.

She had not found Octave either, but it never occurred to her to worry about that.

That house had never been free from the taint of his father's wickedness. Now it was, seemingly, yet Octave toiled on and away from it, for he could find no comfort there. The walk was not difficult, and he knew the way well. The work was in getting away from the house. He had been there so long, through a lifetime and a deathtime, that it was as if attached to him so he had to drag it with him.

He marked the place at the end of the lane where his half of the house had indeed once been dragged. Nothing remained but a green indentation in the rocky slope, and an old bathtub among the low-growing juniper that overflowed with the water that dripped into it from a rusty pipe coming out of the hillside.

At the crossing of the inlet from the sea, the trial became so bitter that he staggered and slipped off the stepping stones and fell down on his knees and thought he might as well stay there as anywhere and become part of the landscape and eventually a stepping stone himself.

He got up nevertheless and went on in wet shoes and with his trousers half-soaked till he reached the High Head and the sheltered niche in the cliff where his brother had once been wont to sit.

It was not snowing as it had been when he last went to look for Angus. The sky was large and the sea stretched out glittering and booming against the granite jumble so a fine spray kissed his cheeks.

They called him Octave because of his range. Now he sang crowding the high end of his third and highest octave, because loneliness filled up the rest of the register and if he ventured there he knew he must cry.

He was afraid Angus would not answer if he called for him crying.

Oh don't you see that broad broad road
That lies across the lily leven
That is the path of wickedness
Some call the road to Heaven

And don't you see that bonnie road
That winds about the hillside so
That is the road to Elfland fair
Where you and I this night maun go

He sang on that hard seat by the sea all afternoon, while other walkers on their summer way looked in at him among the rocks to see where the singing was coming from, and as quickly walked on when he would not stop singing to acknowledge them. After some hours, too, the wind and the spray made a rather intimidating figure of him, sculpting his wispy hair into a Medusian mess, and they were mainly of the opinion that he might be mad.

The milky mist that escaped Raymond as he rejected the demon in him went out the skylight but did not continue rising to join the other clouds. Instead it flew over the ground at the height of a house over the rest of the village and on to the barachois. Arriving there it zipped from place to place, from the boggy foot path to the salt marshes to the drumlin woods, and in each place paused and dissipated into the growing things there and then gathered again and darted on.

On a rocky hilltop by the sea, the mist fragment hovered and circled and then slipped into the cleft of the shattered dead hulk of a tree that had been the enchanted hemlock in which Angle had exchanged himself for Shannon O'Keefe. When the mist slipped out again, it began to spin and compress itself into something like an upright cocoon, which then transformed into two people, one slumped in the other's arms.

With the sea breeze blowing over them and bright sunlight spilling across them, Jenny the Simple sat cradling Angle Daggon's head in her lap, wishing she could run her fingers again through his long hair that when unbraided was like the mane of a lion. Only he had no hair now. And that was not the end of his transfiguration.

Out of grass, she wove a patch for his missing eye. From a fallen limb of the blasted hemlock, she fashioned a crude wooden leg. For his missing hand she substituted a rusty boathook she found on the shore down below.

"Wake up, my love," she said when all was done. "Wake up and see yourself, the very figure of a pirate now."

For clothes he had only her long spreading hair, that lay over his gaunt torso like a blanket of gleaming red gold.

"Wake to the new day," said the Simple, rubbing, in a circular motion, with the tip of one finger, the rose and dagger tattoo on his chest. "Wake and rejoice, oh my love."

Cat and a woeful but at least returned Octave at the puja table in the shrine room sat and contemplated their arrangement of Raymond's favourite things. His red guitar in its open case leaned against the wall beside the shrine, with the light of the shrine candles flickering across the instrument's polished face. Before the guitar was a chair and his music stand with a well-fingered volume of Renaissance melodies transcribed for the classical guitar. On the other side of the shrine, tacked to the wall, was the chart of coastal waters from East Ironbound Island to Chebucto Head that he had used so often in his sailing days that it had fallen apart in the creases of its folds and been taped back together. On a third cushion beside them lay Raymond's laptop computer, open and running, on the screen a blank page in a word processing program, the cursor pulsing, waiting for a word. On the incense table in front of the shrine, crowding to one side the incense burner with its smoking stick of his preferred clove-accented sandalwood, rested the stack of unbound pages of his unfinished commentary on the obstacles and antidotes involved in Buddhist meditation practice, the title page sealed as it were with a coffee cup stain that resembled a Zen ink-and-brush painting of a circle.

On the black-lacquered surface of the puja table, the emptiness bell and the dorje of compassion were ranged in front of a turquoise and gold brocade cloth that for the time being served as a placemat for a dish with a grilled steak and a tall glass of scotch.

On the shrine itself was a framed photo of Cat and Raymond kissing on their wedding day.

Octave said, "I believe that is everything. And though you neglected to mention it, I know from my own observations that the text required for the ceremony is called the *sukhavati*. There was a copy of it in the bookshelf. I have it here. If you like, if you would find it too painful, I can be the one to take the photo from the frame and burn it, so Raymond can move on."

To which Cat replied, "Oh, Octave, I'm sorry. I thought I said. This isn't a sukhavati. We're not here to send Raymond on his way. This is all to invite him to stay. We won't be burning that picture, and I don't need a text."

"Oh," echoed Octave, in a small voice, "so that is why his things are here. I found no mention in the text of that. Only of burning the photo."

"It's all right. I know you meant well. And that is what we would have done if this … if this were business as usual. But it isn't. There's a flaw in the fabric, and Raymond has been back and forth through it. There's a chance he could do it again. In the meantime, well, this will be his hotel room."

There were things he could do that made him wonder.

He could eat the steak dinner and drink the scotch Cat had left him and put on the clothes she brought later. He could type on the laptop she left open and running. He could take the red guitar from its case and play it.

Was he really in between?

Not only that but he could play as he had never played before. He had been a good student in his college days but had never persevered and so had never become more than an indifferent musician who played the same simple pieces over and over. It was the guitar he had loved more than the playing. A handmade Hernandez from Spain with a near concert tone. A ding on one edge had made it affordable. He had sold the rifle his father had given him to pay for it and had never owned a firearm since. He treasured the instrument greatly and kept it waxed and polished though over the years he played it less and less, and rarely at all since he had severed a nerve in his left hand in a kitchen accident, because his thoughts were with Cat leaving home while he was speed-chopping a zucchini with a knife he kept hair-splitting sharp. Yet now his fingers were more limber than ever, and raced up and down the broad neck as if a virtuoso owned them.

He turned the pages of the music book on its stand to Dowland's Forlorn Hope Fancy, a piece he had never attempted because of its level of difficulty, and found to his delight that he could accomplish it with ease. His arpeggios flowed like water, like fire. He took on the rest of the book of antiquarian compositions. There was nothing he couldn't conquer and dominate.

Dressed as he was, he began to feel as if he were giving a concert. Cat had brought his best clothes, including the wedding vest she had made for him of gold and blue brocades with a knot of eternity pattern. He ornamented his renditions and delivered them with the passion of a newlywed.

Remembering their hand-holding reunion, he burned for her. She was his audience. He knew she could hear him. He would go to her now. It was night. He would find her in bed.

He put the red guitar away and confronted the warrior noren.

And changed his mind.

Although the darkness of the demon had dropped away from him, there was something of the pirate captain still with him, a fierceness and audacity that was not like him, and he did not trust it. He would meditate, and then he would go to his wife and embrace her with tenderness instead of lust.

He sat down on his cushion at the low puja table and crossed his legs and settled himself to let his thoughts unwind. And waited. And waited. And waited.

What arose gradually was the sounds of a ship gathering way, sails unfurling and flapping till their lines brought them taut, orders being shouted and men running along a wooden deck, the creaking of cannon being run out. His pulse quickened. And then of a sudden the images surrounded him. The masts and square sails and hustling crew of the *Queen Mab*. The narrow entrance to Rogue's Roost out of which they would burst and hurl themselves upon the unsuspecting merchantman.

The queen's ship that awaited them just outside the entrance. The cannonfire and crashing as his ship was dealt a mortal blow before she could return fire.

The hoisting of himself to the yardarm.

He blinked. He had let his eyes close and had tumbled into the memories of another man. But he was Raymond Kidd. He looked around at his things to reassure himself. His black guitar case, his shrine with the pictures of his teachers in this life above it and the smoking incense below it and on it the glowing candles and offerings and the dorje and emptiness bell, the bookshelf with his dharma books, his refuge name framed on the wall, his open laptop on the puja table, the background image on the screen of grapes ready to harvest in the vineyard of the family home, the open document on which he had typed a title, the flashing icon that showed he had mail waiting.

He abandoned his meditation and checked his mail. He had one message, from lotsawa237@coolboredom.com, an address he had never seen.

The message read:

yo dawg,

what arises like a wave subsides like one
don't leave anyone behind
click <u>here</u> for a good time

yr humble you-know-who

He read it once altogether and then went back through it line by line, trying to puzzle it out. All in all, it seemed suspicious. No one he knew would use *yo dawg* for a greeting. The first line of the body of the text seemed like words of the Dharma, the second like an appeal and also an admonishment. The third line, the invitation to follow the link *for a good time,* was what made his finger hover over the delete button. That made it almost certainly spam or a quick path to the sort of virus that could commandeer his computer. The anonymous closing reinforced that conclusion.

But it also sounded like the sort of trick that Burton Latimer would play. And he was not about to be intimidated by that graveyard bamboozler.

Against his better judgment he clicked the link. When he did, an anonymous browser appeared, and one by one the lost souls of Prospect appeared on his screen as if on streaming video.

The style of their dress depended on the date of their death, and ranged from the homespun of the village's inception in the seventeenth century to the tee shirt made in China with the rapper printed on the front that Turner Charles' son Maxim had been wearing three years ago when he drowned while surfing stoned in a borrowed dinghy. Those who were not within houses dwelt variously outdoors. A child in a nightdress stood under one of the two little bridges in the village, enduring a tide endlessly ebbing and flowing, the tail of her dress streaming forward and back like the one hand of a demented clock. Under the other bridge, two Mikmaq natives outfitted like patchwork settlers floated their jug of rum back and forth to each other each time the tide allowed.

There were few fishermen but many fishermen's wives, some sitting, some standing, all staring out toward the sweetheart-stealing sea. The handful of fisherman who had died ashore adorned the dome of Council Rock near Gordon Daggon's stage, with nets in their crabbed hands that fell apart again as quickly as they could be mended.

Their faces for the most part were so doleful and strained and drained of hope that they did not bear looking at for long. Raymond closed the mysterious browser in which they were appearing and sat there stunned.

The message had cautioned him not to leave anyone behind, and had greeted him as *dawg,* and as Oliver Cole he had been given dog as a name. Emptiness Dog. Howling Cur of Enlightenment. Not as a recognition, he knew now, but as an incentive. He got up again to go to Cat, not for love-making this time but to tell her his teacher had reached him and that his assignment in the in-between was not over.

The noren stopped him cold, as if it were not a flimsy curtain but a real door, shut and locked.

He went back to the laptop and erased the nonsense words he had written there to see if his fingers would impress the keys. In their place, after an hour or so of waiting for the right thing to arise, he typed a title.

A Travellers Guide for Lost Souls

Everything was back to ordinary at last.

Before retiring, she had tended to the men in the house.

She had removed Raymond's untouched steak dinner from the shrine room, transferred the scotch to a regular offering bowl, folded his clothes in a tidy pile, taken the chair and music stand away, closed the empty document on his laptop screen and turned off the laptop. She could still feel his presence. She wished she could hear him play, or read to her the things he might have written.

She had installed Octave once again in the guest room and provided him with a spare computer and left him busy on the Internet. His plan was to find an identity there. It had something to do with getting the birth certificate of someone who had been born when he might have been, considering his apparent age, and who had died as a child, so a life lived would not be in his way. She did not quite understand, but he was quite convinced it would work and allow him to go out in the world and seek employment and so remunerate her for his room and board. The idea cheered him up, and that was good, for he had been sadder than she knew what to do with.

She did not bring up the possibility that the police would come looking for Raymond, and so pester them with an investigation before Octave's identity was well set. At the moment, the official police stance was that they had never arrested her husband. They might not come at all.

It was morning in Prospect.

With the skylight above her swung open, and a concert of seagulls and surf coming through, Cat McCallum lay awake as she had lain for hours, propped up on pillows, her hands folded over her stomach, her head strangely empty and her heart strangely full. The new day's sunshine danced before her on the orange wall. She knew it was time to move on.

She had no idea where to go.

When the change comes, and we don't know our minds, then we're stuck with a stranger, because mind is all we are. All we have left. We think we come here with our bodies, because we can't bear to be parted from them. But the warmth has gone out. They are not what they were. We know that. We admit that to ourselves, but in such a small voice we pretend not to hear it. These illusory forms, that we are only imagining, they continue to deceive us, as a stranger would who does not know or care for us and does not have our best interests at heart. They stand up, they sit down, they look out at a world that is no longer ours, yet they tell us it is. They say that sunrise on the sea, this granite coast, those dear ones, these enclosures at land's end that we have loved as eagles love their eyries, fiercely, all are ours, still ours. And that is not the case, neighbours. These things are the view from a prisoner's cell. We thought we had them but we do not have them now. We are lost souls, trapped by our yearning. All we have is suffering.

It is not too late, however. Introductions can be made. We can be free to come and go, and so continue on our journey, once we know our minds.

These words are sound and emptiness, like an echo. This in-between world is appearance and emptiness, like a reflection. This awareness is a universe of awareness and emptiness.

If you know this, when the universe collapses, you can lead the cheer.

So Raymond wrote, and wondered at what he had written.

End of Book One

(Prospect, Halifax, Dartmouth, Ambergris Cay, Linholme)

Bonus from Jim T. Lindsey

A selection of poetry from
Snapshots from the In Between

Snapshots
from the In Between

Jim Lindsey

A companion volume of verse
to A Travellers Guide for Lost Souls

The Scene with the Beautiful Woman

In the scene with the beautiful woman
no beautiful woman appears.

In the instant the scene is conceived

she turns the sky around
takes refuge in a cloud of unknowing
envelops herself in thin air.

As each single note seeks its chord

the stones shield her
an endless waterway shuffles off her dazzling scent and dainty footprints
her daily affairs submerge her in a different score.

As the hero longs aloud for her particular attractions

she shaves her head and blends into a background of renunciates
her wanted poster kindles countless fires in a universal winter
love itself takes her in where she cannot be singled out.

In the missing scene with the beautiful woman
which plays always and anyway

the constellations absorb all lamentation
and the understudy moon, well-rehearsed,
embarks on its triumphal debut.

Hello Dreamer

A dream never dies, but the dreamer must employ
another eye to see it change. Because we forget, because

the hare in the long grass is still but not hidden
and the breeze in its soft fur is stirring

the sun on the seaway is blinding
and our course takes us into the sun

we cannot cry any more
we have been crying too long

we saw her lose a breast and said she was still with us
saw her lose the rest and said that she was gone

we believe that dreams die
and we are never ready

What We Said by the Beautiful Sea

An ongoing masterpiece
the sea from the cottage
now at high tide now at low
now in fog now in snow

now with clouds of seabirds hovering
as the fishermen disembowelled their catch
now with the last of the fishermen's stages
borne off by the hurricane

Whether upstairs or down though
from one side or the other
through windows clear or rain-smeared, salty or frosted
it seemed to be always the same

romantic seaside scene, the one the bureau
featured in their famous poster, that the tourists
flocked to photo for themselves
as if their mimicry had some secret merit

You know the one, three painted chairs,
red, yellow and white in the year of the photo, in later years
of different colours, facing out on a differently colorful sea
from a dock that was ours, so to speak

Oh how they strove to recapture
that fabulous poster.
Us too. That day the lilies
flamed forth from the flowerbox

behind the chairs, and just beyond
a small laughing boy in a dinghy
not in the picture but off to one side
rowed round and round in a circle.

Our son? It might have been.
A sadness unborn never died.
Hello, and with the same breath, goodbye
is what we said by the beautiful sea.

The Snow in the Closet

Old, middle-aged, or young
how easily we are gulled
into believing
we really are one or the other

Young, middle-aged, or old
this dream of being human
holds us dear, and makes
us so afraid

Whatever age we say
another is already taking us away
I remember asking my mother
was I ever six at all

She had a flower in her hair
There was snow in the closet

We Saw the Wheels Come Loose

We had our names for both the wheels,
the sorrow and the joy.
They altered with the years.
We whispered, "You can do it, Yellow Boy,"
and smoothed a painted mane
or cried into a bloody ear
endearments deafening, had she heard.

So sad and happy still.
At night the crippling weight comes off,
our hearts rise with the sun,
and Ah and Oh we say,
but that's as close as we get now
to calling names. We saw
the wheels come loose and roll away.

We saw the wheels come loose.
No one was crushed.
No wreckage choked the hall.
The train ran on. That form is emptiness
is said to be so out of kindness,
never to dishearten or appall, for there's no harm
in travelling light when light is all.

Where the Cowboy Came to Rest

The sunset was always beyond us.
We never made it there.
They buried us along the way
another broke-down horse and rider.

We never made it there like heroes.
We never left a little woman behind.
The old homestead, where she should have stood waving,
is under a parking lot now.

We never saved her from bad guys or indians.
She left us on the train.
I believe it was raining that day.
You couldn't see anything plain.

My old horse may have turned into dog food.
I couldn't be sure about that.
I remember there was no place to keep him.
Someone said, And you can take off that hat.

I remember the wide open spaces.
That's one thing I'll never forget.
When the nurse said, *The old fart is not eating again*
I was remembering them, from my heart.

The Girl Under The Guvvy

I went down to the sea
to the government wharf
where they waited for me
to come play.

It was warm in the sea
at the guvvy
warm enough to swim anyway
at least for a while.

It's a cold sea, you see, really.
It's only warm where it's shallow
and the sun can work through.
That's what my dad says.

Tommy Robicheau
that chicken
he was scared to go in
so he pushed me.

I would have gone anyway.
At first it's a shock
and yes it takes your breath away
but after a while you don't mind it so much

and then when you're out
at the top of the ladder you shout
as the feeling comes back
in a rush and it's heaven

at least for a moment
and then there's the towel
that your mom makes you bring
lying near.

That's how I would have felt
but he pushed me
the chicken
and I fell and landed funny.

Now I never come out
and I wonder
where everyone went.
I've been under so long

I can't remember much.
I know the crabs are my friends
and Bob the lobster
with the claw long as your arm

but they don't talk much
and I'm never warm now.
I miss the sun, eh?
I miss ... but I won't start.

I can go on for hours,
sometimes days,
and you should be on your way really.
That's what my dad would say.

The Priest in the Glebe House

So call me an idler.
Still, I'm not quite your usual priest.
I didn't hang back out of sloth
Or from love of the cloth
And it certainly wasn't my housekeeper's tea.

No, the past has no collar on me.
I don't walk the halls whispering Mass in the wee hours
or otherwise alarming my less hardy successors.
I couldn't care less.
All I do is go nowhere.

I inhabit this dusty old armchair
(consigned to the attic as my corpse was to the ground)
and keep watch on the village.
With my vision no longer bound
by walls or other petty obstacles

I can see anywhere from Bald Rock out at sea
to the cemeteries along the road into Halifax.
I can see where the Fantome went down, and the Atlantica,
in fact everywhere the lost souls tarry
for they are my consideration now.

They have no other friend, you see,
and though I cannot free them like a warden
I keep my vigil and I send my love endlessly.
What more do you want?
It's very boring, my little corner of heaven.

Last Gift of The Seamstress

I knew the measurements.
They were my own.
I made a bodice
(for the woman that I was

before three babies
and the wear and tear
of gravity
and husbands)

one with sequins and pearl beading
and a heart-shaped
plunging neckline
that would make you stare.

I owned the floor back then
and I could dance all night and day.
I danced as if on fire.
I took their breath away.

Now my own breath is gone
but you can see
my testament to what I was.
It stands up on its own

with stiffeners of whalebone
and that promise of bliss.
It does not need me in it
to charm you like this.

The Guru's Rude Awakening

I'm in my favorite house but not part of the scene anymore.
There's my large-screen TV, my indoor putting green,
my closet of Gieves & Hawkes suits and robes made to order,
and here my wife Tashi and consort Niobe
chatting together on the sofa like the old friends they are
but looking right through me, not feeling my hands
or hearing me lovingly calling their names.

I'm in the realm of lost souls, where the dead stay
when their attachment to life is too strong,
a sort of in-between space, neither here nor there,
no sort of place for anyone, least of all someone like me.
I know the score, that we are empty of any inherent reality
and yet appear like the moon on the water.
I taught that for years, and yet here I linger.

I didn't achieve rainbow body, nor embrace the white light
or even catch the moments when I had the chance.
I lay down on my ear like the Buddha
with my most favoured students around
and when I woke up I was here, neither seen nor heard,
unable to get a drink or even a word
from these two women who adored me.

You there, pray that when you pass
you realize the meaning, and dissolve in bliss
and don't hang around like a trophy, like this.

The Ocean Is Closed for the Season

The ocean is closed for the season.
Hauled and stripped, her booms unshipped,
our playmate sits gathering snow,
her charts by the fire laid out to dry,
her main and mizzen, checked for wear,
to be stowed in the loft, not to mildew.

Rogue's Roost, Bald Rock, East Ironbound, the Ledges,
noteworthy anchorages, islands in the offing, hazards to avoid,
names in flying spray on the wind written large,
an expanse to the landbound no more tactile than a star,
if stars can be seen where they are. And now here we are,
returned to the heathen, with the ocean closed for the season.

Now the armored storms promenade, with the clear days
the coldest of all. More than bulletproof, the space
between Prospect and Betty's Island, three miles out, where autumn saw
a silver anniversary, champagne and cake and more, for the children
kites, kayaks, cranberry-picking, a trip to the lighthouse on the outer
shore
(old Algiers laid out and snoring till the tide reached his privates).

Now Betty's through the kitchen window is our contemplation.
Closed? The lobsterman says no, his red and green lamps in the grey
dawn
glowing as he leaves the harbour, swallowed outside by the seas and the
snow.
And now the amateur sailor concurs. Children, dinners, village issues
intervene,
our own work if we have any, and as the frost flowers mask the pane,
love ever beckoning, an Atlantic within, without beginning or end.

High Flyers

I.
Three miles out, the shore seems relatively insignificant.
It dawns on you the land was never really all that much,
that we ourselves, of water mostly, were always at sea,
always at home, really, beyond being lost or found.

That old salt Victor, he followed his nose,
laughed at compasses and an amateur lost in the fog,
rowed out most every morning never mind age or the weather
till the nets of his calling unravelled

and catcher and caught and the deep were rejoined.

II.
From the cottage, the sea seems relatively distant,
even more than usual with both cove and outer harbour frozen.
What are we seeing, though, anyway, in our subtle blindness?
Reflections conducted by the senses, never the thing itself.

That young stud Evan, he skipped over the ice
and where the waves beat on the frigid shelf
surfed in a neighbour's dinghy till it threw him under.
At low tide we found him, where the big rocks flower

when the ice settles, breaking and blossoming.

III.
High flyers they're called, the reflector-tipped rods on weighted buoys
that mark the big nets farther out.
Fishermen home in on them. Yachtsmen alter course.
Eventually, torn from their tethers by age and the weather,

they make their way onto the rocks
where dreamers wandering the sea cliffs collect them and carry them
home

as souvenirs, or perhaps as reminders of what it is to stand tall and alone,
outfacing the waves of illusion, pointing out to whoever appears

how things are, like it or not, in the uncertain middle of everywhere.

So Childlike We Went Forth

Across the starry sky the fleeting clouds and meteors
across our bundled bodies cold wind from the north, a zero-breaking
blow

two weeks of sickness, one of rain and snow
it seemed that we would never get outside again

the village dreamed around us, surf hammered the shore, space streaked
and flared
while she and I, as well as ever, sat and watched and cried out as they
came

the Leonids, a shower of heavenly light every year, a brainwashing so
benign
so early we woke, so childlike we went forth again

Drowned Rat and Sun

Like a drowned rat in an abandoned swimming pool
be unconcerned

Like the sun that shines always
though clouds intervene
be there for whoever whenever

Like a drowned rat in an abandoned swimming pool
give in completely to change

Like the sun that shines always
though clouds intervene
be an example of uninterrupted radiance

Like a drowned rat in an abandoned swimming pool
let the sunrise suddenly illuminate
your disgusting condition

Like the sun that shines always
though clouds intervene
make even a drowned rat a marvel

The World Called You Love

The world called you love
when already you were becoming a baby

called you a baby
when already you were becoming a boy or a girl

called you a boy or a girl
when already you were becoming a man or a woman

called you a man or a woman
when you were not done with being a boy or a girl

who was not done with being a baby
who was not done with being called love

Two Seagulls on a Dead Seal Floating

Two seagulls on a dead seal floating

were a most unlikely crew
and yet they held their stations as I passed
pausing only to pick and swallow
and till I lost them in the fog behind
were lords of all I knew

lines, course, the straining sails, the wheel.

Walking On

The day will arrive
When you would give all you own
To have never departed

But late on that saddest of days
A child will come out of a door with a flower
A stone will reveal its secret heart of water

The road will end in a field
The field will end in the ocean
The ocean will end in the sky

And you will walk on alone
And lighthearted into the stars

Why I Become a Stranger

The house is built on the edge of a cliff

The sun, if you stare, appears blue

I notice a stranger staring

Sometimes they buckle at the knee
these legs the ocean grew

The lightning resumes her clothing
but forgets the skin

There is a house on my back
that I can no longer support

I want to meet you again
over and over
for the very first time

I want to say sweet unbelievable things
and have you believe me again

The skin of the lightning
is walking away by itself

The legs of the ocean are following after

A Selection of Last Words

Goodbye
says the hunter with his net of chrysanthemums

Goodbye
says the dancer on her crystal cloud

I still love you
says the iceberg that never came so far south

I still love you
says the fountain with its tattoo of tank treads

I will miss you
says the broken mirror with a thousand voices

I will miss you
says the sunrise on the moon

Please be happy
says the missile in its downward arc

Please be happy
says the sweeper of the bones

The Enemy Cannot Be Found

Below the orange tree
is only the dust

In the house of love exhausted
only the echo of the final blow

On the hands of the brother who cuts off your light
the sweat of the fear of his very own death

Listen, reader, whoever you are,
you don't have to box up your heartache
or dress yourself in iron pants
or partake of a meal marinated in shit

The enemy cannot be found

He left his bones in a box made of wind.
Being human, we could wish a fond farewell
or, better, happiness at last
there in the garden before Eden and after the Apocalypse.
Or best of all, right out here under the moon,
peel off his invisible mask and
be done.

Message from the 13th Floor

Later I was having a glass of brandy with a cigarette in my room on the 13th floor. I had the window swung out to let the smoke escape. Suddenly I heard the sound of glass shattering, and looked down at the sidewalk, where a bottle had burst. The people on the sidewalk, at the hotel entrance, were looking up at me. I could see they thought I had thrown the bottle. I waved my finger at them to indicate that it wasn't me. I had a feeling someone would come, and within a few minutes there was a knock on the door and a man from hotel security came in to ask me questions. I told him what I had been doing. He asked if I had seen anything, anyone above me who might have thrown anything. It was an odd question, because the way the window opened out, you couldn't look up. I told him I hadn't seen anything, that his question was very odd, and that I was an 'hombre respetable'. He apologised and left. I lit another cigarette and went back to the window to finish my brandy. I had the strangest feeling. I began to wonder if I had thrown the bottle after all. All those people looking up at me, still looking up at me, felt certain I had. I then began to wonder if I was in the wrong room, if I was even myself. I picked up the bottle of brandy. It began to feel like a bomb. I went back to the window to look at all the staring faces thirteen floors below. They began to look like a target.

All That Is Left

Childhood is gone
and even the far-flung habits of childhood
Who I am becomes a question like the sky
All that is left is this shining awareness
the sun through a gap in the clouds
this undeniable awareness
drain plug of a dream

Snapshots from the In Between, a Companion Volume of Verse to A Travellers Guide for Lost Souls is available from Amazon as an ebook.

Coming from SeaStorm Press Spring of 2013:

Wild Mercy, an Eastern Western

By Jim Lindsey

Chapter 1: Bull of the Woods

I was a different kind of cowboy in a different age. The Wild West had been won and lost forever, and anyway I did my cattle minding in the East, over in southeastern Oklahoma. I rode horses, you bet, and I could rope and brand, but it was all what you might call a less expansive operation. Instead of wide open plains, we had fenced-off river bottom and forested hills. Instead of distant horizons, we had rodeo arenas. Instead of tall tales, we had little mysteries.

I had a horse before I had a job using one. My papa worked for a rodeo company and he bought from the owner, for a dollar, a skinny old used-up splay-footed roman-nosed grey gelding known as Boogeyman, who still had a sinister cast to his eye but was clean out of buck in his bones. Or pretty much. He had managed to retain a fear of snakes or anything snakelike that could still set him off. Any dead limb or piece of rope or shadow of fluttering leaves seen out the corner of his eye would do it. But it wasn't at all like the bucking he was known for. In his prime he had been a real hell-bound train. By the time I got him, it was all he could do to get rid of a dreamy little twelve-year-old like me. Toward the end of his career, the rodeo riders had got to shaking their heads and rolling their eyes when they drew him. No matter what kind of gig got stuck under his rigging, he couldn't be bothered to get mad anymore, and he wouldn't put on the kind of a show the riders needed to win. When the eight seconds were up, they would roll off his back with a laugh and blow kisses at him.

I never made fun of Boogeyman. He meant all the world to me. I called him Bubba, and I spent as much time in his company as I could. I fed him and combed him and rubbed salve on his scars and talked to him in the mornings before school, and after school we went adventuring together. When school was out for summer I pretty much lived on his back. He was mine, about all I had or cared to have, and I was his. You wouldn't have thought that having me was something he cared much for, if you judged by the way he nipped or kicked me whenever I was looking the other way or being absentminded, but I was all he had and he knew that and I knew he knew that, because whenever he managed to get out from under me, he would stand there with the reins trailing waiting for me to get back in the saddle.

Papa understood Bubba too. He knew I was safe with him, aside from a few bumps and bruises from getting bit and thrown, and he let us roam in the evenings as far and as late as I liked. I ate a lot of sandwiches in the saddle and called them dinner and it was all right with Papa. He never liked to sit down to supper with me anyway after Mama passed. Said it ruined his appetite to think of the family he might have had. He preferred eating alone, and he preferred drinking to eating.

I loved my papa. He was unlucky, but he worked hard and he took care of me the best he could given his nature, which was kind of like a wildness always waiting to bust out. He gave me a horse, I think, so I could learn to find my own way if that wildness ever got clean away and up and carried him off, which it eventually did. He came across a dirt runway in a clearing one day with a private plane on it with the door standing open as if he were expected, and he was just that drunk that he got in and tried to take off. He got into the air all right, and made it up about a thousand feet, but then he came down pretty hard about a hillside away and the airplane blew up. His fat old drinking buddy Big Meat, who chickened out on the flight at the last minute, said it looked like a flower, like a goddamn fire flower.

Also he said that the last thing Papa told him before he shooed him away and set the prop spinning was that he figured it was up to each of us to make our own way to Heaven.

That was what it was like at that ranch altogether. Always lots of surprises. That last one of Papa's came later, after Bubba and I in our wanderings had stumbled across a few of our own. Little Wing, for that was the name of the ranch, was a mighty big place, over fifteen thousand acres, and till it dropped into the Red River bottoms it was mostly rolling hills and woodland, with lots of hidden pockets and no one really minding it all, so somewhere smugglers might be bringing drugs in and abandoning planes like the one that put an end to Papa, and somewhere else that old screwloose hermit Cotton Moss could be growing magic mushrooms purely for his own benefit and under their influence calling out from the treetops about the spirits he had seen in the sky and had transferred for safe keeping to the bib of his overalls, and yet elsewhere you could get involved with a marsh so indefinite it would turn you around till you couldn't tell whether you were coming or going, till some part of your mind was persuaded hell would truly freeze over and Oklahoma too before you found your way out.

The owner lived in Manhattan, see, so far away and wealthy he might as well have been a creature from another planet, and anyway the ranch was just investment property for him, something to do with a tax break they said, and so he didn't really care what happened in the vicinity of Broken Bow. He let Papa's rodeo company graze its stock on his property in exchange for a promise to keep up the fences and take care of the roads and supervise some occasional lumbering. His name was Quick, Gabriel Quick. They called him Dirty Dollar till he came on his yearly visits, usually for the rodeo in Archer City, and then it was Mr. Q this and Mr. Q that like he was God on the hoof. He liked me to call him Gabby, and since it was only in private, when I was driving him around in his Cadillac, I did, and I didn't mind it too much. I didn't like the way he looked at me though, all searching and soulful, or the too-familiar way he put his hand on my shoulder sometimes, and I didn't like Big Meat's remarks about me being his chauffeur. "Where you going today? On the back roads again? Making your own way to heaven?"

I did like being tipped. Once Mr. Q gave me five hundred dollars. But I didn't tell anyone. I figured he felt bad about the way Papa died and was trying to make up for it.

But like I said, all that came later. Papa was still alive and kicking that afternoon I came upon the pen with no gate and got introduced to the bull of the woods.

That was early on in my life as a cowboy, just after we had brought our house trailer over from Idabel and settled in to live at Little Wing. I had set out from the barn on my Bubba to see what we could see, and I had gotten us well and truly lost, which was my intention. Any explorer worth his salt has to know how to get lost. If he knows where he is, he is only a tourist. I kept a loose hand on the reins and mostly left Bubba to go where he pleased. You might think he would have just dropped his head and grazed in those circumstances, but no, he was a wandering soul just like me and took his chances every chance he got.

It was one of those sweltering days in late summer when there were always piles of pregnant-looking clouds down south along Red River but never any closer, never bringing any rain. Bubba was keeping to the shade of the woods and threading his way among the pines and post oak where the brush was thin enough to let us through. It was so hot though, even out of the sun, that the sweat popped out all over my body like I was a sponge being squeezed, so hot that the usual vicious clinging cloud of mosquitoes and bar-winged blood-tapping nit flies was not in evidence, as if flying through such viscous air required too much exertion. It was good weather, however, for making detailed observations, everything so still it felt like we were in a painting, an accidentally misplaced masterpiece of dusty leaves and needles, limb overlappings and vine tangles, dry root-riddled creek beds, scattered fragments of bleached-out blue sky, occasional flickers of squirrels on their errands, hidden birds that seemed to moan instead of sing.

I was pleased as I could be. It was like I was in a paradise set aside just for me. I sang Bubba a Johnny Cash tune I had heard on the radio, about going down downtown in a burning ring of fire, as a reward for his superior trailblazing.

The pen appeared with no warning. Bubba was just squeezing through a particularly close thicket, and I had taken off my hat and leaned over to duck some low-hanging branches. A strand of briars caught in my shirt sleeve and tore it and raked the skin of my arm and I was letting the world know in no uncertain terms what I thought about that when suddenly we were out in the broad burning daylight again.

The clearing was square, the same shape as the pen and only that much larger that a boy on his horse could just fit between the woods and the grey boards of the fence. The boards were close set and on foot I would not have seen much, but I was up on Bubba, so I was privy to the whole gruesome sight from the get-go.

The pen was full of dead cattle, all hide and bones, about a hundred head. Had they been live and standing, they would have been packed tight. As it was, leg bones were propped against leg bones, rib cages interlaced like hands folded in prayer, hooves draped over necks as if some of the poor animals had tried to jump out. The jaws of what would have been calves were sandwiched under what would have been their mothers' bellies, as if they had died trying to nurse.

Creeping greenery had begun to join them all together. The stench was no longer strong but when it finally crept over us there at the perimeter I felt as if I had been branded. I wanted to cry and to retch at the same time but I didn't do either. I just held myself together and stared.

Bubba made a long rippling snort as if it were getting to him too, and turned his head as if he didn't want to look anymore. At first I thought he meant to bite me, but instead he just rested his muzzle against the toe of my boot.

It was in circumambulating the enclosure that I saw it had no gate. I steered Bubba around all four sides three full times to make sure, but it was solid everywhere, boards nailed firm to every post. No way in, no way out. The cattle had been brought there to stay. But why?

That question went round in my head like it was stuck in a revolving door. We stayed there till the sun began to sink and the shadows to stretch from the corpses toward us. In one saddlebag I had a ham sandwich that I hadn't touched and couldn't have choked down at that point, but Bubba though oddly fastidious was not nearly as finicky. It was feeding time and so he did what he always did to keep us from adventuring too long. He turned and headed for the barn.

The sense of being watched had come upon me sometime during our discovery, but I had not paid attention. Now, as the reliable old worn-out warrior underneath me threaded his way sure-footedly and unhesitatingly homeward through the thickening obscurity of the woods, I was free to consider this secondary conundrum. Who but me would be out there in that part of the ranch where there was no business to be done, and why they would be watching?

As the sensation of eyes on me grew and I gave in to it more, I knew somehow that whoever was watching was angry, angry with me, and suddenly I was not only wary, I was downright afraid.

I began to catch glimpses of a shadow that was slightly separate from the others, one that disappeared or blended in as soon as I looked directly at it. It flashed around me from all sides and at various distances, sometimes between the trunks of two trees no more than ten feet away, sometimes so far back in the underbrush I thought with relief that I might have been spared, that my pursuer had decided I was not worth the effort.

I wanted to kick Bubba into a run, but I knew that, given the obscurity of the twilight and the closeness of the woods, he was making his way toward his feed trough as fast as he could without hitting anything or losing his footing. Still I gave him a little extra notice with my heels till he worked his way into a trot, by which time I was being dragged at, scratched and whacked by the limbs and vines and bushes he was forced to find his way through so much faster.

He picked up the pace even more as the woods thinned and the open field and sky ahead showed through. I believe that at this point, as was his habit, he would have broken into the rickety rocking-chair lope that was the highest gear he had left if we had not been broadsided at that selfsame instant by a charging shadow.

I had not seen it coming and could not tell what had hit us except that it was something like a truck, something heavy and fast enough to knock us down before we knew what was happening. We landed hard. It drove the breath out of me and I think out of Bubba too, because we both lay there for a minute without moving, me with one leg trapped under his side and him just quivering and batting his eyes as if he were short circuiting. When I was finally able to gather my wits and drag myself free, a great bellowing came from behind us. A couple of saplings shook and shivered at the edge of the darkness we had come from. I could just make out a jet-black head with short and swept-back horns raised heavenward.

And then the bull of the woods took his leave.

Coming from Arcadia House Publishing of Halifax, Nova Scotia Canada in 2013.

Rowga, the Yoga of Rowing

By Jim Lindsey

"Want to meditate for peace of mind and get your exercise and have fun at the same time? At a price anyone can afford? Try *Rowga*. Jim T. Lindsey's forthcoming book *Rowga, The Yoga of Rowing*, shows you how contemplative ocean rowing can enrich your life in all these ways."

Chapter 2 : There is no Typical Session of Rowga.

If you meditate in a shrine room, the situation is always the same. It is always quiet and still and you sit still until you are done. This is not like our lives.

In our lives, even on the most humdrum day, the situation is never quite the same.

On our way to work, a police check might discover our outdated license. At work, we might find that our project has changed unexpectedly. Coming home, it is raining. A family member has emotional news. We are always having to be aware of and respond to circumstances.

So it is with the yoga of rowing. Before each session, you assess the circumstances, and during each session you respond to them. Even after a session, what you do with your boat will depend on the circumstances.

We can practice in this variable way, and benefit from it in a lasting way, because during our practice we are re-introducing ourselves to our basic awareness, which is unchanging and pure and never a victim of circumstances. We are learning to respond while remaining unvictimized. We are returning to a freedom of being we can bring to our everyday lives.

The following is an example of a session of rowga.

Because I live by the sea, I can see from my window that there's sunshine on the water making little sparkling diamonds. The limp flag on Weldon's dock across the cove shows it is calm here in the shelter of the land. Binoculars reveal a ruffled sea outside the harbor, but no whitecaps. A check of the forecast puts the wind from the north at ten knots. The tide tables have the tide going out. The conditions are favorable. Wind and current will be with me going out, and not too strong against me coming back.

The copper cod atop the boathouse confirms the north wind. A stroll to the end of the lane and a view of the Southwest Passage from the harbor to the sea reveals the breakers to be comfortably separate, each abiding over its own set of shoals. Some days the breakers form a solid line across the Passage, but today there is a path to be threaded between them.

I can go out that way if I choose.

There's a chill in the air and some frost on the ground. This is Nova Scotia. Spring forgets itself at times. It will be even colder in the open ocean where there's wind. I duck back in the house for my long johns.

Before I get into the dory, I put in:

> The oars, including an extra set

> A boat hook

> A bailing bucket

> A seat cushion

On myself, I put a life vest; this is ocean rowing—the vest is not optional.

These preparations are all about awareness. Awareness is the essence of rowga. You should always take time to prepare. Your preparations, like mine, can be minimal, but they should always be thorough. This lets you relax in the practice.

Don't bring entertainment. If you take a cell phone, use it only for emergencies. You go unaccompanied onto the big water as you will go alone into the great unknown upon leaving this life.

The soul needs its lonesome adventures.

Before shoving off, dedicate the session to all sentient beings. There is no use in doing this just for yourself. Just say simply, "By the virtue of this practice, may all the beings be happy." That is the best aspiration you can have.

The meditation doesn't happen immediately. The first few moments are all about getting the oars into their oarlocks and the blades into the water before the breeze sets the boat on the rocks.

Then sometimes there's a modicum of socializing to be done. Today a conch sounds across the cove. It's Weldon, who has been out already. At 90, Weldon still fishes every morning before sunrise. He waves and I pause between strokes to wave back. He smiles because blowing the conch is like signaling the start of a race in which I am the only contestant. I smile back because I get it, and because having such neighbors is a genuine pleasure.

I don't stop to chat.

I'm sliding out of the cove and into the harbor at a fair clip with the north wind behind me. I have to keep watch in the rearview mirror mounted on the stern. On my right is some floating seaweed that is hiding a barely submerged ridge of rocks, on my left Ronnie Duggan's dock with its stacks of lobster traps. Ronnie calls out good morning. They are lifting the morning's catch from their Cape Islander to the dock. A cloud of hungry gulls hovers, crying out for more scraps. More, more, more.

I feel the living sea surge underneath as I pull through the narrow granite-bordered gut that is the gateway to the Southwest Passage. The dory lifts. Her flat bottom slaps a little as she drops. I keep an eye on the mirror and the path through the breakers beyond, and at the same time watch the rocky shore and the village houses recede.

I love the thunder and thrill of having breakers near on either side. Nevertheless, it is not a time to be careless. This way out to the sea can be tricky. You don't want to get caught in the door.

Knowing the consequences focuses the attention wonderfully.

Today the swell that is fueling the breakers is more pronounced than the mild northern breeze can account for. A storm a hundred miles offshore three days ago is the cause. This is the result just arriving. This swell is just like the people we meet, who are informed by energies from elsewhere of which we are often ignorant, and for whom the best welcome is just to be open.

Hello great big sea. Shall we go for a ride?

The dory rises slowly up the crests and slips down quickly in the troughs. The meditation proper begins.

The meditation of rowga has two parts, that of the body and that of the mind. The meditation of the body has to do with finding a physical accord with the movement of the waves.

One of the greatest instances of futility in all mythology is that of the Irish hero Cuchulain, enchanted by the Druids into seeing the ocean as an enemy and attacking the waves with a sword.

We ourselves, enchanted by our deep-seated notion of self and other, may instinctively struggle at first as if our oars were swords and the rolling waters our enemy. But the ocean is not our enemy. It is great nature, beyond being our friend or our enemy.

It is alive with a rhythm we can discover and fall in with.

There are no instruments to assist us. We have to feel our way along. When we stop blindly forcing the stroke of our oars, when we give our awareness totally to the rise and fall and carry of the waves and let our rowing coincide, something magical happens. We get the rhythm. We become part of the music of a planet made mostly of water. We know when to rest, and when to pull, and when to rest again.

In a sense, the ocean and rower at this point are no longer two different things.

They have joined.

When we stay in this groove, when we row to the rhythm of the world we encounter, we begin to tap into great nature and our own greater mind. Nagging thoughts of this and that lose their power. We are merely being. The blades of the oars flash in and out like fins instead of swords.

The land shrinks as we leave it behind. Ahead, a mere speck in the mirror, is Bald Rock. The sky is large and gracing us with sun.

We let our awareness expand.

The horizons both landward and seaward might give rise to clouds that might give rise to storms. The north wind nudging us offshore might start to shove; we keep an eye out for whitecaps as a sign of its strengthening. A fishing trawler far out, now just a speck, might end up coming our way and even getting in our way. It is good to be dancing, but we cannot dance in a trance.

There is always much to consider at sea.

This richness of possibilities gives rise to the meditation of mind. Our meditation of body has let us relax, and so our minds have become very spacious and very attractive to all kinds of thoughts.

With our uplifted heart, we might wish a loved one were enjoying the magnificence with us. That wish might lead to memories. Perhaps the reason the loved one is elsewhere is painful. A memory of the empty house we came home to one day might ensue.

Whether joyful or sad, these thoughts with their own vivid storylines might threaten to take over our session. This is good. It allows us to go further. We are on the lookout, in fact, for such wandering thoughts to occur. When they do, when we catch ourselves lost in the future or past, we have a way to engage in the meditation of mind.

Practically, this means letting our thoughts shift for themselves as we come back to each stroke of the oars. We are rowing. We are gripping tooled spruce. At the end of each stroke, we ease our grip to keep our hands from getting cramped or going numb.

We are returning to the cradle of the deep, the rocking of the great expanse.

The wind moves over us; the sparkling sea dazzles all around.

Our return to the moment of being disempowers our wayward thinking. Why? Because there's nothing to our thoughts that they don't get from us. We don't have to ignore them or chase them away. We just cut our fixation. We come back to the ocean, again and again, stroke after stroke. This robs the thoughts of their food, which you might say is our blood, till their innate transparency becomes apparent.

This is the meditation of mind.

We will take thousands of strokes in our session of rowga, maybe millions over the years, and each stroke will be precious because each will propel us not just over the water but also back to our heritage of indestructible sanity.

For me, a session consists of a circuit. When I go out the back entrance through the Southwestern Passage as I did today, I round the harbour islands and come in by the front entrance. Because of the way the coastline bends the wind, this is the most frequent choice. Everything from a southwesterly wind to a northerly one blows in my favour when I go this way.

Today, because there is time and I have you with me, I make a wider loop out. I want to show you the necklace of islands offshore. We leave Bald Rock to starboard, then the grass-topped cliffs of Hopson's Island, then Betty's low woods. We're bowling along with an easy effort. Because you're with me only as a reader, the cold doesn't bother you. It doesn't bother me because, along with the protection of my long johns, I'm warm with the inner heat the rowing generates.

As we near our turning point, buoy AM 62, it becomes frightfully large, swaying back and forth, the bell in its derrick-like housing booming as if to call the congregation of the floating world to the most ancient of churches to hear the most primal of sermons.

I give old 62 a wide berth so as not to be pulled or pushed into it by the wave action. Then I make the turn for home by dragging one oar and pulling with the other till I have the distant steeple of the village church in the mirror.

The 30 minutes out have been no strain; reversing course changes things.

Now the wind is opposing and actually rising as it often does during the day. With her high bow acting like a sail, the dory is pushed seaward. I have to row harder. This is good physically because it gives the heart more of a workout. At the same time, it shifts the balance of the rowga session. The more the rowing is the focus, the less attention the mind needs. What thoughts arise relate mostly to the increasing challenge.

Will I ever get there? Wouldn't it be better to have a motor when it gets like this? I can't pull any harder!

The effort becomes so one-pointed, thoughts like this don't matter much.

If anything, they add more fuel for the reaching and pulling. This back and forth between the physical and mental aspects of rowga is good for developing flexibility. When the ever-arising challenges of our lives on land vary similarly, we will be more prepared.

Finally we regain the shelter of the harbour and the waves disappear. Keeping in the lee of the shore relieves us of the stiffness of the wind. As we work our way in past the village stages and docks, I drop any method and just row, and watch the mirror carefully once again. We are back where things bump.

When the boat grounds on the boards of the ramp at my dock, we don't jump out right away. We sit for a few moments longer, enjoying the transition, regarding with affection the floating world we have left.

You can blow it a kiss if you like.

I sometimes do.

To finish, I pull the dory up the ramp to the high tide mark and tie off bow and stern to the dock. The tide will float her again at some point and so she should always be properly tethered. A couple of old fishing buoys slung from the dock act as fenders to keep the gunwale from grinding. Then I put the gear back in the boathouse— oars, boathook, cushion, bailing bucket—each in its accustomed place, the more easily to be gathered next session.

That is rowga.

Much the same every time, yet always different. In fact, same and different lose their insistence a little more with each outing. As we are born along by the waves, with our practice we are continuously reborn, where everything is simply new.

It's like that.

Now we are back on the land, but we have brought with us, in our bodies and minds, something of the vibrant energy and vast expanse of the sea.

Taking this into our lives—as fearlessness, vitality, equanimity, generosity, as indisputable evidence of indestructible sanity—benefits not only ourselves but also everyone we meet.

About the Author

Stella Ducklow, photographer

Jim T. Lindsey is the award-winning author of two books of poetry, *In Lieu of Mecca,* University of Pittsburgh Press and *The Difficult Days,* Princeton University Press. He has reported for three Texas papers including the *Dallas Morning News.* Jim moved from the San Francisco Bay Area to the province of Nova Scotia in Canada to further his experience as a Buddhist practitioner. He lives in Prospect, a seaside village with a long history and a wealth of storytellers, and is the originator of the discipline of contemplative ocean rowing. His next book, *Rowga, The Yoga of Rowing,* is forthcoming from Arcadia House Publishing of Halifax, as well as an illustrated Canadian version of *The Flaw in the Fabric.*

26284512R00192

Made in the USA
Charleston, SC
02 February 2014